To
John Broomhead
who has helped
me with the great
history of HMS Somerville
I know you love for our past
and its close influence on us

Edward Grant Ries
Christmas 2012

LEGACY
—— of ——
HONOR

EDWARD GRANT RIES

LEGACY
of
HONOR

TATE PUBLISHING
AND ENTERPRISES, LLC

Legacy of Honor
Copyright © 2012 by Edward Grant Ries. All rights reserved.

No part of this publication may be reproduced, stored in a retrieval system or transmitted in any way by any means, electronic, mechanical, photocopy, recording or otherwise without the prior permission of the author except as provided by USA copyright law.

This novel is a work of fiction. Names, descriptions, entities, and incidents included in the story are products of the author's imagination. Any resemblance to actual persons, events, and entities is entirely coincidental.

The opinions expressed by the author are not necessarily those of Tate Publishing, LLC.

Published by Tate Publishing & Enterprises, LLC
127 E. Trade Center Terrace | Mustang, Oklahoma 73064 USA
1.888.361.9473 | www.tatepublishing.com

Tate Publishing is committed to excellence in the publishing industry. The company reflects the philosophy established by the founders, based on Psalm 68:11,
"The Lord gave the word and great was the company of those who published it."

Book design copyright © 2012 by Tate Publishing, LLC. All rights reserved.
Cover design by Rtor Maghuyop
Interior design by Errol Villamante

Published in the United States of America

ISBN: 978-1-62147-499-9
1. Fiction / Historical
2. Fiction / Cultural Heritage
12.09.28

Dedication

Legacy of Honor is dedicated to my wife, Elaine Ries, for her unwavering support and encouragement over the years to turn an idea into a story and the story into this book. She inspired me to discover my Scottish ancestors, some of whom lived through the tumultuous times depicted in this novel, and form my own legacy of honor.

Acknowledgments

I acknowledge and extend my heartfelt gratitude to the following people who provided valuable resource material for this book:

Robert Chambers, Stuart Reid, and Frank McLynn for wonderfully detailed histories of the Jacobite rebellion and its aftermath.

Beccles Wilson, who wrote *The Life and Letters of James Wolfe*, enabling me to characterize that brilliant and courageous leader during his early career in Scotland.

Clan Drummond Society of America for material on the Drummond family of Strathallan and maintainers of the website www.electricscotland.com for a wealth of material.

Contributors too numerous to mention to Internet blogs on Jacobitism, Drummond family of Strathallan, Gordon family of Abergeldie, Kings College, and the Scottish Enlightenment.

Robert Burns, the long-departed but never forgotten poet laureate of Scotland, for penning the words to "Strathallan's Lament," to commemorate the death of the leader of the Strathallan Drummond family in a glorious yet ultimately doomed cause:

> Thickest night, surround my dwelling!
> Howling tempests, o'er me rave!
> Turbid torrents, wintry swelling,
> Roaring by my lonely cave!
>
> Crystal streamlets gently flowing,
> Busy haunts of base mankind,

Western breezes softly blowing,
Suit not my distracted mind.

In the cause of Right engaged,
Wrongs injurious to redress,
Honour's war we strongly waged,
But the heavens denied success.

Ruin's wheel has driven o'er us,
Not a hope that dare attend,
The wild world is all before us—
But a world without a friend.

Prologue

Scotland seen from space is usually obscured by layers of clouds, a principal reason for the lushness of this far northern land. When the clouds draw away, Scotland resembles a gnarled and wizened crone perched on England, wearing a large hat and facing west. Closer, her wrinkled outline and pointed chin resolve into the barren green islands and indented deep blue lochs of Scotland's west coast. The crone's large hat becomes the treeless hills north of the Great Glen that splits the Scottish Highlands from northeast to southwest. Her hunched body becomes the Lowlands descending from the Ochil Hills to rich and populated farmlands clustered around the cities and stretching to thinly settled rolling hills of the border with England.

Scotland has always had a stormy history. The Romans occupied but could not conquer this land of the Picts, the painted people. The Dalriada swept into Scotland from across the narrow Irish Sea in frail boats called birhlins and founded a kingdom on the islands and western coast of Argyll. This violent but cultured people brought beautiful works of art; vibrant folklore; and, ultimately Christianity. They fought the Picts in sporadic wars before merging with them in a still unexplained end of hostilities. Gradually, the intermingled people became known as Scotti or Scots.

The Vikings arrived across the North Sea from their ice-bound homeland in high-prowed dragon ships. At first, they pillaged the northern and western coasts, carrying off everything of value.

They inflicted unspeakable atrocities on the helpless, who vainly begged for mercy. The raiders sailed away before resistance could organize, leaving heaps of dead clustered about monasteries and farmsteads. The Norse returned many times to war and trade and finally stay. They coveted the land, so like their home strands in Norway, but with milder weather. They intermarried or brought wives and children to strongholds and settlements they built along the coasts, bays and inlets. Their early settlements coalesced into small kingdoms across the western islands, Highlands, Isle of Man, Northern Ireland, and Orkney Islands.

For three hundred and fifty years, the Norse ruled the land. But the descendants of the Scotti remembered their ancient heritage. Early in the twelfth century, they began a war under leadership of a tribal chieftain, Somerled, son of a Scottish father and Norse daughter of the King of Man. After twenty years of brutal warfare, Somerled drove the Vikings from the land and had himself crowned Lord of the Isles. His victory was short lived, for a disgruntled servant slew him at a victory celebration.

The Scots had scarcely driven the Norse from the Highlands when invaders came from the south. Scotland's kings brought Norman ways and followers from recently conquered England. Norman nobles and knights introduced a feudal organization that existed uneasily with the ancient clan system of loyalty and allegiance bound by blood. Scottish kings gave charters of lands to favorite nobles, many of whom already possessed lands and titles in England.

Stone castles built by Normanized nobles soon dotted the countryside, replacing old fortifications of wattle and wood. These castles were the most distinctive signs of Norman occupation. Some loomed over dark glens from craggy hilltops; others were easily defendable, engulfing tiny islets in the middle of lochs; still others were reachable only by stone causeways. Towns and hamlets grew up around fortifications. Great families maintained and improved principal castles. Feuds decimated some families, and their castles fell into disuse. Others were torched or thrown down in the frequent wars that ravaged early Scotland.

Gray bracken and purple heather crept into cracked walls of abandoned castles, hastening their erosion into ill-defined mounds. In the imagination of medieval Scots, these mounds became places of legend inhabited by ghosts of the long dead. People avoided them at night and in fog that crept low over the moors and glens. Herdsmen, shepherds, and travelers claimed to have seen shadowy forms and strange music when passing by, pipes playing long-forgotten piobroachs or battle songs while eerie voices enticed them. By contrast, castles maintained by lords and clan chiefs were places of vibrant life and bustling activity. Fortified and well supplied, they were places of refuge and defense from invaders.

Legends claimed that the Drummond family originated in Hungary. The first authentic record shows that a son of Malcolm Beg became Steward of the earldom of Strathearn in 1255 and signed charters as Sir Malcolm. Over centuries, Drummonds shared in Scotland's great victories and its shameful defeats. There were many more of the latter than the former.

Drummonds were staunch supporters of Robert the Bruce, playing an important role in guerrilla campaigns after Bruce rebelled against England's King Edward the First, frequently called "Hammer of the Scots." King Edward sought to crush Scottish independence after the untimely death of King Alexander, swiftly followed by that of his infant daughter, which left the Scottish throne vacant. Edward the Second dispossessed the Drummonds for fighting for Bruce and seized their castles and lands. Robert the Bruce fought on, with his wife, daughter, and mother held by the English as hostages and three of his brothers executed.

Drummonds fought courageously at Bannockburn in 1314 when the outnumbered Scots caught the larger English army on boggy ground. The Scots cut down the mired English cavalry and trapped the foot, who could not escape across the river. Thousands of English soldiers died, but more drowned fleeing the fearsome Scottish battle-axes and claymores. Although the Scots won a great victory, the English refused to sign a peace treaty. The Scots fought on until, after fourteen more years of war, the English had had enough and English nobles forced Edward the Second to recognize Scotland's right to its own kingdom.

The victorious King Robert was generous to his loyal followers. He and his descendants tied the prominent families to the royal family by bonds of marriage. Margaret Drummond married King David the Second in 1369. Annabella Drummond became the wife of King Robert the Third and bore the son who became James the First, establishing the long line of Stewart kings.

King James the Fourth of Scotland gave the first Viscount Strathallan permission to build a fortified home on Machany Water in Perthshire in 1490. Over the next hundred and fifty years, the family became highly influential in Scotland. Succeeding Viscounts enlarged the original structure, adding floors and rooms to make it a—comfortable home for their numerous families and guests. They built gardens with walkways around trees, shrubs, and flowers, which became a gathering place during long summer days.

Cromwell destroyed the keep of Strathallan during the savage English Civil War that finally embroiled the Scots. The family patiently rebuilt it. While not as magnificent as Drummond Castle a short distance away on the other side of the village of Muthill and owned by distant relations, it was one of the more magnificent properties in the Highlands. Lawns and flowers presented a majestic vista to visitors approaching the castle.

Gun ports punctuated walls, while a high balustrade provided a wonderful view to strollers, looking down from atop the twenty-foot wall to smooth reddish stone that paved the inner courtyard and wide gardens on the other side. Beyond the gardens lay stables; carriage house; kennels; and workshops for smiths, farriers, and mechanics.

At night, torches ensconced in wall brackets or mounted on movable stands illuminated the inner courtyard and castle walls. Strollers enjoyed the evening air without hazard, as they traversed the gardens and paths. No one could miss signs that this was fundamentally a fortified citadel as well as a family home. Sentries stalked paths below the walls at all hours. Guards with muskets and pikes stood at the small kiosk before the great iron gates. Servants patrolled castle grounds with leashed mastiffs. On every interior wall and gracefully framed by magnificent Persian tapestries hung rosettes of shining pikes, long-handled halberds with ominous hooks for unseating riders, oiled muskets with stocks shining with fresh linseed, and matched braces of pistols gleaming blue in the dim light. Doors were heavy oak, bracketed with thick iron braces to hold massive bars fitted into deep recesses cut into walls. The castle had four large stone chimneys, stained dark from long use. While these were working chimneys providing outlets for smoke from fireplaces below, chinks between stones also provided roosts for ravens that made the castle grounds their home. The attached kitchen, easily reachable from the main building, also had chimneys above commodious ovens and fireplaces hung with spits and hooks.

The Drummonds had designed their home for lavish entertainment as well as defense, traditional for a viscount of the realm. On the main floor stood the viscount's well-appointed study, sitting rooms, a library, magnificent ballroom where at least two hundred guests could comfortably assemble, and a dining room with a massive horseshoe table seating a hundred. A curving marble staircase wide enough for three abreast led to comfortable family living quarters. Three floors were spacious enough to serve as home for the viscount and his large family of children and grandchildren as well as frequent guests who stayed for periods ranging from a few days to months.

At the end of covered walkways on the roof could be found the Viscount's small domed observatory and extensive glass-roofed greenhouse where Lady Margaret raised hothouse flowers and salad vegetables. Anyone walking into the greenhouse was swept into a tropical world incongruous with the gray weeping skies and bitter winds of a Scottish Highland winter. Yellow daffodils, blue jonquils, lacy ferns, gardenias, jasmine, and purple orchids crowded the small greenhouse in a riot of color. They provided a kaleidoscopic variety of sights and smells in the tropical island floating against the gray sky, visible through tree ferns and the curved glass roof spattered with raindrops. Lady Drummond loved to sit on a stone bench in a secluded bower in her greenhouse. She referred to it fondly as her Andalusian garden. She stayed for hours during the short days reading novels and travelogues and dreaming of tropical islands far from the grimness, darkness, and biting cold of the Highland winter.

Over the oaken double entry doors, the family crest hung from heavy bolts. Expressed in hammered black iron were the symbols of the family, an out-of-crest coronet and goshawk with wings expanded. Circling the crest stood the family motto, "Gang Warily." Indeed, that was the behavior of the Drummonds, "Go carefully."

Drummonds were prominent in the turbulent world of Scottish politics and finance for three hundred years through strong connections with other influential families and careful application of strength. They sided with the Stewarts in the 1688 and 1715 risings and were punished severely after those rebellions were crushed. The Drummond family of Strathallan, with the Viscount at their head, had been cautious since the last rising thirty years before. They were landlords with well-managed and productive properties. From the castle and offices in Crieff, Edinburgh, and Perth, they controlled farms, flocks, fisheries, toll roads, canals, distilleries, banks, and mercantile establishments. They were modestly wealthy, but not so wealthy that they were too frequently a target of suspicion by the government in London. The Drummonds of Strathallan had many armed retainers but no standing army. Through wise marriages and clan alliances, they could count on many staunch friends, but there were always some who wished them ill.

Political fortunes of the Drummond family spiraled downwards after William and Mary seized the throne and Catholic James the Second fled in 1688. Drummond men were among the first to rally to John Claverhouse, nicknamed Bonnie Dundee, and fight in the narrow gorge of Killikrankie. The outnumbered Highland army won that battle but lost the war, since Bonnie Dundee suffered a mortal wound and died within days. His death took the spirit out of the rising. The rebels, filled with despair and without organized leadership, drifted away. Within a month, the rebellion that started with such promise died out. King William exacted savage reprisals against the rebels. The Highlanders nursed their resentments and waited for another opportunity.

In 1715, economic conditions in Scotland were worse than ever. The union with England in 1705 brought prosperity to the Lowlands, but not the Highlands. Queen Anne, last of the Stewart monarchs, died childless, and Parliament offered the throne to an obscure branch of the royal family, the solidly Protestant Elector of Hanover in northern Germany. The loyal clans rose, and the countryside flared into rebellion again, under James the Third, the young arrogant son of James the Second, newly arrived from France. Once again, the rebels won battles, although outnumbered and outgunned.

They inexplicably withdrew from the bloody battlefield at Sheriffmuir when they could have pursued and defeated the exhausted government troops. The discouraged James the Third fled back to France. He never returned to Scotland, but many clan chiefs and their sons remained in communication with him and dreamed of the day when he would return and they could throw off the yoke of the hated Hanoverians. Lowland Scots, especially those in the newly prosperous cities of Glasgow and Edinburgh, tended to side with the government, which further isolated the Highlanders.

At the opening of this story in 1743, it had been thirty years since the last rising on behalf of the Stewarts. The Hanoverian King George the Second, sitting on the throne of the unified kingdom of Great Britain, and his ministers were suspicious of the families and clans whom they labeled 'Jacobites' once staunch supporters of King James the Third, but with no solid proof of disloyalty. Spies masquerading as merchants and travelers were everywhere. Information and rumors were bought and sold in every town and village. Although Scotland was outwardly peaceful, military garrisons of well-guarded forts frequently sent patrols to march through the countryside. They were watchful of every gathering, made surprise visits to search castles and homes of suspected Jacobites for weapons, and pried into every international post and shipment. Indeed, the Drummonds, as well as other clans who had risen in the past, "gang warily."

The Drummonds of Strathallan became enmeshed in the events leading to the final rising of the Highlands, the '45, that separated and nearly destroyed them. Into this world of intrigue and violence came young James William Drummond, born on a spring morning in the year 1738, who learned to live with a legacy of honor through the tumultuous years that followed.

Chapter One

The pale disk of the mid-winter sun emerged above the eastern hills and reflected off the snowy hills and glens of Strathallan in dark rose and violet hues. A gray-feathered sea eagle perched atop one of the standing stones of Dalchirla above the road that ran from Glen Artney eastward to the village of Muthill and the crossroads leading to Strathallan Castle. In the dim morning light, her grey-and-white feathers were indistinguishable from the mottled, dark-gray stone.

The sun slowly rose into a cloudless blue sky. There had been a heavy snowfall over the previous three days, but the clouds had flown eastward with the gusty breeze. Sunlight winked and glittered on thick layers of ice on the banks of Machany Water and the numerous small ponds scattered across the meadows.

The eagle was not hunting, having dined on a luckless hare the evening before, but human activity on the road made her wary. She saw four horsemen approaching. She dropped from the stone pillar, and with strong beats of her broad wings, spiraled upward to find a rising thermal. When the horsemen were mere dots against the snow behind her, the eagle uttered a defiant scream and turned eastward away from them along Machany Water.

∽

Donald Cameron and his three companions halted to watch the eagle rise from the standing stone. The chief pointed skyward. "I feel a strong kinship wi' that ern, floating sae serenely in the heavens. Damn all political strife and machinations o' deceitful men and nations! Gie me such freedom tae hunt and live far frae strangers wi' only kith and kin by me, fed and housed among rocks and glens o' my ain land," he muttered.

His horse nickered and tossed her mane.

"Whoa! Easy, my pet!" He pushed back his blue bonnet with the tall eagle feathers that denoted his status as clan chief. His saddle creaked as he leaned forward to pat the stamping mare's neck and cheeks and speak to her soothingly.

"Why are we here, my bonnie companions, romping through the snaw on the verra last day o' the year?" enquired Donald Cameron.

One of the men trailing behind him spoke plaintively. "Ye are the chief o' Clan Cameron, Lochiel, and a force tae be reckoned wi' in the west. It seems tae me that Strathallan should hae come tae Lochaber tae visit ye, and nae the other way around. If so, we could be sitting by a roaring fire at hame and nae here, trampin' through the snaw and freezin' our arses."

His companions voiced their assent with a curt, "Och, aye!"

The massive chieftain twisted in the saddle to better see his companions. His horse, well trained, wheeled smartly to face the three riders.

"Because, my guid and faithful dunniewassels, while Camerons and MacDonalds hae stout hearts, strong arms, and broad claymores, they dinna hae the other ingredients o' a successful rising."

"And what might those be?" inquired Alexander MacDonald, with a trace of a sneer.

Donald Cameron looked at him from under hooded lids for a long moment before speaking softly. "Political connections and gold, Alex, o' which the Camerons o' Lochaber and MacDonalds o' Armadale hae precious little. Neither do the MacKenzies, MacLeods, McNeils, Keppoch, or any o' the other clans o' the western Highlands and islands. We hae come all the way to Perthshire to seek them. We certainly canna find them by pleading with the Campbells. They support the Hanoverians to the teeth! Those wha gae tae Inverarry seekin' help seldom come oot again."

Donald Cameron pushed back his flowing auburn locks, smoothed his mustaches, and leaned over the pommel. "Nae, lads. Ye must heed my counsel. We are here tae celebrate the festival o' Hogmanay wi' our auld friends, the Drummonds o' Strathallan. We may"—the chief paused and looked at each of them in turn to assure their attention—"hae occasion tae sit and talk over auld times and the future behind closed doors wi' gentlemen wha are also guests come tae celebrate the holiday and Drummond hospitality. But"—he paused again and then spoke forcefully—"there is news I expect tae hear aboot the king o'er the water, but must hold it close. There may be a rising soon, or perhaps there will be nae rising. Ye will nae speak a word tae anyone other than those I point out tae ye o' anything other than holiday cheer. And see that ye take nae more than a wee dram betwixt yer lips. If your tongue gets loose and starts tae wag, I may well cut it oot. And I willna be careful o' whatever else comes oot wi' it."

He grinned hugely, revealing strong, white teeth, and pulled his long dirk half out of its scabbard to make his point. His companions did not share in his amusement but sat grim-faced in their saddles.

Lochiel stopped grinning, grunted, and said, "Let us gae tae Strathallan Castle before me belly thinks me throat is cut."

The others, glad that their tempermental leader had finished his peroration, laughed heartily and followed him.

※

As the eagle flew eastward along Machany Water, she passed over the mill of Drummond. The wheel was not turning, and no one was in sight since the last day of December and the first day of January was a holiday throughout the Highlands and most of the Lowlands of Scotland. She soared over Muirside, Bridgehill, and the falls of Ness with only an occasional beat of her powerful wings to sustain her altitude in the updraft. To the left rose the gray spires of massive Drummond Castle and the village church at Muthill. Far in the distance lay the cattle fair town of Crieff.

The sea eagle turned southeastward, away from the stream, to fly over extensive woods of fir, pine, and juniper that stretched south to Tullibardine Station, across Murray lands, where the military road came north from Stirling and the Bridge of Allan. The road past Strathallan was a dark streak of mud and slush in the white far below her, revealing that at least a few other travelers had come that way. Along the road rolled a post coach heading northeast. The driver, perched on his high seat, with a heavy woolen wrap around his legs to keep out the invasive cold, pulled on the reins to slow the team. He leaned down and spoke loudly enough so that his passengers could hear.

"Aye, 'tis a lovely sight on a fine morning! After three days o' snaw, it is guid tae see a clear sky again. That eagle is going eastward at a guid pace. The wind is strong up there but pleasant doon here among the trees."

"Ach! Get a move on, driver! I did not pay ye an exorbitant fare tae malinger all day staring at a silly bird!" bellowed a harsh voice from inside the coach.

The driver sighed and whipped up his reins. Simon Fraser, the eleventh Lord Lovat, was a great man but a very impatient and irascible one. The driver leaned down to shout into the coach. "Will yer lordship and lady be wantin' tae stop at Tullibardine Station for a bite or fer necessity?"

Simon Fraser shouted back, "My throat and bladder are in excellent condition, my guid man, but my gout objects tae frequent stops. Drive on tae Strathallan. Lady Lovat and I expect an excellent midday repast and dinna wish tae be late."

The driver raised his whip in acknowledgement and cracked it over the team's head. The coach lurched through a deep pothole and sank to the wheel hubs in the thick mud. With the driver shouting and the team straining against the axletrees, it pulled out, straightened, and lurched in the direction of Tullibardine

Mill and the Strathallan estate. The driver smiled as he heard cursing from inside the coach.

Simon Fraser shouted, "Damn, ye clumsy lout! Watch oot fer potholes and ruts! Four years past, a driver broke an axletree on this road not far frae here, and me, my wife, and daughters had tae ride bareback all the way tae town! I will nae hae that again, with this damnable gout crippling me!" The driver could hear Lady Lovat trying to calm her husband, but obediently, he slowed down and kept the coach in the middle of the road.

*

The sea eagle soared over the standing stones west of Auchterader and turned lazily north with the swirling breeze. A few minutes of flight brought her over Tullibardine Mill, also not turning, and directly over the considerably slowed coach carrying Simon and Lady Fraser. Below the eagle stretched thick woods surrounding the stately lawns and gardens of Strathallan Castle, coated in white around the ice-laced lake. A small forester's crofthouse lay on a knoll in the western woods about a mile from the castle. Outbuildings and stables surrounded with foot and hoofprints in the snow fringed the castle grounds.

The bird soared over the castle and Machany Water beyond, past the point where the Machany joined the Earn at Kinkell Bridge, where the road veered north to the town of Madderty and the ruins of Inchaffray Abbey. She caught another strong updraft, turned eastward, and was gone into the sun, heading toward the Perth lowlands and her home near the bitter cold and stormy North Sea beyond.

Below the eagle's track, Sir William Drummond, fourth Viscount Strathallan and Machany, stood on the exposed portico at the rear of the castle. He felt the chill breeze penetrate his cloak and settle into his joints. His thinning hair was iron gray, and he was feeling all of his sixty-four years. He reflected that he was at an age when he should be comfortably enjoying his children and grandchildren rather than contemplating conspiracy to fulfill a promise made long ago to a youthful king who had lived his entire life in exile, except for those brief heady months in 1715. Fulfilling that promise filled him with dread for himself and his family.

Sir William looked up to study the flight of the sea eagle. He reflected that while his honor called for fulfilling the promise, it carried a high price. Was he prepared to pay it? A young and dashing William Drummond had fought at Sheriffmuir in 1715 in a bloody battle in which no man could tell which side had won, but the Jacobites had abandoned the field, so the other side claimed victory. King James the Third, called the Young Pretender by the Hanoverians, offended his Highland loyalists with his disdainful and proud manner and fled to France rather than fight on, never to return to Scotland. The abandoned rebels made what accommodations they could with the hated "German lairdie." On this last day of the year, 1743, James's young and charismatic son, Charles Edward Stewart, exiled in France, was conspiring to put his middle-aged father on the throne of the unified kingdoms of England and Scotland.

Sheriffmuir lay only miles down the road toward Stirling, but nearly thirty years had passed since that fateful battle. Few remembered and the site was visited only by browsing cattle and ghosts of the men who had died there so pointlessly. Then the crown had been reasonably lenient toward the failed rebels. William Drummond had himself escaped punishment and banishment for fighting. Would he escape if the Drummonds of Strathallan rose again?

William had married Margaret Nairn thirty-one years ago, before Sheriffmuir, when he was thirty-three and she only nineteen. Margaret was a stunning dark-haired beauty who grew to be a strong woman, bearing thirteen children, of whom nine had survived childhood illnesses that took away four of their babies, who now lay beneath their small tombstones on a knoll beyond the castle's gardens. She was the strong-willed matron of her family and as passionate a Jacobite as her husband.

Viscount William sighed and turned his thoughts to his children and grandchildren. Of their nine surviving children, all but three were at Strathallan for Christmas and Hogmanay. Margaret, the eldest, lived with her planter husband in Jamaica. Anne lived with her husband in London, where he managed a portfolio of properties for Scottish magnates. James, his eldest son and his wife, Euphemia, lived at the castle with their only child, little James William, a tousled-haired, sturdy blond boy nearly six years old. Little James William Drummond, the only son of his heir and nicknamed Jamie, had been born at Strathallan on the sixth of April of 1738. He was christened, as were all Strathallan Drummond family members, in the Episcopal church at Muthill. His father, James, had called the boy Jamie from the beginning, and the nickname had stuck.

Clementine was a tall, dark-haired young woman of twenty-two with poor marital prospects because of her plain face and rail-thin body, but she had a good heart. William, aged twenty, was in the army and stationed in Ireland. John was now nearly nineteen, tall and handsome with dark hair and eyes, unmarried, and usually in the company of two or more lovely girls. Emilia was sixteen, pert, short, blonde, and engaging. She was superbly athletic and an excellent rider. Andrew was seventeen and a student at the University of St. Andrews and home for the holidays. Henry, the youngest son at thirteen, was just starting to grow. He was a natural leader who should become a soldier. However, he aspired to be a lawyer or financier, as did his brother Andrew.

Charles Gordon was eldest brother to his son James's wife, Euphemia, and Laird of Abergeldie since his father's untimely death ten years before. He and his wife, Alison, had brought their four children from Abergeldie in Aberdeenshire for the holidays. Charles was a man who took his responsibilities seriously since his father had died when Charles was only twenty-four, leaving a large family for Charles to lead and a terribly mismanaged inheritance to put to rights. William wondered about Charles's political leanings since the Gordons were Catholic and Jacobite. Charles was taciturn and evasive whenever the subject arose. Their family consisted of Peter, age fourteen; William, age six; Alison, age three; and twins David and Margaret under two.

Three days before, a storm had struck unexpectedly with roaring winds that ripped leaves from the trees and coated the entire region with ice and snow. The skies cleared, and no snow had fallen since the previous night. Ice glittered and sparkled in the trees.

Trapped indoors by the snowstorm, the children were underfoot and restless. Maids worked busily "touching up" rooms and rearranging furniture to accommodate the expected crowd of guests. Gardeners labored through the morning, clearing snow from walks, porches, and paths and brushing icicles from trees and shrubs to better show off the stately winter gardens. Days earlier, workmen brought cases of fireworks labeled in Italian from Perth and stacked them in a special shed situated well away from the mansion for safety. They locked the door and posted a guard to deter youthful pranksters. Musicians arrived in mid-morning, uncased their violas and cellos, and set them up for tuning and practice in the ballroom. Pipers and drummers assembled out of doors to practice, since untuned bagpipes were an assault on the ears.

For weeks, servants stacked provisions in larders and pantries from floor to ceiling. Now that the days of celebration had come, they brought them forth, dusty bottles of well-aged wine and champagne from the cellars, wiped carefully and set to chill in tubs of snow. Kitchen helpers brought meats from the smokehouse at the back of the garden: hams crusty with peppercorns and wood ash, haunches of salted venison, and saddles of beef and lamb. Before dawn, servants brought baskets of charcoal from the kiln and arranged pyramids of the black chunks in fireplaces and under ovens. When the burning coals developed a white ash coating, they knocked them down and prepared the ovens.

Bakers worked ceaselessly in the hot kitchen mixing, kneading, and shaping loaves that, in the hot ovens, would rise to become dark-crusted and tasty breads, scones, and rolls. Pies and cakes sat cooling on shelves. Crocks of freshly churned butter and rounds of white and yellow cheeses lay on tables. Cooks seasoned joints and set them to roasting on spits turned in the fireplaces by bored scullery boys. The kitchen helpers peeled, chopped, boiled, mashed, and seasoned turnips and potatoes to make the beloved "neaps and tatties" thick with butter and cream. The mingled aromas of baking breads, roasting meats, boiling carrots, and pies spiced with cloves and cinnamon wafted through the kitchen and out open doors into all the rooms.

The numerous children of the family and guests who had arrived early were agog with excitement. They were distracted by the delicious smells and abandoned indoor games to stand transfixed in hunger. Any child who moved too close to the kitchen was stared down by the frowning Mister Dobie, the major domo, guarding the kitchen doors.

Adults were distracted as well and frequently checked clocks and pocket watches as they wished away the slow morning in anticipation of the joyous evening. Nannies and tutors anxiously called children away from the busy servants, who were furtively slipping them buttered scones; raisins; and slices of an unheard of treat, Spanish oranges. Cooped up during the storm, the children exploded with energy when red-faced and plump Mrs. MacRobie flounced downstairs to announce that the sun was out and the children were allowed to play in the snow before the servants swept and shoveled it away.

❧

Jamie Drummond was tall for his age but too young to venture into the snow-shrouded gardens on his own. He was constantly accompanied by either Mrs. MacRobie, the head nanny, or her fifteen-year-old daughter, Agnes, who already had the plump shape of her formidable mother and the same shapeless mass of red-gold hair. Agnes bundled Jamie into heavy trews, two woolen shirts, jacket, hat, gloves, and boots. He squirmed throughout the ordeal, anxious to play outside.

Agnes opened the bedroom door. Jamie saw Will Gordon, also age six and dressed in heavy outdoor clothing.

"Come, lad," said Agnes. "Hold hands wi' Will sae ye dinna get separated."

"Get separated?" inquired Will. "Agnes, we canna get lost up here."

But Agnes insisted. Reluctantly, the boys gave in. To pique Agnes, they raced down the long hallway past the formidable portraits of somber Drummond ancestors who stared down severely from the walls. When they reached the end of the carpeted hallway, their boots skidded on the marble landing at the head of the stairs. The boys lost their balance and teetered on the edge for a long moment while Agnes shrieked. She was too far behind to catch them. Holding hands, the boys tumbled down the stairs and landed in a sprawl but unhurt at the bottom.

Agnes took the stairs two at a time until she stood over them, red-faced and breathing heavily. She scolded them severely and picked up each one and felt arms and legs with anxious fingers.

"Ach, ye wee mon," she scolded Jamie. "Ye gie me such a fright. Ye are both lucky indeed tae nae be busted. Hold still until I get ye ootside safe and sound."

When she was satisfied that they were unhurt, Agnes sent them to the door that faced the gardens at the back of the castle. She swung it open and, like a mother goose, led them out. Sunlight reflecting off the expanse of snow blinded them. They covered their faces with their gloved hands and squinted against the light until they could see. They tumbled off the porch. Jamie found that he could run fast, plant his feet, and skid across the crusty snow. He caromed off Will, who had stopped just in front of him. Both boys went down like bowling pins. They impulsively rolled in the snow.

"Look!" shouted Will.

He waved his arms and legs back and forth like a marionette. His limbs had scooped away the snow into the pattern known to children everywhere as a snow angel. Jamie rolled over and repeated Will's performance. Soon, all of the dozen or so children in the garden were making their own patterns. The boys jumped up to stamp out each other's patterns.

The children were full of energy after being cooped up for days by bad weather. They organized a mock battle and began choosing sides. Already, they were busily building snow forts and stockpiling snowballs. They chose the two oldest boys, Henry Drummond and Peter Gordon, as team captains. As the sides formed up on opposite ends of the wide lawn, Alison, assisted by Peter, scooped up the three younger Gordon children. Jamie loudly protested that he and Will were old enough to play and had lots of practice. Jamie went off chasing other children and pelting them with snowballs, with a strong and surprisingly accurate aim.

Clementine looked helplessly at her father, who waved his assent from the portico. He shivered in the cold but stayed to watch the children's battle.

In a moment, the air was full of whizzing missiles. Smaller children accumulated piles of ammunition on both sides of a line scratched in the snowy field that separated the small armies. Peter Gordon, carrying an armload of snowballs, raced toward the line separating the armies. Defenders rushed up but were badly fooled as Peter feinted left, veered right, spun and fired two snowballs. Both landed squarely in the faces of two surprised boys. With an exultant shout, Peter launched an attack on Jamie, running to intercept him. Jamie made up for his deficient size with speed and accuracy. His missiles hit the older boy in the face and chest. Peter flung up his arms to defend himself and dropped his armload of ammunition. Other boys pelted him as he scrambled away on all fours.

"Ho, Peter! Ye're at our mercy! No quarter, no quarter!" they shouted.

"No quarter asked!" he shouted back.

"No quarter given!" they responded and continued to pelt his exposed haunches.

Eventually, Peter escaped to his own side.

Girls watched for a few minutes and then joined the fray. Breathless, with faces reddened by cold, the children on one side raced toward a defended hedge. Shouting children poured around the hedge in a counterattack. Those aggressive enough to fight back were pelted mercilessly until they fled or fell. These luckless souls were joyously rolled in the snow by the victors until they surrendered and were led off to a makeshift prison of cut pine boughs. Finally, everyone was too out of breath to continue, and a truce was declared. The nannies, who had stood by to watch and cheer the combatants, led the happy children inside to a hot lunch and warm milk laced with a bit of the punch reserved for the evening's celebration. Viscount William Drummond chuckled to himself as he followed a manservant who had come to announce the arrival of the coach bearing Simon Fraser.

The gouty old man stumped up the broad steps while servants gathered his luggage from the boot. The coach rolled away to the carriage house with a crunch of gravel before Simon reached the top of the long marble staircase. The Viscount clasped his hand warmly and pulled him inside.

"Greetings, my auld friend. Ye look half-frozen. Please join us fer tea and perhaps something stronger."

Simon grimaced with the pain of his long ascent and said, "Aye. I must remember, William, that I am nearing eighty and nae longer the man I once was. I need a place where I can pull off these accursed boots and raise my leg. Tea is guid fer warming the mouth, but rum punch would warm my belly better."

The Viscount grinned suddenly and motioned to Mister Dobie, recently freed from guarding the kitchen. The major domo nodded understandingly. "A brimming bowl, a hot poker, tobacco, and pipes are waiting in your study, my lord."

"Call James and John, Mister Dobie, if ye please, and ask them tae join us. Oh, and ye had better invite Charles Gordon as well."

Simon Fraser was not above a small joke. "Ach, aye. Do invite the Laird o' Abergeldie, my near neighbor in the frozen north. Some warm punch will help unpinch his prim mouth and might make him almost jovial."

Mister Dobie carefully kept his face impassive, but the Viscount nodded goodnaturedly.

"Charles hae had a difficult life, since burying a father and salvaging his financially mismanaged estates at a young age. Such burdens would sour most men."

Simon nodded but observed, "Aye, but he is now rich and well endowed with five children and a guid wife. He should be a happy man. However, I sense that he hae few feelings o' enjoyment. Where does he stand politically?" William shook his head and placed a finger beside his nose.

Simon grinned toothily. "Ah. On the fence, as I suspected." He moved off on Viscount William's arm toward the waiting punchbowl and a good pipe.

After lunch, Lady Euphemia, Jamie's mother, came to the bedroom where Agnes MacRobie was removing Jamie's sodden outer clothes and preparing him for a nap. Jamie was a healthy and active boy with grey eyes and a mop of unruly blond hair. He was a replica of his father at the same age who stared down from the family portrait that hung in the main hall.

Euphemia smiled at her ruddy-cheeked son and tousled his hair. She told him excitedly, "Your papa arranged for Italian rockets at midnight. The sky will be lit with all the colored fires of the rainbow. The men will fire them o'er the castle gardens at twelve. Ye may stay awake and watch, but promise me that ye will then gae straight to bed. 'Tis traditional fer big people tae stay up long past twelve, but ye need sleep."

Jamie squirmed with pleasure. "Please let me stay up, Mama. I will be ever so guid."

Euphemia reached down to tickle him. "And guess what your papa hae done."

Jamie frowned and shook his head.

His mother said, "He hae written yer name on the biggest rocket in the box! I will make sure tae tell ye before it gaes off."

Jamie shrieked in delight while Euphemia laughed, and Agnes backed away and covered her ears.

"Ah dinna ken aboot rockets, mum," she said and shook her head disapprovingly.

"Oh, Agnes, ye need nae be afraid. They are just big toys."

Agnes's scowl deepened, and she said crossly, "Sech toys belong on castle walls. We ca''em cannons. Nae, mum. I weel sta' here and kiver me ears when they fire the rockets."

"That's fine, Agnes. Send Jamie upstairs tae bed as soon as the fireworks show is done. Now, please dress the lad fer dinner as soon as he hae finished his nap. The Viscount will order dinner to start at precisely eight o'clock, but we expect mair guests tae arrive anytime now."

Jamie climbed onto his bed. Agnes drew the curtains shut and blew out the candles. The room was dim in the fading light of a short winter's afternoon. She drew up a chair in the corner next to the window and took up her stitchery to while away the time while Jamie napped. The boy tossed for a few minutes and tried to engage her in conversation. Agnes shushed him, and he soon fell asleep. The maid hummed softly and sewed while the light faded to dusky rose and then to twilit gray.

※

The Drummond men and Simon Fraser talked long over the tea, punchbowl, and food. Servants called out the Viscount several times to welcome more guests, including the Cameron party, MacDonalds, Forbes, Strahans, Hays, Lord George Murray and his brother the Lord of Tullibardine, and others. The study grew noisy, crowded, warm, and smoky.

The arrival of Lochiel added greatly to the joviality of the group, far more than the influence of the warm punch. He was an unquenchable wellspring of amusing tales, anecdotes, and wry jests. Finally, with a glance at the dark windows, William Drummond rose.

"Your pardon, my honored guests, but it is time tae prepare fer the celebration. Mister Dobie and his attendants are here tae direct ye tae yer rooms. Ye hae twa hours tae rest and refresh yerselves." The Viscount chuckled goodnaturedly. "It takes me that lang tae dress myself these days. Dinner will be at eight sharp."

In the faint light from torches, servants completed preparations for the Hogmanay celebration. They wrapped paper and twigs in wire netting, attached short handles of heavy cord, and dipped the bundles in a large vat of melted grease and laid them to harden. These would become flaming balls for men and older boys to swing after dark. They collected dry juniper branches from where they had been laid to dry in the byre's loft to be used for the saining of the house. They placed drinks and sweets on a table by the entrance to offer to the man to be the first foot crossing the threshold after midnight, a sign of good luck to come. These Hogmanay traditions were centuries old and still practiced in most Highland households.

As early twilight turned to darkness, guests from Crieff, Muthill, Auchterarder, and other places in southern Perthshire began to arrive. They were locals who did not expect to stay the night. Carriages arrived frequently and rolled up the center drive and through the open iron gates of the torch-lit castle to the rhythmic clop of their horse's hooves. They circled until they came to the broad marble staircase before the great doors. Wheels crunched on the snow-covered gravel and slowed as drivers pulled back on the reins. The horses stood steaming while footmen sprang down to open carriage doors and extend folding steps so that ladies and gentlemen could dismount. Servants in Drummond livery directed drivers to park their carriages in designated spots in the vast inner courtyard.

With footmen and servants assigned to assist guests, drivers gathered to warm themselves around fires in stone rings along the side of the courtyard. While they waited in the cold, servants carried out and set up tables and stools. To the applause of the crowd gathering in the courtyard, servants began arranging trays laden with a working class feast of roast goose, bread, vegetables, and plenty of beer.

"Huzza, huzza for our Viscount and his lady!" they shouted as they jostled for places at the feast.

After the crowd finished their meal, servants brought great flaming puddings studded with citrons and raisins from the kitchens, along with tubs of spiced wine. The servants put irons to heat in the fires and passed wooden cups. The crowd shouted approval when the servants withdrew the glowing irons from the coals to thrust them into bowls filled to the brim with the wine-laced punch, causing it to sizzle and smoke. Immediately, the happy and talkative crowd pressed forward around the bowls. Outstretched arms passed mugs to be dipped and passed back. The grinning crowd repeatedly toasted the Viscount and his lady, the makers of their feast, Andrew the patron saint of Scotland, and various dignitaries until the punch ran out. Servants hurried forward to replenish the empty bowls and reheat the irons.

Dressed in keeping with the customs of the mid-eighteenth century, bewigged and powdered guests in fluttering great cloaks climbed the marble steps illuminated by flaring torches mounted in wall sconces. Passing through the entrance, they left the flickering light of the courtyard and entered a great hall with soaring stone walls lit by rows of enormous cut glass chandeliers blazing with the light of hundreds of candles. The guests gathered in the great hall to be received by the dignified, grey-haired Viscount and his wife, Lady Margaret. Streamers of plaid, silk, and satin presented a varicolored display as guests crowded into the receiving lines. A murmur of voices and soft music filled the hall and floated up the stairs.

When Jamie woke to the muffled sounds from below, the room was fully dark. Agnes relit the candles and pulled open a drawer in a tall chest and took out shirt, knickers, and jacket for Jamie. In a few minutes, she had him dressed. She pulled out his freshly tallowed shoes with the silver buckles and bent to push them on his stockinged feet. She tied his cravat while ignoring Jamie's little choking noises. She took up a brush and spent some minutes fussing with his unruly hair. Sighing, she finally dipped her fingers into a small ceramic pot, rubbed them together, and with deft strokes, patted scented pomade onto his hair. She smoothed it with her fingers and brushed it. She led Jamie to a tall mirror so that he could look at his elegant reflection.

"Now," she told him. "Ye must practice walkin' and bowin' like a fine gentleman. We canna have the grandson of the Viscount fallin' doon and lookin' the fool, not in sech fine clothes."

After a few minutes of practice, she stood him in a corner and pretended that she was a lady being presented to Jamie. He put a hand before his stomach and another behind his back as Agnes had taught him.

"My lady," he intoned.

Jamie bowed until he was bent double. He held the pose for a long moment. Agnes curtsied. "Verra guid, indeed!" she pronounced. She held out her hand. Jamie linked arms and walked with Agnes around the room. After a lap, he released her arm, faced her, and bowed again as she curtsied. Agnes giggled with pleasure. Jamie laughed loudly and clapped his hands. The bedroom door clicked open. A tall, thin servant dressed in black livery stood in the opening.

"Lady Drummond hae requested that all children assemble fer a final inspection. The reception has already started," he intoned.

He frowned severely. "Young lady, such frivolity is fine fer Hogmanay celebrations, but nae before the Viscount hae welcomed the guests and certainly nae before grace is said before dinner."

The servant sniffed disapprovingly, turned on his heel, marched out, and shut the door. Agnes and Jamie both made faces at the closed door. Agnes took Jamie's hand and led him down the hall. They entered a room just past the grand staircase, where children were gathering for their inspection and instructions. After a few minutes, a satisfied Mrs. MacRobie released the children to go downstairs for their formal presentation.

It was thoroughly dark outside, but the interior of the castle was lit with ensconced torches, lamps, and candles. The hubbub of voices downstairs nearly drowned out the music from the ballroom. Jamie stopped at the head of the staircase and sucked in his breath. He had never seen such a display. The lamplight winked off the cut glass chandeliers, jewels in the women's hair, and the men's medals and buttons. Jamie squeezed Agnes's hand tightly.

"Do I hafta gae down there, Agnes?" he asked plaintively.

"Aye, laddie," she whispered. "But be brave. Do yer bowin' and be done. There'll be a plate o' guid meat and other victuals for ye in the dinin' room off the kitchen with the other children. Then, after a' that, the rocket show will start and ye can take off the fancies and tae bed wi' ye."

Jamie puffed out his cheeks, squared his shoulders, and marched down the rest of the marble steps. As he walked slowly downward, he stared at the brightly lit and animated faces. He recognized his grandfather, William Drummond, Viscount Strathallan, and his grandmother Margaret. They were finely dressed, with the Viscount in a coat of dark blue and trews of spotless white. His chest was adorned with medals. Jamie saw the pommel of his grandfather's sword, with gold inlay, protruding from the scabbard that hung at his left side. The Viscount wore a tasseled red tartan sash over his shoulder. Lady Drummond wore a formal gown of light blue silk and a plaid across her shoulders. Her dark hair shot with gray was done up on top of her head and pinned with bright jewels.

Nearby stood Jamie's parents, James and Euphemia Drummond, he dressed in uniform and sword and she in an elegant, long gown of burgundy. Jamie saw his aunts and uncles and guests, most sporting long sashes of the tartan cloth that had recently become fashionable for formal wear. Many other people, most of whom Jamie did not recognize, crowded the hall and streamed into the dining room. Jamie found the noise of the many intermingled conversations jarring and unpleasant. He felt a twinge of panic, which he fought down. He was determined not to embarrass his family.

Marching up to his grandfather to pay his respects was like walking through the trees of the forest. The top of Jamie's head scarcely reached the midriffs of the men standing in the hall. Jamie was afraid that they would step on him, but they moved away as if by magic from the path of the oncoming children.

Jamie saw the elegantly dressed men and women looking at him with smiles and some with open grins. The women were whispering to each other. Jamie put on his most serious look as he marched up to his grandfather. He stopped suddenly by his mother's side. His grandfather and grandmother stopped talking and turned to look at him expectantly.

Jamie said gravely, "Guid evening, your grace and my lady," and bowed stiffly.

Jamie's grandfather nodded and smiled. His grandmother beamed and clasped her gloved hands and raised them to her mouth. Jamie turned and took the arm of Rachel, a pretty blonde girl of seven, whose father was the Earl of Atholl. Very solemnly, they slowly walked toward the dining room set aside for the children.

A few of the ladies and gentlemen standing nearby applauded politely. Jamie heard his grandfather talking as he walked away.

"A fine lad, James. Aboot six years auld, Euphemia, my dear?"

Lady Margaret said, "So tall and handsome, just like his father when he was a wee lad." She paused for a moment, as if lost in reflection. "Except for the blond hair. Do ye think that it will turn dark? Our James and John were both blond until they were nearly twelve. Now see them! The handsomest and darkest men in the Drummond household!"

The rest of the conversation was lost to Jamie, as he and Rachel drew further away.

Jamie audibly sighed with relief as they cleared the noise and bright lights of the great hall. Rachel disengaged his arm as they entered the children's dining room, gave him a little shove, and headed for the far side of the room to join other girls. Jamie wiped his damp forehead, which mussed his unruly hair. He stood uncertainly near an end of the horseshoe-shaped table.

Agnes appeared suddenly and grasped his hand while wiping tears from her eyes with the other. She led him to a chair near the head of the table. He climbed up, and she pushed him close to the table. Agnes smiled approvingly and tied a cloth around his neck that covered his shirt and cravat.

"Aw, Agnes, I willna spill," Jamie complained.

"Ach, lad. Ye're wearing fine clothes and yer mum will nae want ye ruinin' 'em. I will stay here wi' ye tae make sure."

Jamie wrinkled his nose but said nothing.

It was a tasty meal made memorable by entertainers and jugglers performing between courses. The children chattered amiably and clapped after each performance. Jamie made a mighty attempt to keep up with the larger boys in consuming the rich food, but Agnes put her hand over his plate to restrain him.

He looked down and saw that suddenly, his plate was gone. He was irritated and scowled at Agnes.

She leaned forward and whispered in his ear, "Ye'll make yerself sick if ye eat mair. Remember, laddie. There will be cake, pie, syllabub, and other guid things tae come."

After the sumptuous dessert, adults and children gathered in the great hall, with older children standing behind their parents and mothers holding younger ones on their laps. Soft string music played in the background. When everyone was seated, Mister Dobie advanced to the middle of the hall, holding a heavy wooden baton as tall as himself, decorated with silver bands. He thumped the baton on the oak floor three times, and everyone quieted. Servants threw open the tall doors at the end of the room.

Standing outside were rows of pipers and drummers dressed in ornate uniforms with tasseled tartan plaids flowing down their backs. Everyone craned to see. Jamie heard the ruffling of the drums and low drones as the pipers inflated their bagpipes. Suddenly, the high-pitched skirl of the pipes filled the hall, and a roar of approval rose from the diners.

Pipers and drummers marched into the dining room, splitting into files to traverse the long tables on both sides of the hall. Everyone rose, cheering and waving. The musicians, still playing, assembled in two rows behind William Drummond. After the pipers played several tunes, the leader raised his baton and the music stopped.

The Viscount rose. "Gentlemen and ladies, I bid ye welcome," he intoned quietly.

Another cheer erupted, which stopped expectantly when the Viscount bent to pick up a glass. He lifted it high and began to speak. Although his voice was soft, the sound carried easily.

"Here's tae the King, tae his happiness, health, and long life."

There were subdued growls from down the tables. The Viscount held up his hand and shot a warning look in the direction of the sounds.

"Ye ken o' whom I speak!" said the Viscount in a loud and clear voice. "Have a care fer yer own health and happiness!"

The growls subsided. The men rose and raised their glasses. In unison, they shouted, "Tae the king!" and drank. The women, seated, did the same.

William Drummond turned to smile at his wife's upturned face and said, "Here's tae the finest and most loyal companion that a man e'er had, wha hae been by my side fer mair than thirty years. She brought happiness tae ease my sorrow after the loss o' four o' our children. Long life, health, and happiness tae her."

With a roar and scraping of chairs, everyone rose, raised their glasses, shouted, "Tae Lady Drummond!" and drank.

The Viscount sat down. Servants bent forward to refill glasses. Jamie's father rose and toasted the Viscount's health. Others rose to offer toasts to Lord Lovat; Lord Murray; clan chiefs; lesser dignitaries; and of course, Saint Andrew, Saint Columba, Robert the Bruce, and William Wallace.

Jamie drifted off to sleep, since the toasts continued for a long time. He was startled awake when the Viscount raised his hand and a single piper stepped forward. He inflated his pipes and began to play a mournful and traditional tune, a piobroach, commemorating a long-ago battle fought by the Drummonds. Jamie noticed that men and women standing around the table had linked hands and were swaying in time to the melancholy notes. He was strangely moved by the swelling and falling notes of the pipes but drifted off to sleep again since the tune went on and on.

Jamie woke when his father picked him up out of his chair.

"Wake up, wee man! It's time fer the rockets tae fly!"

Jamie yawned and rubbed his eyes mightily with his fists. The pipers and drummers, playing a lively tune, led the crowd streaming out of the ballroom. Servants handed out cloaks as the guests moved out of doors into the inner courtyard. Jamie's breath puffed in a cloud as soon as he left the warmth of the castle.

People stood in knots on the paving stones of the courtyard with their arms crossed against the cold. Little clouds of steam rose from every group.

Torches and bonfires that ringed the courtyard dispelled some of the moonless darkness. The horses stamped and whickered in their paddock nearby. Grooms moved to the carriages to put blinkers over the eyes of the horses and hold their reins. They did not want rocket explosions and flashes panicking the horses. Servants moved quietly among the lamps and torches to snuff them. The courtyard was soon enveloped in darkness. For a while, nothing happened. Jamie grew restless. He was tired and cold. He wanted nothing but to go to sleep. He leaned against his father's leg, and his head nodded.

Jamie suddenly snapped awake. A bell tolled twelve times in one of the castle turrets, marking the end of the old year and beginning of the new. Young men brought out and lit the fireballs from a sizzling match. They marched around the courtyard, swinging the flaring balls on their short ropes. The glowing balls made arcs in the darkness that dazzled Jamie's eyes. The assembled crowd applauded and cheered loudly. After three trips around the courtyard, they doused the balls in the fountain.

Someone called, "Wha will be the first foot, Lady Drummond? We're a' here, already! Do ye expect a stranger this nicht?"

A raised torch illumined her face. She shrugged and said nothing.

Lochiel stepped forward and said loudly, "Nae one here is taller, darker, or mair handsome than Donald Cameron! Wha will gainsay me?"

There were jeers and catcalls, but no takers stepped forward. He raced up the steps and crossed the threshold, returning holding the plate of sweetmeats and cup, which he drained at a gulp.

"But where is yer gift fer Lady Drummond?" came a voice from the darkness.

Lochiel grinned hugely and reached beneath a fold of his great kilt. From an inner pocket, he extracted a large bottle and held it aloft.

"A bonnie gift, my lady. 'Tis the finest Bordeaux ever smuggled fra' oot o' France!"

The crowd cheered madly as he handed the gift to Lady Drummond with a deep bow. She laughed and took the bottle from his outstretched hand.

Suddenly, Jamie's father reached down to pick him up. As soon as he was settled, James whispered, "Look!"

Jamie swiveled his head around and saw nothing unusual. Then he heard a loud pop and whoosh as the first rocket headed skyward, trailing sparks, closely followed by another and then another. Jamie watched the three arcs climb upward and was vaguely disappointed. Red, yellow, and green flashes suddenly split the sky.

Boom! Boom! Boom!

The muffled explosions reberberated, and a curtain of multi-colored light flashed and sparkled across the sky. Jamie jerked spasmodically in his father's tight grip and flung his arms outward in surprise and delight. His eyes were shining, and he squealed his glee. Over the succeeding fifteen minutes, rockets raced skyward, exploded, and then died in sound and flaring light.

After a long pause, Jamie's father whispered in his ear, "They are getting ready tae launch yer rocket, son, the one with yer name on it. Watch and listen."

There was another pop followed by a deep roar as the rocket ignited. Jamie hugged his father close and shivered. The big rocket made a whizzing sound as it rose into the dark sky. The audience gathered in the inner courtyard gasped in anticipation. From the sky came a dull *boom!* as the rocket exploded. In less than a second, there was a crackle of many smaller explosions accompanied by vivid flashes of multi-colored light. The large rocket was a canister of a dozen smaller rocket charges. The multiple explosions filled the sky over the castle and lit up the tall turrets.

As soon as the light faded from the sky, a guardsman standing on the outer wall walk of the castle shouted, "Fire!"

Other guards standing by cannons on the castle parapet touched burning matches to the powder charges. The cannons tucked behind the castellated wall facing the front of the castle fired in a rippling crescendo of sound.

Boom! Boom! Boom! Boom!

The crowd cheered and clapped wildly. Happy children danced up and down and ran in circles. Jamie shouted himself hoarse.

When the fireworks show ended, his father took Jamie inside and handed him to his mother, who hugged him and passed him to Agnes MacRobie. Although Hogmanay evening would continue for several more hours for adults and older children, it was far past time for youngsters to be bedded down. Jamie laid his head against Agnes's shoulder and was asleep before she mounted the stairs. He opened glassy eyes momentarily when she laid him in his bed and snuffed the candles. She kissed his cheek, said good night, and softly closed the door. Jamie heard her receding footfalls down the hall. He closed his eyes and slept.

Much later, the sound of laughter from below woke him. He was disoriented and sat up. He had been dreaming of the fireworks. In the dim light, Jamie noticed that his bedroom door was half open. Obviously, someone had looked in on him while he was sleeping and had forgotten to shut the door.

Jamie clambered out of bed. The moon had risen in the clear sky, and soft light filtered through the curtains. He padded out the bedroom door and down the hall. When Jamie reached the railing, he knelt and then crawled to the top of the stairs. He peered down into the entry hall. Several men were standing by the doors, talking and laughing boisterously. Three older girls were sitting on the bottom step, also talking and laughing. Suddenly, one of the girls glanced up and saw Jamie peering down from the top step.

"Look!" she cried and pointed up the staircase. "We hae awakened our little prince. Let's bring him doon fer a proper coronation."

Giggling, all three raced up the steps. Uncertain of their intentions, Jamie scrambled back toward his bedroom. The girls caught him easily and carried him, struggling and legs kicking, down the staircase. The men watched the proceedings with curiosity. The girls told them that they were staging a coronation and invited the men to join them.

At one end of the ballroom, a dais had been set up with large comfortable chairs for the Viscount, his wife, and other dignitaries. No one was sitting there, but groups of people stood and sat in various places around the spacious ballroom. The orchestra had departed, and no one was dancing. The girls deposited Jamie in the largest chair.

One dark-haired girl said, "We canna have a proper coronation wi'oot a crown."

Another girl leaped up and ran to the kitchen to get shears and paper. She fashioned a coronet and brought it back. The third girl ducked into the vestibule where guests stored their cloaks and coats and returned with a white fur wrap.

People drifted toward the dais to watch.

The girl who had suggested making the coronet loudly announced, "The time hae come fer all guid Scots to crown their proper prince."

Many of the people, clearly amused, applauded. Others stood silently.

"He is a brave prince and true, come frae o'er the sea tae join us and make our Hogmanay celebration complete."

At these words, the clapping died away. Jamie looked up as the girls solemnly pulled the fur wrap around his shoulders and placed the paper crown on his head. They curtsied to him, and

Jamie clapped his hands in delight. The girls joined hands in a circle and sang to him.

When they finished, one of the girls plaintively asked, "When will the real prince come tae be wi' us?"

Another asked, "Will he raise the Stewart standard once again?"

At this, the three young men who had accompanied Donald Cameron, wearing great kilts, tartan sashes, and other accoutrements of Highland dress, moved to the front and raised their voices in a loud, "Hurrah! Hurrah! For Bonnie Prince Charlie! Hurrah for King James! Hurrah fer the House o' Stewart!"

Others cheered and raised their fists. Some voiced angry shouts and placed their hands on the dirks in their belts. In a moment, the ballroom was in noisy pandemonium. Jamie cried in fright. He yanked the paper crown from his head and flung it to the floor. He threw off the fur robe and climbed down from the would-be throne.

In a moment, Jamie's father was in their midst. He stooped and picked up Jamie, who clung to his neck, sobbing. He turned to the suddenly quiet group gathered around the dais.

"Hush!"

He pointed his free arm accusingly at the stunned and suddenly sober girls. "Ye are but foolish children. This game that ye hae invented tae entertain yerselves hae serious consequences. Ye dinna ken wha is listening and taking down yer words. Ye should be ashamed tae hae frightened a wee bairn. Such talk should be only behind closed doors among those wha know how tae close their mouths and keep them shut!" He turned to the others assembled in the ballroom. "Many wish fervently fer a return o' the king o'er the water and his son, the Bonnie Prince. Aye, they do, and none mair than I. But taking up arms is a most serious undertaking because it requires the risk o' everything." He paused and whispered, "All titles, estates, perhaps life itself. Time and time again, many o' those loyal tae the Stewarts and their cause lost their properties, fortunes, and even their lives in failed risings. Many were attainted and lost their ancestral homes, fortunes, and freedom fer years. Others lost their courage and ran awa', tae their everlasting shame." He shook his head slowly. "Nae, I canna wish fer such an outcome fer my family and friends on such a joyous nicht."

The young Highlanders muttered defiantly.

James continued. "Be silent. Nae one questions the courage o' the Camerons, MacDonalds, MacGregors, and others who hae fought bravely many times. If a rising promised a reasonable hope o' success, ye know wha would be in the forefront tae take up arms and risk all."

A young Highlander, clearly a Cameron from the clan badge clasping the sash that girded his thick chest, growled, "Aye. Our chief Lochiel would rise, and sae would many chiefs in the west. But wha' o' ye? Wha' o' the Drummonds?"

James took a deep breath and sighed. "Would he? Your clan chief, the Gentle Lochiel, is in the next room. I doubt that he is sae certain in his own mind, but ye should ask him yerself. If Charles Edward Stewart came o'er the water to raise his standard, he would find many stout souls with strong arms, broadswords, and targes, I am sure. Yet, brave souls and strong arms hae nae artillery and few other weapons. Will the Bonnie Prince bring them? Many are undecided. Some would do their utmost tae oppose him. They hae muckle artillery and many guns. Perhaps the prince and those wha rise wi' him would succeed. Perhaps they will lose…again. Perhaps the French would send men, guns, and money. Perhaps they will abandon us tae our fate…again."

He sighed and, looking down at his drowsy son, stroked his hair.

"Now is nae the time tae speculate, though the very air carries rumors aplenty. Let us see what the future brings. Let the clan chiefs consult while wise and loyal clansmen remain ready for war, if need be, or peace, which we all pray God tae hae. Now, be silent and let nae word o' this pass yer lips after this nicht. Above all, dinna frighten children wi' yer loose talk. Remember this evening's fine Hogmanay celebration and Drummond hospitality. Enjoy the guid company, guid wine, and guid food. Then, gae hame in peace and quiet."

The entry hall was hushed. Jamie's father carried him upstairs and comforted him with soothing words. The subdued guests drifted away.

When James Drummond came downstairs again, he quietly rejoined his father, brother John, Lord Lovat, Lord Murray, Lochiel, and other clan chiefs in Viscount William Drummond's study behind a locked door. Charles Gordon had gone to bed, refusing to participate in the discussion. The Gordons were Catholic and Jacobite but not willing to support open rebellion. No one in the room spoke up to persuade him.

Over glasses of port and a large map, the men returned to discussing possibilities and probabilities of rebellion until nearly dawn. William Drummond spoke little except to ask probing questions. Simon Fraser was argumentative but coldly logical. Lochiel and Lord Murray were passionate but refused to commit, and James Drummond cautioned everyone to be discreet and patient.

"Rebellion is brewing, and there is hope o' a successful rising in the Highlands tae put King James on the throne in place of that hated German, George. However, no one kens how far the French will gae tae provide real support, and none kens the resolve o' the English Jacobites, who say they despise the Hanoverians but hae nae risen in the past. How much influence will the hated Campbells exert on the western clans in their support fer King George and his ministers? How much steel is there in the backbone o' the young prince? There is much to risk and nae enough intelligence. We need information in order tae make reasonable decisions."

Lord William Drummond spoke up. "We need an intelligence-gathering expedition tae be completed before the end o' January. James, ye will return with Lochiel to Arisaig in Lochaber tae meet with Jacobite agents due tae land there frae France. John, ye will accompany Lord Murray tae Carlisle and Newcastle tae meet with English Jacobites tae evaluate their intentions. Lord Lovat, can ye meet wi' the northern clans and bring us word?"

He looked levelly at each man in turn. All nodded.

Viscount William stood wearily. "Weel, gentlemen," he said. "We hae used enough candles fer ain evening. Let us retire."

⁂

In midmorning, those sleeping at Strathallan Castle assembled in the great hall to watch the ancient Highland saining or blessing ceremony, presided over by Lady Margaret Drummond. She carried a pot of water "from a dead and living ford" scooped from Machany Water near the ruined chapel at Drumness. Leading an entourage from room to room, she and her daughters dipped their fingers and sprinkled the water on the people, beds, and carpets in each room. Servants lit partially dried juniper branches and set them to smoking by sprinkling water on them. They put these into damp baskets and carried them throughout the castle to fumigate the sealed rooms. The acrid smoke caused everyone inside to sneeze and cough uncontrollably. When servants finished fumigating every floor of the castle, they repeated the ceremony in the outbuildings. When they finished, servants doused the smoking branches and flung open doors and windows to welcome the fresh air of the New Year. Viscount Drummond himself served the restorative, a fine Scotch whiskey to guests and family members in filagreed silver quaiches. Following that rite, adults and children assembled in the dining room for a leisurely and sumptuous breakfast.

Chapter Two

It was an unseasonably mild day in mid-March. The sun shone brightly, but the air was still brisk. Gusty winds swept across the lawns and gardens at Strathallan, still spotted with heaps of melting snow. Euphemia Drummond stood pensively before a mirror in a downstairs hall. She had discovered a wrinkle at the corner of one eye. She examined the thick dark locks that hung down her back for signs of gray. She found none, for she was only twenty-five, but the strains of the last year were telling on her constitution. She felt anxious and suffered from sleeplessness. She was still as slender as her girlish portrait that hung on the wall, in which she stood in a garden bower, wearing a white frock and leaning on a frail gazebo among beds of flowers and blossoming trees. She wished herself there or riding among the mountains of lovely Abergeldie with her long-dead father instead of languishing in this house of intrigue in late winter.

She heard the heavy garden door slam. Jamie turned the corner and raced down the hall.

"Jamie! Shh!" she whispered severely.

He stopped abruptly as he tripped over a table leg. Euphemia groaned. The lad crawled to his feet and stood up. He walked with exaggerated slow steps until he reached his mother's side. Then he boiled over with excitement.

"Mama!" he whispered loudly.

"What?" she whispered back.

"Papa is back, and the chief o' the Camerons is wi' him. They're putting awa' their horses."

Euphemia's hand flew to her mouth. She felt a surge of dread.

"They bring news o' the French fleet and army, I ken."

She spun and ran toward the Viscount's study. Jamie stood uncertainly for a moment and then raced after her.

Within minutes, Viscount William greeted his eldest son, James, and Donald Cameron and ushered them into his study, along with his younger son, John Drummond.

Euphemia came to the entrance and beckoned to her husband. "James, ye must tell me what is transpiring. I have endured much heartache these past weeks, with intrigue all around me. Yer secrets are safe with me."

The Viscount looked pained and turned to the others questioningly. Lochiel smiled but said nothing, simply raising his big hands and letting them drop.

James said, "It would make things easier all around, Father, but…"

He turned to his wife. "If we fail and ye are questioned, ye will face the same rope and ax that we face. Can ye bear that?"

"Ye know I can, James," she whispered, "willingly."

He nodded but jerked his thumb at Jamie. "Get Agnes tae take Jamie ootside."

Euphemia gaped. "I'd forgotten that he followed me," she said weakly.

Jamie piped up, "I willna tell any secrets, Papa. I willna."

James reached over and patted his head affectionately.

Lochiel spoke up with a growl. "Lad, if ye learn a secret and tell, we'd have tae cut oot yer tongue."

Jamie stared at him open-mouthed. "Papa said that ye are an ogre."

Everyone burst out laughing, Cameron loudest of all. He slapped his knee.

"The Gentle Lochiel, an ogre. See my sharp teeth!" He bared them in a grimace and growled again.

Jamie backed up a step.

When the laughter subsided, James said to his son, "Nae, Jamie lad. Donald Cameron is as gentle a man with lads and lasses as any man can be. He only likes tae pretend tae be rough. He is mair a bear than a man, but nae an ogre wha eats children."

Jamie nodded and put in bravely, "Weel, he'd better nae try or I'll hae tae fecht him."

There was shocked silence in the room, except for Euphemia's exclamation.

"Ach! Sae violent, my son!"

Viscount Drummond smiled and said, "The lad is a terror. Ye must be careful, Lochiel."

Cameron laughed again and said, "I won't eat ye, lad. Someday, we'll gae hunting together like auld friends. I'll teach ye how tae shoot."

Jamie brightened. "Oh, will ye? I'd like that sae very much."

Cameron smiled affably. "I promise, lad. Yer papa will bring ye tae Lochaber. We'll hunt a stag together."

Agnes MacRobie appeared before the door of the study and held out her hand. Jamie took it and followed her to the kitchen.

James turned to Euphemia and asked in a low voice, "Please ask Mother tae join us."

Once Jamie was gone and Lady Margaret arrived, James shut and locked the door so they could discuss the news from France in addition to John Drummond's report and that contained in a letter just received from Simon Fraser. In Cameron territory on the west coast of Scotland, Donald Cameron and James Drummond had met with two spies who had ridden hard from the southern coast, bringing news carried from Brittany by smugglers. The Royal Navy had turned away the French convoy sailing toward Scotland's Hebrides. It had been loaded with French and Scottish Jacobite troops, arms, ammunition, and money. The English had caught up with them off the west coast of Ireland. Rather than risk capture or being run aground, the convoy had turned back to French ports.

As if this was not enough gloomy news, John Drummond reported on his unsatisfying meetings with English Jacobites. While they wanted to support a rising, without solid evidence of arrival of French arms and money, they would remain uncommitted. They had resisted John's plea that French help would be forthcoming with a strong showing of English support. Simon Fraser's news was equally gloomy. The clans of the northern Highlands—Sutherland, Caithness, Ross, and Aberdeen—almost all refused to commit themselves. The Huntley Gordons were the key to obtaining support of other northern clans. They wanted to support the king over the water, but the presence of a large and alert garrison at Inverness made them wary.

With a sigh, Lochiel said, "Aye. The situation is the same in the west. Fort William's garrison is strong and alert. There are patrols traversing Argyll constantly. Everyone is wary in Wester Ross, Lochaber, northern Argyll, and the isles." He pounded his large fist on the table. "They all speak the same weel-chosen cautious words. If….if…if the prince brings troops, guns, and artillery, we will support him. If…" He slumped in his chair. "However, wi' this bad news, we must wait." He sighed heavily. "We must get word tae the clan chiefs. There must be nae musters. Arms and ammunition must be weel hidden and guarded."

There was desultory conversation for a while that led to no better decision.

William Drummond looked around the room, sighed heavily, and said, "This is difficult and very saddening. I think, gentlemen, we share the conclusion that there is nae other choice but tae send messengers tae deliver the grim news and urge the clan chiefs tae do as Lochiel suggests. Let us then wait to see wha' further developments take place in France."

Everyone nodded assent, and James unlocked the door. At dinner that evening, the mood was somber. Even the children sensed that something had gone wrong, but there would be no answers to any questions. In the morning, Donald Cameron rejoined his followers, who had slept overnight in the forester's croft on the edge of the Drummond property out of sight of inquiring eyes, and rode west toward Rannoch Moor. James and John Drummond selected trusted servants to carry the message to Jacobite supporters across the Highlands, Lowland estates, and towns.

The mild but short days of late winter gave way to spring and finally to the long days of summer. Jamie's routine was daily lessons taught by Euphemia, Clementine, and Emilia in a spare room, followed by play out of doors or riding. Evenings were taken up with study. There was always time for sitting in front of a crackling fire with his father; Uncle John; Uncle William home on a brief leave from military duty; and his grandfather, William. Admonished by his mother, he noticed but did not say anything about the frequent furtive visits of strangers to the castle grounds. Most of the strangers did not come to the castle itself but stopped at the forester's croft in the western woods. There was always a servant posted there to convey news of their arrival to the Viscount through Mister Dobie.

The exception to the daily routine was on Sundays, when the family stepped into coaches emblazoned with the Strathallan Drummond coat of arms for the mile-long ride to the village of Muthill. They worshipped in the squat eleventh-century stone church with the incongruously tall spire added three centuries later. The church was built of reddish stone and sat on a rise at the edge of the village. Although the church bore the ancient marks of its Catholic origins in the architecture, it had been Anglican for two hundred years. The Drummonds always sat in their family pew. As all the others, it was of dark red cherry wood and marked with a brass plate with the Drummond name and coat of arms.

The seats were hard, but there were soft cushions for the women, the Viscount, and his wife. William Drummond seldom came, protesting duties, but everyone knew that he was Anglican in name only. He brought his children to be christened, paid tithes, and made frequent bequests that enriched the church. However, he and his wife Margaret maintained a prie dieu above which hung a dark wooden crucifix. They prayed regularly in their rooms in the traditional Catholic way. Every year or two, a priest came to the castle secretly, and William Drummond would call the family together to listen to the priest say Mass, take confession, and administer the sacrament of wine and wafers. However, the Viscount's children and their wives and husbands were outwardly Anglican and attended church regularly, to avoid difficulties with the crown.

On a warm day in mid-summer, the children sat fidgeting on the hard benches during the droning sermon of the stern white-robed minister. Occasionally, Jamie felt the pressure of his mother's hand on his shoulder or knee. It was a gentle but firm reminder for him to sit still and stay awake. He was annoyed with a pesky fly that kept circling his nose. Exasperated, he raised his left hand very slowly and suddenly swatted. He missed the fly but slapped the back of the pew in front of him. The minister stopped his sermon at the unexpected sound and glared at Jamie.

Jamie swiftly discovered that his mother was capable of unimaginable cruelty. Jamie felt her thumb and index finger close around his earlobe. She pulled him steadily to her side. He tried to resist, but the pain in his ear quickly persuaded him that a Jamie with two ears was far better than a Jamie with only one. He giggled as he imagined what he would look like with only one ear. Euphemia's sharp fingernail dug into his earlobe. It was more than he could endure.

"Ouch!" he yelped loudly.

The minister once again glared down from the lofty pulpit. Jamie gave up and slid obediently next to his mother, who shifted her grip from earlobe to arm. She maintained her grip until, mercifully, the sermon ended and the entire congregation rose to sing the hymn "Praise God from Whom All Blessings Flow." Escape was the blessing for which Jamie yearned.

After the sermon, the Drummonds and other landed families who owned pews in the little church laid a picnic on the grassy lawn in the shadow of the church's ancient bell tower. After eating to repletion, children played on the grass while adults lounged in the shade of the leafy trees that crowned the knoll. The children roamed everywhere around the church, except inside the low red stone walls of the cemetery, with its rows of weathered dark gray stone slabs with faded lettering. Jamie knew that many of his ancestors were buried in the churchyard. The stones had once all been upright with lettering precise and clear. Years of wet Scottish winters, freezing, thawing, and shifting soil had tilted and weathered the stones so badly that they could hardly be read, except the newest. Many of the stones were unstable, and the children had been warned to beware of touching or standing near them. Jamie's mother told him that before he was born, a little girl had been crushed by a falling headstone. She showed him where the little girl was buried. He was careful to avoid the cemetery entirely. In mid-afternoon, servants packed up the remains of lunch and families returned to the church for another two-hour service.

On most Sundays, the Drummonds worshipped at the Muthill church. When winter weather turned the roads to mud and made travel difficult, the family prayed in the castle's chapel and invited the minister to visit them for dinner. Occasionally, they visited other churches close by in Perthshire. The Viscount's favorite was in a village near the cattle fair town of Crieff two and a half miles from Strathallan castle. Fowlis Wester lay in a hollow north of the road from Crieff. Along the road, the coach passed Pictish standing stones and ancient burial mounds.

The twelfth-century church of St. Bain stood in the center of town, next to the village green. The Earl of Strathearn had built St. Bean's Church, so there was a close tie with the Drummond family of Strathallan. The chapel was severely plain and edged with stone arches. Inside stood rows of heavily worn benches of dark wood and simple unpadded wooden kneelers for parishioners. The building was not remotely like the elegant and massive cathedrals in Perth and Aberdeen, but the ancient church had an air of reverence that impressed young Jamie. The interior was musty, dark, and quiet with a quaint echo even when the chapel was filled with people. The church's vaulted ceiling was the most impressive feature. One could see that the dark brown wooden arches of the ceiling fitted closely together and curved gracefully upward to form the interior of the tall spire.

After the sermon, while the congregation slowly filed out to talk under the trees, Jamie stared at the Pictish standing stones. Inside the church was the real wonder. There was a light gray stone slab with a crude carving of two horsemen and animals on one side and on the other a man leading a cow wearing a bell, followed by six other men. On another stone was a chiseled scene of two priests seated in chairs flanking a Celtic cross. On a third was Jamie's favorite, a rough sketch of a whale and a man about to be swallowed. To answer his son's questions about the meaning of the drawings, James took down a Bible from a shelf in the entry and read him the story of Jonah and the whale.

Jamie asked his father, "Papa, what is the meaning of the stone with the cows and men?"

James thought for a moment, with his finger on his chin. "Nae one kens the meaning, Jamie lad," he replied. "The people wha carved the stones are lang dead. They couldna write, so they told stories from memory fer centuries. Finally, people forgot the stories and all we hae left are the auld stones. Everywhere we look, Scotland is filled with such mysteries o' the past.

"I think," James said, "that the people wha carved the stones were just telling stories aboot their ain lives. They herded cattle, just as ye see herdsmen bringing them in during the cattle fairs in Crieff." He pointed to one of the slabs. "See that bell? It is just like the the bell up in the tower that was ringing when we arrived at church."

His father smiled gently and said, "Ye see, Jamie, they were people just like us. They measured their wealth in land, cattle, and men just as we still do. Fathers and mothers loved their children. They fished, hunted, and farmed. They fought wars when there was nae choice. They probably even looked like us. They were yer ancestors."

Jamie tugged at his father's arm. "Tell me aboot the auld times and people. Will ye, Papa?"

James put his arm around his son's shoulders. "I will, Jamie, but nae now. Storytelling should be in the dark in front o' a guid fire after our bellies are full. I'll tell ye then."

Together, they stared at the stone. Jamie wet a finger and touched it to the gritty stone. Slowly, he traced the outline of the man leading the cow.

All Drummond men were excellent storytellers and loved telling stories to the children in the evenings. His grandfather told the oldest and longest tales. Uncle John stood and acted out parts, flailing his arms vigorously in imaginary swordplay with grand gestures. James sat quietly and sketched his stories with words and the tone of his voice alone. Sometimes, both told parts of stories that fitted together like a puzzle. Most of the stories ended in a single evening, but sometimes they required several evenings to tell. Jamie loved to stare into the fire during the storytelling. In his imagination, the flickering shapes in the fire and shadows on the walls were dragons, horses, warriors, and other participants in his father and uncle's verbal dramas.

Jamie loved to hear stories of the early history of Scotland. The past of his homeland was peopled by giants, witches, trolls, kings, and knights who fought dragons and rescued beautiful maidens from lonely castles. He went to bed dreaming of Viking marauders in their long ships with dragon-headed prows, Saint Columba who brought Christianity from Ireland to the tiny isle of Iona in the Hebrides, or Somerled who drove the Vikings from Argyll and Kintyre.

Jamie and other Drummond children played games in which they reenacted long-ago battles. They raced down the hill behind the castle with wooden toy swords to the small bridge over the lake to reenact the Battle of Stirling Bridge where William Wallace and Andrew Murray defeated the English. They found a small cave, whose entrance was obscured by gnarled old willows behind the castle garden, and pretended that they were Robert Bruce and their brave ancestor Malcolm Drummond, who sat watching the spider patiently spin its web, teaching patience to the future king of Scotland.

Lady Margaret, Euphemia, Clementine, and Emilia sat close to the flickering candles to have enough light for their needlework but seldom participated in storytelling. Examples of their excellent stitchery hung on the walls of many of the castle's rooms. One winter's night, Jamie urged them, over their protests, to tell some stories. Reluctantly, his mother laid aside the tapestry on which she had been sewing. Jamie sat spellbound as his mother recited the tales of Scheherezade to the sultan, *The Arabian Nights*. She did not finish the first story that evening. She broke off, just as had Scheherazade, and insisted that the children go to bed.

"But, Mama, it's such a wonderful story, and ye are such a guid storyteller. May we stay up until ye finish the story?" Jamie asked hopefully.

She ignored his plea and ordered him to bed. He sighed loudly and grimaced to signal his great disappointment, but she was obdurate. The next night, Jamie did not have to be told to finish his supper. He was done and in place by the fire before anyone else. His mother settled herself and waited for the others to gather while Jamie fidgeted. She began the tale exactly where she had left off. It was nearly two weeks before Euphemia told the last tale.

Jamie begged for more, but his mother said, "But, Jamie, there is nae mair. The princess and the sultan lived happily ever after. The end."

Everyone burst out laughing, but Jamie sulked.

The children were so taken with the tales that Clementine and Emilia spent nearly the whole winter working with them in acting out the tales of the Arabian nights dressed in borrowed sheets, silks, and satins fashioned into robes and turbans.

One evening after listening to his father recite the story of the great victory of the Scots over the English at Bannockburn, Jamie asked, "Papa, why was Robert the Bruce able to defeat the English army when there were so many of them in Scotland and we canna do it?"

James did not answer his son for a long time. He sat gazing into the fire thoughtfully. To his son, James Drummond was an affable and gentle father who loved playing with children, laughing and romping with them.

Jamie looked at his father's face, which was grimmer than Jamie had ever seen it. "Papa? What's wrong?" asked Jamie plaintively.

James put his hand gently on Jamie's. Finally, he spoke. "Those glorious days are past, my son. Scotland had tae make an unhappy union with the English. Before that, Parliament took the throne awa' frae the rightful king and gave it tae a usurper frae Holland and then tae a German prince, a distant relation tae the Stewarts. We Highlanders fought the English twice tae restore the rightful king tae his throne. While we fought bravely, we lost. Now, we are too weak tae fecht back. We must wait until a better time, but someday, we will have our rightful king again. Perhaps it will happen in your grandfather's lifetime, perhaps in mine, perhaps only when ye are a man. We must be wise and patient. Someday, ye will learn tae fecht as a man must if he values honor and freedom. The English and the Lowlanders will nae give us freedom easily. We must take it."

He looked into the fire and was silent for a space. Then he said, "We dream o' our glorious past and yearn fer a yet mair glorious future."

Jamie looked at his uncle, John, who also sat staring into the fire. Jamie's grandfather sat in his great chair nodding slowly, his eyes glistening.

James reached into his jacket pocket and extracted his new watch, which was fastened to his pocket with a finely worked silver chain. He flipped up the engraved lid and stared at the face.

"Humph! It's almost nine o'clock. Your mama will be here shortly tae wonder why ye are nae upstairs already, Jamie. Now, off tae bed with ye. Morning will be here soon. Ye start yer lessons tomorrow."

Jamie gasped. "What lessons?"

"Ah!" James grinned. "Yer mother hae nae told ye? Ye hae a tutor arriving by coach tomorrow frae Aberdeen."

"Where will I gae tae school, Papa? In town, with other boys?" asked Jamie.

"Why, here," his father replied. "I hae hired Doctor Archibald Thomson tae tutor ye, several o' yer cousins, and some neighbor children from Aberruthven, Tullibardine, and Auchterarder whose fathers will help pay the tutor's salary. The schoolroom is already prepared and stocked wi' books, slates, and everything needful."

Jamie's grandfather seldom said much around the children. Now, he leaned forward in his chair and took Jamie by his right hand. He stared intently into his eyes. "I expect ye tae be obedient tae Doctor Thomson. He is a strict tutor and, unlike us, a staunch Presbyterian. He is nae here tae teach ye religion by my strict instructions, but he will awake in ye a desire tae do yer best, sae learn the lessons that he will teach. He'll open yer eyes tae yer own possibilities. We live in an exciting time, Jamie. The world is changin' quickly, and auld ways are changin' as weel. Whether we hae peace or war, ye will need many kinds o' knowledge tae survive in this world. Ye canna depend on auld traditions as I hae done. Ye need to be exceptional at languages, history, geography, natural philosophy, logic, rhetoric, mathematics, and law, things that ye dinna yet understand. But Doctor Thomson will teach ye and prepare ye fer the world, as yer father will prepare ye fer yer responsibilities as leader o' the Drummond family. Ye are my eldest son's son. He is my heir, and ye are his. Ye hae great responsibilities, and must grow in knowledge and wisdom accordingly. I will arrange other tutors fer ye, sae that will grow strong in body and spirit. Ye must learn o' leadership, horses, weapons, and management o' estates and lands. Tae be a Highland gentleman, ye will need all these skills and many others."

The viscount shifted in his chair and frowned.

"In spite o' the usefulness o' book knowledge and a strong body, ye must learn the age-auld lessons of honor, honesty, thrift, integrity, and respect fer others, especially honor, lad. When ye hae naught else, always hae honor. Ye canna buy it with any amount of gold and silver. Honor will guide a boy and a man all his life. Honor is what makes a man a man and nae an animal wha kens naught but tae follow his nose and root fer food, wha will betray those wha trust him because o' power, greed, or political advantage."

Jamie giggled at the thought of following his nose and rooting for food but became solemn when he saw the fierceness of his grandfather's gaze and felt the trembling of the big creased hand pressing down on his.

"Ye will someday be a man, Jamie, a guid, strong man like yer father and become his pride and joy as an honorable son wha can be trusted tae always do the right things. Ye are part o' a strong family that has survived nae because o' this castle, wealth, or lands but because we hae integrity and honor. Ne'er forget that. Ne'er lie. Ne'er cheat. Always pay what ye owe. Ne'er take advantage o' someone weaker. A strong man hae nae need o' that. Always do yer best. In all that ye learn, in all ye do and where'er ye gae, live as an example o' what it means tae be a Drummond, especially after ye are grown tae manhood and we are nae there tae guide ye. Ye must choose the right course by yerself then. Ne'er let another man choose it fer ye."

Jamie frowned and said, "But, Grandpapa, I dinna ken what all those words mean."

His grandfather's expression softened, and he said gently, "That's why ye hae us and Doctor Thomson tae teach ye."

William Drummond released his grandson's hand, touched his cheek gently, drew him into a strong hug, and then released him. Jamie was troubled by the seriousness of his grandfather's speech. It frightened him in a vague way. He was very impressed by the intensity of his voice, and he could see tears glistening on his furrowed cheeks. The Viscount wiped his eyes fiercely, as if he were ashamed to be seen weeping before a child.

Then, in a husky voice, he commanded, "Time fer bed, lad. Off wi' ye now."

Jamie looked intently at his grandfather hunched in his chair.

Impulsively, he ran back into the old man's arms, hugged him tight, and whispered, "Thank ye, Grandpapa. I love ye." Then he walked to his father and buried his head in his shoulder.

James could not speak, but patted Jamie's shoulder lovingly. Jamie stepped back and turned around to see Agnes MacRobie standing behind him, tears trickling down her cheeks. Jamie seized her hand and pulled her toward the door. Together, they raced up the stairs.

Chapter Three

Jamie discovered quickly that young Doctor Archibald Thomson was everything that his grandfather predicted. He was tall, thin, and plain of face and dress, befitting one raised in the strict Lowland Presbyterian tradition. He was ungainly while walking and had a tendency to stop suddenly on his perambulations to gaze into the distance as if on the horizon he could see the solution to whatever puzzled him. The children in his care quickly gave him the nickname "gilly gaupus" but never used that insulting term in his presence.

Archibald Thomson was a strict disciplinarian, as the children discovered, and adept in accurately throwing pieces of chalk at sleepy students. He carried a short stick capped with a metal ferrule and frequently used it to rap disobedient lads over the knuckles. He was visibly uncomfortable around women of the household and halting of speech in social gatherings. However, in the classroom, he underwent a remarkable metamorphosis. He had a passion for learning that infected the students.

It seemed to Jamie that Doctor Thomson was knowledgeable on every topic. He could recite wondrously long passages from memory and draw on a wealth of examples when teaching mathematics or logic. He kept a small botanical collection in the classroom and spent hours in the solar and gardens with Lady Margaret. He accompanied the gardeners to examine plants and collect specimens. Jamie was amazed to see him peer at a flower or leaf and recreate it in chalk on a slate with a few deft strokes.

Over the next year, Jamie proved an adept pupil. He pleased Doctor Thomson and his parents in rapidly outdistancing the other students of his age in nearly every topic. He became a voracious reader. Several times, his grandfather found him in Strathallan's library, poring over books that had gathered dust for decades. However, Jamie did not spend all of his time in study. He completed his assignments quickly in order to race down to the stables. He helped the grooms with chores and learned the traits of each horse. He looked for every opportunity to exercise and ride as many horses as the grooms would allow. James frequently took Jamie to the woods, where he taught him to load and shoot a fowling piece. Jamie shot a duck that startled him by flying from cover in the tall grass right at his feet. Jamie proudly carried the duck home, where the cooks plucked, cleaned, and roasted it to a brown crackling finish to serve as a centerpiece of the next night's supper.

James also taught Jamie archery, using targets set up on the castle lawn. With a few lessons, Jamie showed that he was an excellent shot at close range, with hopes of developing proficiency with a full-sized bow as he grew in strength and stature.

In the late summer of Jamie's seventh year, Jock McRae came to live at the castle. Jock was a retired soldier of indeterminate age who had fought with William Drummond at Sheriffmuir. After the Jacobites scattered, Jock had left the country as a mercenary soldier, serving in Flanders, Austria, and Italy. He returned briefly when opportunities dried up and bought a commission in the Black Watch regiment with his earnings and prize money. His military career ended when a musketball broke his left arm, which, in healing, shrank until it was noticeably shorter than his right. The injury did not impede McRae's ability to ride and shoot, so Viscount Drummond hired him to tutor Jamie in riding and the military arts. He had no wife and lived alone in a cottage on the castle grounds. Immediately after his arrival, he took down and inspected all the blades, guns, and pikes in the castle.

He set up a small forge before his cottage and could be seen in the evenings cleaning and repairing weapons and the Viscount's stock of hunting guns. He became popular with the grooms, who recognized in his way with horses the excellent abilities of a professional cavalryman.

Jamie had ridden almost since he could walk, gradually moving up from small ponies to the gentler horses. Not long after Jock McRae's arrival, the veteran invited him and his aunt Emilia to ride.

"I need tae explore the grounds, and I hae need fer a guide. Ye twa are perfect fer that purpose," he said.

Emilia noticed that Jock had saddled a recently acquired chestnut mare for Jamie. The horse was taller and more spirited than his usual mount. Emilia whispered to Jock that Jamie had never ridden such a large animal before.

"Ach," he responded. "The lad needs a leetle challenge sae he will grow. I hae watched him ride, and hae tested this animal. He'll soon learn tae control her."

As soon as Jamie approached, the mare looked down at the boy holding her reins and whickered gently. Jamie reached up to pat the mare's nose. He stepped up on the mounting block and clambered into the saddle. They rode out, tousled-haired seven-year-old perched high on his new mount, lithe seventeen-year-old girl, and the old cavalry soldier. Emilia rode a little behind Jamie to watch him. She saw quickly that Jock was right. The boy had a sure and confident touch with the mare. All three cantered along the path through the trees leading eastward from the stables. Soon, they came out onto pastureland dotted with grazing sheep.

"Steer clear o' the sheep, Jamie!" called Emilia.

Obediently, the boy guided the mare between the animals. Once clear, he kicked his mount into a slow gallop, with the other riders following. On the far side of the pasture, the mare vaulted the low railing with ease. Jamie found himself on the road leading to Kinkell Bridge over the River Earn. The drumbeat sound of the mare's hooves on the hard-packed road after thudding on the soft turf of the well-clipped pasture was exhilarating.

"Wha-ho!" shouted Jock from well back on the road. "Hold up, laddie!"

Jamie slowed the mare to a walk to allow the others to catch up.

"I'll hae tae put a halter on ye tae hold ye back, lad!"

Jamie grinned and shouted, "I love this horse!"

The mare whinnied appreciatively.

On succeeding days, they explored every part of the extensive grounds of Strathallan Castle. They took trails along Machany Water to Brackenhill, Culdees, and the ruins of Drumness Abbey. They discovered the old forester's croft on a knoll in the western woods, secluded in thick trees not far from the military road that ran between Tullibardine Mill and Muthill. The croft house puzzled Jock McRae. He circled the building and then bade them dismount while he closely examined the outside. Weeds had grown up around the building, but the door was secured with an unrusted padlock and the hinges were freshly oiled. Emelia peered through the windows. She saw shelves along a wall, stocked with boxes and bottles.

"Humph!" exclaimed Jock as he peered in. "'Tis nae abandoned. Someone's been living or visiting here, for sairtan."

Emilia spoke up. "James mentioned something aboot using the croft fer meetings with visitors because none are tae ken they are here."

Jock grunted. "Aye, it is nae guid fer us tae be snoopin' around if the Viscount dinna want anyone tae ken he is entertainin' visitors. We must be gone, and nae talkin' tae anyone aboot what we hae seen."

They remounted and moved off the knoll until the croft was hidden in the trees. Jamie wondered who the visitors might be who did not want to come to the castle. He resolved to sneak back for time to time to check, but winter closed down with a heavy snowfall, and walking and riding through the woods became too difficult.

On a day in early November, while the Gordons were visiting from Aberfeldie, James and John Drummond brought exciting news. They were taking Jamie and his Gordon cousins, Peter and William, west for two weeks to Lochaber, homeland of Clan Cameron, for a stag hunt. Young William Drummond was home on leave from his military posting in Ireland and would join them. Charles Gordon declared that winter hunting was not to his liking and declined the invitation. James, John, and William bundled the boys into a coach, but the men rode for most of the long journey. They took the road north from Strathallan through Crieff to Aberfeldy along Loch Tay, across Rannoch Moor, over the pass where heavy snow bogged down the coach for an hour, then down into Lochaber to the Cameron stronghold at Achnacarry.

The trip took two long days, but everyone was restored by a grand feast presented by Donald Cameron and his brothers. There was food and drink aplenty, music, dancing, and telling of old tales around a roaring fire. The Drummonds presented fine gifts of whiskey, dirks, and belts to the Cameron men, and jewelry of silver and precious stones for their ladies. After two days of merriment, Donald Cameron gathered for the hunt. Dark clouds threatening rain raced across the sky, with occasional breaks of sunshine.

Jamie enjoyed the riding in the steep, hilly terrain of Lochaber with the other boys and young Cameron clansmen assigned to escort them. They could not maintain the same pace as the hunters and were quickly separated from them. From time to time, they heard hunting horns, baying dogs, horses crashing through underbrush, and distant shots. As the early dusk enveloped them, the boys and their escort turned back, disappointed at having missed out on the chase. The only stags they saw were the three heavy antlered specimens stretched out at the lodge by the proud hunters.

That evening, the Drummond and Cameron men drank innumerable toasts and ate venison roasted over open fires as they sat at long trestle tables, their breath smoking in the frigid air. Before the men butchered the animals, Donald Cameron invited Jamie to come forward to wrap his arms around the neck of the big stag felled jointly by himself and James Drummond. After the butchering, Lochiel made a gift of the magnificent rack of antlers to Jamie. A second set went to Peter and Will Gordon to take home to Abergeldie.

After the meal, the Cameron brothers sat drinking until late with the Drummonds. Jamie and the other boys sat up with them. The talk was of prospects for a rising and intentions of the Bonnie Prince. The men spoke openly, for in the stronghold of the Camerons, there was no one of the opposition to overhear them. The conversation was speculative since no one knew anything definite. Jamie, tired to exhaustion by the long day of riding, quickly lost interest. Bundled in a heavy bearskin and leaning against Lochiel's massive shoulder, he drifted off, awaking curled up before the hearth as servants built up the fire for breakfast.

Three days later, in a drizzling rain, they started on the long journey back to Strathallan, where Jamie proudly presented the antlers to his grandfather. Within days, a carpenter had mounted the antlers high above the fireplace and the set to go to Abergeldie on a polished slab of oak.

At the annual Hogmanay celebration, James Drummond announced that Charles and Alison Gordon had invited them to spend a month at their home in the north as soon as spring came. Alison was expecting another child and wanted Euphemia to be with her.

The children did not mind the incessant rain that turned the roads slick, though several times they had to stand on the side of the road while the driver and footmen used shovels, pry bars, and ropes to dig out the coach when it sank to the hubs in the muddy quagmire. Jamie especially enjoyed having a month away from classes with Doctor Thomson. Anticipating the spring break, the tutor loaded Jamie with schoolwork and additional studies and exercises until the day the family departed. In addition to his clothing, Jamie lugged a large case of books assigned by Doctor Thomson.

Jamie loved Abergeldie on first sight. His first view was of towering hills on either side of the narrow strath along the River Dee, as the coach jounced along the rough road from Crathie. The estate ran for miles along the river through the district known locally as the Mains of Abergeldie. The castle took its name from the Gaelic *abhir-gile*, meaning "confluence of the clear stream." The horses strained to pull the coach up the long grade after they turned off the main road. When they cleared the crest, Jamie saw a rocky hill towering darkly beyond the rushing, boulder-filled stream. Euphemia leaned forward and gripped both James and Jamie's arms in excitement.

"That is Craig-na-ban. I remember the first time I climbed that hill as a girl. It was so difficult at first. As I grew up, it was such a pleasure and not a labor at all to race up. I would stand on top to admire the magnificent view and breathe in the fresh, fresh air." She pointed to the stream. "And that's the River Dee, and on the other side, high up is Mount Geallaig, even higher than Craig-na-Ban. Frae the top, there is an excellent view o' the snaw and ice that is around Lachin-y-Gair most o' the year. The glens are sae deep up there that they are dark most o' the day. That's why we call it dark Lachin-y-Gair." Euphemia clapped her hands and pointed to the bridge over the foaming stream. "Look! We can see the castle! All this land that we have been passing fer nearly half an hour is a' part o' Abergeldie."

Jamie watched as the driver pulled hard on the reins to slow the team, and the coach slowly turned onto another road beyond the bridge. The route leading to the castle was much rougher, and the coach rumbled and swayed through thick stands of Scotch pine, fir, larch, and birch. As they neared the castle, the trees thinned and Jamie could see manicured gardens and lawns surrounding it. The coach pulled into the curving driveway to the castle entrance.

Jamie saw that the castle was massive and marked by a turreted square block tower. His mother continued to tell the history of Abergeldie.

"It's very auld, Jamie. My ancestor, Alexander Gordon, the first Earl of Huntley, acquired Abergeldie almost three hundred years ago. Over the centuries, people have added rooms, and now it is three stories high, with cellars and a spooky auld attic. You'll love exploring it, but ye must be careful."

She paused, and Jamie asked, "Careful?"

The coach lurched to a stop, and the driver leaned down to call, "Abergeldie, my lord!"

Footmen hurried forward to unload the family's luggage, open doors, and place steps for passengers.

Jamie persisted. "Why be careful, Mama?" Jamie did not see the faint smile on his father's lips.

Euphemia leaned forward and whispered, "Because the castle is said tae be haunted by the ghost o' French Kate, or Kitty Rankie as they called her at Abergeldie. She was a French girl wha once served at the castle. She was secretive, and very soon after her arrival, other servants suspected her o' practicing black magic. They went tae the earl and accused her. Kitty was arrested and tortured, and they pronounced her guilty o' being a witch. They kept her in the dungeon o' the castle."

"Dungeon?" squeaked Jamie.

"Aye, and they tortured her with red-hot pokers pressed tae the soles o' her feet, until she confessed. Then they took her up on that hill over there. They tied her tae a stake and piled dry brush all around and set it on fire. She went up in a greasy cloud o' smoke. Her ghost is still angry aboot that and hae been seen drifting around and muttering doon in the cellars o' the castle late at nicht since that day."

Jamie shivered, and looked searchingly at his mother. Finally, she smiled.

James burst out laughing and said accusingly, "Ye are just making up that story, Mama, just like ye did wi' the Arabian nights!"

Euphemia's smile vanished. "Ye think I am?" she said in a low voice, as she turned to dismount from the coach. "Ask Peter if it isna true," she said and held out her hands for Jamie to climb down.

Charles Gordon was standing on the portico of the castle as the coach crunched to a stop. For one of the few times in Jamie's memory, his uncle smiled as he embraced his sister and shook hands with James. Within seconds, the five Gordon children—Peter, William, Alison, Margaret, and David—surrounded Jamie, chattering excitedly. The Drummonds settled into the rooms assigned them, and Charles gave them a tour of the castle.

Late that afternoon, Jamie had the opportunity to ask Peter about the ghost of French Kate. He was afraid of the other children laughing at him for his fears, so he asked Peter privately. Peter was fourteen and nearly as tall as his father. Peter listened to Jamie's retelling of the legend with a serious face. As he finished the tale, Peter nodded slowly.

"I am sorry tae tell ye this, Jamie, but yer mother is right. She really did live, and she really died as Aunt Euphemia said."

Before Jamie could react, Peter gripped his shoulder.

"But she has nae appeared tae any o' our family fer a very long time. Papa had a priest come tae the castle when I was little tae pronounce an exorcism. It dinna work perfectly, but now French Kate stays doon in the cellars. The dungeon is there, and she only appears at nicht. So, dinna gae doon in the cellars at nicht. Ye might hear her clattering and groaning aboot though," mused Peter thoughtfully.

Jamie persisted. "Is there really a dungeon doon there?"

Peter nodded his head. "Ach, yes. Would ye like tae see it? It is only a couple o' empty rooms now. Nae torture implements, nae chains, and nae manacles fer a hundred years. They are just rooms where the servants store unused tools and things."

"Nae now," said Jamie cautiously. "Perhaps later, when I get used tae the idea."

"Are ye afraid, Jamie? It is all right if ye are."

Jamie responded, "Weel, I'm nae afraid, but I am careful."

At that, Peter burst out laughing and clapped Jamie on the shoulder.

"Come, cousin, let's gae riding. I want tae show ye some o' the grounds. But first, let's find Will. He will want tae come along."

The month passed quickly. The children spent mornings in studies, Jamie included, but afternoons were for play, riding and tramping in the woods during good weather and playing indoor games on inclement days. Several times, James and Euphemia led the older children on hikes up Geallaig and Craig-na-Ban. They also went to the village of Crathie several times and to a lavish costume ball at Braemar Castle, with all of the children dressed as pirates. Jamie even built up courage to visit the dungeon and the stuffy attic, where the children pulled out old toys and clothing from chests and an old armoire thick with dust. Jamie found a trunk filled with seventeenth-century Restoration wigs with long curls and another filled with medallions and jewelry.

Euphemia and Alison were delighted with the find and helped the children with reshaping and fitting the wigs and cleaning the old clothing. Euphemia was exceptional at painting, and for two long rainy afternoons, she posed the children in the solar while she worked on a large canvas. When she finished, the entire family viewed it and pronounced it a masterpiece. Charles proudly hung the painting in a downstairs hall.

All too soon, the idyllic month was over. Alison Gordon had an easy and short labor and gave birth to a little girl named Anne by her parents. The Drummonds decided to stay an extra week to enjoy the new child. Then it was time to repack and return to Strathallan. Jamie was almost in tears as the day of departure arrived. He had come to love Abergeldie and its high mountains, deep woods, dark lochs, and especially his friendship with his Gordon cousins. James and Charles announced that as soon as the children finished classes in early summer, the Gordon family would come to Strathallan for a month. This news softened the blow of departure.

It was warm and clear weather the morning of departure. The Gordon and Drummond adults embraced, and James and Euphemia herded Jamie into the coach. Everyone shouted their good-byes excitedly as the footmen fastened the last strap on the boot and the driver took his place.

Jamie leaned out the window precariously to shake hands with Peter and Will. "And dinna bring French Kate!" he shouted.

"Jamie, sit doon before ye fall oot!"

Euphemia grabbed Jamie by his collar and banged him onto the seat. The coach picked up speed as it headed for the bridge over the River Dee.

Jamie returned to Strathallan filled with anticipation of the promised visit. Doctor Thomson shocked him out of his pleasant reverie with a wrathful denunciation of the poor quality of Jamie's work during the stay at Abergeldie.

"It is obvious from yer lack of answers tae my questions," said Master Drummond, "that ye have been slacking while ye were gone, as if it were merely a holiday. Ye hae nae completed the readings and other work assigned. I am not just angry. I am furious with ye, sluggard!"

He turned and left the classroom. The other students were silent. They sat staring at Jamie. Doctor Thomson returned within minutes and beckoned for Jamie to follow. They marched side by side in silence to James Drummond's office. He went in, and Jamie waited miserably outside the door. He could hear voices raised behind the thick oaken panels. Finally, the loud voices subsided to murmurs.

After nearly an hour, James opened the door. Doctor Thomson stood with arms crossed tightly across his chest. There was a red flush on his cheeks, and his lips were thin and tight. Jamie stood before his father with fear tingling along his spine. James's angry words washed over him, with occasional comments from Doctor Thomson. He bowed his head, for he knew that he had not been diligent and no excuses would be acceptable. Jamie felt a flush of shame that he had disappointed his father, but he also felt hot indignation that he should be punished while everyone had had such a good time on their holiday. He bit his lower lip tightly and said nothing, although he was shaking with suppressed anger. Finally, his father's outburst died away since his anger was forced to impress his son with the seriousness of doing well at his studies. James did not believe in beatings in order to enforce discipline, but he had already agreed with Doctor Thomson to inflict punishment. Jamie gasped on hearing the harsh sentence but resolutely bowed his head and kept silent. He knew that arguing would not work. His father and his teacher were implacable.

James tonelessly imposed the punishment: no outside play, no horseback riding, no sports. Meals only would interrupt schoolwork until lessons were caught up and Doctor Thomson was satisfied. Sundays were excepted. If lessons were not caught up before the Gordons arrived for holiday in July, then Jamie would spend the entire time confined to the schoolroom. Jamie was stricken by the harshness of the punishment but only nodded when his father asked if he understood. He did not trust himself to speak. James was puzzled by Jamie's response: no excuses, no arguments—only mute agreement. He felt a brief urge to lecture his son about honor and responsibility, but the boy's puzzling acceptance negated his desire. Doctor Thomson looked smugly satisfied. He opened his mouth to say something, but Jamie's undefiant behavior deflated him, so he only nodded.

"Fine then, my lord. It seems that this affair is settled. If there is nothing more, Master Drummond and I will return tae the classroom and begin work."

James held up a restraining hand. "Doctor Thomson. Ye will provide me a daily report on Jamie's progress. How long do ye think that it will take fer him tae satisfy all delinquencies?"

Doctor Thomson stopped his movement toward the door. He shifted his balance from foot to foot as he stroked his long chin thoughtfully. "Weel, that depends on the lad, does it not, my lord? If he is as determined as he appears, I think that the remaining time may be sufficient. I intend to leave on sabbatical before the end of June to Geneva to do research for a book I am writing on the life of John Calvin, the great Reformation divine."

"Ah, yes, John Calvin, the tutor o' Mister Knox, wha brought Presbyterianism tae Scotland. I dinna agree with that man's philosophies but find him a very compelling figure in history. Ye see, I dinna believe that God hae predetemined the fate o' anyone. Were I tae believe that, I would find myself a hopeless skeptic." James settled back in his chair. "I wonder, Doctor Thomson, if such men ever thought that their words and actions could have deleterious as well as beneficial effects upon the world? That we, twa hundred years after the schisms o' the sixteenth century, are still bent on oppressing and killing each other o'er their fine points o' doctrine?"

Doctor Thomson smiled. "Aye, my lord—a fine question. We could pose the same question today of political figures and institutions concerning their inflammatory rhetoric, which seems designed mostly to reinforce the convictions of their followers and not to convince their critics. There are men who fight and die every day over their principles, if one can call them principles."

James responded, "Indeed, Doctor, it is a tumultuous world. We live in a swirl o' conflicting ideas and principles. I pity and pray fer the young such as Jamie, since it is fer them that we struggle tae improve our world. Let us hope fer their sakes that we succeed, if e'er sae slightly. Freedom withers when it breathes polluted air."

Archibald Thomson stood still for a long moment and then smiled and inclined his long chin in a brief nod. "Aye, my lord. I pray that the emerging Enlightenment pervades more minds than heretofore." He turned and tapped Jamie on the shoulder.

"Come, Master Drummond. Let us return tae our labors."

That night, in the privacy of their rooms, Euphemia Drummond paced restlessly as James recounted the meeting with Jamie and Doctor Thomson. She stopped and nervously repositioned a vase of spring crocus on her boudoir table then turned suddenly and faced James, who was sprawled comfortably on the settee. She was clearly incensed. James recognized her mood and knew better than to remonstrate with her.

"Dinna ye think we are being somewhat o'er harsh wi' Jamie?" she inquired with some heat. "It seems tae me that we are both guilty of dereliction o' responsibility, since we dinna maintain a close watch on his studies. I dinna recall ever asking him his progress. Ye hae nae said whether ye inquired." She paused.

James said nothing; only shook his head slowly.

She sighed deeply and sank onto a chair, facing him. "We were all having a guid time, James. Now it is the lad wha must pay the price fer our frippery, but nae us. As his mother, I find it quite unfair. But, what are we to do with him?"

James treated this as a rhetorical question and did not answer.

The silence stretched, and James heard only the pleasant crackle of the fire in the corner hearth. There was a soft thud, and the flames spurted and popped as a log collapsed in the glowing pile.

James ran his hands through his dark hair and shook his head. "My love, it is Jamie wha must do the studying. He stands tae benefit frae the experience. He enjoyed the holiday and will hae mair guid times once the school term is o'er. He must learn discipline sometime, and this is as guid a time as any. But his response puzzled me greatly, and Doctor Thomson was amazed as weel."

Euphemia raised an eyebrow. "How sae?"

James raised his hands expressively and turned them over. "Jamie hae always been an excitable and vigorous child, emotional, decisive, and quick tae anger. He is impulsive and expresses that anger physically. He is a young man o' action." He chuckled and lowered his hands. "I hae seen him quite indignant when he feels that he or any other person hae been wronged. This time was different."

James looked at the fire. Euphemia waited, resisting an urge to prompt her husband.

"Nae hot denials, nae claims o' injustice…he was uncommonly meek. It is nae like him. Oh, he is still unco proud, and I can see the defiance in his eyes. Our lad is changing, Euphemia. He is starting tae think aboot consequences and responsibilities."

Suddenly, he laughed and leaned back, stretching his long legs.

"Aye, we'll see the auld Jamie frae time tae time as a wee champion struggling tae correct injustice, but I think that he is much mair inclined now tae reason and weigh the consequences before acting."

Euphemia had risen while he talked. She sat down on the settee beside him. She tucked herself in close and began to stroke his hair. "I feel that ye are quite right, James. Our wee lad is growing. Sae much like his father."

James shook his head. "Nae. He is similar tae his grandfather, mair practical than I am. I am too much a romantic, a believer in the rightness o' causes regardless o' consequences. That explains my infatuation with our Bonnie Prince and his cause."

Euphemia nodded and snuggled closer. "Ye must hae dreams, my love, but be a man of action when the time comes, as we ken it will…someday soon."

James nodded and drew her closer. "Aye, someday soon."

After a long pause in which they both seemed lost in thought, James suddenly said, "I will monitor Jamie's work daily and ensure that Doctor Thomson is nae excessively harsh. Jamie will only benefit frae this trial."

Euphemia disengaged, walked to the window streaked with spring rain, and stood staring into the darkness. She idly ran her finger through the mist coating the glass and drew Jamie's initials, *JWD*. Abruptly, she turned to face her husband.

"I know ye are right in this, husband," she said softly, reaching up to wipe a tear that had suddenly welled from her eye and fallen onto her cheek. "I love him too much at times. He is our only child, James, our only child in all these years. He is the center point o' all our hopes and dreams. Perhaps soon, we will hae another child and I will be able tae divide my affections and motherly protection. But right now, it is hard, verra hard."

James rose from the settee and held out his arms. She moved soundlessly into them and buried her face in his shoulder, too consumed with her feelings to speak.

―※―

Jamie's days were filled with classes, study, and assignments. He was too consumed by activity to note the quick passing of the days. Before the Abergeldie Gordon family arrived on a warm day in late June, Jamie had satisfied and even impressed his tutor and father. Trees leafed out, birds nested, and spring flowers bloomed in riotous colors, but Jamie saw none of these events. He had so engaged himself in studies that he did not take advantage of his tutor's occasional inattention to sneak outside. He had called forth a determination that amazed even himself. He began to realize that he was overcoming bad habits that sapped his concentration. He worked and avoided daydreaming and wasting of his suddenly precious time. He missed his outside activities in the continually lengthening and warming days of late spring. Especially, he yearned for daily rides on the forest paths with Emilia and Jock McRae, who stayed away from Jamie while he worked out his punishment.

The morning before the coach bearing the Gordons drew up at the entrance to the castle, Mister Dobie found Jamie sprawled before a fireplace, reading a book.

"Pray put down the book, young master. Yer father desires ye to attend him in his study. Doctor Thomson is already there."

Jamie flung down the book, thanked Mister Dobie, and raced downstairs to the study. Thomson sat in a side chair, with his knees drawn up. Jamie thought that he looked strangely like a human grasshopper. There was a battered black valise at his side, along with his coat and top hat.

James interlaced his fingers and studied Jamie appraisingly.

"School is now finished, Jamie. Doctor Thomson is leaving Strathallan fer the summer and wilna return until autumn. He hae given me a glowing account of yer diligent study and progress. I commend ye, lad. Ye hae made an amazing turnabout and hae performed excellently in all disciplines. He believes that ye hae great promise tae be an exceptional scholar. I hae made arrangements tae retain his services as tutor when he returns. He is going tae the continent tae study and write and hopefully tae enjoy the beauties o' summer in the mountains o' Switzerland. Ye are hereby released frae durance vile and may enjoy the summer frolicking with yer cousins and friends in the straths and glens. Jock McRae assures me that yer horse will remember ye and that ye hae nae forgotten how tae ride, although yer bottom may ache fer a few days frae yer inactivity." James raised an admonitory finger. "But we expect that ye will devote some hours every day this summer tae reading. Here is a list o' his assignments fer ye."

He held up a sheet of paper and then laid it down on a corner of his desk. Jamie glanced at the paper but remained silent.

"He also asks that ye tend his botanical collection in the greenhouse, with the help o' the gardener."

James leaned over his desk and plucked some papers from a stack and held them out to Jamie.

"He asks that ye examine these sketches. If ye see any o' these specimens flitting around while ye explore the woods, Doctor Thomson asks that ye use his net, bottles, and chloroform that he is leaving ye tae catch and prepare them fer mounting. He is leaving his materials and display cases fer that purpose."

Jamie turned to look at Doctor Thomson with wonder. Archibald Thomson smiled genially and nodded.

"Ye are a very bright young man, Master Drummond. With yer newfound diligence, I have every confidence that I shall return in October to find my collection not only cared for, but greatly expanded. Do ye accept this assignment?"

Jamie nodded vigorously. "Ach, aye! I will do my best fer ye, sir!"

The tutor extracted his pocket watch, flipped up the cover, and said, "I say, it is almost eleven of the clock. The coach going south to Stirling must be nearly here. Well then, I am off, my lord."

He turned to pick up his hat and adjusted it firmly on his head. The tall hat only accentuated his height and spare figure. He draped his coat over his arm and, stooping, picked up the valise. "My luggage is already out front with the footmen."

James rose and gripped the tutor's hand and shook it vigorously. "My thanks fer all ye have done fer Jamie and the other children this past year, sir. I look forward tae welcoming ye back tae Strathallan when the leaves turn golden."

James put his arm around Jamie, and together, they followed Doctor Thomson to the front entrance. Mister Dobie opened the double doors to reveal a coach rounding the curving drive, closely followed by another.

The first coach slowed, with a jingling of harness, crunch of gravel, and squeal of brakes against wheel rims. After the first coach stopped, the driver put down his whip. Turning, he reached down to rap on the glass of the passenger window.

"Strathallan Castle, my lord."

Footmen began unloading luggage. The coach door opened.

James called, "Charles! Allison! Welcome tae Strathallan! Step doon and come inside. Ye are in just time fer lunch. Certainly, the children are hungry already."

Charles Gordon laughed. "Nae only the children. I'm famished frae the long ride and could eat the lead horse myself."

He helped his wife down while she juggled her newborn in a small basket. The four older Gordon children dismounted from the other door and ran shrieking to surround Jamie, who leaped down from the top of the staircase to meet them.

The second coach approached slowly and stopped behind the first. A footman dismounted; collected Doctor Thomson's luggage; and, loosening the leather straps at the boot, stowed them inside and rebuckled the straps.

With a, "Good-bye, everyone," Doctor Archibald Thomson boarded the coach.

Everyone turned to wave as the driver expertly maneuvered the coach to begin the journey south to Stirling, from where another coach would take him to Edinburgh and the ship to the Continent.

Within days, the Gordons settled into the routine of the Drummond family. The adults tended the small children and left the older ones in Peter's care. That lad was exceptional in organizing activities to fill the long summer days. The first few days were consumed wandering the extensive grounds around Strathallan. The woods were abundant with small game. Peter convinced the cooks that a brace or more of plump hares would be an excellent addition to the menu. Peter and Jamie rummaged in the storehouse behind the stables and found an old game trap. Peter examined it carefully and began taking it apart. Jamie was disturbed.

"Wait! Wait, Peter! What are ye doing? That's our only trap!"

"I ken that. Now watch," said Peter softly. "We need aboot four mair traps if we are tae hae any hope o' catching mair than a single hare, and a single hare makes a puir meal fer such a large family." Peter leaned back on his haunches. "Ye see, Jamie, how the trap is made with curved withies knotted in a framework wi' heavy twine. We need tae gather many mair withies. I found several hanks o' twine in the storeroom. Now, do ye see how the withies curve inward? The hare goes in here tae eat the carrots and turnips that we use as bait but canna get oot again. The back o' the cage is hinged and released with these twa catches. That's how we take oot the hare. We can get the blacksmith tae fashion mair catches. We anchor the cage by pushing a stake inta the soft earth. Then, we fasten the stake tae the cage with mair twine."

"Very ingenious, Peter! You're making a pattern wi' the pieces o' this cage."

Peter nodded, "Exactly so. Let's get tae work then. Ye, David, and Will start gathering withies frae the stream bank. Just make sure that they are the same length as these. I'll gae talk with the blacksmith about making the catches. When we have all o' our parts, we can start assembling the traps."

Within a few days, the boys had a goodly supply of finished traps. They decided that the woods adjoining a clearing near the forester's croft contained evidence of the hares' presence and was a good spot to place the traps. They wheedled vegetables from the cooks and set off for the meadow to place, stake, and bait the traps.

The next morning, the boys headed for the meadow right after breakfast. The first trap lay at the edge of the woods, but the vegetables inside were untouched and wilted. The second trap held two hares, which skittered about nervously as the boys approached. Peter unlatched the cage and pulled out the hares, clubbing them on the back of the neck. He tied them by their back feet with a leather thong and handed it to Jamie, who hefted the hares proudly.

They had some difficulty finding the third and fourth traps in the thick heather. One was empty and the vegetables untouched. They were combing the heather for the last trap when Peter motioned the boys to be quiet. He held his right hand with the palm out and waved it downward. The boys sank to their haunches.

"What is it, Peter?" whispered Jamie.

Peter pointed across the meadow. "There are four horsemen headed this way."

"Why would they leave the road? Do ye think they are highwaymen?"

"I dinna ken, Jamie, but they should nae be here. Sit still and watch."

The horsemen moved in single file across the meadow. All were armed. The lead two carried pikes, and Jamie could see that the riders wore broadswords. All were wearing tartan and bonnets sporting sprigs of plants, which indicated that they were Highlanders. The fourth rider, bringing up the rear, had flowing auburn locks below his bonnet, which bore three long eagle feathers.

"He's a clan chief," murmured Peter. "What is he doing here?"

Jamie whispered excitedly, "I ken wha he is! He is the chief o' the Camerons. His men call him the Gentle Lochiel. He is a guid friend o' my papa's."

"Then we will greet him and bid him and his men welcome."

Peter rose and waved his arms to gain the attention of the riders.

The riders wheeled left and approached the boys.

Donald Cameron dismounted and extended his hand. "Ach, Master Drummond. Ye have come part way tae welcome us tae Strathallan. We are headed tae a forester's croft near here by instructions frae yer father. Do ye ken it?"

Jamie spoke up. "Aye, I ken it and can lead ye tae it quickly." He waved his hand in a circling motion. "These are my Gordon cousins frae Abergeldie, Peter and William. We are trapping hares."

"And I see that ye are most successful." Lochiel laughed.

"My lord, we can guide ye straight tae the castle if ye wish."

"Nay, laddie. Our instructions are tae await yer father and Viscount Strathallan at the forester's croft. Lead us there and then run tae the castle to tell them that Lochiel hae critical news tae impart."

Peter said, "Lend me a horse, and I can bring them quickly."

Lochiel nodded to his men. With a sigh, one man dismounted and offered Peter the reins. Peter took them, vaulted into the saddle, and headed across the meadow eastward toward the castle. Jamie led the group up the narrow path leading to the croft. The door of the croft was unlocked.

Lochiel chuckled. "The roof is sae low that I must nearly kiss the ground tae enter."

The Cameron clansmen preceded their chief into the croft house.

Lochiel turned to speak to the boys. "Now, lads, we must be aboot men's business, and ye must be aboot takin' the hares tae the kitchen. When Peter returns, hie ye back."

Jamie nodded and said, "My lord, the gift o' antlers looks fine indeed on the wall o' my grandpapa's study."

Lochiel laughed uproariously. "I kennt that the Viscount would like them. Perhaps next time we hunt, 'twill be a bear. Ye hae best select a place tae put the big skin." He put his rough hand on Jamie's shoulder and said gently, "But, wi' my news, it may be a lang syne before we can hae that hunt, I fear."

Within the hour, James and his father William Drummond rode up the path to the croft with Peter, who dismounted and returned the horse to the Cameron who lent it.

James gathered the boys a few yards away, while the Viscount and Lochiel entered the croft and shut the door. James sat on a fallen log and motioned the boys to sit.

"Lads, ye hae knowledge o' that which ye should nae hae, that Lochiel is here and dinna wish it known. This is a most serious matter, and I am asking ye tae think before ye talk tae anyone. Concealing the presence o' Lochiel and his clansman at Strathallan is important tae me and the safety o' the Drummonds and Gordons. Do ye understand that?"

James looked at each boy steadily and waited while each nodded.

"It's important tae yer weel-being and that o' yer sisters, mothers, and fathers. Nae one talks. Now, finish yer hunt fer hares and return tae the castle."

"Aye, Papa," whispered Jamie.

"Aye, Uncle James," the other boys said in unison.

James stood and patted Jamie on the shoulder. "Now gae hame and try very hard tae nae look sae serious. Ye hae some fat hares tae take back. Ye are successful hunters, sae gae back and talk aboot that."

The boys walked to the meadow and checked the fourth trap. They found a hare inside. That time, Will killed it and laced a thong around its feet. As the younger boys turned to head across the meadow toward the castle, Peter spoke up.

"Jamie, show Will tae the castle, but take yer time. I'm going back tae listen under a window o' the croft house. Something very important is going on."

Jamie rounded on Peter. "What are ye doing? Ye gave yer word!"

"I gave my word tae nae talk with anyone at the castle aboot Lochiel and his men being here. I dinna gie my word tae nae listen. I have a terrible feeling that this is aboot a rising. This news affects others, nae just the Drummonds. It concerns the Gordons o' Aberfeldie also. Now gae, but gae slowly sae I can catch up wi' ye before ye reach the castle."

Peter raced back up the path toward the forester's croft.

Jamie and Will moved slowly and rested frequently. They went back to each trap and rebaited it with fresh vegetables. They reached the small stream that ran into the lake behind the castle.

They sat down on the stream bank to wait. They heard Peter coming before they saw him. He was gasping for breath and collapsed on a stump for a few moments before speaking.

"It is as I feared," he muttered in a low voice. "The news is spreading fast. The Bonnie Prince landed in the western isles five days ago."

"So he is bringing an army frae France," said Will.

Peter shook his head. "Nae. He came alone. 'Tis difficult tae believe. He sailed frae Belle Isle with twa ships, but the British Navy intercepted ain and forced it back tae France, sae the prince came on wi' only eight supporters. My God, only eight men. What kind of an army is that? The other ship carried fifteen hundred firelocks and eighteen hundred broadswords, ammunition, and money. Lochiel kens that the prince sent the ship back wi' instructions tae make a second attempt tae bring on the weapons, at least. But nae one kens if they can get through the blockade. Some of the Islesmen and Highlands clans hae already joined the prince. Others, like Lochiel, are nae certain what they will do. But the prince thinks that he will gather an army in a few days and the whole o' the Highlands will rise. There are already runners carrying the fiery cross tae the north and west."

"What will my papa and grandpapa do? What did they say?"

"They are sending oot messages calling fer a meeting of Jacobite supporters next week at Crieff. They plan to use the cattle fair as a cover fer the meeting.

Jamie cut in. "We were all planning tae gae tae the cattle fair."

"All the principal families will be there, according tae yer father."

"Will Lochiel stay?" asked Jamie.

Peter shook his head. "He is returning westward tae consult wi' other clan leaders." He had regained his normal breathing. He stared at Jamie and Will. "If we keep a wary eye on the forester's croft, we may see much mair, but we must nae let our fathers learn that we ken anything at all. Agreed?" He held out his hand and gripped Jamie's and Will's. "Now, let us hie tae the kitchen and get them started on a fine stew."

Chapter Four

The Drummond and Gordon families were excited by the boys' success. Charles was especially pleased that Peter had shown such ingenuity in designing and leading the boys in producing and setting the traps.

As the families gathered in the dining room, Charles stood to remark, "I thought that ye would be lucky to snare a brace, lads, but ye brought back four, and sae plump they are. They clearly love the fine vegetation at Strathallan. In the north at Abergeldie, hares are nae so fat, with less tae eat."

Peter was exceptionally pleased with himself. He raised his nose to sniff the aroma drifting from under the covered platter brought in by a beaming server. "Ahh, delightful!" he exclaimed as the server whisked off the lid to reveal a succulent stew of chunks of meat and vegetables and a rich brown gravy under a crusty layer of biscuit.

"There is just enough fer each tae have a hearty taste," offered the server. "The cook is busy disjointing the roast guinea fowls fer the main course."

James stood and rapped a knife on a glass, which tinkled softly. The room quieted immediately.

"They offer their apologies, but the Viscount and Lady Margaret are absent. They are visiting Marquis and Lady Murray at Tullibardine. We must thank Peter, William, David, Jamie, and the cooks fer the fine stew that graces the table this evening."

Everyone clapped, while the boys grinned hugely.

"After we hae eaten and the plates are cleared awa', I have invited Mrs. MacRobie tae attend us. She hae an important announcement tae make. Now, I will say grace and we can proceed with supper, after which we will listen tae Mrs. MacRobie's news."

After the prayer, everyone chattered excitedly as servers ladled the stew and biscuit. All agreed that it was wonderful and the boys were charged with the task of trapping more to allow everyone to enjoy a full bowl. Servers brought in the main course. Throughout the dinner, the conversation was brisk. Jamie listened attentively. He was disappointed that there was no discussion or even a whisper about the visit of Donald Cameron and his news of the landing of the Bonnie Prince. Once or twice, Jamie caught Peter looking at him significantly. Jamie touched his spoon to his lower lip. Peter nodded and repeated the gesture.

Suddenly, Jamie felt his mother's fingers close over his hand as she leaned close to whisper, "Put down the spoon, Jamie. Whate'er is bothering ye?"

Jamie laid the spoon on his napkin and whispered back, "Naething, Mama. Peter and I are agreeing that we need to gae hunting again this week."

Euphemia looked at her son calmly. "I ken yer mind, Jamie Drummond. I think...I think that ye and Peter are up tae something."

Jamie's heart thumped so hard in his chest that he was certain that his mother could hear it. His throat constricted, but he said as quietly as he could, "Only hunting, Mama."

Euphemia whispered back, "Then see that it's only hares that ye are hunting."

She looked deep into his eyes and smiled. Jamie quailed under that direct look.

Servers cleared away plates, bowls, silver, and glasses. There was a knock on the door, which was opened quickly by the major domo. Mrs. MacRobie, Agnes, and a tall young man stood in the entrance.

James stood and extended his hand in a brisk welcoming wave. "Come in, come in. Pray join us fer dessert and a glass o' port."

The three servants came forward uncertainly and took seats in chairs at the end of the table. Jamie wondered what was happening. Agnes, in particular, looked extremely nervous. She wrung her hands until they showed white. The young man looked equally nervous. Mrs. MacRobie, on the other hand, was flushed and beaming.

Jamie's mother caught her breath and whispered, "I ken what is aboot tae happen!"

"What, Mama?"

"Shh, Jamie. Mrs. MacRobie is ready tae speak."

James stood and again rapped a knife blade on a glass. The ringing sound quickly quieted the diners. "Mrs. MacRobie hae an announcement tae make that we are most pleased tae receive, although it causes us all a modest amount o' grief because o' our loss. But"—he smiled broadly—"our grief, as the blessed Saint Paul says, is swallowed up in happiness." He turned to Mrs. MacRobie. "Please, madam, tell us yer news."

In an automatic gesture, Mrs. MacRobie rose and curtsied. She cleared her throat and raised her voice. "My lords, ladies, children, and household staff, I hae such wonderful news!" she burbled. "Ye ken my daughter Agnes, wha hae served the Drummond family since she was a child. I hae been a fortunate mother to raise her and hae her devoted help since Mister MacRobie's untimely death…" She paused to dab her eyes with her kerchief and then took a deep breath and plowed on. "Weel, since that time, we have been sae happy here. But now she is going awa'—" Her voice broke, and she paused. Again, she dabbed at her eyes, which were turning red. "She has met Mister Robert Sandilands, a fine young man who serves as a butler at Blair Castle. They met last summer when we were visiting family in Atholl. He hae asked fer her hand, and she and I hae accepted. They are tae be married in September.

She is taking a position right awa' with the Murray family at Blair sae they can be together. Isna this wonderful news?"

Everyone except Jamie stood and cheered. Jamie was transfixed. He had known Agnes all of his short life. She couldn't be getting married. She was so young. He knew that men and women married and lived together, but he could not understand why they couldn't live at Strathallan.

His mother reached out and took his hand firmly in hers. She bent down to his level and whispered, "Jamie, ye will be all right. It is time fer Agnes to get married. She is a woman now. It is also time fer ye tae grow up. Sae smile, and nae tears."

Jamie gripped her hand tightly and whispered back, "Aye, Mama, but I love Agnes sae much."

The strain on his emotions overwhelmed him. Euphemia saw her son's face pucker and his eyes squeeze shut. She pulled him close to smother his sobs. Agnes stared at her with a strained smile. Euphemia nodded, and Agnes disengaged from her mother's arm. She walked around the table and bent low to hug Jamie.

"Jamie, I promise ye that I will come back to visit ye here at Strathallan as often as I can. I will even bring my baby."

Jamie looked up through streaming tears to ask loudly, "Ye are having a baby?"

People turned to stare. Agnes blushed to the roots of her red-gold hair. She shook her head violently while Euphemia laughed.

"Not yet, ye silly goose. Later, when…when." She stopped. "Aye, much later, after…"

She looked at Euphemia beseechingly.

Euphemia finished her sentence. "When the time is right, Agnes will hae a baby and will come tae visit us sae we can meet the wee thing."

Agnes nodded vigorously. "Aye, laddie. When the time is right. Certainly nae before. Now please hush aboot a baby."

Jamie dried his tears on the front of his mother's dress, pulled free of her embrace, and threw his arms around Agnes tightly, overbalancing her so that both sprawled laughing on the polished oak floor.

Later that night, Jamie waited until sounds outside his room quieted. He pushed back the coverlet and crawled out of bed. He tiptoed to the door, knelt, twisted the knob, and gently pulled it open just enough to allow him to peer out at floor level. While the bedroom was dark except for a quarter moon glistening through the lace-covered window, the hall was dimly lit by candles mounted in amber glass wall sconces.

Soon, a servant would come to douse the candles, but Jamie had enough light to navigate the long hall to the room where Peter and Will were sleeping. Jamie could hear murmurs of adults talking downstairs, but nothing from inside his cousin's bedroom. He cautiously tapped on the door. There was a shuffling sound, and then the door opened a crack.

Peter whispered anxiously, "Ach, Jamie. Get in here. We must talk."

He reached out to grip Jamie by the sleeve and tugged him through the door. The boys sat on Will's bed in the moonlight.

Peter opened the conversation. "I heard my father say tae my mother that John Murray is coming tae visit Strathallan on Thursday. He is coming tae meet the Viscount; yer father; yer uncle John; members of the Murray family of Tullibardine; and others. They are going tae meet at the forester's croft tae talk about Bonnie Prince Charlie and the rising."

Jamie was confused.

"Who is John Murray, Peter?"

Peter leaned forward and said, "He's a secret agent o' the king o'er the water, as he hae been fer years. He is here tae stir up rebellion in Perthshire. My father despises and distrusts him. He is a troublemaker."

Jamie said intensely, "My mama suspects that we are up tae something, Peter. I dinna know why she suspects. Only that she does. She warned me this evening that we must stay oot o' trouble. I canna disobey her. Ye can gae, Peter, but I canna do it."

Peter sat quietly for a long time. Then he said, "I dinna ken what is happening, but I think ye are right, Jamie. I'll gae and listen at the forester's croft. I know how tae hide. Ye and Will shouldna gae. It will look suspicious fer all three o' us tae approach the forester's croft. Ye will gae east in the woods tae place the traps."

Jamie shook his head sadly. "Sae, there is going tae be war, Peter. What will yer family do?"

Peter sighed. "My father does nae wish tae support a rising, but he hasna truly made up his mind. He dinna think that yer papa hae really decided either. Yer grandpa went tae visit the Murrays at Tullibardine tonight. I wonder what they will do." He shrugged. "Right now, our families dinna ken what is happening with the Bonnie Prince and the French. We just have tae wait and see."

Jamie nodded. "Ye sound like my papa."

The jingle of harness and the loud voice of a driver woke Jamie shortly after dawn. He rose and shuffled to the window while wiping sleep from his eyes. Outside, the steady rain made visibility difficult. Looking down, he saw a footman struggling with luggage while two laughing figures dashed down the steps to the waiting carriage. It was Agnes and her betrothed leaving Strathallan for their new home in Blair Atholl. Jamie felt an aching hollowness. Agnes had told him at dinner the night before that they were leaving early. He did not think that, in spite of her promises, Agnes would be returning to Strathallan Castle anytime soon.

He wondered, *Will others whom I love be leaving soon?* He was vaguely frightened, in spite of his mother's assurances. His father had told him stories of war and heroic actions.

In those stories, soldiers fought and either won, died, or ran away. There was never a mention of pain or suffering. Jamie visualized the weapons mounted on nearly every wall of the castle: glistening pikes, broadswords, bows, and battle-axes. He suddenly had a vision of battle so real that he staggered back from the window. His ears filled with the sound and tumult of battle: trumpets and pipes calling, men at arms fighting with shields interlocked and swords clashing, smoking cannons roaring, knights on mighty destriers charging, and pikemen bringing down riders, all engaged in glorious deeds, struggling in the intensity of battle. He saw fallen horses thrashing and men falling, crying out, and lying still on that visionary battlefield.

Suddenly, the battle was over and the knights and men at arms were gone, leaving only the dead on the field. Jamie saw himself walking across a meadow churned to a muddy morass by horses's hooves and wagon wheels to where fallen soldiers lay sprawled in inglorious poses. The faces of the fallen were obscured by the visors on their helmets. He reached down to tug at a visor, which came up with a snap. He stared down into the dead soldier's face. The eyes were staring and unseeing; the lips grimaced over bloody teeth in a final rictus of pain. It was Peter's face.

A knight in a torn and dirty white surcoat and armor lay face down in the grass with his sword still clutched in his dead hand. Jamie tugged with all his strength on the knight's other arm until the heavy body rolled slowly toward him and then crashed over onto its back. The visor on the knight's helmet was down. A large and spreading splotch of red marred the front of the knight's surcoat around a spot where a broken-off arrow had punctured it. Jamie reached for the visor and then stopped, his fingers shaking uncontrollably. He could not will himself to bring his fingers down to touch the visor. Then he saw the sprig of holly with the red berries pinned to the surcoat. A thrill of fear shot through him. Holly was the plant badge of the Drummond clan.

Jamie looked wildly at the bodies of knights and men-at-arms around him. Everywhere, he saw holly badges. He saw a banner stained with blood and torn nearly in half, still fastened to a broken flagstaff, lying between the bodies of two soldiers.

He clutched at the banner and carefully pulled to reveal the Drummond motto, "Gang Warily," emblazoned on it. The stiff breeze fluttered the banner in his hands. Suddenly, it pulled free and flew away on the wind, the only sound on that silent field of the dead.

The vision closed abruptly, and Jamie staggered and fell against his bed. His breath came in deep sobs, and his head spun. He shut his eyes tightly to keep the vision of death from returning. He was still lying on the floor when there was a soft knock on the door. Jamie was locked in the daytime nightmare and did not hear it.

The knock sounded louder, and Will's voice called, "Jamie, are ye in there?"

A few moments later, the door opened and anxious eyes beneath a tousled shock of brown hair peered in. Seeing Jamie lying on the floor in a stupor, Will ran to find his brother. Peter rushed in and, kneeling, began rubbing Jamie's clenched hands and stiff arms.

"Will!" he shouted. "Find Uncle James. Quickly!"

Jamie began thrashing from side to side, murmuring, "Nae! Nae! They are dead! They are a' dead!"

Peter's fright was evident in his high-pitched voice as he called to Jamie. Just as James, followed by Euphemia, burst through the bedroom door, Jamie's eyes opened. His head ached abominably, but he recognized his father's face as through a fog.

"Jamie, lad. Whatever happened tae ye?"

His father picked him up and laid him gently on the bed. Euphemia gave a low cry and clutched Jamie's hand. Peter sat down on the room's only chair and began to shake.

"I thought he was dying, Uncle James. He was a' stiff, and when I tried to wake him, he began to scream a' kinds of strange things, as if he was possessed."

Jamie struggled to rise. "I want tae get up now, Papa."

James pushed him back down. "Wait, Jamie. Something has happened tae ye. We need tae understand before ye get up. Do ye remember anything?"

Jamie passed his hand before his eyes.

"I was dreaming, but I was already awake, standing over there watching Agnes leave. The coach woke me, and I went tae the window tae watch. It was raining, and the window was misty. Then, it was as if I was in another place. I saw knights and soldiers fechting a battle."

James said nothing, but his gray eyes contemplated his son while he continued to hold his hand. Euphemia knelt on the floor and held Jamie's other hand and smoothed his hair.

"And then what happened, Jamie?" she murmured.

Jamie's body was still trembling but beginning to relax.

"It was sae real, Mama. I was standing in a grassy field churned up by horses' hooves. There was a strong wind blowing. I could see flags and banners streaming. I could hear trumpets and pipes. There were knights on horseback and soldiers and cannons firing. I watched the knights and soldiers charging. They fought, and some began falling. Then, suddenly, the battle was o'er and the knights and soldiers gone, except fer the dead. I walked tae where a group o' them hae fallen. I bent down to look at one o' them and…and…"

A wailing cry burst from Jamie, and his body stiffened. James held on tightly, but Euphemia jerked back reflexively. James looked toward the door to see Charles and Alison Gordon, along with several servants, all with deep concern on their faces. James shook his head slowly, and they left. A minute or two passed before Jamie was calm enough to continue.

"It was Peter, Papa. He was dead, lying in the grass. I saw his face when I pulled up the visor o' his helmet. Then I turned o'er a knight and saw the sprig of holly on his surcoat and there was blood o'er his front. A' the dead men had holly badges on their coats. They were Drummonds. It was terrible. Do ye think that I saw the future, Papa?"

Peter stared wide-eyed at Jamie, his hands clenched and white on the arms of the chair.

James bit his lip and was silent for long moments.

Euphemia stared into his eyes while she continued to stroke Jamie's hair. "Do ye think the lad hae the sight, husband?" she whispered.

James shook his head. "No one in our family hae the sight. If we had, we would have fared better in the '15 rising, and we would be enormously rich now."

Euphemia blew out a gusty breath. "The sight is nae about such things, James. It is a gift. It provides a vision o' the future tae warn people o' what is tae come, guid or bad."

James shook his head again. "Nae. This dream is nae aboot the future. It's aboot the past, but Jamie hae heard things recently that make him very anxious, sae I think…" His voice trailed off. It was a way for him to gather his thoughts. Finally, he spoke again. "If the soldiers were knights and men-at-arms, I think ye were seeing the past, Jamie, nae the future. If they were wearing visored helmets, I think that ye were remembering the tale I told ye earlier o' the Battle of Flodden Field, when so many valiant Scots, including our own kinsmen, the Drummonds, fell fechting the English. Let us think aboot this. Ye said that there were armored knights on horseback and men-at-arms, but also cannon. Flodden Field was a terrible loss, and many o' the flower of Scottish nobility and knighthood fell that day. The Drummond family suffered terrible losses, as did most o' the great families o' Scotland." James gripped Jamie's hands again and looked intently into his son's eyes. "Can ye see that now, Jamie?"

Jamie's face was solemn, and he slowly shook his head negatively.

James sighed and continued. "Fer many months now, ye have heard talk o' a rising, with the possibility of fechting. I think that such talk, which should nae hae been said in yer hearing, has made ye worried. Can ye see that, son?"

Jamie nodded slowly.

"Yer mind associated that worry with a story I told ye aboot a great battle which the Scots lost. Yer mind jumbled those worries about those ye love, yer family and clan, with a story frae the past."

Jamie's face cleared, and he nodded again. "I understand that, Papa, but I dinna wish tae see those things."

Euphemia looked at her husband reproachfully. "Ye are such an artful storyteller sometimes, James."

He shrugged helplessly.

Euphemia continued. "Jamie, yer head is filled with worries. There hae been a lot o' talk aboot the Bonnie Prince and the king o'er the water returning, but men have been saying that fer many years, because they try tae keep their hopes and dreams alive. But it is only talk. If it ever amounts tae mair than that, we will tell ye and we will gae tae a place where we will be safe." She looked at her husband. "I think fer a time that Jamie should nae sleep alone. Let us ask Charles and Alison if Will or Peter can sleep with him. Would ye like that, Jamie?"

Jamie nodded vigorously, but a corner of his mind had stored away the horror of battle, and he knew that he could not forget it easily. And so it was arranged that Peter would move his things while the servants set up another bed in the spacious room. There was no recurrence of the strange and disturbing waking dream, and everyone relaxed, concluding that it was an odd combination of youthful anxiety and overactive storytelling that had brought the horror of war for a brief moment to Strathallan Castle.

The bad dream also put an end to Peter's plan to inform Jamie of what was being said by visitors to the forester's croft. Two days later, in late afternoon, the boys picked up the traps, augmented by their work to six, along with two bags of garden clippings to bait the traps. They trekked eastward into the woods. After a half-mile of hiking, they came to a broad meadow where Peter found evidence of droppings and cropped vegetation. He pointed out likely spots for the boys to install traps and left at a run back along the trail.

Jamie stood watching Peter until he disappeared from sight and then shook his head resignedly and accompanied Will to where they decided to place the first trap. It took the boys two hours to place, bait, and conceal the six traps. The sun was sinking toward the western horizon, and a cool breeze had begun to ruffle the tall grass and bend the heather in the meadow. Peter had not returned, so the boys began the trek back to the castle. They had just entered the outer path of the formal garden when they heard loud voices from beyond the first row of decorative shrubbery.

Will stopped and placed a restraining hand on Jamie's chest. The boys knelt down in the shrubbery to listen. They had a clear view of two figures on the path not fifty yards away. Jamie recognized the rumbling voice of Jock McRae and heard Peter's indignant shout.

"I was nae doing anything wrong!"

"Then, ye should nae hae been skulkin' around the forester's croft, Master Gordon," growled Jock McRae. "I saw ye lying in the bushes nearly under the window. Ye were listening tae the conversation inside. I want ye tae tell me what ye were doing there. If ye willna do that, then I intend tae pick ye up by the scruff o' yer skinny neck and haul ye in front o' Viscount Drummond and yer father. Ye can explain yerself tae them."

The boys leaned forward to better hear Peter's subdued answer.

"Please dinna report me, Master McRae, I beg ye. I meant nae harm. I was only being curious since I saw Lochiel, the Cameron chief, here and I heard him talking about Bonnie Prince Charlie's landing frae France."

Jock roared, "Ye were only curious? There are serious doings aboot in the Highlands, lad, that can hae great consequences. These are matters fer yer elders, nae ye."

Jamie and Will heard Jock sigh heavily as he sat down on a cut-off stump at the edge of the garden path. He patted an adjoining stump.

"Sit ye doon, lad. I dinna wish tae get ye in trouble wi' yer father or my master. But ye are headed fer trouble, sure. And ye will certainly get caught. And if ye tell others what ye discover, it can place yer family and the Drummonds in great danger."

Peter retorted, "But there are great events happenin' in the Highlands and islands just now. They could affect me as weel as my family."

Jock sighed again. "Ye will understand, lad, in guid time. If naething happens, what ye dinna ken canna hurt ye. If ye will be affected, ye must trust ye father tae tell ye." He held up an admonitory finger. "When ye hae a need, ye will be told. And that is nae now. Ye must nae tell what ye heard in the forester's croft or wha ye saw enter or leave. Better ye rip oot yer own tongue and leave it here than tell another soul. Someone could die because o' what ye hae heard. Do ye ken what I say?"

Peter looked at his feet for a long time. Jock McRae waited patiently for him to answer and looked slowly around the garden. Finally, Peter's head came up, and he looked directly at Jock.

"If I swear nae tae talk or write anything that I heard, ye willna tell my father?"

Jock nodded. "Aye, lad. I trust yer word. I will say naething."

Jock raised his voice and turned toward where Jamie and Will squatted behind the shrubbery.

"Come oot now, lads, and join us."

Jamie and Will gasped but did not move. Jock rose from his seat on the stump.

"I've known ye were there fer five minutes or longer. Ye think ye are quiet as mice, but tae an auld hunter, yer scuffling along the path was as if ye were stumbling and crashing aboot." He snorted in disgust. "I can also see yer shadows against the tree behind ye. Now, come oot, ye rascals."

The boys, shocked by Jock's ability to see them in what they thought was a secure hiding place, came forward slowly until they stood side by side before the old soldier.

"Sit doon on the grass, lads," Jock ordered in a low voice.

He waited until they were seated and began.

"I ken ye be lads wi' unco abilities and wisdom, far greater than yer fathers realize. Ye also hae a great desire tae hear secrets, and that can be yer undoin'. The Highlands are a dangerous place today, though I can say frae lang experience that they hae ne'er been safe, nae in my lifetime. We hae had many lang years o' peace, though the Highland clans have been unhappy wi' the German lairdie on his stolen throne. There are people goin' aboot stirring up the clans, but fer seventy years, we hae had armies o' English and Lowlanders at Fort William and Fort George and fortified places between wi' the objective o' ensuring that there is nae rising, nae armed force tae threaten their king's peace. Pah! If not fer such armies and forts, the Highland heather would hae been aflame lang since. Now there is a rumor that the Bonnie Prince is in the islands. We hae heard such rumors afore, and naething hae come o' it. Yer fathers are concerned. They hae a great longing fer and loyalty tae the king o'er the water, but there is much at risk: their lives, lands, and families. They must hae a strong hope o' success and support. They need opportunities tae confer and gather information sae they can make intelligent choices fer themselves and fer us. Perhaps the prince will bring enough support to make the risks worthwhile. Perhaps the prince will gae back tae France in a few days and the Highlands will return tae an uneasy peace. Lads, ye must trust yer fathers as they struggle wi' their weighty responsibilities. Essential tae that trust is that ye be silent and tend tae yer own affairs. Are ye prepared tae shut yer mouths, or do I rip yer tongues oot here?"

The boys, wide-eyed at the threat, shook their heads vigorously.

Jock leaned forward. "So it will be our little secret, eh? I trust ye, lads, but I will be close by. If I hear that any o' ye hae talked, there will be consequences. Perhaps, I should chain ye up inside the tower…"

He left the sentence and its menace hanging and stood up.

"Weel, lads, it is getting on toward the gloaming. It is best that ye be getting hame. I need to exercise the horses tomorrow on a long ride. Can ye be ready by an hour after breakfast? It promises tae be a lovely summer day fer a ride. I think we can convince yer mothers to let ye gae and the cooks tae pack a nice lunch." With those remarks, he turned and walked slowly up the garden path toward the castle.

※

Several days later, after the midday meal, James Drummond gave the boys permission to accompany him and his brother John to the cattle fair at Crieff on horseback while the women and younger children would make the trip by coach.

"Lads, this is nae the Michaelmas cattle fair held in mid-October, when drovers bring thousands o' cattle tae Crieff tae sell tae English and Lowland factors and contract wi' drovers. This is mid-summer, and most o' the cattle are still grazing and putting on fat. This is mair o' a farmer's and merchant's fair. There will be a few cattle sold, since families and herdsmen need money tae last them through the summer. Crofters' wives will hae booths where they will be selling products o' their crafts. Lowland merchants, tinkers, mercers, knife makers, jewelers, and others will hae booths as weel, tae sell their wares. The women will want tae browse through the booths. Charles, John, and I plan tae meet wi' leaders o' some o' the local clans tae discuss affairs and gather news. There will be entertainers, jugglers, acrobats, and such, performing on the square opposite the tollbooth. There will also be sporting competitions such as weight tossing, wrestling, and rough-and-tumble fighting. Jock McRae will accompany ye on the ride into town and tae the entertainment. I expect ye tae stay there until we join ye aboot noon."

"There is a lovely glen a short distance north o' town where Mister Dobie has arranged tae set up a pavilion where we will enjoy lunch. We will rest there until late afternoon, when we will return ta' Strathallan." He raised a warning finger and punched it in the air to emphasize his instructions. "First, ye must stay awa' frae the cattle pens. Highland cattle are restless when penned up, and their horns are sharp and dangerous. So dinna approach the fences o' the corrals. And stay awa' frae the drovers. Drovers are rough men. Highland, Lowland, and Sassanach drovers are all the same. They carry dirks and sgain dubhs. They drink and can get argumentative and violent. Third, there may be cutpurses and thieves in the crowd. Being young, ye will probably be beneath their notice. But stay in the entertainment area and dinna wander off. Fourth and last, I understand that the sheriff will be hanging some cattle thieves in early afternoon. Some folk consider that great entertainment. I dinna agree. We will be in the glen during that ghastly spectacle, though the thieves may still be hanging on the gibbet when we ride back through Crieff on the way hame. I'm sorry to hae ye see such a spectacle, but it is a cruel and necessary part o' our system of justice." He paused. "These are the rules, lads. If Jock finds ye disobeying any o' them, he will march ye straightawa' tae yer mothers and ye will spend the day with them browsing the booths."

The boys groaned and looked downcast by the threat.

James waited for them to nod to acknowledge their understanding of the rules that he had laid down. Then he smiled. "It will be a memorable outing, and ye will hae a great time if ye obey the rules." He raised his hands and clapped them together. "That is all I hae tae say. Now, off wi' ye. 'Tis time fer bed."

The next morning, as soon as breakfast was cleared away, Jock McRae met Jamie, Peter, and Will at the stables. The midsummer day promised to be hot and humid. Grooms had already saddled horses for the day's ride to Crieff. As Jamie approached, a smiling young groom produced a step stool and placed it next to the mounting block. Another groom tugged on the horse's reins to position it so the small rider could reach the shortened stirrups.

"Time tae ride tae the tryst, Master Drummond," he said in a low voice.

"Ye cut a fine figure, sir," said the second groom.

Jamie climbed from the stool to the mounting block, steadying himself against the horse's flank. He took the reins from the groom and inserted his booted left foot in the stirrup. His gloved hand grasped the reins. As soon as he was ready to mount, Jamie nodded to the groom, who shifted his grip to the horse's bit. Jamie vaulted upward, crossing his right leg across the mare's back to settle himself in the saddle. The grooms moved away to help Will mount. Peter, tall and lean at fourteen, easily swung himself into the saddle. Jock McRae, in spite of his loudly proclaimed infirmities, was an accomplished horseman and into the saddle before the grooms moved toward him with questioning looks. Jock led the boys from the stables up the path to the graveled driveway in front of the castle to await the two coaches carrying the Drummond women, girls, and servants to the tryst.

Jock and Jamie led the caravan along the rutted road that ran to the main turnpike between Stirling and Crieff. The group clattered over the small stone bridge and approached the intersection with the turnpike. They reined up to wait for the coaches and remaining riders. While they were waiting, two carriages and nearly a dozen riders approached from the south.

When the entourage came closer, Jock recognized the Murrays of Tullibardine. He turned to Jamie and said, "That will be the Marquis and his wife in the lead carriage. I recognize his brother, George Murray, coming up on the big bay stallion. He is a fine military man wi' a long history o' fighting on the continent. Their wives and maidservants are in the second carriage."

George Murray pulled up as his horse came abreast of the coaches turning into the roadway from Strathallan Castle. James and John Drummond cantered around the coaches to greet him.

"An unco sunny morning, Lord Drummond!" George Murray exclaimed.

"Aye, Lord Murray, it is indeed. A fine morning for a tryst, a guid opportunity fer the wives and children tae enjoy an outing and fer us tae meet. Will ye be coming tae our gathering in Crieff tae discuss…"

There, his voice dropped so low that Jamie could scarcely hear.

"News o' interesting doings in the western Highlands?"

George Murray's eyes flicked left and right to take in the others in the Drummond party.

"Aye, along with my brother. However, I dinna expect tae make any decisions. The information available is sketchy, and it will be best tae move carefully, if at all. And remember this, James." He used his knees to urge his horse closer until his horse's flank nearly touched James's left boot. "We must beware the Campbell's claw stretched oot fra Argyll, even tae Crieff. I would nae be surprised tae find some here sympathetic tae their cause, which is the same thing as saying the cause o' the Hanoverians."

James nodded in agreement.

"Where is your father on this fine day? Already gone tae Crieff?" called Marquis Murray from the lead carriage.

James shook his head. "He is laid up with a touch o' the gout and nae comfortable either riding or sitting. John and I will bring back whate'er news we discover."

"A miserable affliction." Lady Murray sniffed, leaning from her carriage window. "Brought on, nae doubt, by excessively rich living."

John smiled but replied with a slight edge in his voice. "Aye, my lady. Sae most believe, but modern medical science is thinking perhaps the disease may be hereditary and nae caused by rich food or drink. Father hae always been careful in both regards. If nae hereditary, it may hae been caused by excessive exposure tae the cold and damp o' military campaigns."

Lady Murray looked taken aback, her lips pursed in a sour expression. Not desiring to start an argument, she conceded, "Aye, that may be. It is a most painful and annoying affliction. Tell yer father that we sympathize wholeheartedly."

John touched the brim of his wide hat respectfully. "I will, madam." James pulled his horse's neck to the right and wheeled away. "Let's awa' tae Crieff then before the crowds arrive!"

The two parties moved off along the road. They rode through the village of Muthill and proceeded toward Crieff. As they neared the town, they passed increasing numbers of country people walking, pulling carts piled high with produce and baskets of chickens and ducks, and leading cows. The growing crowds slowed their pace.

Jock leaned back in the saddle and blew out his breath gustily. "Waall," he drawled. "Naething fer it but tae wait fer a space in this crush o' humanity sharing the road wi' us. 'Tis still early, and there is only a mile mair. Ye know, Jamie lad, the military built this road aboot fifteen years ago, to permit them tae quickly race inta the Highlands tae put doon risings o' the clans. If the clans were tae rise today, it would be a week before an army could get through this tangle." He laughed, pleased with his own joke. "I near broke my back working on the stretch north o' Crieff when I was a young soldier. Aye, it was difficult labor. I blistered my hands and walked aboot like a cripple every nicht fer months." He laughed loudly, remembering those difficult days.

Jamie interrupted the old soldier's reverie with a question. "I thought ye were a mercenary soldier on the Continent."

Jock nodded. "Aye, I was fer years after Sheriffmuir. But kings and princes run out o' money to pay mercenaries, and I hae tae move on. Finally, there was nae mair employment as a mercenary fer a time. There was naething else tae do but come hame tae the Highlands. I worked on this road. For a while, I was a guard at Eileen Donan Castle near Fort William. That's the McRae castle. Then the Black Watch needed officers and the Campbells paid weel, sae I bought a commission with my mercenary prize money. It was guid duty and mostly overseas. Now, I am reapin' the benefits o' my own lang-ago labor." He chuckled again.

Jamie persisted with another question. "Will ye become a soldier again if there is a rising?"

Jock dropped the reins, took off his hat to wipe away sweat, and then brushed back his iron-grey locks. He put his hat on again and picked up the trailing reins. "Nah, lad. Too many nichts spent freezin' in the open on the hard ground. Rheumatism hae set inta my auld bones, along with a fragment of that German musket ball in my arm that is startin' to pain me. I hae a lot o' enthusiasm fer the king o'er the water, but nae lang tramps and rides fer me, I'm thinkin'. But I can teach young laddies the mechanics o' war right weel." Jock changed the subject by turning in his saddle and waving to Peter and Will to advance. When they had caught up, Jock said, "Do ye lads ken the history and significance o' the cattle trysts at Crieff?"

When he received headshakes of denial, Jock launched into a history lesson.

"Waal, *Crieff* in the Gaelic language means 'tree.' Fer hundreds o' years, Highlanders hae been coming south tae Crieff to sell their black cattle tae markets south, especially across the border tae England. Every year, there are twa trysts and sometimes three, but the Michaelmas cattle sale in October is the biggest. Drovers come early tae put up fences in the fields and on hillsides. Thousands o' the shaggy beasties get driven in, until the fields and hillsides are black. Drovers bring cattle frae all o'er the Highlands, some frae as far awa' as Caithness, Sutherland, and Ross, and even frae the Hebrides, brought tae the mainland in boats. The drovers take many days tae bring on the cattle, so they can fatten up along the way. The cattle business is difficult, lads. The drovers are a wild lot, wi' drinking, carousing, and fighting. Some men are lazy or dishonest and try their hand at thieving cattle frae drovers along the trails and sometimes right frae the fenced pens.

"Just short o' James Square, ye will see a gibbet called the Kind gallows, because o' all the cattle thieves hanged there fer stealin' kind o'er the years. It's a rough and swift justice, and many hae their necks stretched on an accusation. But cattle in the Highlands are mair than only money, lads. For Highland families, the twa or three heads of cattle they assign to a drover mean food on the table, and their loss means starvation or want through a cruel winter. The Kind gallows hae also received its share o' cutpurses, sharps, and highwaymen. 'Tis tradition hereaboots when passing the gallows on which the condemned still hang tae touch our hats and say, 'God bless ye, and the De'il damn ye.'" He chuckled. "I dinna like most o' the merchants in Crieff. They are stiff-necked Presbyterians wha love the Hanoverians. They resent the high-spirited Highlanders, although they profit hugely frae their custom. I would tip my hat and say tae them, 'The De'il bless ye and God damn ye.'"

The boys giggled at his mild profanity, and Jock McRae laughed uproariously.

He leaned close to Jamie, winked, and said in a low voice, "Personally, if there comes a rising, I am fer burnin' doon this damned town, as we did after Sheriffmuir, but yer grandfather hae invested heavily in the town and will protect it."

Peter spoke up. "Master McRae, I hae heard that Rob Roy spent much time in and around Crieff. Is that true?"

Jock looked up, his face filled with reminiscence. "Aye, lad, he did. In many respects, I agree wi' the guid burghers of Crieff, wha called him a troublemaker. In the Gaelic, men called him Raibeart Ruadh, Red Robert MacGregor, because o' his red hair. The McGregor clan was outlawed fer their depredations, and he went by the name o' Robert Campbell since his mother was a Breadalbane Campbell."

He interrupted his tale by pointing suddenly. "We are turning here. Yonder is Gallowhaugh and Gallowford Road leading past the gallows. Turn tae the left, lads, sae we can get through the press toward James Square where the merchant booths are set up. Follow me!"

As they moved up the street toward the square, the noise of the gathering crowd grew louder, and Jock had to raise his voice to be heard.

"What was I sayin'? Ah, yes. Rob Roy was a tall and braw lad in his youth and unco brave. He fought at Sheriffmuir in the rising o' seventeen fifteen. I met him there, though in later life, he was concerned about his reputation, so he claimed that he was nae at the battle. Four years after that disaster, he was wounded at Glenshiels when the Spanish came in a poorly-supported attempt tae help the king o'er the water regain his crown. Fer a time, Rob was a respected cattleman. This was when cattle taking and selling protection against thieves was a common way of life in these hills and glens. Rob borrowed money to increase his herd, but his chief herder disappeared wi' the money and the cattle. Sae, Rob Roy could'na pay back the loan. The authorities branded him an outlaw. They ransacked his house at Inversnaid and burned it down. Luckily, his wife and family got awa'. Rob waged a blood feud against his creditor, the Duke o' Montrose, for that terrible act. He hid in the hills around Crieff for years and sometimes rode armed through the town wi' his men. They caught him and put him in gaol several times, but he was finally pardoned. He died an auld man peacefully in his own house at Balquhidder aboot ten years ago. Although he was pardoned, he ne'er forgave Montrose for his great crime agin his family."

"What crime was that, Master McRae?" asked Peter.

Jock hawked and spat into the street. "Injustice, lad. Rob McGregor lived wi' it his whole life. In his youth, his father was imprisoned unjustly fer treason. His mother died while his father was in prison. The auld man was broken in health when he was released and died o' sorrow soon after. Rob Roy grew up with injustice and spent a guid part o' his life fighting tae correct it. It cankered his soul and drove him tae commit many violent acts. Tae a true Highlander, the man is a symbol o' courage and resolution in the face o' injustice. They honor him for that, and many's the time flowers mysteriously appear on his grave, up at the Balquidder kirk."

Jamie had listened thoughtfully and spoke up. "He sounds just like Robin Hood."

Jock laughed.

"Aye, lad. In many ways, he was like Robin Hood. Perhaps Rob was an appropriate name for them both."

Abruptly, Jock stopped talking and steered closer to the boys. Everyone was staring at the troop of red-coated soldiers marching three abreast with measured tread along the street toward the square, led by a mounted officer in a tall black beaver hat.

"Bloody lobsters," muttered Jock. "Here tae keep the peace, though I doubt that anyone is in a mood fer trouble today. Many's the time, though, I've seen them wade in indiscriminately against men, women, and children wi' fixed bayonets to break up a feud or fight."

They neared James Square, filled with a surging throng crowding the close-set booths and stalls of the merchants. The noise was deafening. The smoky smell of roasting joints and entire lambs turning on spits wafted on the summer air. Hucksters held aloft sweetmeats impaled on long sticks as they passed through the crowd. Jamie pulled up to admire a juggler in a gay multi-colored costume entertaining a small clot of children on the edge of the crowd. Suddenly, he felt a tug on his reins. He turned to recognize Malcolm, one of the grooms, with his hand on the horse's bridle.

"Time tae dismount, young Master Drummond. I'll lead yer horse tae the glen where we will be setting up the pavilion fer the family."

Jamie jerked his head around to see Jock and Peter dismounting.

"But, Malcolm, where is the mounting block? I canna get down wi'out it."

Malcolm shifted the bridle to his left hand and extended his right. "Yer a braw lad, but still only seven years auld, Master Drummond. I can take yer weight easily."

Jamie was uncertain, but not wanting to show fear in front of his cousins, he dropped the reins, gripped the front of the pommel, stood up on his left leg, and swung the right over the horse's withers. Malcolm encircled his body and lowered him effortlessly to the cobbles without releasing his grip on the horse's bridle. Jamie was impressed with Malcolm's strength.

"I can hardly wait tae be big and strong like ye, Malcolm," he said.

The groom smiled genially. "Ach. Ye will be taller and heavier than me someday, Master Drummond. Ye are only seven, and I am seventeen. Ye will be surprised by how much growin' ye will do in ten years."

Jamie sniffed. "It couldna be soon enough to suit me, Malcolm."

"Patience, lad." The groom laughed.

Jamie retorted, "Ye sound like my mama. She always says 'Patience, Jamie.' I hate that word."

"So do all young men," responded the groom cheerfully, leading Jamie's horse away.

Jock led the dismounted boys toward where James and John Drummond still sat their mounts.

James leaned down. "Jock, take the lads around tae see the sights. Here are some coins they can contribute tae the entertainers and use tae buy sweets. We will be going tae a meeting at the Drummond Arms Hotel. I saw Lord Lovat's coach moving that way. He must hae come doon frae Inverness and stayed the nicht at an inn outside the town. I'll lead the Murrays there. We will meet ye in three hours, or if we are going tae be late, I will send a groom tae find ye and guide ye tae the glen where we will assemble fer lunch."

Jock nodded agreement and reached up to take the small purse from James's gloved hand.

The next three hours disappeared in a delirious whirl of activity. Tightly gripping hands, the boys hung close on Jock McRae's coattails as they wandered through the throng. They followed the sounds of dogs yelping and growling. In a corner of the square stood a large cage where a black bear sat, restrained by a short length of chain. The panting beast licked blood from a tear in its glossy coat. On the grassy verge nearby, three dogs lay licking their wounds from a fight with the bear, which the boys had heard but just missed seeing.

On a small platform of rough planks stood a fiddler sawing frantically at his instrument while stamping his foot to keep the beat. A boy rattled a snare drum while a piper played a reel, the skirling notes rising above the noise of the jostling crowd. The boys pushed through the people listening to the music to find another scene.

A group gathered close around a chubby bald man standing behind a narrow table on which stood three upside-down tin cups and a small pile of coins. The man moved the cups around deftly. Jamie was amazed to see his fingers flash with incredible speed. He lifted a cup and then another to show the crowd nothing underneath. With great deliberation, he raised the third to show a silver coin. The crowd cheered.

"Risk a penny, win a silver shilling!" he called in a loud voice. "Wha will chance a penny fer such a prize?"

Jamie could hear Jock's low voice in his ear. "Ne'er take such a chance, lad. The game is crooked as the man's ugly nose. His hands move sae quickly that ye canna see him slip the coin under the lip o' the cup, but he is a cheat, for sairtan." Jamie watched three men in a row attempt to guess the cup with the coin underneath. All failed to guess correctly, and the chubby man scooped their pennies into his purse.

They wandered through the stalls and booths. Jock slipped the boys coins from time to time to buy sweets, pastries cooked in bubbling hot grease and drizzled with honey, dense bannocks studded with currants and chunks of dried apple, and hard candy wrapped tightly in twisted colored paper.

They watched a trio of dancing dogs barking joyfully while hopping to a tune scraped on a battered fiddle by a one-eyed man. Jamie tossed a penny in the old man's hat lying by his foot. The man nodded and smiled, revealing gaps where teeth should be.

Suddenly Peter pulled at Jamie's sleeve. "Come on. There's a rough-and-tumble bout starting over there."

Jamie and Will looked expectantly at Jock McRae, who assumed a pained expression but reluctantly moved toward the sign advertising the bout.

They pushed their way through the crowd to a raised platform topped by four stakes lashed together by strands of heavy rope to form a square. In that enclosure stood two brawny barefoot men stripped to the waist. One was a tall, broad-shouldered, smooth-shaven youth with long, dark hair tied behind his head with a leathern thong. The other was an older and shorter barrel-shaped man with hairy muscular arms, dark beard jutting from his chin, and heavy eyebrows that met in the middle of his forehead. His dark, greasy hair was hacked off at the level of his chin.

A fancily dressed man stood in the ring with his hand up. Above the roar of the crowd, he pointed at the younger man and shouted, "I gie ye Andrew Graham o' Gartmore. He hae laid low the last seven men tae face him!"

There was a torrent of cheers.

Then the man pointed to the older bearded contestant. "And on this side, I gie ye the Irishman Patrick O'Neill o' Antrim!" When the chorus of boos died down, he turned to the fighters and shouted, "Gentlemen! Will ye fight fair or rough-and-tumble?" The contestants muttered something that Jamie could not hear, whereupon the man shouted, "Rough-and-tumble it is!"

The crowd roared their approval.

The well-dressed man stepped out of the ring down to ground level. He held up a pistol, and the crowd quieted. The contestants faced each other. The crack of the pistol signaled the start of the bout. The two men sidled around the ring, hands clenched, taking tentative swipes at each other while the crowd surged and roared advice.

Suddenly, the burly man went into a crouch, drew his arms to his face, and leaped at his opponent. The youth stepped aside deftly and landed a blow on the side of his attacker's head. The older man tumbled to the boards, rolled, and sprang to his feet. The contestants circled, and once again, the older man crouched and charged, but the youth stepped aside and retaliated with a swift punch to the older man's left eye. Blood ran down his face and stained the boards. The circling and occasional blows went on for a few minutes until the crowd became restless and began to hiss.

Suddenly, the fight changed. With blood leaking from his damaged eyebrow, the bearded man crouched and sprang to his right, colliding with the youth chest to chest. The combatants fell to the boards with a crash. The bearded man fixed his hands in his opponent's hair and rolled astride him. With a firm grip in the other's hair, he hammered the back of the youth's head onto the boards repeatedly. The youth retaliated by pulling his opponent's face close and fixing his teeth in the man's right ear. The bearded man howled and released his grip to clutch at his damaged ear. The youth sprang to his feet, spitting out the fragment of ear, and rushed his opponent. They circled the square, raining blows on each other without losing their feet. The faces of both men were soon streaked with blood.

The end came suddenly. The Irishman got his powerful arms around the youth's chest and squeezed him in a bearhug. They waddled around the square, fastened together, occasionally banging into the corner posts and threatening to tumble into the crowd below. The youth thrashed in the grip of the bearded man and pounded his face until the man's nose erupted in a shower of blood. Suddenly, the trapped youth smashed his forehead against his opponent's face. Blinded by blood, the bearded man howled and released his grip. The youth staggered back, gasping for air. Sensing the change in the match, the yelling crowd surged toward the ropes.

The bearded man rushed the youth again, knocking him to the boards. Seizing his opportunity, he leaped into the air and landed on his opponent's chest with his knees. The youth rolled away. The Irishman rose to his feet and launched several vicious kicks at the stomach and groin of the youth, who howled piteously, and thrashed about on the boards. The Irishman kicked him in the head, and he lay still. The youth's head lolled to one side. The blood-drenched Irishman hovered over the prostrate form, and then recognizing that his opponent was unconscious, spat out a gobbet of blood, grinned, and raised his own hands exultantly. The bout was over.

Someone sloshed a bucket of water over the unconscious youth. His legs kicked spasmodically. Two men dragged his body through the ropes and down onto the grass. In a few moments, he awoke with a groan and sat up. The crowd, which had exploded in boos and hisses when the bout ended, pulled the bleeding victor over the ropes and seated him in a wooden chair. Someone passed him a scrap of blanket that he used to wipe his face. He lifted the bloodstained blanket and waved it around his head. The joyous men who had bet on the Irishman lifted the chair over their heads and paraded the victor around the square. A mesmerized Jamie felt a hand on his shoulder.

"Enough o' this insanity," growled Jock. "They are like rampaging bulls, beating and scarring each other fer life fer nae guid purpose, except tae fill and empty other men's pockets. Let's move on, lads."

They moved to a quieter corner of James Square, where a slender woman dressed in a simple belted dress, whose dark hair was streaked with silver, sat on a chair under a vine-covered arbor while a small crowd stood silently listening to her play the clarsach. As she plucked the strings of the small harp, she sang old melodies in a mixture of Gaelic and Broad Scots. Jamie felt strangely moved by the lilting music of the harp and the woman's clear, high voice.

Vair me o ro van o
Vair me o ro van o ee
Vair me o ru o ho
Sad am I without thee.

When I'm lonely, dear white heart
Black the nicht or wild the sea
By love's light, my foot finds
The auld pathway to thee.

Vair me o ro van o
Vair me o ro van o ee
Vair me o ru o ho
Sad am I without thee.

Thou'rt the music of my heart
Harp o' joy, oh *cruit mo chridh*
Moon o' guidance by nicht
Strength and light thou'rt tae me.

"What is she singing, Master McRae?" he whispered. "I dinna ken very much Gaelic."

"She is singing an auld sang of the sea and islands. She is frae the Outer Isles, lad. This is Maggie MacLeod. I ken her weel frae auld times, when we were both young. I met her when we were both seventeen, when she came tae Eileen Donan tae sing fer the McRae chieftain. She sang and played fer many years as she wandered frae place tae place. She is mair than a singer, lad. She is a bard, like those o' ancient times, bringing news and preserving the auld tales and sangs. Some people believe that she can prophesy, that she hae the sight."

Hearing the roar of the crowd assembling for another rough-and-tumble bout, he snorted and jerked his thumb in the direction of the fight.

"She is worth mair than her weight in gold, but those fools prefer tae be entertained by blood. Let this be a lesson tae ye, lads. Here is spiritual strength and nourishment fer the soul. There, pah!" He wiped the moisture from the corners of his eyes.

Jamie pretended not to notice.

A servant dressed in Drummond livery found them there, wrapped in the magic of Maggie McLeod's voice.

"All is ready. Shall we gae tae the glen? 'Tis not far. The walk will whet yer appetite, and the shade will be welcome after the heat o' the sun."

Jamie held out a hand toward Jock, who reached into his scrip and extracted the small purse that James Drummond had given him. He passed it to Jamie, along with some coins of his own. Jamie walked forward to drop the coins onto the plaid shawl spread at the singer's feet. He smiled at her and turned to go when she suddenly stopped playing. She set down the harp and looked him in the eyes.

"Stay, laddie," she said in a soft voice. "Ye, yer friends, and Jock McRae are different frae the others hereabout. I see it in yer faces and the way ye linger while others move awa' after a time. Yer hearts are touched by the auld melodies. My homeland is the tiny isle o' Eirisgeidh in the Outer Hebrides. It is a wild and rocky place, where the spirit sings in the stormy sea and the wind that whines around the auld croft houses."

Jamie nodded, wordlessly, transfixed by her dark blue eyes and the smile that played at the corners of her mouth.

"Lad, yer life is aboot tae change in ways that ye canna expect. When beset by troubles that seem tae o'erwhelm ye, remember the strength o' yer own soul and the traditions o' yer family, clan, and nation. They are precious and the foundation o' yer soul. What ye are and what ye may become depends on what ye start with.

Yer soul is rooted in these hills as I am in the western islands far awa' where my heart dwells. Ye may gae tae the ends o' the earth, and my soul tells me that ye will someday, but yer blood and heart will always be tied tae the legacy o' this land and its people. Remember, lad. Honor, integrity, and loyalty tae kith and kin are what will make ye great, nae matter where ye wander."

Her eyes flicked to Jock McRae's face, and she smiled. He smiled in return and bowed to her.

She whispered, "Gae with my auld friend. Tell him that I remember him frae when he was a handsome and impulsive youth. I loved him then, and I think he loved me, but our paths led us tae far different places. Now, he is auld, like me, wi' honor and virtue written in every line o' his face. His heart was e'er guid and true. Listen tae his wisdom and heed his lessons. They will help prepare ye fer what is tae come."

"What is tae come?" whispered Jamie.

"Enough, lad," she whispered back. "Yer heart is nae yet ready. Just heed what Jock tells ye." She took his hand in hers.

It was cool to the touch. He could feel callouses on her fingers from years of harp-playing.

She squeezed his hand tightly. "People think that I am a seer, but only some o' what I say comes true. I canna even see my own future clearly. I see only what the sight permits me tae see fer the benefit o' others. People are staring at us now," she said, "and wondering what secrets I am telling ye. Now gae, lad."

Jamie plucked up his courage. "Will ye sing me another sang that will help me remember what ye hae said tae me? And in Scots? I canna understand much o' the Gaelic."

She looked deep into his eyes and, reaching out, touched his cheek tenderly. She picked up the clarsach from her lap, and plucked a haunting melody. Closing her eyes, she lifted her head and sang:

> Oh, tae him tae the land o' passages
> Gliding on a distant sea.

Set him doon beside the sunset-shadowed sky
Tae dwell where the eagles fly.
Far awa' I see the gleaming peaks
Hov'ring high above the earth.
Silently, in stately majesty
They usher oot the sunset fading north.
Rank on rank, the somber cedar trees
March awa' their endless miles.
Evergreen, where sight hae ne'er seen
They cover every hill and clothe the solitary isles.
Frae the shore the ravens call his name.
On dusky wings, they wheel and whirl.
Raucous cries, their haunting lullabies,
Like ancient voices frae another world.
Scarlet flames the brilliant columbine.
Sapphire spears the lupine blue.
Buttercups and silver fairy drops
Weave a fragrant carpet glist'ning in early morning dew.
Frae the deep, the great leviathan
Points his brow tae the air.
Crystal white, it breathes a fountain bright;
Then it plunges back, its fanning flukes obscure.
Icy blue, the glacier's sculpted cliffs
Crumble down tae the bay.
Floating ice, a seal's paradise
And the thundering echoes fade awa'.

Jamie backed away slowly until he felt Jock McRae's hand on his shoulder. When the last note faded, the audience was still for a moment and then cheered Maggie McLeod until they were hoarse. A shower of coins landed on the plaid shawl, bouncing and rolling. She rose slowly; bowed, smiling to her audience; and carefully packed the clarsach in a black velvet bag, which she slung over her shoulder. Then she knelt and picked up the coins and shawl. She came forward to envelop Jock in a tender embrace that lasted for long moments. The crowd watched silently. Then, without a word, she turned and left.

Jamie said nothing to anyone of the meeting with Maggie MacLeod, but Peter told everyone. Jamie was bombarded with questions when they reached the glen. Her reputation as a bard and seer was widespread in the Highlands. Jamie admitted to being confused by her words and could offer little more than a vague outline of what she had told him, except that she foretold of trouble and travel to faraway places. James and Euphemia exchanged concerned glances but said nothing.

The children and adults ate themselves to repletion on the fine food laid out on cloth-bedecked trestles by servants from the huge wicker hampers, wine for the adults, and cold water from a nearby freshet for the children. After lunch, Jamie dozed in the shade cast by a copse of old trees. The men gathered some distance away to smoke and talk about their morning meeting while the women exchanged and admired their purchases in the fair's stalls.

Peter wandered close to where the men were sitting. He stretched out in the shade and pretended to sleep. The men stopped talking and looked at him desultorily. Jock laid down his pipe, rose, and walked over to nudge Peter with his foot. Peter's eyes flew open. He stared into Jock McRae's grim face and jumped to his feet. He returned resignedly to where the other boys were dozing. Jamie looked at Peter questioningly.

"Nae luck," growled Peter. "All I heard was that nae one seems tae hae decided what tae do aboot the Bonnie Prince. He is still hanging around Glenfinnan, bein' entertained by various chiefs. Lord Lovat is particularly undecided and will return tae Inverness in the morning tae talk wi' the chiefs in the north. My ears are particularly attuned tae my father's voice. He is adamant. The Gordons are Jacobite tae the core but convinced that now is nae the time fer a rising. Then Master McRae surprised me by kicking me rudely wi' his foot."

Jamie leaned forward to whisper all that Maggie MacLeod had said. Peter was very impressed.

"I dinna believe in the sight, but Maggie MacLeod hae a reputation fer hearing most o' what passes fer news in the Highlands and islands," he observed. "If she sees trouble coming, then I believe that she kens that the western chiefs are ready tae rise. That is her message. I canna ken the travel part o' her prediction and all the rest aboot eagles and trees and ravens and glaciers. Time will tell."

It was late afternoon, and the air much cooler when the families rose to prepare for the return journey to Strathallan. The sun was sliding down into the west, sending long shafts of dusty light through the canopy of trees when the servants loaded the hampers in the boots of the coaches and handed the women inside. The boys and men mounted, with Jamie and Will hoisted into the saddle by the grooms. The cavalcade wound its way onto the road that led back into Crieff. The crowd thinned appreciably as the horses clopped up Gallowshill Road.

Jamie, with fearful anticipation, glanced toward the gallows where only a small handful of people stood. Hanging from the gibbet were three figures dressed in shabby jerkins and trews, inert in the still warm air, with heads lolling and hands tied behind their backs.

"Jamie! Come here!" came the crackling voice of James Drummond.

Jamie tore his gaze away from the gallows and urged his horse forward until he came up next to his father.

James sighed. "I was afeared that ye would see that. It is a pity that men can sink sae low that they commit such crimes that the law deems them irretrievable reprobates. Ye will see many such on nearly every crossroads in the land."

"Perhaps, Papa, they had nae choice but tae steal."

James reined up, and his horse stopped. James laid a gloved hand on his son's shoulder. "My son, men always hae choices.

God dinna create them thieves. Rather than steal, they could work. Even when caught and convicted, prisoners can petition a judge tae transport them. Better tae sweat and slave in the mines and fields o' the New World than tae kick out yer life on the gallows. Besides," he said grimly, "it is a natural process of selection. These men were stupid and impulsive, in addition tae being unprincipled, and they were caught. Now they will steal nae mair. Intelligent thieves find ways to nae get caught. Take Henry Morgan, for example, an accomplished pirate wha was successful enough tae rise tae become governor of Jamaica and a belted knight approved by the crown."

Jamie thought for a moment and then said, "Sae, Papa, the best thieves are in the government."

At that remark, James burst into hearty laughter shared by the other men. He reached over to cuff his son affectionately. "My son, the eminent philosopher, hae spoken a great truth!"

The next day, the Gordon family completed their packing and took the carriage north to their home in Abergeldie. Before leaving, Peter led Jamie and Will into the garden. With considerable distress, he gave them the news. His father, as Laird of Abergeldie, would not join any armed force for the prince and would forbid his tenants permission to do so as well. Charles Gordon was utterly convinced that a rising against the armed might of British authority was not only foolhardy but also suicidal. He would provide support with money and arms, but only so secretly that the transactions could never be traced to his family or properties. Only if the Gordons of Huntley came out would Charles Gordon change his mind.

A few days later, Jamie woke to the realization that only another month of summer remained and he had yet to venture into the woods and meadows to collect a single specimen for Doctor Thomson. After breakfast, he went to the greenhouse to gather his tutor's sketches, nets, bottle of ether, wool pads, and collection bottles. He placed them in a wicker basket and brought them downstairs. Leaving it on the front steps, he raced inside to tell his mother that he was going into the woods until lunch.

He found her in the solar, talking with Lady Margaret, his grandmother. He waited until Euphemia noticed him. Then he told her of his plans.

"Jamie, it might nae be guid tae tramp through the woods alone. I think yer father would enjoy helping ye. He is in his study, writing letters. Gae and ask him."

Jamie followed her advice and sought his father. He heard voices inside and rapped gently on the closed door of the study. John Drummond opened the door, and Jamie stepped inside. His father sat quill in hand at his polished oak desk and looked at Jamie expectantly.

"Papa, summer is getting on, and I need tae start collecting specimens fer Doctor Thomson. Mama suggested that ye might like tae come along."

Jamie took a deep breath and held it as his father considered. John glanced at James. "Weel, brother, I can finish that letter for ye. We've already agreed on the contents. Ye should gae wi' Jamie and enjoy this fine day."

James set the quill down in its horn stand and stood up. "Since I was instrumental in persuading Jamie tae take the assignment fer his tutor, I should hae some involvement in its satisfaction. Come, Jamie. The woods and meadows should be dry since we hae nae rain fer a few days, but as a precaution, I will pull on some boots. Do ye have the materials Doctor Thomson left?"

"Aye, Papa. I put them in a basket just outside."

Father and son walked down the hall toward the entry. The doorman pulled open the tall doors. A light carriage crunched on the gravel driveway and slowed to a stop. The driver hopped down from his seat and pulled open the carriage door. Two men stepped out.

The younger man, obviously agitated, called brusquely, "It is imperative that ye send fer Viscount Strathallan immediately!"

Lord George Murray and his brother, the Marquis of Tullibardine, had arrived at Castle Drummond for an unannounced visit.

James called from the top of the staircase, "Lord Murray! Pray come in fer some refreshment!"

Over his shoulder, he said in a low voice to the doorkeeper, "Notify the viscount that we have unexpected guests wha need tae see him as quickly as he can get here."

The Marquis of Tullibardine and his brother walked slowly up the steps.

When they reached the top, George Murray said, "No refreshments please. We hae nae time tae stay. We will wait here."

William Drummond arrived a minute later. As he walked out into the sunshine, he said, "My guid neighbors, please come in and we can talk."

George Murray was agitated enough to blurt his news in front of Jamie and James Drummond. He spoke rapidly and with some agitation of spirit. "Lord Drummond, it is happening already. News has come tae me that the Prince is in Moidart, looking fer additional followers. Lochiel is calling oot the Camerons fer him, and the McDonalds o' Keppoch are joining them. No one seems tae ken how many swords they will bring, but there will be at least a thousand. Alexander MacDonald o' Sleat and Norman MacLeod o' MacLeod are refusing tae meet with the Prince and offering many pretexts. The intentions o' the other clans are unknown. Clan Ranald, MacDonnells, and MacDougalls are undecided, but favorably considering sending men and arms."

The Viscount observed mildly, "That's nae news, George. It's little mair than we hae heard fer several days."

George Murray smiled grimly. "That is nae the significant news, neighbor. What we came tae tell ye is that General Sir John Cope is readying an army in Stirling tae move north tae the Highlands within days, with seventeen companies o' infantry and cannon. He hae heard rumors of the landing. He is determined tae find and capture the Bonnie Prince and what he believes tae be his growing army of French and Highlanders."

His voice rose and he ran his fingers through his gray hair. "My God, man. They could be here in less than a day after leaving Stirling. We could nae possibly stop or delay them. We must send word west tae the Prince and Lochiel immediately. Almost certainly, Cope's army will proceed tae Crieff and then tae Aberfeldy, Rannoch Moor, and Lochaber. After they pass here, we canna get through safely. We must also send a courier tae bring news tae Lord Lovat in the north."

William Drummond turned to see Jamie and James staring at him. He pondered for a moment. His lips tightened into a thin line, and he nodded decisively. "I see that the time for keeping secrets is past." He beckoned to his son and then turned to the Murrays. "Come, my lords. Please join me in my study. James, find and bring John."

James replied, "He is in my study, writing." He turned to Jamie. "Nae a word tae yer mother or grandmother. I will tell them in guid time what must be done. Now, get ye gone and find Jock McRae. Tell him tae join us in yer grandfather's study forthwith."

James spun on his heel and ran to notify his brother. Jamie raced off to find the old soldier. The wicker basket lay unheeded.

Chapter Five

Jamie found Jock McRae at the blacksmith's forge near the stables, reshaping a bit for his horse. He held the bit flat against the anvil with heavy tongs and delivered sure, hard strokes with a short-handled heavy hammer. Jamie watched the hot metal flake off the bit under Jock's blows. Jock set down the hammer and examined the bit at arm's length. At last, he grunted with satisfaction and took a step to the quenching barrel, where he plunged the red-hot metal into the dark water. Jamie jerked back as the metal hissed and sputtered and steam rose to momentarily envelop him and the blacksmith. Jock looked at Jamie.

"What is it, laddie?"

"I hae a message fer ye frae my grandpapa. Ye must come immediately to his study. My papa was most insistent."

"Do ye ken why the laird is calling me, Jamie?" he growled, irritated to be pulled away from what he considered an essential task.

"It must be important, Master McRae. The Murrays are here. It hae something tae do wi' an army marching north."

"Damn," breathed the old soldier. Jock McRae set the smoking bit down on the anvil and turned to the blacksmith.

"Prepare another bit to match this, Archie. I will return as soon as I can, which may nae be soon."

The blacksmith nodded.

Turning away, Jock smiled at Jamie and said, "I thank ye, lad, for finding me sae soon. Lead on, and I will follow as fast as these auld legs can move."

After Jamie led Jock to Viscount Drummond's study, the men shut the door and locked it. Jamie wandered to the garden and sat on a bench in the sun. He thought about returning to retrieve his net and bottles but decided to wait to see what would happen when the meeting in his grandfather's study ended. A servant emerged to run to the stables. He returned a few minutes later with Alexander MacKenzie, the Drummond master of horse. The two men disappeared inside the castle. Jamie followed a discreet distance down the hall from the study. The low murmur of voices from behind the door rose abruptly. Moments later, the door opened, and both Murrays stepped out.

George Murray turned back and said with some heat to someone inside the room, "We don't understand enough yet tae make such a commitment! I pray ye wait three days, gentlemen. If there is positive movement and support frae the west and north, then I say we march."

A sharp voice urged him to return inside the room, and the door was again shut.

Jamie decided to wait a bit longer, but he knew it was time to leave when Mister Dobie turned the corner and saw him.

"Come, Master Drummond. No eavesdropping. It is nearly eleven o'clock. I believe that the cook has just set oot some nice bannocks to cool. I wager that ye would enjoy a wee sample wi' milk. Come now."

He took Jamie's arm in a firm grip, lifting him to a standing position and placing an arm around his shoulders. Jamie felt himself propelled toward the kitchen. Sure enough, the promised warm bannocks were there, along with cold milk. Many minutes passed, but Mister Dobie finally left, and Jamie took the opportunity with the cook not looking to escape. As he passed the viscount's study, he saw that the door was open and the room empty.

Hearing footsteps, he shrank back against a door. He saw his grandfather and the Murrays join three men standing in the vestibule, all booted and spurred for riding.

William Drummond handed a sealed packet to Alexander MacKenzie. "Alex, take this letter tae Lochiel, the chief o' Clan Cameron. Bypass Crieff tae avoid detection by the government spies there. Gae by way o' Aberfeldy and then by Loch Rannoch tae Lochaber."

"Aye, my lord. I remember the way frae last year's hunting party."

"Ye know what intelligence we seek aboot the arming and gathering o' the western clans. We also need tae ken the Prince's destination and intentions, because o' our commitment, decided fer Drummonds, but nae yet fer Murrays. Gae and return quickly. Take twa companions and six horses. It is crucial that ye return wi' news as fast as ye are able. On yer return, ye must be extraordinarily careful because General Sir John Cope's army is on the move. We know not its destination or route."

Alex MacKenzie bowed and left.

John Drummond spoke up. "My task is to ride north tae find Simon Fraser at his Lovat estates near Inverness. Given his gout on his last foray to Strathallan, I dinna doubt but that he is still laid up at hame. However, he hae promised to meet wi' the northern clans. We must understand their intentions, given the prince's presence in Lochaber. I believe that I can reach Inverness in twa days and return in another twa, Father."

William Drummond nodded and embraced him.

"Gae with all speed, and take ain or twa trusted companions wha are excellent with pistol and sword. The road north teems with highwaymen."

"Aye, father." John's spurs jingled as he walked with measured steps across the marble entryway.

The Viscount turned to his eldest son. "James, tae ye I entrust the task o' riding tae our Perthshire properties tae raise the levy. In every sense o' the word, yer task is tae take the fiery cross tae our lands and prepare the muster. Those possessing arms should bring them and whatever ammunition they can carry. For those wi'out arms or insufficient, we hae enough in the armory tae equip them. Return wi' as many men as are ready tae march or ride within three days, and be back within five. I am committed, although we still await the Murrays' decision, tae deliver at least three hundred fully armed men as soon as we learn where the prince is gathering the loyal clan forces."

James nodded agreement with his assignment and turned to leave. William Drummond stayed him with an upraised palm.

"I will stay here and, with Jock McRae's help, place the castle on a ready footing, muster all available men, and prepare an encampment fer those wha will be coming here temporarily."

James embraced his father, shook hands with Jock McRae, and left. Jamie turned and fled back up the corridor toward the back of the castle. Troubled by his conflicting emotions of excitement and dread, he returned to the garden and sat down on a low stone wall. He stared at the speckled fish circling in the pond in the center of the lawn. Suddenly, a shadow fell across the grass.

Startled, he looked up to see Emilia smiling at him. The sun caught her blonde locks and made them appear as a halo around her face.

"Oh. Hullo, Aunt Emilia," he said.

"Oh, Aunt Emilia, is it? Sae formal! Weel, Jamie Drummond, I see that I surprised ye, but ye dinna sound excited to see me." She peered at his face for a few moments and then sat down on the wall next to him. "I see. Ye saw or heard something o' what happened this morning, did ye? The whole castle is buzzing aboot the Murrays' visit and the abrupt departure o' my brothers." She sighed. "I ken that ye are troubled and just a little frightened. I am very frightened, Jamie, nae because o' what is happening but because o' what might happen. We just dinna ken the future. We have tae watch and wait, and that is the worst state o' all, nae understanding whether tae be frightened or composed." She put her arm around his shoulders and hugged him tight. "Ach, Jamie!" she said. "We canna let ourselves be overwhelmed in our ignorance. We need tae stay busy while we wait. Papa says that we canna leave the castle grounds, but we can do something."

Jamie brightened. "I know what tae do. I hae an assignment frae Doctor Thomson tae be completed before he returns in October. I must explore the gardens, meadows, and streambeds tae find and net insects fer his collection."

Emilia clapped her hands in excitement. "I can help ye, Jamie. I've been all o'er the grounds. I know lots o' places where we can find butterflies, beetles, dragonflies, and water bugs."

After lunch, Jamie showed Emilia the sketches. They retrieved the wicker basket from the doorman and set off to scour the meadow and watercourses east of the castle. It was very warm, so the insects were not moving very fast and were easily netted. Jamie wielded the net, and Emilia placed captured specimens in the bottles with the ether-soaked wicking. By the time the sun moved down the western sky and the meadows began to cool, a strong breeze came up and made netting impossible. They were very pleased by their haul, over twenty excellent specimens. They spent the next morning in the classroom mounting, labeling, and storing them in Doctor Thomson's glass-covered display cases.

After lunch, Emilia suggested that they exercise the horses. She had laid out an obstacle course with jumping hurdles and flag-draped pylons in a cleared field close to the stables. Several of the grooms joined them in running the horses through the course. It was hard not to notice the creation of a tent camp on the far side of the cleared field and the arrival of two score armed men to occupy it. When they rode back to the stables, they saw many more men unsaddling and wiping down their mounts. The stalls in the stables were full, and grooms put the additional horses in temporary paddocks that they had constructed the day before.

In the castle, men were taking down broadswords and pikes from their age-old positions on the walls and hauling them to a makeshift armory next to the blacksmith's forge. The rasp of steel on the grinding surface of the large blackened wheel drew Jamie's attention as the stone spun under the blade's edge, causing a shower of sparks in the fading light of late afternoon. The blacksmith's assistant stopped the wheel long enough to swat with his apron at the flies gathering on their neglected meal. It was obvious from the growing stack of blades that they would be sharpening far into the night and through much of the next day.

As they returned to the castle, Emilia pointed to where men-at-arms were busily oiling the small cannons that punctured the crenelations in the castle's walls. Hay wagons lay turned on their sides in a semi-circle around the front and sides of the castle. Heavy barrels were roped together and stacked in the spaces between wagons to form a makeshift barrier. Jamie saw that wheeled gun carriages now stood at several places around the barrier. A platoon of about thirty armed men wearing jerkins bearing the Drummond coat of arms on the left breast stood in formation before the castle entrance, listening to instructions from Jock McRae, who faced them wearing a scabbarded basket-hilted broadsword hung low on his hip.

Jamie and Emilia made their way to the garden behind the castle, where a sentry met them and waved them through another barricade of wooden hurdles and bales of hay. Emilia broke the silence.

"It is strange how the castle hae changed in only a day. I'm surprised that we call it a castle at all." She sniffed and continued as they approached the rear entrance, also now guarded by a sentry. "A castle is surrounded by a moat and a curtain wall all around. Inside the moat is a drawbridge and portcullis. In the middle o' the castle is a donjon or keep, also wi' stout walls. The walls hae slits through which soldiers can shoot. Strathallan is only a manor hourse dressed up tae look like a castle. I suppose the sentries are here tae prevent a mob frae attacking, but they could ne'er stop an army. I suppose we could climb up on the roof and pour boiling oil down on the heads o' attackers."

Jamie burst out laughing. "We can do that, Emilia! Let us winch up a big pot and tip it over."

Emilia hugged him. "Ye are such a silly goose, Jamie Drummond. But if an army does come, we will show them that we fecht like lions. Come. We'll be late fer dinner."

Later that evening, as he prepared for bed, Jamie peered down from the window. Sentries wearing white bandoleers over their chests, with muskets slung over their shoulders, walked with measured tread around the castle. He stood watching the flickering torches casting gigantic shadows of marching soldiers across the lawn. He thought about the dream that he had standing at that very window of the soldiers lying dead on the field. He thought of Peter Gordon lying still with unseeing eyes. But Peter was safe at Abergeldie.

Jamie pulled back the curtains of his bed and blew out the candle, plunging the room into darkness. He knelt beside the bed, pressing his hands tightly together and bowing his head. He prayed for Peter's safety, knowing in his heart and mind that war would soon come to envelop them all. He prayed for Alex MacKenzie riding through the night somewhere over Rannoch Moor, his uncle John heading for the northern Highlands, and his father somewhere on the roads of Perthshire.

He prayed longest for his mother, who, at dinner that night, had burst unaccountably into tears when someone mentioned his father's absence. He prayed for himself that he could be brave when danger came near and that he would not again see the terrible dream of dead soldiers. Reassured, he climbed into bed and closed his eyes. He did not expect sleep to come swiftly, but within minutes, his anxieties floated away, and he drifted into a dreamless sleep.

The next morning, Emilia pulled Jamie aside.

"Jamie, we must stay closer tae the castle today by order o' my father. But I know where blue butterflies are gathering. Do ye ken the hilltop near the forester's croft?"

Jamie nodded and said excitedly, "There is a meadow close by, where we put the traps tae catch our first hares. We were mair successful there than anywhere else."

Emilia cut in. "It is less than a mile frae the castle. Not even fifteen minutes brisk walk will take us there. And it is weel distant frae the main road. There is a patch o' blue thistle there, and it is sae pretty. We can catch yer butterflies and be back within an hour."

They gathered up the net and bottles with an agreement that this time Emilia would catch the butterflies. As they left the castle garden, they walked east to the stream and cut back through the woods. They had an excellent view of the main road, which lay at the base of the slope. There was no one in sight. A light breeze played across the meadow, ruffling the tops of the heather. As they neared the patch of tall thistle, they saw a cloud of butterflies with iridescent blue wings. Unfortunately, the butterflies hovered directly over the prickly thistle, which was in full summer bloom, bearing large, bright-blue flowers. Emilia looked doubtfully at the patch of thistle. She held the net toward Jamie.

"I changed my mind. They're yer butterflies. Ye must catch them."

Jamie stared at her, his face changing as he recognized what she was implying. He backed away. "Ach, Emilia. Ye are only afraid o' fallin' into the thistles. Ye are a coward!" he accused.

She blushed and bit her lip. "I suppose I am cautious, but no coward." She sighed resignedly. "Weel, I must do it. I promised."

She pulled back the net and walked around the patch. Reaching on tiptoe, she swung the net gingerly at a butterfly that had separated from the blue cloud to fly close to the edge of the thicket.

"Gotcha!" she exulted, pulling back the net and examining the creature fluttering in the confining folds of netting. Jamie held the bottle, and with numerous finger pokes, they succeeded in coaxing the butterfly inside. Jamie pulled away the bottle and screwed on the lid tightly. Suddenly, Emilia dropped the net and clutched his arm so tightly that Jamie almost cried out.

"Shh! Get doon! Look there! Soldiers on the road!"

Jamie squatted and looked to where she was pointing. Sunlight scintillated on the weapons of red-coated soldiers marching three and four abreast up the road from Stirling. At the head of the formation rode men on horseback. Jamie carefully set down the bottle with the butterfly inside, fluttering helplessly.

"What should we do?" he whispered.

Emilia's voice was strained. "They hae not yet seen us. If we move too swiftly, some of the dragoons will be up here in a flash. We must crawl slowly until we are on the other side o' this patch o' thistle. Then we run back hame tae bring word tae my father that soldiers are here. Put the bottle in yer trews, but leave everything else."

The breeze brought snatches of commands along with the rumble of the gun carriages and caissons on the rutted road.

"Stop! Lie still!" Emilia commanded.

Jamie craned his neck and peered down the slope. The column had stopped, and soldiers were crowding the edge of the road, standing in a line.

Emilia giggled when Jamie whispered, "They are all just standing there, taking a piss!"

"Then we wait until they button their trews and start marching again," she said.

The soldiers milled about on the road, drinking from canteens and adjusting their gear. Jamie saw a mounted man ride down the ranks of soldiers, barking commands. In less than a minute, the soldiers were all back on the road and moving forward again. Emilia and Jamie crawled slowly around the thistles.

After what seemed an eternity, Emilia urged him in a tense voice. "Now, run!"

Taking advantage of the cover offered by the thicket, they raced back over the meadow and entered the trees. Breathing raggedly, they neared the sentry-guarded barrier across the path to the formal gardens.

The sentry looked at them disinterestedly until Emilia gasped, "Soldiers! Hundreds o' soldiers on the road tae Crieff!"

Leaving the children doubled over to catch their breath, the sentry turned toward the castle, bawling, "Captain o' the guard! Soldiers on the road!"

Jamie, kneeling panting on the path, felt hands around his shoulders and looked up into the grim face of Jock McRae.

"Quickly, tell me everything that ye saw, lad."

Emilia had recovered more quickly than Jamie and gasped. "We were near the forester's croft catching butterflies. We saw them...doon on the road, hundreds o' redcoats marching north... mounted men and wagons wi' cannon."

"How many men?" queried Jock roughly.

Emilia shook her head.

Jamie blurted, "We dinna ken. They were still comin' up the road when we ran awa'."

Jock straightened and then turned and shouted, "I need a man tae ride tae the forester's croft!"

A groom swung into the saddle and trotted to him. With a few words of instruction, Jock waved the rider back the way that Emilia and Jamie had come and then turned toward the castle. A sentry came on the run.

"Master McRae," he called, "Three mounted men approaching at the trot frae the main road!"

Jamie and Emilia followed Jock McRae around the southern wall of the castle until they could see the three men approaching and then stopped behind a blooming rowan tree. They sat down on the lawn, out of view from the path, so they could listen and watch through the greenery and white blossoms. Jock advanced to the far end of the graveled driveway and stood facing the oncoming riders. They slowed to a walk and stopped. They sat so silently that Jamie could hear the breathing of the horses and the creak of their leather harness as the riders shifted in their saddles.

Jock waited silently, right hand resting easily on the basket hilt of his broadsword.

One of the riders raised his hand in greeting and said in a high-pitched voice, "I am Subaltern Reginald Briggs, of the staff of General Sir John Cope." He did not introduce his companions. "Who are you, and what is this place?"

Jock waited a moment and then replied in a deep voice, "My name is John McRae, master at arms tae Lord William Drummond, Viscount o' Strathallan, a loyal subject of his majesty. Ye are standing at the entrance tae Strathallan Castle, ancestral seat o' the Drummond family o' Strathallan."

The young officer responded, "The general is taking this army north to seek out and destroy a military force that recently infiltrated His Majesty's dominions. Have you heard any news of such a force hereabouts?"

Jock took his hand from the hilt of his sword and waved it in a northward direction. "We have heard nae mair than a rumor that such a force landed in Lochaber some days past, but we canna confirm the news. Nae one hae come o'er the mountains tae inform us. I suggest that ye seek fer information in Crieff. It is less than an hour's march northward."

"I dare say," murmured the young officer, who spoke with a strong Midlands English accent. He gestured to the overturned hay wagons and interlaced barrels surrounding the castle. He leaned forward and asked, "And what, Master at Arms, is the meaning of these…fortifications? Do you expect trouble?"

Jock responded, "Aye. The Viscount Strathallan ordered these fortifications erected because of the risk frae brigands and thieves raiding hereabouts. If the general's army will bivouac in or near Crieff, we are relieved and can dismantle them, assured o' the safety of the Viscount's family and estates."

The subaltern shook his head. "Nay, there is no possibility of that, although the army will be resting for a day or possibly two in Crieff before moving north. I suggest that you keep the barricades and sentries because affairs will undoubtedly be unsettled for some time to come. Good day."

"Guid day tae ye, sir," responded Jock.

The officer raised his hand in a turning motion and pulled his horse's reins sharply to the right while gigging the horse with his boot. His companions followed as he completed the turn. All three kicked up dust from the dry roadbed as they urged their horses into a canter on their return to the main military road.

Jock let out his breath in a gusty sigh. "Aye, guid day tae ye, Sassanach, ye great pox on the arse o' humanity," he growled. Over his shoulder, he called, "Stand easy, lads, but stand alert."

As he walked around the side of the castle, Emilia rose from her position under the rowan tree and called, "Master McRae! What meant ye by saying that my father is a loyal subject of His Majesty?"

Jock McRae stopped and grinned broadly. "I spake nae lie, lass. Yer father is a loyal subject of His Majesty o'er the water. Our Sassanach visitor didna ask the question properly." He drew his broadsword and saluted Emilia, who curtsied with a wide smile.

As the day drew toward evening, an exhausted horse and rider appeared, riding low in the saddle across the meadow east of the castle and leading another horse. This was a most unusual path for a visitor to take, so the sentries immediately hailed him as he drew near. He straightened in the saddle and took off his hat. It was Alexander MacKenzie, spattered with mud and at the end of his strength. He staggered as he dismounted and a groom rushed to help him. He gasped for breath as he leaned on the young groom.

"Cope's army is at Crieff. He hae dispatched patrols on the roads in all directions. I hae tae ride overland south tae Machany Water but encountered a patrol outside o' Muthill. I finally crossed the road near Tullibardine. I rode o'er the Murray lands until I reached Kinkell Bridge and then turned back sou'west across the North Mains, forded Machany Water again, and then turned fer hame. I am done in."

Jock McRae accompanied MacKenzie to the garden, where Jamie was sitting with Emilia. The door to the solar opened, and William Drummond beckoned the men inside. Jamie and Emilia could easily hear their conversation through the thin wall of the solar.

Jock McRae spoke first, his rough voice carrying well. "Sit ye doon here, Alex. Take a draught o' Bordeaux. 'Twill revive ye."

There was silence for a space.

Alex MacKenzie spoke. "Thank ye, Jock. My Lord, the prince is on the move and hae an army."

William Drummond exclaimed exultantly, "Praise God! I was beginning tae think that this adventure would end like all the rest, in crushed hopes and dreams."

Alex MacKenzie's voice was hoarse from his arduous journey but could easily be heard. "The prince raised the rebel standard at Glenfinnan twa days ago on the nineteenth. He hae brought aboot twa hundred o' Clan Ranald's men. Lochiel arrived wi' seven hundred guid men, but ill-armed. Keppoch arrived that day wi' aboot three hundred and fifty men decently armed. That gave him a force o' nearly thirteen hundred men, with more arriving in small groups throughout the day and evening. By the time I left late the next morning, young Glengarry and his MacDonnells hae come in, raising the entire force tae nearly twa thousand. I fear me, however, that they are mair strong arms than swords, pikes, and muskets. I saw that they did hae swivel guns, though naething that ye might call by the noble name o' artillery."

He stopped, and William Drummond mused. "It is amazing. They now outnumber General Cope's force. I saw by means o' a very fine telescope mounted on the roof that Cope's force numbers aboot seventeen companies o' foot and some cavalry. Cope has nae artillery train tae speak aboot. I saw a few guns that might be anywhere frae twa tae three pounders and four mortars, accompanied by suspiciously few caissons o' powder and ball. The foot companies looked only partially equipped with arms, and the supply train was also short. I suspect that tomorrow or the next day might see reinforcements, but Cope has a pressing problem in that he must secure his line o' supply, Stirling, and Edinburgh against the possibility o' a rising in the Lowlands or French troops landing in his rear. He is in a very unenviable position."

Jock's voice cut in. "Alex, do ye hae any intelligence on the prince's route o' march? How will those who wish tae join him find him?"

Alex sighed. "I think that events hae galloped beyond his ability tae foresee. I dinna sense that he hae thought that far ahead. He needs leaders to direct the forces flocking in tae support him and mold them tae become fighting forces. Ach! Right now, except fer clan chiefs, there is nae military organization. He will hae tae counter Cope's movement in the Highlands and prevent him joining wi' the garrisons o' the northern forts. If he evades Cope, I believe that he desires tae proceed eastward toward Aberdeen or Perth."

The conversation stopped since dishes began clattering.

"Ah, food!" exclaimed Jock. "Ye look famished enough tae tear inta a horse, Alex. Fill yer stomach, and we will converse wi'oot ye fer a while. As far as we are concerned, everything seems tae turn on what General Sir John Cope chooses tae do."

William Drummond demurred. "I dinna agree, Jock. Cope is nae his own man. He is a neat and fussy staff officer. Unfortunately fer his government and fortunately fer us, he is an uninspiring leader. Risk-taking is nae in his nature. I expect that he will collect his forces, arms, and supplies fer a few days and wait fer higher authority tae push him tae take action. As long as he stays at Crieff, we canna move frae here. I am nervous about how tae explain a muster o' three hundred armed men at this location. We might hae tae disperse them again if Cope dinna leave Crieff soon. We can ill afford some snooping officer mair intelligent than the young pup wha came here this afternoon. I will also send a courier tae intercept James and instruct him tae refrain frae bringing any troops here until Cope leaves."

Mister Dobie interrupted their conversation to bring word that John Drummond had already come in, also having to evade the army camped around Crieff. In a few minutes, John's voice carried through the solar wall, raised in anger by what he had to report.

"Father, I will nae speak the profane comments I was going tae utter aboot Lord Lovat. However, let me say that he dithers worse than an auld lady. He canna decide whether tae support the prince or nae, although he is now on Scottish soil. He has done naething, naething tae urge the northern clans tae support the rising. Until the prince himself confronts Simon Fraser, I doubt me that the gout-infested slug will take a stand ain way or the other. I met with the Gordons o' Huntley and several other leaders wha are waiting tae see if the prince shows up with a substantial and weel-equipped army."

William Drummond spoke up. "That is, indeed, bad news. They are like men wha wish tae bet and win on a horse race, but only after the horses are nearly at the finish line." He sighed audibly. "I think it essential that we leave soon and move north and east tae bring some leadership that the prince will badly need. I am ready as soon as Cope moves oot o' our way. However, I need tae speak with George Murray this nicht or tomorrow at the latest.

He met with John Cope this afternoon, as the army marched past Tullibardine, tae offer his services tae the government."

There was a sound of a dish crashing to the floor and a loud clamor as the other men in the solar all shouted at once. William Drummond raised his voice, most unusual for the affable Viscount.

"Sit doon, gentlemen! I beg ye tae listen! He was there merely tae assess Cope's plans and scope o' authority. He hae none. Cope dinna gae outside tae take a piss wi'out permission frae the secretary o' state fer Scotland, the Marquis o' Tweeddale. That worthy is far awa' in London, and his instructions are hopelessly outdated since it takes days fer a courier tae reach Cope. Tweeddale is an incurable optimist and will undoubtedly push Cope tae some rash act. George and I agree on that." He pounded his fist on the table. "And hae nae fear. Lord George Murray is the prince's man and the best tactical leader that Scotland hae tae offer."

At that point, a sentry entered the garden, headed in their direction. While the sentry could not see them in the gathering gloom, Emilia decided that it was still a good time to retreat from eavesdropping. She tapped Jamie on the shoulder, and they stepped noiselessly away to evade detection.

Two days later, in the evening after dinner, Jamie stood outside his parent's rooms, stricken with emotion. Through the closed doors, he could hear his mother's tearful pleas.

"Please. Please dinna leave, James. It is far tae soon tae make such a commitment. What if it all falls apart and the prince flees? What will ye do? The authorities in London will declare ye a traitor and banish ye, or worse."

His father's calm voice responded, "We hae discussed this many times, Euphemia. This is a commitment that I must make, fer honor's sake. I am my father's heir. God help me, I believe in this cause. If affairs proceed badly, I advise ye tae flee tae yer brother Charles at Aberfeldie. He will shelter ye and the boy until I can come fer ye. But affairs will nae gae badly. The prince is gathering his loyal men by the hundreds and soon by the thousands. Supporting this cause is the right course fer me; my father; and my brother, John. Every bone in my body feels that it is the proper thing tae do."

Euphemia Drummond's voice trembled as she asked, "And when must ye leave?"

James answered, "At dawn. Cope's army is now moving into the mountains northwestward. We will travel eastward tae Blair. We hae heard that the Prince hopes tae recruit the Atholl men thereabouts. Lord George Murray is coming with us and will bring his men. Cope is a fool and will nae be able tae trap the prince's growing army. We will take the Drummond muster but leave enough men to safeguard Strathallan frae all but a military attack in force. Ye will be safe frae marauders and bandits. Father is leaving Jock McRae behind tae command the guard. The auld veteran is furious, being a double-dyed Jacobite, but he realizes how much he is needed here. Perhaps later, he can join us. Now come and sit wi' me, dear wife. We hae sae little time left together."

Jamie's throat constricted, but tears would not come. He heard his mother wail and, turning, fled up the corridor to his room.

Much later, Jamie heard a knock on his bedroom door. He shut the unread book on his lap and opened the door to see his father and mother standing outside. They entered and sat on either side of his bed. Jamie noticed that his mother appeared composed, though her eyes were puffy and red. His father broke the silence.

"Weel, Jamie, lad, I hae sworn an oath of allegiance to King James the Third, which means that I must leave tae help his son, Prince Charles Edward, regain the throne fer his father."

Jamie stared into his father's eyes and nodded slowly. His mother reached to grip her son's hand.

"I leave at dawn in company with yer grandpa, Uncle John, Lord George Murray, Alex MacKenzie, and others. Yer Uncle William is loyal tae the Hanoverians and will continue serving in the military but safely distant, in Ireland. Yer Uncle Andrew arrived this evening. He took leave frae his studies at the university tae lead family affairs here. Jock McRae, Mister Dobie, and servants beyond military age will stay." James leaned forward. "Jamie," he said in a soft voice, "I would stay if I could, but a man o' honor must keep faith with his allegiance. That is mair important than comfort, safety, money, or even life itself. I will return as often as I can, but I canna say when that will be. Obey yer mama in all things, and be diligent in yer studies when Doctor Thompson returns in October. Master McRae will be busy safeguarding Strathallan and maintaining communications wi' us as we travel. He will hae little time fer riding and other lessons." He smiled. "But I hae a worthy volunteer. Yer Aunt Emilia is here and will tae ye in hand. She is a difficult taskmaster. When she has finished with ye, ye will ride like an Arab."

Jamie brightened.

"I will miss ye, Papa, but I understand. Ye must do what honor requires."

James leaned forward to enfold his son in his arms for a long moment. Tears brimmed in Euphemia's eyes and trickled down her cheeks.

Jamie whispered, "Ye canna take me wi' ye, Papa? I do nae eat much or take up much space."

James held him at arm's length and smiled but shook his head slowly.

"There is a risk o' fechting, and I canna be distracted in order tae protect ye. While ye are here in our hame, ye weel be safe. Now, it is far past time fer ye tae be sleeping. We hae mair preparations before we depart."

His parents rose and moved to the door. Euphemia blew out the candle in the sconce by the bedside. In the suddenly darkened room, Jamie saw them link hands as they left, shutting the door behind them. That simple act of parental love reassured his troubled mind. He fluffed up his goose-down pillow and lay back.

Jamie opened his eyes to a rose-streaked sky. He padded to the window and pulled it open to let in the gentle westerly breeze.

He knew that his father and the others had left since he had been awakened momentarily by their voices and the nickering of horses as they departed before dawn. He opened his door and walked down the corridor to his parent's suite. The door was open, and his mother stood in her nightdress, looking down at the path leading westward through the avenue of tall pines.

"They are gone," Jamie said matter-of-factly.

His mother smiled, though her puffy eyes showed that she has spent a sleepless night.

"Aye, they are gone, riding off tae meet the prince. Pray God that our prayers keep them safe and assure their early return. How aboot breakfast? Would ye enjoy bacon, shirred eggs, toast, and porridge with fresh cream and strawberries served in the garden?"

Jamie clapped his hands, eyes shining. "Aye, Mama. It all sounds wonderful!"

Euphemia pulled on his ear and said, "My guid lad. There is nae benefit tae body or soul in pining. What is done is done. We must fulfill our duties and live life as best we can while we wait."

Between Emilia and his mother keeping him constantly busy, the days of late August slipped into early September. Couriers brought letters first from Blair and then Perth. His mother read him portions. It seemed that the prince's small but growing army had outmaneuvered General Cope and forced him north to Inverness while they occupied Perth. Lochiel's brother, Archie Cameron, had conducted a surprise attack on the barracks at Ruthven that convinced Cope to seek refuge in the north, although the attack in force failed to dislodge the sixteen stout defenders. Cope's move north permitted the prince's army to move eastward to Blair Atholl. It entered Perth two days later to no resistance.

At a council of war in that town, the prince appointed three lieutenant generals: the Duke of Atholl, William Drummond, and George Murray. James Drummond was appointed a colonel in command of a battalion within his father's regiment. John

Drummond sailed surreptitiously to seek French aid, to include Scottish troops serving the French crown, the Royal Eccossais, and a commission for a French regiment, artillery, and money to recruit additional troops to be sent to Scotland before the end of the year. On the eleventh of September, the growing rebel army moved out of Perth and crossed the Forth at the Fords of Frew, well south of Strathallan. The government forces fell back on Edinburgh, so the prince's army followed them.

By late September, the first frost came to Strathallan. News arrived that the rebels had taken position outside Edinburgh. The outmaneuvered General Sir John Cope had marched south from Inverness to Aberdeen and taken ship southward to Dunbar. Another letter proudly told the story of how the rebels had surprised the guards at the gates early in the morning and had taken the city of Edinburgh without a fight.

A third letter related how the rebels won a great victory over the forces of John Cope at Prestonpans, a few miles outside Edinburgh. While the opposing armies maneuvered for hours in the fields bordering the Firth of Forth, the actual combat at Prestonpans lasted perhaps eight minutes.

Euphemia read with relish, "While we were inexperienced in positioning and employing our forces – mostly consisting o' undisciplined clansmen, our losses were few, and the government forces were beaten handily wi' great loss o' men, arms, and provisions. Cope fled the field, and his army is destroyed. Huzzah fer our brave lads!"

The first of October was the date originally agreed for the return of Doctor Archibald Thomson from Geneva to resume teaching at Strathallan. He did not arrive on that date or during the succeeding week. A letter finally came posted from Amsterdam that Dutch authorities were not allowing ships to sail to Scottish ports. Archibald Thomson wrote that he could think of no solution to the dilemma. He could sail to an English port, but that would necessitate him somehow making his way across the border or traveling by way of Ireland and, thence, across the Irish Sea, which he considered hazardous. The letter ended with his regrets and his decision to return to Geneva to await safer conditions.

Euphemia and Emilia Drummond resolved to teach the children themselves. They set up the classroom and contacted parents on surrounding estates about their plans. School began on the succeeding Monday morning. At first, the children assumed that the women would be gentler in discipline than Doctor Thomson. They were mistaken.

On Wednesday of the second week of October, Emilia was teaching French grammar when the door burst open to reveal James Drummond and Alex MacKenzie in military uniforms, grinning broadly. Euphemia leaped to her feet with a shriek of joy. She rushed around two rows of tables to embrace her husband.

"Papa!" shouted Jamie, upsetting his chair in his haste to reach his father.

After disengaging himself from his wife, James Drummond shouted, "I bring the most excellent news! Father hae been assigned tae command at Perth, but before he takes up that post, he is coming back tae Strathallan, bringing the Bonnie Prince fer a gala ball on Saturday. We hae less than three days tae prepare fer the royal visit!"

The children screamed in excitement. All order was lost, as distracted children danced around the room. Euphemia breathlessly dismissed classes until the following Monday. Preparations were rushed as servants cleaned, rearranged, and decorated castle and grounds. After dinner on Thursday, Jamie sat reading in a corner of the dining room while his parents talked with Alex MacKenzie and Jock McRae. Little meaningful was said until Euphemia rose to excuse herself. Inexplicably, she had forgotten about Jamie curled up in a corner. Jamie kept his nose in his book, and everyone ignored his presence.

In a low voice, James leaned over the table and said to the others, "I am very concerned about the state of military affairs. While we hae succeeded far beyond our hopes, our leadership is divided and weak. Father is indecisive and a bad judge of battlefields. He made several mistakes at Prestonpans that could hae been disastrous. Oliphant of Gask, his second in command, is nae a credible leader as weel. That is why they are being sent tae Perth while the remainder o' the army prepares tae move south. It might actually be a blessing and keep the auld men safe. Aberdeenshire and Banff are in the guid hands o' Lord Lewis Gordon. Simon Fraser hae finally come around tae the patriot cause and has rallied Inverness and the far north. The rest o' the Highlands rule themselves, in accordance with ancient clan loyalties. God can only know what will happen there, with the forts still in government hands. We canna hold Edinburgh and wait for the French. We did receive some arms and gold, but nae enough. Only three ships got through, and there are now government warships in the Forth to blockade it. Our cavalry is scarcely five hundred horse. We did receive some experienced French military advisors and gunners. But we need artillery and hae little."

Alex MacKenzie interrupted, holding up thumb and forefinger. "A canny artillery commander, Colonel James Grant, wi' experience in France, but only thirteen field pieces, all wee guns. We hae six ain and a half pounders captured at Prestonpans, four brass four pounders, and ain brass carriage-mounted cannon o' uncertain size. We also hae six unreliable mortars fer dropping hot shot on the heads o' the enemy. We will certainly face far stronger artillery frae Southron forces. We canna hope tae neutralize their much heavier artillery. Our only hope is tae outmaneuver or surprise them while they are nae properly positioned. It is a pitifully small army with which tae launch an invasion, but the Hanoverians are in three separate forces scattered around the country. They will employ some Dutch, German, and Swiss troops wha are very professional but hard tae command. The prince's advisors believe that many government forces, under threat o' invasion, will defect tae our side and that the mostly Catholic north will rise and join us. It is a wonderful thought, but wha can ken what they will actually do?"

As the master of horse fell silent, James spoke. "Tae outmaneuver the divided Hanoverian forces, we must exploit those divisions wi' decisive leadership. We hae Lord George Murray, but some o' the prince's advisors dinna agree wi' him and waste much time squabbling. Murray knows the terrain o' northern England. The mountains o' the west country favor Highland tactics. I expect that Murray will argue fer a movement south by way o' Carlisle. Winter weather is coming on and the Hanoverians might quickly lose their will tae fecht in uncomfortable conditions."

Everyone chuckled, knowing how English armies preferred the comfort of remaining in garrison during winter.

"But I am very concerned about our Bonnie Prince. He must discipline his advisors, stop the bickering among his commanders, and learn tae trust the judgment o' George Murray, else…" His voice trailed off. He stared at the others, who shook their heads grimly.

James rose. "Weel, gentlemen, we hae thrashed and thrashed, but it appears that our course is set, fer better or worse. We must do all we can tae advance our cause. I believe that my cause is now a just rest, and I am leaving tae seek it."

The others rose.

James, turning toward the door, glanced back to see his son still huddled at the far end of the table with his nose in his book.

"Jamie, lad!"

Jamie pretended to be startled and leaped to his feet. "Ach. I am sorry, Father. I was sae preoccupied with my study o' this book, that I forgot tae gae tae bed."

James reached his side and affectionately ruffled his hair. "Then tae bed wi' ye, lad. Since Mama is yer schoolmaster, it is best that ye get plenty o' rest. Otherwise, she will ensure that ye hae a hellish experience when ye fall asleep in class."

Jamie tucked his book under his arm, bade everyone a good night, and scampered from the room.

Jock stood looking after him and rumbled, "He is a very attentive lad, my Lord James, and an exceptional actor. He sat and listened tae every word said here." He held up his hand. "Nay, I am nae concerned aboot whether he talks tae others, fer he keeps a tight counsel on his tongue. But I wonder how much he understands."

James shook his head admiringly. "How much, indeed? But next time, we check every chair and under the tables fer him and post a trusted servant at the door."

Jock barked a laugh. "Better check the windows, as weel, my lord."

※

There was great excitement at Strathallan as everyone awaited the arrival of Prince Charles Edward Stewart and Viscount William Drummond, traveling together in an ornate state coach from Edinburgh. The weather was frosty, with a strong wind whipping dead leaves from trees and a low cloud layer scudding across a sky that promised freezing rain or sleet. Guests arrived early and rapidly filled the ballroom, where servants finished lighting the glittering chandeliers.

Jamie sat stiffly waiting in a nearby room with Emilia, Andrew, and Henry, freshly arrived from university studies in Aberdeen. Emilia, dressed in the height of fashion recently imported from the French court, wore a sleeveless, low-necked burgundy brocade gown over a smock with puffy, frilled white sleeves and petticoat with a very wide pannier. Her long, blonde hair was piled under a white wig. She wore a simple locket on a gold chain. Her shoes, peeking from under the edge of her long gown, were of silver-and-blue brocade with low heels.

Andrew and Henry wore fashionable white wigs with tight curls, but Jamie was bareheaded, in keeping with court fashion for children, with his hair brushed back and clubbed at the nape of his neck with black ribbon. Jamie kept inserting a finger between his high collar and neck until Emilia leaned close to flick a jeweled finger at his hand.

"Stop it, Jamie!" she said reprovingly. "Ye will stretch the fabric so that it will look like a piece o' bacon wrapped around yer neck!"

Everyone chuckled, but Jamie, stung, dropped his hand.

They could hear soft music start up from the orchestra brought from Stirling, over the rising murmur of the crowd gathering in the ballroom. Suddenly, a servant opened the doors to the room and Euphemia Drummond entered. She wore a gown similar to Emilia's but of a startlingly bright blue silk with a gold embroidery stomacher in front and trumpet-shaped three-quarter-length sleeves with red ribbons. Multiple coils of white pearls adorned her long neck. She wore her dark hair piled high, with jewels pinned around an eagle's feather. Diamonds glinted in bracelets on her wrists. Jamie gasped. He had never seen his mother look so lovely or so decorated.

"Mama, what is wrong wi' yer face?"

"Why, naething is wrong, Jamie," she replied.

"It's all white and red!" he responded.

Euphemia opened her mouth to speak, but Emilia cut in.

"That is makeup, Jamie. It's a white cream covered with rice powder, and that is red rouge on her cheeks. 'Tis tae make her mair beautiful."

"Aye," he breathed. "And it does!"

Euphemia dimpled with pleasure and curtsied. "Why, thank ye, James William Drummond. Ye are a verra sweet lad, and ye hae a special way wi' the ladies." She turned to face the others. "The Prince is due tae arrive soon. I suggest that ye take the time tae practice yer introductions wi' Mister Dobie since he will be announcing the guests. I will send him in momentarily."

She turned and swept out of the room, leaving behind a scent of powder and cologne water.

Mister Dobie was soon satisfied, after correcting the bows and turns of the young men several times. Emilia and Clementine had no difficulty with their curtseys. Just as they were finishing, they heard an increased level of noise from the ballroom, followed by silence. It was clear that the Prince and Viscount had arrived. The orchestra shifted to martial music to announce their arrival.

Mister Dobie left abruptly to reassume his duties as chamberlain. A few minutes later, Mrs. MacRobie opened the doors and beckoned them forward. When Jamie stood before her, she sighed and shook her head. She reached down to undo and rebutton his waistcoat. Then she took him by the shoulders and spun him around. She tugged at the shoulders of his coat to straighten it and then spun him back and pronounced him ready for presentation.

The ballroom blazed with light. Jamie took several deep gulps of air to quell his rising nervousness as he surveyed the scene before stepping down to the marble floor. Mrs. MacRobie motioned them to one side, where they joined the other Strathallan Drummond family members. Jamie was transfixed by the panoply of colors. The women wore long gowns of every color of the rainbow. Most wore the newly fashionable gowns with smocks and petticoats, but some women wore old-fashioned hoop skirts. Most men wore long coats in somber colors, but there were many in military uniforms of red, blue, white, or black with ceremonial swords.

In a clear strong voice, Mister Dobie announced the presence of Prince Charles Edward Stewart, as well as other dignitaries. The ballroom erupted in thunderous applause that lasted for several minutes. When it subsided, the smiling prince moved forward and held out his hands, palms down. The room hushed instantly.

Jamie stared at the resplendent figure of the Bonnie Prince. He thought that he had never seen so handsome a man. He wore a white wig, and his face was pale with makeup, but his eyes were clear and his features smooth, as lovely, he thought, as those of a beautiful woman. No wonder people were attracted to this handsome young man. He exuded confidence as he addressed the crowd.

"My friends, we wish to begin by thanking you for coming in such inclement weather. We wish to especially thank our good friend and most loyal supporter, William Drummond, Viscount Strathallan, and his noble wife, Margaret, and their family for their faith in supporting our glorious cause for so many years."

The audience erupted in applause once again. When they subsided, he held out his hands for quiet.

"Without their unflinching loyalty and the support of so many others, we would not hae come this far. Our armies have grown daily, and we have gained great victories over forces sent to oppose us. We have laid the necessary groundwork for our allies in France and England to join us. We will now go south to claim victory and the crown in London!"

Wild cheers resounded in the ballroom.

"Viscount Strathallan will command our forces, which will remain behind to defend our homeland. We pray to God Almighty that he will continue to bless our armies with victory so that we will soon be able to lay down our arms to enjoy the peace that we so richly deserve in a land free of Hanoverian tyranny!" The prince stepped back.

The clamor in the ballroom was so intense that Jamie had to hold his hands over his ears.

After the applause died down, the Viscount stepped forward to announce that the Prince would receive as many as chose to come forward, with the Drummond family at the head of the receiving line. Dutifully, Jamie held his mother's gloved hand, which she stretched out over the voluminous folds of her silken gown. It was all he could do to move forward and avoid stepping on the gown. After his grandfather and grandmother bowed and curtsied before the Prince, it was the turn of James Drummond's little family. The Prince shook hands gravely with James.

"My good companion and Colonel, are ye ready to accompany us to Newcastle or Carlisle town?"

"Tae London, yer grace. Walking all the way, if necessary."

The Prince smiled winningly at Euphemia, who swept her gown into a curtsey, murmuring, "My Prince, this is a very special day indeed fer me and my family."

The prince nodded. "Our thanks for your gracious gift."

Euphemia straightened and looked puzzled.

"My gift, yer grace?"

"Aye. Your gift of your husband. He is one of our most trusted and talented leaders. We regret taking him away once again. We will return him to you as quickly as possible."

"Ach," she gushed. "I understand. He is yers to command, My Prince."

Again, the Prince smiled his dazzling smile. "And this handsome lad?"

James intoned, "May I present my son, James William Drummond o' Strathallan, Yer Grace."

Jamie took a step forward and bowed stiffly.

The prince extended his hand to take Jamie's, who felt the strong, cool fingers envelop his.

"What a pretty fellow!" exclaimed the Prince. "We warrant that as your firstborn son, he is also intelligent and uncommonly brave."

"Aye," James responded with a little laugh. "He sometimes gives his tutors fits, but he is very quick in mathematics, languages, and horsemanship."

"Languages?" inquired the prince. He looked at Jamie and said, "*Ainsi vous êtes habile avec des langues. Avez-vous jamais été en France?*"

Jamie quickly replied, "*Pas, mon prince aimable, mais un jour moi espèrent faire ainsi. Je comprends que c'est une belle terre.*"

The Prince smiled broadly once again and said, "Aye, France is indeed a lovely land for the most part, and we do hope that you get an opportunity someday to visit. It was our home for a very long time, but now we are in Scotland, our true home and by far the loveliest land on earth. We pray that we will all be able to enjoy it in peace and freedom."

Their meeting was at an end, and Euphemia took Jamie's hand to lead him away. The Prince was already greeting others. When they reached the edge of the ballroom, James pumped his son's hand enthusiastically while his mother's hug almost drowned him in billows of blue silk.

"Ye were magnificent, my son!" she gurgled happily. "I could almost weep fer joy. How could ye answer him sae quickly?" Without waiting for a response, she turned on her husband. "For shame, James, tae run the risk o' embarrassing the lad in that way."

"I hae nae fear o' that, wife. The lad is almost uncannily brilliant. I heard him conversing with Emilia in French yesterday. He has a natural knack wi' languages." He tugged at his upper lip and mused, "I wonder how he would hae handled a question in Latin?"

Jamie responded, "Nae as weel in Latin, Papa. I am glad that the Prince asked in French. Can I gae upstairs tae change? I dinna like this suit."

"Soon," murmured his mother. "Ye must endure the praise o' at least a hundred people wha were knocked off their pins by yer conversation wi' the Bonnie Prince."

Jamie suffered through numerous handshakes and hugs from dowagers and young ladies before finally escaping to a corner. He had hoped to sit with Emilia, but that young woman was continuously being asked to dance by the officers and gentlemen who hovered around her. Finally, Jamie had had enough and wandered to the staircase. When he saw that no one was looking, he raced upstairs.

Chapter Six

Two days later, the tranquility and order of the castle were restored. The prince's party and other guests had already departed. In a drizzling cold rain, the viscount and a small party of officers left early in the morning to ride to Perth, where William Drummond took command of the forces left behind in Scotland while the bulk of the army moved south toward the border and England.

Andrew and Henry returned to Aberdeen to resume their studies. With all Drummond men gone, Lady Margaret declared that she felt perfectly adequate to administer the affairs of Strathallan. She had run the household since her marriage to William Drummond over thirty years before. James and John Drummond, accompanied by Lord George Murray, Lord Atholl, and at least a dozen other officers, traveled eastward to Dalkeith, where the army mustered for the move south scheduled for the first of November. James took command of the forces previously led by his father.

A week later, Euphemia called in Jamie to read him portions of a letter.

"'We left Edinburgh on the thirty-first o' October. The first division o' troops encumbered by our small artillery and baggage trains left Dalkeith in clear but cold weather over muddy roads the next day. They are headed southward through Peebles and Moffat. Our division, mair lightly equipped and encumbered, left Dalkeith twa days later by way o' Lauder and Kelso. We stopped fer a day tae adjust the order o' march and await some provisions, and then headed westward through Jedburgh and Liddesdale to rejoin the other division, north o' Carlisle. The Prince hae taken the advice o' George Murray tae follow the westward route tae England, which enables us tae avoid General Wade, wha expected us tae gae south toward Berwick and Newcastle. General Wade, leading the Hanoverians, must be terribly confused because our reconnaissance patrols report that he is still encamped around Newcastle. Our plan is tae besiege Carlisle, sae that it nae be a thorn in our side as we move southward. While the wet weather is what we typically expect in November, it makes the roads sloppy and difficult tae traverse fer foot, cavalry, and wagons.'"

Jamie lived for the letters from his father. The weather was terrible, curtailing most outdoor activities. His days and evenings were taken up by schoolwork. The only times he saw Emilia were in the classroom, when she was teaching or admonishing him for not finishing assignments, which was often, for he was so distracted that he had trouble completing them.

Jock McRae was frequently gone, shuttling between Strathallan and Perth on duties for the viscount. The family still found time on Sunday for the weekly trip to the church at Muthill, where Jamie sat dozing through services, followed by the interminable sermon. The parishioners at the church either did not know or did not care to comment on the invasion of England by Bonnie Prince Charlie's forces. It was as if they lived in a different world than that which Jamie inhabited, in which his nights were filled with dreams of battle and anxious loneliness.

On the twenty-second, another letter arrived from his father. Euphemia invited Jamie into her suite, where she settled him before the fireplace, where crackling blue flames played and pine knots snapped and spat sparks before settling into glowing orange coals that gave off a steady and comforting heat. His mother took some time to shuffle the pages before she began to read.

"'Our information about the enemy's composition and intentions is wildly contradictory. What I would nae gie fer a decent intelligence service. It would be worth several men's lives tae know the truth. The prince assigned me tae command the siege o' the town o' Carlisle. We established a battery o' artillery about three hundred yards frae the East Curtain, a straight section o' the town wall between the Scotch and English Gates, so named because their orientations are toward Scotland and England, north and south. Colonel Grant, in charge o' the artillery, after observing the first shots causing little damage, remarked that the four-pounders are incapable of knocking down a barn door and he regrets forcing the horses to tow them frae Edinburgh. Neither townspeople nor garrison hae stomach enough to make a fecht of it. General Murray is becoming somewhat of a nuisance. In spite o' my receiving the order tae conduct the siege, he is proposing a new plan o' attack, without presenting it tae me beforehand. His behavior strains our friendship, fer he is behaving as I would expect a rival and nae a friend. The council o' war rejected his proposal. Until his troops spend time in the trenches relieving the Perth men, he has nae cause or knowledge tae propose another solution. By five o' the evening yesterday, nae strategy was necessary, fer the town garrison hung a white flag offering tae surrender. I refused tae accept it, unless they also surrendered the castle, fer investing the town while the fortifications o' the castle are still occupied would be foolhardy. Before their commander, if indeed they had ain at the time, could reply to my proposal, troops in the castle mutinied. Some went o'er the wall. Others forced their way through the gates and ran awa'. By dawn, the commanding colonel and some invalids who lacked the mobility tae flee were all that were left tae defend the castle. We sent word that unless they surrendered, we would fire the town. Upon hearing this threat, the commander capitulated. This morning, I required the remaining garrison tae lay down their arms and hand o'er arms, ammunition, and horses. I required that the aldermen and mayor o' the town greet the prince at the town gate, offer him the keys, and proclaim King James the Third at the Mercat Cross. They looked ready tae explode at this humiliation heaped on their surrender, but they had nae choice but comply.'"

Euphemia and Jamie beamed at each other at this report of James's success in commanding the siege of Carlisle. She continued reading.

"'My joy at this triumph o' our arms was spoiled by an act of silly pique on the part o' Lord George Murray. He was sae angered by the council o' war's rejection o' his proposals that he resigned his commission in a letter tae the prince, offering tae serve in the trenches wi' the common soldiers. The prince was equally angry and accepted his resignation. However, Atholl and the other colonels, including myself, interceded tae urge the prince to reinstate him because we need his abilities and fortitude in command. He hae done that. I see somewhat of a lack o' confidence in my own abilities by the council, and in the interest o' our cause, I am ready tae step aside fer a man of ability whom I still consider a friend. I am deeply concerned by the friction between His Highness and Lord Murray. The best course fer the cause would be fer the prince tae listen mair favorably tae Murray's proposals. His Highness is wildly optimistic in spite o' lack o' evidence tae support his position. Murray is extravagantly pessimistic, exhibiting negativism in spite o' encouraging evidence. My hope is that the council o' war will mediate a middle path between their extremes.'"

Euphemia laid the pages of the letter on the table next to the lamp. She stared into the flames for a long time. A log crumbled with a thump in the fireplace, sending up a shower of sparks.

"Oh, Jamie, this winter is truly a trying time fer yer father. He is entirely devoted tae the cause o' the House of Stewart. I pray that this misadventure—aye, I am convinced that it is that—will end soon and in such a way that Scotland can gae her own way, wi'out England, which we can ne'er conquer. If only the French were tae send true help in the form o' stout men and artillery, and nae only promises. They always promise, promise, promise but ne'er come in adequate strength."

Jamie moved to her side. She reached to embrace him.

❦

On the second day of December, another letter arrived from James Drummond. Euphemia waited until after the evening meal to summon Jamie to read the letter together. She broke the seal on the envelope and spread the pages. After a brief perusal, she blushed, turned over the first two pages, and began to read from the third.

"'We held a council o' war on the eighteenth. Once again, we rehearsed the courses o' action open tae us, whether tae return tae Scotland, stay at Carlisle waiting fer the enemy tae make a move or obtain reinforcements, or press on. The prince is all fer pressing on tae London. He is utterly convinced that the English Jacobites are numerous and ready tae rise; that we will receive a growing number o' defections frae demoralized government forces; and the French will finally land troops on the southern coast o' England tae draw away defenders wha would otherwise reinforce General Wade, wha is moving south slowly frae Newcastle, sae our spies and scouts tell us. We hae a heavy and cumbersome baggage train that slows progress tae scarcely a crawl. Since we hae a garrison in Carlisle, the council proposed tae leave a considerable portion o' the baggage there, along wi' much ammunition, and camp followers. This is certainly a relief tae me, fer we can move much faster. I now report tae General Murray, sae we marched on the twentieth, followed a day later by the prince's division. We got tae Kendall on the twenty-second, but when we reached Penrith, we sent mair ammunition back tae Carlisle since our pack animals are exhausted and the roads in such puir condition. Being thus lightened, we were able tae make better time and reached the city o' Manchester on the twenty-ninth. We were prepared tae invest the city but discovered tae our amazement that an element o' the vanguard, consisting o' an intrepid sergeant o' my regiment, John Dickson by name, his doxie, and a drummer took action. These three took the surrender o' the garrison wi'out any other help! We also received some volunteers sufficient tae form a regiment under the command o' Francis Townley, a Lancashire gentleman wi' experience in the French army. This regiment is a regiment in name only, fer it consists o' twa hundred men, less than the garrison we left in Carlisle. If the remainder o' the English are as demoralized as the men wha surrendered in Manchester, perhaps the prince is correct and London will fall tae our tiny force.'"

When she finished, Euphemia folded the letter, creased it with her thumbnail, and sat thoughtfully tapping it against her teeth. She started when she realized that Jamie was still sitting opposite her.

"Schoolwork, Jamie."

Jamie looked up. "Aye, Mama. I was just waiting tae see if there was any mair news."

She shook her head reluctantly. "We'll just hae tae wait."

Nearly a month passed, and there was no more news from the south. Jock McRae was concerned enough to saddle his horse and ride to Perth, although the weather was dirty, with sleet coating the road with ice. He rode from the castle at dawn and did not return for four days. In his absence, a heavy snowfall covered the roads with more than a foot, followed by freezing rain and more sleet. Shortly before dark on the fourth day, grooms saw a horse plowing through crusted drifts to its withers. Jock rode with a plaid wrapped around his head so that only his eyes showed under his shaggy grey brows. There were frozen icicles in the wool over where he breathed through his mouth. He brought his horse to a stop before the castle and put up a mittened hand to knock off the ice.

The horse stood snorting clouds of steam, trembling with exhaustion. Two grooms pushed bodily through the drifts. Jock handed the reins to a groom while the other helped him out of the saddle. Mister Dobie met him with a blanket and led him to the roaring fire. He pushed down the frozen plaid to reveal his bearded mouth. A servant handed him a mug of mulled wine and stood ready to refill it. Lady Margaret and Euphemia Drummond arrived to hear his news. Jamie hovered in the background.

"Aye, the conditions frae Perth were evil, wi' snaw, sleet, freezing rain, every form of moisture in the air and on the ground. The roads are bogs in which a man can fall and ne'er be seen until spring. I hae been in the saddle since dawn just tae come frae Methven. The wind and blowing snaw made travel the first day frae Perth nearly impossible."

Lady Margaret inquired anxiously, "Would it nae be better, Mister McRae, fer ye tae rest a while before talking? Ye can stretch oot here and impart news when ye hae regained some strength."

The old soldier straightened and shook his head vigorously, spraying drops of water from the snowmelt trapped in his hair and beard.

"Nae, madam. Another mug o' the wine will set me up sufficiently. My jaws are unstuck enough frae the cold tae speak."

A servant extended a third mug and a towel to dry his hair. He took the towel and wiped the back of his neck, face, and beard and returned the towel to take the proferred mug of warm wine.

"Ach, that's better!" he exclaimed as he leaned back. He looked at the waiting women, now joined by Emilia and Mrs. MacRobie. He began to speak, choosing his words carefully and avoiding looking directly at any of them. "The news at the Lieutenant General's headquarters was sketchy, but the evening before I left, a rider came in wi' dispatches. General Drummond was guid enough to call me tae him after he addressed his staff officers and sent information tae the various posts. The prince's army experienced great success on the way south. Let me see. They were in Manchester on the twenty-ninth and left the next morning. The army entered Derby on the fourth."

He paused as the others interjected comments of amazement at that news. They were within days of reaching London. Jock interrupted them.

"During the pause in Derby, however, the Royal Prince met with his commanders, wha advised him tae abandon the movement south. His Highness was utterly confident in success. He believed that there was a rising underway in Wales. Lord Kilmarnock had the guid fortune tae capture an intelligence officer on a reconnaissance. Murray sent him back tae Derby tae be interrogated. Based on what that officer told him, Murray interrupted the prince's confident declaration that he was ready fer the army tae march tae London the next day. Murray told him that it was the council's opinion that they had tae retreat north while they still had the chance. Murray followed up that astonishing declaration by saying that the army had done all that could be expected o' them. Murray said…"

Jock's voice grew strained. He stopped to rub his hands over his face.

"He said…he said that the army had marched tae England ready to join with anyone wha would rise with them tae support King James. Howe'er, in the areas through which they passed, they encountered far mair enemies than friends. The French troops that hae been promised hae nae come and dinna appear tae have made any reasonably believable plans tae come soon. They hae nae sent any money or arms or the least advice telling the prince what he should do. Even if the army met and defeated the forces o' the Duke of Cumberland, they would lose hundreds of men and still hae tae face seven thousand o' the King's army around London. Certainly less than five thousand Scots ne'er thought that they could put a king on the English throne alone."

Jock's voice trailed off. He stared into the fire, squeezing his big hands together so hard that they could hear the knuckles crack in the silence. Composing himself, Jock went on.

"Only James Drummond was prepared tae support continuing the march. The others advised an immediate retreat, but were uncertain o' the preferred route, since they hae little knowledge o' the whereabouts o' General Wade's forces. The prince came unstrung, as ye might expect, seeing his hopes dashed at a stroke. He flew into what can best be described as a passion. The correspondent, wha sent Viscount Strathallan a report o' the meeting, was Colonel Sullivan, who described the prince taking this course o' action harder than anything anyone hae seen before, but he was obliged tae consent. None o' the officers could speak tae him fer the remainder o' the day as they prepared the army tae depart."

"God in Heaven." Lady Margaret gasped. "We are undone. What will become o' our nation, our homes, and our husbands? How can they now win this fecht?"

Jock's head came up, and his countenance grew stern. He half rose out of his seat with the forcefulness of his response. "My lady, they can win in the way Robert the Bruce won, by biding time, choosing his place o' battle, wearing down the enemy with small forays, then melting awa' until he could reduce the enemy and gain the advantage o' place and numbers, by ne'er surrendering!"

Lady Margaret put her hands over her face and rocked back and forth.

Euphemia's crumpled face revealed the emotional strain that was taking its toll on her. She turned to Jock and pleaded, "Where is my husband? Where is John? Where is the prince's army now?"

Jock resumed his narrative. "They stayed ahead of Cumberland's army, which chased them north, but were unable tae come tae grips wi' them. What saved them frae being forced tae engage Cumberland were some tactical errors committed by his subordinates. I'm certain that the fat young royal Duke's nose is weel oot o' joint because he was outmaneuvered sae neatly. There were also false threats o' a French landing in his rear that stymied him. James Drummond took a group of Hussars ahead, riding hard fer Scotland tae get reinforcements and locate his brother with the Royal Eccossois and the other units come frae France. The prince had earlier sent John Drummond to escort the French troops tae a rendezvous. By the fifteenth o' December, the prince's army caught up with Drummond and his Hussars at Kendal. The army met with much confusion because troops hae been ordered tae forage fer provisions, which delayed their departure fer Penrith. The Prince left a garrison tae defend Carlisle wi' the accursed thirteen-gun artillery train that proved sae useless in England that none fired a shot. The prince's army, including Glengarry and Appin reinforcements, recrossed the border on the twentieth. The unfortunate garrison at Carlisle is now under siege by Cumberland's army. They are only three hundred strong and willna be able tae hold oot long."

Jock took a refilled mug offered by an attentive servant and drank deeply. He continued.

"John Drummond brought the Royal Eccossais and the French units ashore, but it was a close-run series o' near disasters that led tae troops being scattered frae Peterheid all the way tae Stonehaven and Montrose. Unfortunately, a Lieutenant General Handasyde arrived tae occupy Edinburgh after the prince's army abandoned it in mid-November. This general got wind o' the landings and took measures tae prevent troops frae passing across the Forth. Another piece of bad news is that Lord Lovat finally and publicly committed himself, only tae be seized and locked up in Inverness. However, the auld fox escaped on the nineteenth and hae gone into hiding somewhere in the north. Now, there is a loyalist army planning tae march on Aberdeen. We dinna ken their strength and are rushing reinforcements tae hold the city."

Lady Margaret had again risen from her seat with her hands over her mouth. "What o' Andrew and Henry?"

Jock held up his hand.

"They showed up at their father's headquarters in Perth three days ago. Apparently, they heard the rumors and decided that it would be guid tae decamp. They dinna wish tae publicly declare fer the prince, being young lads yet, but neither do they wish tae be recruited by the loyalists. They are staying at an inn in Perth and continuing their studies in seclusion."

"Thank ye fer that news aboot my youngest sons, but what aboot John?" Lady Margaret asked and resumed her seat.

Jock continued, "John Drummond still faces the challenge o' bringing his troops and heavy guns tae a rendezvous with the Prince's army, but we dinna yet ken where or when. The Viscount expects another major battle after the first o' the year, since the young Duke o' Cumberland is naething if nae tenacious. He is like a bulldog that clamps down and ne'er lets up until it is either victorious or dead. It is in the interest o' the cause to see him ignominiously defeated or killed. Then, either the French come in or the prince must sue fer peace in some form. And now, I am utterly spent and must either sleep in my room or collapse here for ye tae tend my puir carcass."

Euphemia rose and, reaching forward, took Jock by the hands, eyes brimming. "Jock McRae, ye are a most excellent man and a guid friend. Thank ye fer risking the storm tae bring us encouraging news o' the safety o' those we love. We grieve fer what might hae been a swift resolution fer the young prince and his hopes o' a crown fer his father, yet the die is nae finally cast fer the outcome. Powerful forces are at work, and we canna foresee what will happen. We can only hope and pray now that the war is coming north."

She released his hands. "I ken that ye must be hungry as weel as exhausted. I will hae the cook bring a platter and a pint tae yer room. Mister Dobie already arranged fer servants tae lay a fire, sae yer room will be as warm as toast by now."

❦

There was no Hogmanay celebration at Strathallan that winter and only a simple Christmas since none of the Drummond family came home for the holidays. Jamie enjoyed a brief respite from classes, but to keep him busy, his mother assigned additional reading about travel to exotic places. Sitting by a roaring fire, he closed his eyes and dreamed of far-off India, Cathay, and the new world of savage peoples and exotic animals.

The thirtieth of January was a warm, clear day after a bad storm lashed Strathallan with high winds and rain that melted away much of the heavy snow. The late afternoon light was fading to a dusky rose hue when a rider trotted through the slush and mire that lay on the road leading to the castle. The solitary guard at the gatehouse acknowledged him since he was a well-known young officer on the staff of the Viscount. He rode straight through the open stable door and handed the reins to a young groom.

Pulling off the saddlebags, he slung them over his shoulder and, after a few words of instruction, walked up the path. The servant who greeted him took him at once to Lady Margaret in the warm and comfortable rooftop solar. She accepted the packet of letters he produced and directed a servant to bring refreshments and another to send word to Euphemia, Clementine, and Emilia to join them.

By the time the women reached the solar, the young officer had devoured a goodly portion of the refreshments. He jumped to his feet immediately on their arrival.

Euphemia stepped forward and extended her hand. "How guid tae see ye, Lieutenant Grant."

William Grant bowed over her hand and brushed it with his lips.

"Lady Drummond," he murmured.

"Aye." She laughed and turned her head to look at Lady Margaret, Clementine, and Emilia. "Lady Drummond, Lady Drummond, Lady Drummond, and Lady Drummond. In the interest o' simplicity, Lieutenant, please address us by our first names."

Somewhat abashed, the young officer nodded. He sat down as soon as the four ladies had taken their seats in a row on the wide sofa facing him.

"Are ye here to give us a narration o' events or only tae deliver letters?"

William Grant frowned and shifted in his seat while he composed his thoughts. "Both. I am sent by my general to tell ye o' another signal victory by our cause, at Falkirk."

"So close, and we dinna ken," said Lady Margaret in a low voice.

"With the weather, madam, few are available tae bring news. Men canna be spared tae courier letters except fer matters essential tae military business."

Emilia saw the Lieutenant glancing at her and met his gaze boldly, offering him a dimpled smile. A flush reddened his cheeks and he looked away.

"Pray, continue, sir," urged Euphemia in a soft voice.

Lieutenant Grant gazed into the fire for a moment. "The prince's army moved north tae occupy Glasgow and on the fourth o' January farther north toward Stirling tae rendezvous with John Drummond's forces, which hae moved south tae meet them. Those troops hae successfully slipped the cordon put up by the enemy and met with the Prince's force at Bannockburn, truly an excellent omen. While the bulk o' the forces bivouacked in the surrounding area, Lord Murray took the Highland clan regiments across tae Falkirk and established cavalry posts at Elphinstone, Callendar, and Airth."

He paused, and Euphemia murmured, "Aye, we hae heard that mounted troops were in and around Callendar."

"Three days later, on the seventh, the town leaders of Stirling surrendered their arms. In order tae besiege the castle at Stirling, there was a lot o' maneuvering tae get the French guns doon." Lieutenant Grant stopped to take a sip from his glass. "While Lord John Drummond's Royal Eccossais remained in Stirling, the rest o' the forces moved toward General Hawley's government forces at Falkirk. Drummond was assigned tae conduct a feint tae lead awa' the enemy frae Lord Murray's troops moving through the Torwood tae attack them. The actual battle began at four o'clock in lowering light and stormy weather. Government dragoons launched an attack on the MacDonalds, who mowed them doon. When they retreated, the impetuous MacDonalds ignored orders tae stand. They chased the loyalists down the hill, drawing the rest o' our troops wi' them. The storm broke, and conditions became chaotic, with the strong wind blowing directly at the enemy. The storm was sae severe that General Hawley ordered a withdrawal of the government forces back tae Linlithgow rather than have his men lying in the open all night. Both sides suffered light casualties because sae many ran awa'. Falkirk was a victory fer our side, but there was confusion on what tae do next except continue the siege o' Stirling castle."

He stopped again to take a sip. The women glanced at each other but said nothing.

Lieutenant Grant clearly had something further to say. He sat with his head down as if deep in thought and then, without looking up, spoke slowly. "The prince's council of war advised strongly, against his desires, which he heatedly expressed, tae abandon the siege o' Stirling Castle and retire north. Cumberland is now in Edinburgh and preparing tae move west in pursuit. We canna fecht a second battle wi' depleted forces with sae many men running awa'. The intention o' the commanders is tae spend the winter adopting Bruce's tactics tae isolate and reduce loyalist strongholds before taking the offensive again in the spring wi' expected reinforcements."

Euphemia erupted. "Expected reinforcements? Frae where? The French?" She made a disparaging sound deep in her throat.

"We hae some French fechting wi' us, madam, but I dinna ken the information on which the council based its decision. They are buying time."

Lady Margaret broke the silence. "If the army retires north, then we here at Strathallan will be exposed tae the loyalist army. I willna leave my hame. I hae lived here since my marriage and will wait here fer my husband. Unless he orders me tae leave, I will stay."

Emilia whispered, "I will stay wi' ye, Mama."

Clementine knelt on the floor beside her mother and gripped her hand tightly. "And me, mother."

Euphemia sat tight-lipped and silent.

Lady Margaret asked, "What o' Perth?"

Lieutenant Grant said heavily, "If Cumberland comes north, then Perth is unsafe and will be evacuated. Lord William Drummond will move north toward Inverness tae intercept the prince's army." He looked pleadingly at the women. "He hae sent me here tae urge ye tae gae quickly before Cumberland's army enters the Highlands. When he does, it will be impossible to leave northward, and there is nae safety southward."

Lady Margaret said in a controlled voice, "I will stay and wait fer my husband." She looked at Euphemia. "Ye are the wife o' a rebel officer, my dear. I advise ye tae take Jamie and fly tae Aberfeldie. Ye are a Gordon, and Charles will shield ye. I am certain."

Euphemia stared at her for a long moment. "But sae are ye a wife and mother o' rebels."

Lady Margaret took her hand and smiled faintly. "But I am auld, and that may provide me security that yer youth and beauty will nae provide. And ye hae Jamie tae think aboot. Ye must leave, sae pack only what ye need and gae quickly."

Euphemia hesitated. "Will ye escort me tae Aberfeldie, Lieutenant Grant?"

He shook his head slowly. "I canna help ye, my lady. I must follow my commander. But I canna leave ye desolate and will stay until morning if need be. Is there a reliable man wha can escort ye tae Aberfeldie?"

Lady Margaret spoke up. "I choose Jock McRae to accompany ye, my dear. I would trust him with my life. I will assign him that task."

Euphemia asked, "But do ye nae need him here?"

Lady Margaret replied, "I will be saving the auld soldier by sending him wi' ye. He is loyal tae the cause and this household. He would end his days on the point o' a pike or sword defending me. There is nae need tae waste the life o' another guid man wha is stubbornly loyal. I will order him, and he will get ye there safely. I will also order him tae stay until yer father or James comes tae relieve him. I am certain that Charles Gordon will take him in, fer although he is Jacobite tae the core, Mister McRae hae made no public declaration nor taken up arms."

Lady Margaret stood up. "Excellent! Then we are decided. Lieutenant Grant, please convey my thanks tae my husband in Perth, and tell him that I await him here. My cooks will prepare ye food that ye can pack in those saddlebags. The grooms will give ye a fresh mount since yers is probably exhausted frae the long trek through the snaw."

Lieutenant Grant rose; saluted the three women; and followed the grim-faced servant who had stood stiffly at the door, taking in the conversation. Euphemia hugged Lady Margaret tightly.

Emilia, in a low voice, said, "I will give instructions to Mister Dobie to bring Jock McRae to yer suite, instruct the grooms tae prepare a coach, and then return tae help ye talk tae Jamie and pack his things."

The Drummond family ate their last meal together at Strathallan in near silence. Euphemia had met with Jock McRae alone in her suite before dinner. The grizzled veteran took the news of the retreat calmly since he had already heard snatches of rumor for several days.

"I foresee a repeat of the events following the fifteen rising, madam. Lord Murray is correct. The only course of action open tae the rebel army is to adopt the Bruce's tactics, either in the mountains o' Mar or the western Highlands. Maintaining a substantial force in the wild is very difficult, with soldiers near starvation. They must live and fecht on what they can take frae the enemy, and such tactics are damnably difficult on their families, wha might be seized by the government as hostages. Ye are right tae flee north tae Abergeldie."

At that point, Euphemia told him of Lady Margaret's recommendation for him to leave Strathallan to escort her and Jamie north. Jock rose to his feet and paced the room in great agitation, stopping now and again to ask a curt question. Lady Margaret had known the old soldier's temperament. He would not leave without her express order. They discussed taking Lady Margaret by force and then dismissed it. The action, even if successful, would forever estrange them from her.

Finally, Jock agreed with Euphemia Drummond's decision, though his misgivings about the ruthless Duke of Cumberland were deep.

"I will see ye safely tae Abergeldie, but I reserve the right tae return here tae see after the welfare o' my mistress and follow the instructions o' the viscount. He hae paid me guid money fer my faith and dedication," he rumbled. "In an earlier age, he would be my liege lord and hae claim on my service even tae the laying doon o' my life. Honor requires nae less. I must obey my lady." He rose from his seat before the fire and faced Euphemia. "I will gae tae Lady Margaret and pay my respects and then prepare a coach and horses fer the journey. I will select three grooms wi' the best horsemanship tae accompany us, sae we can take turns drivin' and guarding, ain on horseback in the van and ain on horseback trailin', in case o' brigands on the roads. See that we hae food in sufficiency fer all, since stopping at country inns during the day is nae wise wi' such a large party, but only at nicht. We hae a spacious coach wi' a private cuddy fer personal affairs, if ye grasp my meaning, my lady. Ye should be comfortable enough, though it is an arduous journey that will take us three days or mair, wi' the roads in such pitiable shape. Hae ye told Jamie what is afoot?"

She shook her head. "As soon as ye leave tae arrange affairs, Master McRae, I will speak wi' my son. Lady Emilia is preparing food, bedding, and other necessaries fer us. There is nae time to send word tae my brother, the Laird o' Abergeldie, so this visit will come as a surprise, if not a shock. He hae nae openly declared fer the prince. Although the Lord o' Lovat marshaled a number o' the Gordons, my brother is nae among them. I dinna ken how he will feel aboot sheltering a sister whose husband is a Jacobite leader."

"Are ye worried that he will turn ye awa'?" inquired Jock with evident concern. "Must ye become a fugitive?"

Euphemia smiled. "Nae. My brother dinna wear his emotions on his coat, but he is loyal tae family. Ye must remember that I was born a Gordon. The blood ties are strong in the Highlands."

Jock nodded in agreement. "In the west as weel, my lady. Nae matter how far I hae roamed, when I hae returned to McRae country, I am always counted as kin."

Jamie took the news with more calmness than his mother expected. Being privy to multiple conversations about the progress of the army seemed to have steeled the boy to the prospect of flight. His mother asked him why he seemed so prepared to leave.

"Mama, do ye remember last summer when Maggie McLeod told me my future, that I would travel tae far places?"

She frowned, looking puzzled. Then remembrance dawned. "Aye, laddie, I do remember. Do ye think she hae the sight?"

Jamie responded, "I dinna know, Mama, except that she seemed sae wise. There was nae reason tae invent such a tale tae amuse the crowd because they were nae close enough tae hear her say those things. And I did hae a dream or twa, so I am thinking that I do believe her prophecy, and I am ready to start on what might be a great quest."

She laughed and ruffled his dark gold locks. "I love ye sae much, my son. Ye are unco brave. Now, this is a journey that we will take together, tae safety, where we can wait fer yer papa tae fulfill his duty tae the prince and then come hame tae us. I pray that it dinna become an adventure. None o' us kens what the future holds, but we will face it together."

They held hands as they walked to where Lady Margaret and Emilia sat waiting in the solar. Mister Dobie and Mrs. MacRobie stood by the door. They had scarcely arrived when Jock McRae joined them. Lady Margaret put down the rosary that she held in her hands. Then she wiped her reddened eyes and broke the silence.

"It's late, my dears, and time fer ye tae depart." Her voice broke, and she said querulously, "Now come and kiss me. The Blessed Christ and the Virgin alone know when we shall see each other again."

Jamie threw himself into his grandmother's arms with a cry. That brought a round of sniffles from everyone and tears from Mrs. MacRobie and Emilia. Mister Dobie directed a question to Jock McRae.

"Are ye carryin' sufficient arms fer protection?"

Jock held up the fingers of his right hand and touched them one by one with his left index finger.

"All men wi' guid broadswords. A brace o' pistols and a dirk fer each man. Three muskets wi' powder and ball in the coach. And this, as a way to stop abuse o' an unarmed woman."

He held up a sgain dubh in its scabbard, which he passed to Euphemia, who smiled and slid it into her bodice.

"I feel like a Highland lass again," she said brightly.

Mrs. MacRobie spoke up. "There are three hampers o' food, wine, and cider in the coach, my lady, which should see ye tae Abergeldie."

Euphemia embraced her mother-in-law and whispered her thanks. Jamie hugged everyone, and then it was time to leave.

The coach was large and heavy, which made travel hazardous on the path through the avenue of trees, stark and black in the wan moonlight. However, the six horses were fresh. The groom driving the coach was experienced and knew the path to the main road well enough to avoid the potholes and rocky bumps.

Jock took the van, positioning himself a hundred yards ahead of the coach, with a groom riding a hundred yards behind. Jock did not expect an ambush on Drummond property or anywhere before Crieff, but he did expect to encounter loyalist patrols as they skirted Perth. His plan was to drive through the night and the next day until they reached Dunkeld, where they would sleep in a post house and rest the horses before pressing east to Blairgowrie and and then north to Netherton for a second night. Jock anticipated spending a third night somewhere in Badenoch on the old military road through the mountains and reach Abergeldie in late afternoon three days later.

The trip went uneventfully, except for a loyalist patrol that stopped them shortly after leaving Dunkeld. Once they identified themselves as Gordon family members journeying to Abergeldie and clearly not harboring anyone on the list held up by the captain leading the patrol, he waved them on. Jamie remembered the journey as an interminable round of swaying, lurching, eating, sleeping, stepping into the wonderful privacy cuddy that held a wooden chair with a large crock underneath, and returning to his seat for more swaying, lurching, and sleeping. He noticed that his mother never seemed to sleep, except when they stopped in the post houses. She stared through the curtains at the dark, leafless trees passing.

The road was empty most of the time. They rode for many miles before they saw other travelers, who were mostly on foot.

As they entered the mountains after Badenoch, the uphill going became difficult and the road rutted and slippery. Not knowing the road, the groom driving the coach slowed until the horses were moving at a walk. Near the end of the journey, he did not want to risk a broken axle or wheel.

Suddenly, the coach stopped. Soldiers armed with muskets and broadswords had stepped out to bar the road. Jamie craned his neck to see what was happening. Jock dismounted and stood facing the soldiers. A brief conversation in low tones ensued. A sergeant stepped out of the bushes beside the road and joined the conversation. After a short pause, he walked to the coach and peered through the curtains at Euphemia and Jamie. Then he took off his hat and swept it low in a bow.

"Lady Drummond, ye may ride in safety frae here tae yer destination at Abergeldie," he said courteously. "My Lord General Murray controls the land all the way north tae at least Inverness."

The sergeant and his soldiers faded into the dark bushes and were gone.

Jock decided to send a rider ahead to Abergeldie with notice of their arrival. That worthy trotted off up the curving mountain road. The coach resumed its creaking journey up the steep grade. They stopped once just short of Braemar while Jock talked to a rail-thin pastor riding an ancient mule, who was out in the sub-freezing weather to visit a sick parishioner.

As they approached Crathie, about an hour from Abergeldie, Jock hailed a group of riders trotting their horses toward them on the road. The lead rider turned out to be Charles Gordon, accompanied by his Master of Horse David Lindsay and six grooms, all armed, arriving to provide an escort for the Laird of Abergeldie's eldest sister. Charles Gordon released his reins and leaned down from his saddle to tug at the latch on the coach door.

When the door opened, he expertly slid off his saddle directly into the open door, almost falling into his sister's lap. Given his reputation for taciturnity and solemn demeanor in public, his youthful impetuousity was surprising. David Lindsay caught his mount's reins in his gloved hand. Utterly relieved by his sudden arrival, Euphemia hugged her brother and burst out laughing.

On the ride to Abergeldie, she told him of all that had happened and everything that she knew.

Charles listened grimly, and then said, "Conditions are tumultuous here in the north. We might almost call it civil war. If the rebels are moving north toward Inverness, I must wonder what yer father-in-law, Viscount Strathallan, will do. He must abandon Perth and move north as weel. Loyalist forces are swirling through the mountains and along the coast. We dinna ken exactly where they are on any given day or what they intend tae do. Everyone is fearful. While I will do my duty as a brother and laird o' the family, I am worried about repercussions."

Euphemia frowned. "Repercussions?"

"Aye, sister, repercussions. James is a publicly declared outlaw, as is his brother John and the viscount. Until matters settle themselves, it would be best if we are discreet in wha knows that ye are here. If they ask, ye are here fer family matters and it is a short visit."

Euphemia nodded. "I understand that there is risk, Charles, but I will do naething that would compromise yer neutrality. The man who hailed ye as ye met us is Jock McRae, a retired officer of the Black Watch and a former mercenary. He is a faithful retainer who although Jacobite in spirit, hae taken nae public steps tae support the cause, and hae nae taken up arms against the government. Please allow him tae stay wi' us until events settle themselves."

Charles nodded agreement. He turned to Jamie with a smile.

Jamie smiled back from where he lay burrowed in pillows and blankets. "Hullo, Uncle Charles. Thank ye for allowing us tae come tae visit unexpectedly. How are Peter and Will? Do ye hae a horse that I can ride?"

Charles gave the boy his hand and said, "They are both fine and will be unco pleased that ye are coming. Aye, we still hae the same horse that ye rode last spring."

Jamie said in utter seriousness, "But I was nae much o' a rider last year. I'm sae much better now and can ride a much bigger horse."

Charles looked at his sister, who quirked an eyebrow.

"It sounds as if ye are ready tae ride the master of horse's stallion," Charles said in jest.

Jamie did not take it as a jest and said, "Oh. May I? I can hardly wait tae try."

"Ye are sae brave and sae braw, lad." His uncle chuckled and reached over to ruffle his hair.

On a morning two days after their arrival, Jock McRae felt that Euphemia and Jamie were settled enough for him to return to Strathallan with the grooms. He felt uncomfortable leaving Lady Margaret, in spite of her advice to stay in the north. Over Euphemia's objections, he readied the coach for the return journey. However, it was a journey that never happened. Before they could hitch up the team, a courier trotted across the bridge over the frozen river to Abergeldie castle. He brought news from General William Drummond. Euphemia waited until her brother and sister-in-law; sister Jean; Peter; Jock; Will; and Jamie were seated in the parlor to break the wax seal on the letter. She looked down for a few moments to read ahead before attempting to read aloud. After a minute of intense concentration, she dropped the letter into her lap, covered her mouth, and burst into copious weeping.

Charles stood up, walked to her side, put his left arm around her, and picked up the letter. He studied the first page and then disengaged his arm from his still-weeping sister and returned to his seat. His brows furrowed with intense concern as he read. His wife, Alison, holding a nursing baby Ann, urged him to read aloud.

"'Dear daughter-in-law, Lieutenant William Grant returned tae my headquarters just in time tae join us in evacuating our headquarters in Perth. He assured me that ye and Jamie are being escorted north by our ever-faithful Jock McRae. We received other news that James and John are reunited and moving north toward Inverness. The Prince's army abandoned Falkirk on the first o' February, apparently only hours ahead of the Duke o' Cumberland's troops. With Stirling Bridge broken, the army moved north by way o' the Fords o' Frew. It breaks my heart tae report that they abandoned the wounded tae the tender mercies o' the enemy, along with the heavy guns that John brought sae laboriously frae France. They then blew up the powder magazine in St. Ninian's church tae keep it oot o' the hands o' the enemy.'"

Charles closed his eyes for a moment and then took a deep breath.

"'The next day, the western clans marched o'er the hills toward Inverness, while Lord George Murray took the rest o' the forces up the coast road through Fife and Stonehaven toward Aberdeen. The weather is sae dirty and the roads sae treacherous that I doubt that Cumberland will advance further than perhaps Aberdeen, until spring. We are now joined up wi' George Murray's forces and moving north as rapidly as we can, but the weather is severe. The worst news I hae saved for last. My dear wife Margaret, stalwart supporter o' the cause, is paying a heavy price fer her loyalty. Cumberland's men confiscated Strathallan and converted it tae an officer's billet. The servants were permitted tae stay, but my dear Margaret hae been arrested and is being conveyed tae Edinburgh tae be imprisoned there in the castle for nae mair crime than tae be married tae the Viscount Strathallan. Emilia and Clementine were allowed tae leave wi' their clothes tae join their sister Margaret in Kinross. Andrew and Henry are nae oot in support o' the cause and will return tae Aberdeen tae resume their studies as soon as the roads permit passage. I dinna think it safe tae visit ye in Abergeldie and impose on the hospitality o' the laird, so we will bypass it on the coastal road north tae Inverness. I sincerely hope fer a quick yet favorable outcome o' our struggle but must be prepared to give all fer as long as the prince needs my services.'"

Charles stopped and wiped his eyes. He dropped the letter on a table and passed his hand over his eyes. "Ach, the suffering that the people o' this nation must endure because o' their unending conflicts." Charles turned to Jock McRae. "And what will ye do, Mister McRae? Ye can stay here fer as long as my sister needs ye, or ye can gae north to join Viscount Strathallan."

Jock thought for some time while everyone waited in silence. "My heart tells me tae gae north, but I ken that I can do little guid there. I fully expect that the viscount would dress me doon fer coming and then send me back tae be wi' Lady Euphemia until Lord James Drummond can come fer her. I will accept yer invitation. What aboot the grooms, horses, and coach?"

Charles responded, "I daresay that eventually the government will conduct an audit of the Strathallan property and notice that the coach and horses are missing. In the meantime, we will keep them safe and employ them frae time tae time. The grooms are another matter. They are men and nae property. They should choose their own course o' action. They can return to Strathallan, and I believe that the army would treat them as they hae other servants caught up in this business, as non-combatants. They may choose to seek employment elsewhere, as others are doing in these unsettled times. I will hae the master o' horse look in his accounts tae see if he hae need fer grooms. I trust that they are excellent employees or ye would nae hae brought them on this dangerous journey, Mister McRae." Charles turned to his sister. "We hae ample room sae ye may choose yer own suite, sister, as weel as space fer Jamie, though he may hae thoughts o' his own o' being closer tae Peter and Will. Ye can look o'er the available rooms and choose. Tomorrow, I will also introduce ye tae our children's tutor, Oliver Forbes. Since it appears that ye are here fer a stay that we can nae longer consider short, the lad should nae be away frae studies sae long. I will instruct the master o' horse tae select rooms fer Mister McRae. There is also room fer the grooms in the servants' quarters, at least until they decide their future."

Euphemia looked puzzled.

Charles asked with some concern, "What is wrong, dear sister?"

Euphemia responded, "In the coach on the way here, Charles, ye were quite concerned with the length of our stay and emphasized that it hae tae be short. What has happened tae change that opinion?"

He looked out the window at the frost-glazed bare trees swaying in the wind. In a low voice, he said, "Because I love ye, dear Euphemia. Now that Strathallan hae been taken, ye need a hame fer yer wee family. Abergeldie can be that hame."

His voice caught. "Of course, I am concerned fer the security o' the family that I head, but our ties as brother and sister are deeper than our political differences. I dinna ken how lang this rebellion will last before it burns itself oot, but I will do all that I can tae keep ye and Jamie safe."

Chapter Seven

Jamie settled into the routine of life at Abergeldie. He moved into a bedroom next to Will and across from that of Peter. Since he and Will were the same age, he wore some of his cousin's clothes until Euphemia could arrange for new suits, shoes, and other items. She had brought what money she could from Strathallan to meet their needs. It had traveled securely in a secret compartment in the coach to protect against the possibility of discovery if they were assaulted by highwaymen. Charles, not naturally generous, provided a modest allowance for his sister, since he knew that all Drummond lands and accounts had been seized by the government. No one knew when, if ever, those properties would be restored.

The sheer isolation of Abergeldie was an inconvenience but also proved a safeguard from constant movements of rebel and government military units in the area. Abergeldie in its deep glen was over seventy miles from Inverness and Elgin to the north and Stirling to the south. Aberdeen on the coast lay forty miles to the east. Travel on mountain roads was difficult until spring warmth melted the snow and ice. Abergeldie was a tranquil place, and Euphemia and Jamie were satisfied to enjoy its serenity and security.

※

Euphemia met with the Gordon family tutor, Oliver Forbes, to discuss Jamie's education. She found him younger than she expected but altogether competent. She also found the tutor stiff and somewhat humorless. He seemed to lack the passion for learning exhibited by Doctor Archibald Thomson. However, that worthy gentleman was still languishing in Geneva. She wrote Doctor Thomson a long letter, describing the Drummond family's current circumstances and notifying him that his possessions, including his collection of biological specimens, were stored in the classroom at Strathallan. Because military officers were using the castle as a headquarters, she did not believe that the collection was in danger of being destroyed or damaged. She promised to send a letter to the Duke of Cumberland to urge him to safeguard the tutor's possessions. She wrote it and gave both letters to a Gordon servant to post.

Master Forbes interviewed Jamie at some length after he had completed classes the next day and requested a meeting with his mother to report his evaluation. Euphemia received the tutor in her sitting room. He entered and stood somewhat uncomfortably in the center of the room, facing her.

"Please, Master Forbes, sit yerself and be comfortable."

He sat awkwardly on the edge of an ornate chair on the other side of the fireplace. She sensed his discomfort in her presence and smiled to make him feel more at ease.

"Lady Drummond, I held a lengthy conversation with your son."

She noted immediately that he took great pains to hide the burr of his native Aberdeen accent. She felt that he was trying to sound like an Oxford-trained scholar.

"I was deeply impressed with the boy's ability to read and grasp the subjects that I am currently teaching. He is well beyond what I expected to find for his age. He is not quite eight years old. Is that correct?"

She nodded, watching his face closely.

"I found Jamie conversant in French and with excellent reading and writing abilities in that language but somewhat deficient in Latin. I can correct that shortcoming rather quickly. He writes excellently in English and hae absolutely no fear of reciting and standing to explain his learning. I suspect that he is a bit of a showoff with his superior knowledge and impatient at times."

She broke in. "And he can be manipulative of adults and jumps fences on occasion."

Oliver Forbes looked confused. "I beg your pardon, madam. Jumps fences?"

Euphemia laughed. "What I mean, Master Forbes, is that he understands rules set down by those in authority and chooses tae ignore them fer his own reasons that I sometimes dinna fathom."

The tutor rubbed his chin reflectively. "Oh dear. Then I must discipline him."

Euphemia held up her right hand with index finger extended. "I think that ye must be careful, Master Forbes. My son's thirst fer knowledge is great, and he takes liberties tae hear and ken what is going on around him. Ye see,"—she leaned forward and lowered her voice though there was no one else in the room—"he dinna think that he is but seven years auld. Discipline him if ye must, but ye will gae much further if ye continually challenge his mind and expect much mair than ye should frae a child o' his age. Discipline should be yer final recourse fer flagrant disobedience. When he asks ye why something must be done or why it must be sae, ye hae best hae a ready answer. If ye feed his inquisitive mind, he will respect ye. If he respects ye, he will do anything fer ye. That, Master Forbes, is yer challenge, tae fill up his mind as a sponge soaks up water."

Oliver Forbes nodded slowly. "I have never dealt with a child this bright, Lady Drummond, but I will take what you say to heart. I enjoy a good challenge."

Oliver Forbes was good to his word. Jamie was somewhat taken aback by the scope of what Master Forbes expected of him but responded well. The weather was still bitterly cold, so outdoor activities were not a distraction to learning.

Twice a week, rain or shine, Jock McRae met Jamie, Will, and Peter at the stables. Together, they explored the glens around Abergeldie. The snow still lay on the hills that towered to the north and south of the River Dee, so they avoided climbing the slippery trails that led to the heights. Jamie loved the long rides to the villages of Craithie and Little Mill.

On a Saturday in mid-March, the clouds cleared away eastward and the sun warmed the air. Jock led the boys on a ride all the way to a country inn, the Boar's Head, where they dismounted and ate a filling meal before riding farther into Glenmuick before returning home. All the way up the Muick, Jamie gazed on the snowy heights.

Turning to Peter, he pointed and said, "What is up there, Peter?"

Peter rode closer until they were nearly knee to knee. "The prettiest place I hae ever seen, Jamie. Up there, lying in a rocky bowl, is a clear loch in whose water the peaks are reflected frae all directions. That is Lachin y Gair."

Jamie asked, "Can we ride up there?"

Peter shook his head. "Nae, but in summer, when enough o' the snaw and ice melts, we can. We'll pack a lunch and ride up this glen tae its end, tae the Spittal o' Glenmuick. There is a steep trail there that twists and turns through pine trees and a high meadow aboot a hundred times before it reaches the lip o' a crater. Ye will ne'er forget the first time ye reach the crest and peer across the chasm tae view the loch. The trail is dangerous coming doon though, sae we hae tae be careful. We may hobble the horses partway and finish the climb on foot if the trail is too wet and slippery. But the effort is worth it. Ye will see. I even think that yer mama would like tae come. Let's ask her."

Jock looked back over his shoulder. "Aye," he rumbled. "'Twill do her ladyship much guid tae get oot in the fresh air fer a time. I can see her up there in the meadow, gathering flowers and making garlands. 'Tis a great suggestion, Master Peter. Let us propose it."

When they returned, they crowded around Euphemia and proposed the trip. Her eyes shone with remembrance of trips to the loch when she was a girl.

"An excellent idea, lads. We will gae as soon as we can depend on the flowers blooming on the hills. I suggest the middle o' May. But I hae nae been in the saddle since last year. I will be sore indeed if I do nae do some riding and walking beforehand." She rubbed her thighs while uttering a low groan.

Everyone laughed.

On the third of April, letters arrived for Euphemia. She broke the seal on the first and read it quickly. It was from an officer on the staff of the Duke of Cumberland. The officer assured her that the military officers who now occupied Strathallan had the government's authority to do whatever they wished with the property to which the Drummond family had forfeited all rights by taking up arms against the king. He assured her, however, that they were gentlemen and had not in any way damaged the property, which would revert to the crown on their departure. They had identified trunks, boxes, and specimen cases marked with Doctor Archibald Thomson's name and set them aside to claim whenever he returned to Scotland. She resolved to send the tutor a letter with that news as soon as possible.

The second letter was from James. She read it eagerly twice through before calling Jamie to her rooms. He sat on the edge of his chair, listening intently, for the letter provided news of his father's activities and expressed his love for his wife and son.

"'We are now stationed near Inverness, which I must confess tae be a small and somewhat squalid place, with none o' the magnificent estates that make the southern Highlands sae pleasant. We are encamped on a hill somewhat west o' the town center. We hae sufficient supplies that the men are reasonably well-fed, but we do nae hae enough tents tae provide all soldiers adequate shelter and must shift them frae place tae place. George Murray went south through the Cairngorms tae attack government outposts near Atholl. Blair Castle itself is in government hands. Assure Jamie that the servants are all safe, including his dear Agnes, who evacuated tae Aberdeen as soon as the attacks commenced. It appears that all o' Murray's valiant efforts were fer naught, for he hae tae abandon the captured outposts and return tae Inverness. He came back yesterday with very few casualties. Cluny's men remain at Badenoch tae guard the southern approaches. Ye may rest assured that Abergeldie is safe, since it is nae on the military road tae Inverness.'"

Euphemia set down the letter and glanced at Jamie with grave eyes. He showed no signs of distress, so she picked up the letter and continued reading.

"'In Murray's absence, father was assigned tae command an expedition north tae destroy Loudon's loyalist army. We scoured the Moray Firth fer fishing boats sae that we could bypass the Dornoch Firth, which extends inland fer a considerable distance. James Moir slipped past the patrols and reached Tain by dawn. We crammed eight hundred troops in the boats and made them depart in the teeth of a fog sae thick that men in adjacent boats could nae see each other but had tae maintain contact by using signal cords passed between them. After hours o' drifting aboot, they ended up on the same beach frae which they departed. We hae mair success when they effected a landing on the other side of the firth early in the morning. They took the enemy by surprise. By the time they discovered our troops, we had all eight hundred men on the beach. The enemy hastily retreated, dumping supplies and reserve ammunition. Some surrendered, but others were sae demoralized that they retreated westward all the way to the Kyle o' Localsh and are now huddled on the Isle o' Skye.'"

Jamie's mother took up another page.

"'The French are still trying to send reinforcements, but what is landing is pitifully deficient. Last month, they tried tae send an Irish regiment in French service but ran across the ever-present Royal Navy and were captured. A ship got through the blockade and landed at Aberdeen on the twenty-second with a hundred and thirty men and saddles. But there were nae horses. Twa units were ordered to turn o'er their horses tae these unfortunates. Some ships arrived off Aberdeen, but that city is now in the hands o' the enemy, and the ships turned back to Dunkirk on the French coast. In another piece o' bad news, on the twenty-seventh, a French ship carrying a large amount o' gold and some troops and officers was chased until they ran aground at Tongue in the far north and were forced tae surrender. The gold got ashore, but ended up in the pockets o' loyalists and charlatans. Gold seems tae hae that effect on men o' little honor. It seems that everywhere we turn, our best efforts come tae naught and salvation lies just oot o' reach.

'We are now back in Inverness. I expect that we will see mair action soon, since some o' Cumberland's forces are now at Huntley. There was a sharp action at Keith Kirk, six miles frae Huntley. We lost a few men, but the casualties tae the cursed Campbell loyalists were satisfyingly large, wi' over seventy lost. Campbell was unlucky in picking such a well-defended outpost and paid the price by being badly mangled and left fer dead in the hot action. The River Spey, defended by John's men, is now the boundary between our forces and those o' the enemy. I believe, dear wife, that we are approaching a time o' crisis, in which we may weel be positioning ourselves fer a decisive battle. The weather is moderating daily, and Murray is confident that we will soon have an opportunity tae either crush or inflict such significant casualties on the loyalists that they will be forced tae retreat or sue fer an armistice. I am confident that we nearing the end o' this business.'"

Euphemia set down the letter and, with tears trickling down her cheeks, looked at Jamie, who sat silent and dry eyed, staring into the flames.

Sunday the sixth of April was Jamie's eighth birthday. The weather was cold and threatening showers, so Euphemia and

Alison prepared a festive lunch for the family in the solar. They pulled the curtains back to reveal the gardens. The trees were still bare but showed promise of leafing out soon. Crocus and forsythia bloomed, and gardeners had pruned the hedges and swept dead leaves from walkways. Inside the warm solar, servants piled a table at one end with sandwiches, bowls, a huge tureen of steaming cock-a-leekie soup, and an enormous cake. Another table held wrapped birthday presents.

It was a festive occasion, with streamers hanging from the frosted glass ceiling.

Charles invited Jamie to sit in the place of honor. He asked, with some trepidation, "I dinna hae tae gie a speech, do I?"

Charles shook his head. "Not unless ye plan to put us all tae sleep this afternoon!"

There was a burst of laughter, and Jamie sighed in relief.

Soon, everyone had full plates and cups and, very quickly, full stomachs. Euphemia and Peter took turns bringing presents for Jamie to unwrap. In addition to toys, there was a mysterious gift with no indication of its donor. Jamie unwrapped it to reveal a leather-bound book with its title stamped in gold on the cover: *The Life and Heroick Actions of the Renoun'd Sir William Wallace, General and Governour of Scotland*, William Hamilton of Gilbertfield, William Duncan, Glasgow, 1722.

Jamie carefully opened the cover to reveal his name written in flowing script and a handwritten note. Jamie stared at the signature: Margaret McLeod. A thrill coursed through his veins.

"Can ye read it, Jamie?" asked his mother softly, looking over his shoulder.

"Aye, Mama," replied Jamie. "It is in very simple script. It is the words frae her sang last summer in Crieff, in English and Gaelic." He paused and ran his finger down the page. "She says, 'The adventure hae begun. Ye may nae be ready tae read and understand this book, but ye will very soon. Treasure the example o' the life and heroic deeds o' William Wallace, Scotland's greatest hero. The story o' his life will gie ye solace and encouragement when the road seems hard and yer afflictions too great tae bear.'

"It is a wonderful gift, Mama. How did she know where tae send it and the date o' my birthday?"

Euphemia shrugged in wonder and took the note from Jamie's hand. "Perhaps she does hae the sight. A man on horseback in Highland dress brought the package yesterday and left without saying mair than to give it tae ye today. It is a mystery."

That evening, Peter came to Jamie's room as he was preparing for bed. He softly shut the door behind him and then threw himself into a chair and looked at Jamie for a moment before speaking. "Jamie, ye are sae much younger than I am, but I hae always felt that our spirits are very similar. What would ye do, Jamie, if ye were auld enough tae fecht fer the cause?"

Jamie contemplated his bare feet.

"'Tis an unco difficult question, Peter. I dinna know much aboot weapons and fechting and such. I'm guid on horseback, so perhaps I could be a dragoon someday. But I am little, sae they would probably make me only a courier. Since my papa went tae fecht fer the prince, I would follow him."

Peter shifted in his seat and did not speak. Jamie knew that something was troubling his cousin, so he waited.

Peter looked up, and his voice trembled. "My father dinna believe in the cause as yer papa does. He canna make up his mind frae day tae day. He believes that James the Third is the rightful king, but nae enough tae commit himself tae fecht. I think my papa is a coward because he refuses to fight fer his convictions. My grandma's brother is at Carlisle and is probably in prison now. Uncle Archie Primrose is an auld man, and he went tae serve because he believes in the cause. The loyalists are in Huntley and will soon be in Inverness. I ken that there will soon be a battle tae decide which side will win. Now is the time fer brave and loyal men tae decide."

"Peter!" exclaimed Jamie sharply. "Ye are only fifteen years auld. No one expects ye tae fecht, and there is nae langer time tae drill and learn tae fecht properly. Ye are yer father's heir. Ye will be Laird o' Abergeldie some day. Ye canna do anything foolish."

Peter sat still for a very long time, gnawing on his lower lip. Finally, he stood up, and moved toward Jamie, who stood to face him. Peter hugged him fiercely, smiled, and said, "Ye are right, cousin. I canna do anything foolish, but I must do something."

Jamie looked at him quizzically.

Peter rose and punched his shoulder affectionately. "Guid nicht, cousin."

While Jamie sat at breakfast the next morning, eating a bowl of steaming porridge and cream, Jock McRae strode through the door, calling loudly, "Laird Abergeldie! I need ye quickly!"

Alison Gordon stood in the doorway for a moment and then turned and ran up the stairs. Moments later, Charles came down, shrugging himself into a coat.

"Mister McRae, what seems tae be the problem?" inquired Charles, looking at the veteran's troubled face.

Jock McRae wiped the rain off his face. "A groom told me, yer grace, that twa o' the horses are missing frae the stables this morning."

Charles asked, "Perhaps the stall and stable doors were nae closed properly and the horses wandered awa'. Did the grooms search the grounds?"

Jock said heavily, "There is nae need tae search. Two bridles and a saddle are missing as weel."

"Do they suspect that the stables were robbed in the nicht?"

"That is possible, my lord, but there might be a simpler explanation. I spoke with Mister Lindsay, and he reported something troubling tae my ears. He told me that yer son Peter was in the stables quite late, looking aboot wi' nae guid reason tae be there. He offered Mister Lindsay a weak excuse about havin' lost something there on Saturday and then left, saying that he would return tae look fer it in the morning. I suggest that ye check his bedroom. Perhaps he rode oot tae spark with some neighbor lass."

Charles shook his head in disbelief. "Do I think that he would do that in a driving rain? I dinna think he would." He ran to the staircase and shouted, "Peter! Come doon now!"

Jamie pushed back from the table, leaving his porridge uneaten. "Uncle Charles! I do nae think that he is up there. There is something I must tell ye."

Charles spun about and looked at Jamie. "What is this, Jamie lad?"

Jamie faced him. "Peter was in a very peculiar frame o' mind last nicht. Just before I went tae bed, he came tae my room and shut the door. He talked very strangely aboot the cause and why brave and honorable men should fecht fer it."

Peter's words about believing his father a coward ran through Jamie's mind, but he could not say them.

"I think he went tae join the rebels, sir."

Charles sat down heavily on the stairs and put his face in his hands.

Jock stepped close and said, "I will gae after him wi' Mister Lindsay, my lord, if that is yer wish. Lindsay saw him just before ten last nicht. It is now seven o'clock in the morning. He hae at most a nine-hour start on us. He must be headed toward where the Prince's army is encamped at Inverness. There are twa roads that he could hae possibly taken. Ain veers off toward Huntley and Keith and then on through Elgin to Nairn, but we know that area is infested with Cumberland's troops. The other route is through the mountains tae Grantown-on-Spey. There are twa choices frae there. Ain road goes through Nairn and the other through Cambridge tae Inverness. That route is the safest, tae stay oot o' the clutches o' the loyalists."

Charles sat for a moment with his head down and then rose to his feet.

"I will gae wi' ye. I canna lose my oldest boy. Gie me a minute or twa wi' his mother. Hae the cooks prepare food fer the trip. We must leave within the hour."

Charles left to talk with Alison, and Jock hurried from the room. Jamie bounded up the stairs with Will. They opened the door to Peter's room to find the bed not slept in. There was a note folded on the pillow. Will snatched it up, and the boys headed back downstairs, calling for Charles. He unfolded the note and read quickly.

"He is headed fer Inverness tae join the army!" he said in a strangled voice. "We must leave quickly!"

The rest of the household waited in apprehension all that day for news and through the night into the next day. The children were so distracted by Peter's disappearance that they could not concentrate in class. Oliver Forbes, seeing the state of the children's minds, was merciful and terminated school early. Rain poured down in sheets, and a chill wind blew from the west. Twilight came down over Abergeldie, and the servants lit lamps. The rain stopped, but the wind blew harder. The cooks served dinner, but no one was hungry. Everyone ate listlessly.

Suddenly, the dogs started barking. Alison and Euphemia, followed by the boys, jumped to their feet and ran to the entry hall to peer into the darkness. They could make out silhouettes of three men on horseback splashing their way up the long drive from the river. As they neared the pools of lamplight glowing at the front of the castle, Alison recognized her husband. She yanked open the doors with a glad cry and rushed out. Grooms met the riders and took the reins of their mounts and led them away. The three riders were clearly exhausted, walking with uncertain steps to the entrance, where they stood, dripping. Alison wordlessly embraced Charles, burying her face in his wet coat. Euphemia, with Jamie and Will on either side, stood with arms folded against the cold, looking solemnly at Jock McRae and David Lindsay.

Jock raised his hands in an expression of helplessness, and then dropped them to his sides before hoarsely breaking the silence.

"We failed. We tried tae get through on the road tae Grantoun, but there was a loyalist patrol holding the bridge o'er the Spey. They gave chase, but we outran them. We tried several side roads tae get past, but the fords across the Spey are in full spate and dangerous. There are loyalists on the road tae Nethy Bridge as weel."

He stopped, and David Lindsay took up the tale. "On the way, we inquired at post houses. We were on the right road, for several people saw Peter riding the big bay and leading the other horse. I dinna ken how he made it past the loyalist patrols, but he must hae crossed the bridge o'er the Spey before they got there. It was the merest chance that he got through, and we failed." Charles held a sobbing Alison close. His voice was near breaking. "We can only pray that our boy gets through and someone wi' intelligence turns him back or puts him tae work in a safe place weel awa' frae the fechting. I will send a letter tae Viscount Drummond, but it might be days before it reaches him and we receive his response."

Jock and David Lindsay touched their forelocks and stepped back. Euphemia said gently, "Ye did all that ye could. Please come in tae warm yerselves. We'll hae the cooks lay oot some victuals fer ye. Then, ye need tae change into warm clothing and sleep."

※

In their isolation in the mountains, the inhabitants of Abergeldie received little news of the clash of rebel and government forces in and around Nairn. Charles, David Lindsay, and Jock McRae rode to Crathie or Braemar every day, hoping to hear news of events in the north.

After a week of fruitless trips, they returned with a scrap of news from an itinerant merchant who had been to Nairn. There had been frequent running skirmishes for several days. Cumberland had ordered the concentration of his forces in anticipation of a decisive battle. The rebels had barely contested the government forces crossing the Spey on April 12, choosing to withdraw toward Nairn. The merchant saw the rebels retreating from the town, followed closely by government troops pouring in before he himself decided that the town was far too dangerous.

"I spent the nicht in an abandoned house on the southerly edge o' Nairn, my lords, lately occupied by the rebel garrison. There was still food on the table and a fire burning. The only remaining occupant was a puir cat, sitting by the fire. I ate the food, fed the cat, and at dawn fled southward yester e'en o'er the mountains, bringing oot only a fraction o' my wares, all that my puir mule could carry," he said mournfully.

Charles paid for the man's beer and placed a guinea coin on the table in recompense for his information. As they rose to leave, the merchant laid a hand on the laird's arm. Charles looked searchingly into the man's face.

"I almost forgot, my lord. There is another piece of what might be news," he said in a low voice, looking around. "I heard it frae a blacksmith wha reshod my mule at Little Mill. He hae visited his sister the nicht before. That would be on Monday, at Dalcross, near Kilravock Castle, and hae just returned at dawn."

"And what news might that be?" questioned Jock McRae.

The merchant leaned close and said, "She was taking eggs tae market at Balloch and saw parties o' rebel officers walking aboot on Drummossie Muir. There was also cavalry there."

As they walked to their horses in the persistent drizzle and prepared to mount, David Lindsay muttered, "Drummossie Muir? 'Tis a terrible place tae fight a battle. All flat, it is, and a perfect killing ground fer artillery." He stopped and gazed into space and mused, "Unless Cumberland is foolish enough to let the Highlanders get close enough for a clear run wi' broadswords."

Jock McRae held out his gloved hand and counted his fingers. "The merchant said that the blacksmith's sister hae seen them there on Monday morning. He met the blacksmith on Tuesday morning. It is now midday on Wednesday. God in heaven! There might already hae been a battle, and we dinna ken the outcome. Dare we ride tae Speybridge to learn mair?"

Charles shook his head. "The day is already far advanced. I suggest, Jock, that we return tae Crathie tomorrow and then send ye tae Grantoun to listen fer news. Ye look too auld and harmless tae be a rebel soldier."

Jock scowled, but David Lindsay and Charles laughed heartily.

There was no news on Thursday, so Jock left for Grantown early Friday morning, leading a spare mount. The weather was cloudy, but there was no rain. He kept his mount to a slow trot to preserve the animal's stamina. As he approached Cock Bridge, he pulled up at sight of a group of mounted soldiers advancing. Close behind came columns of foot soldiers in a loose formation. At Jock's hail, the horsemen reined up. Jock trotted closer.

"Guid day, tae ye, gentlemen. I am Jock McRae, in the employ o' the Laird o' Abergeldie. What means this formation here in the Cairngorms?"

One of the riders urged his horse forward. "I am Captain Andrew Alford of Lord Ogilvy's Regiment. We are in a hurry, man, coming frae the disaster at Culloden, wi' many wounded. This is the lead party, wi' Lord Ogilvy comin' behind wi' the rest o' the regiment."

Jock's craggy eyebrows shot up. "Disaster? What kind o' disaster?"

Captain Alford looked back up the road for a moment and then turned toward Jock. In a heavy voice, he explained, "The prince's troops were exhausted frae a futile and badly executed nicht march on Nairn. But without artillery or much cavalry on such a level field, it was hopeless tae expect a Highland charge tae break the loyalists. We lost thousands in the space o' twenty minutes. Few got close enough tae engage wi' broadswords. They were cut down in rows like ripe wheat. Our regiment was in the center o' the first line, and I was in the middle of thick action there, sae I must profess ignorance o' the rest o' the battle. Most rebel troops fled west and north, and I think they are hoping tae regroup."

A young Subaltern edged his horse forward. "Abergeldie, did ye say?"

"Aye. I came frae Abergeldie this morning," Jock told him.

Captain Alford sheathed his sword and extended a gloved hand. "I am sorry tae say that we hae bad news fer ye. We are transporting the body o' William Drummond, Viscount Strathallan, killed on the field at Culloden. His son, Lord James Drummond, gave instructions tae Lord Ogilvy to take the body tae Abergeldie, since his wife is there."

Jock reeled in the saddle in sudden grief. "Ach, my puir Lord Drummond. His wife lies imprisoned in Edinburgh Castle. His children are scattered frae here tae Aberdeen. The loyalists hae taken Strathallan. We canna even bury him on his ain land. How did Lord Drummond die?" growled Jock.

Captain Alford shook his head, raised his right arm momentarily, and then dropped it helplessly. "He commanded the left w' the MacDonalds, which caused nae end o' discontent, for the MacDonalds always hae claimed the right tae fecht on the right wing. I heard that he hae trouble getting the McDonalds tae charge. The ground was sae mucky that footing was perilous. General Drummond rushed tae the Clan Ranald regiment, seized their colors, and told them tae come wi' him. Finally, they followed and got within a hundred yards o' the loyalist right several times, but the fire was withering. I dinna see the general fall." The captain's voice was strained, and his face worked as he struggled to control his emotions. "I spoke tae a soldier wha was there. The MacDonalds were regrouping fer another charge when the General was hit by at least twa balls. The men eased him tae the ground, and young Gordon, wha had just returned frae conveying a message tae General Murray, threw himself doon on General Drummond's body tae shield him. That is when the lad was shot twice in the hip and a ball furrowed his shoulder. Seeing that the General was dying, Colonel Sullivan ordered the soldiers tae pull the lad tae the side while he saw tae the last rites."

"Last rites?" queried Jock.

"Aye, the Colonel, being Catholic, understood what the General wanted. He called fer John Maitland o' Careston, chaplain tae the Forfarshire regiment. The priest came on the run, saw the General's condition, and decided tae administer the last rites. Maitland took an oatcake frae his kit and poured a wee bit o' whiskey and put them tae the General's lips. He whispered his thanks, though he was fading fast. He ordered Colonel Sullivan to see that the Gordon lad was taken tae a place o' safety. General Drummond closed his eyes with a sigh and expired peacefully. That is where some o' our Ogilvy troops found him. They couldna' leave the lad, not with Butcher Cumberland orderin' his soldiers to dispatch the wounded. I canna tell ye what happened tae the General's sons, Lords James and John Drummond, except that I heard that they were wi' the troops retreating westward."

Captain Alford shook his head as if to clear the memory from his mind and restore him to his current duties. "Do ye ken where we can find medical help for our men?"

"Aye, Captain," responded Jock, "but none 'til ye reach the village o' Crathie. After that, ye pass by the castle o' Abergeldie, and then ye come tae Braemar. Ye will probably find a physician or twa in Crathie or Braemar, but none at Abergeldie, though the servants and ladies will offer such assistance as they can."

Captain Alford asked, "Will ye come wi' us tae show us the way?"

Jock bowed his head for a moment and then looked up and wiped his eyes. "Aye, Captain. 'Tis my duty."

The captain said, "The foot are coming up now. We must be moving."

"Then lead me tae the wagon so I can identify the Gordon lad ye mentioned. I came this way looking fer Peter Gordon, the missing son o' the Laird o' Abergeldie."

"Follow me," urged the Subaltern, while the other officers wheeled their mounts and resumed their journey.

They trotted past the columns of disorganized troops, many of whom were stumbling in their weariness, until they reached the small supply train at the back of the loose formation. They found a wagon drawn by a single mule with four wounded soldiers lying in the back like so much cordwood, swaying with the motion of the wagon. A fifth soldier sat behind them, showing no apparent wounds but staring blankly and shivering uncontrollably.

The Subaltern rode close to the wagon and reached over the side to pull the blanket off the face of one of the wounded.

Jock leaned close. "Aye," he breathed, "it is Peter Gordon. Three balls, ye say?"

The Subaltern nodded. "Mercifully, he is unconscious now. He was raving wi' pain earlier. He is nae even a soldier, puir lad, just a younker. He was General Drummond's courier and tried tae protect him after he was shot. The boy still lives, but those balls must come oot soon. Otherwise, gangrene will set in and kill him for sairtan."

Jock turned to the Subaltern. "Hae ye administered anythin' tae suppress the pain?"

The Subaltern lowered his head. "We hae nae mair medications. Our surgeon was killed and his bag lost when we retreated frae the field at Culloden."

He pointed a finger at Peter. "He is only a lad, but we gie him a wee dram o' single malt Scotch frae time tae time. I believe that is what put him tae sleep and enables him tae take the lurching of the wagon better."

"I suggest, sir, that since we are aboot twa hours frae the Bridge o' Gairn, that I ride ahead tae Crathie tae find at least ain physician willing to come oot and join us tae provide such succor as is possible for these puir lads. I will leave my spare horse here wi' ye."

He lifted the spare horse's reins and offered them to the officer, who, in turn, tossed them to a man sitting on the high board of one of the wagons full of wounded.

"Sergeant, here is a bareback mount for ye," he called.

The officer followed Jock as he galloped past the columns of trudging men for a swift conference with Captain Alford. The riders wished Jock good luck and Godspeed as he galloped back up the road toward the Bridge of Gairn.

As he neared the outskirts of Crathie, Jock stopped at an inn to inquire about physicians in the village. A frowzy maid drawing water from the well next to the inn directed him to the house of the town's only physician. Jock tossed her a shilling coin and galloped onward. He found the house easily, dismounted, and twisted the reins around a lantern post. Unlatching the gate, the old soldier followed the path through a small and tidy garden to the entrance. There was an ornate knocker in the center of a substantial oak door bound with brass. Jock banged the knocker vigorously, awakening a dog, which began barking. After Jock's third impatient bang, a tall, balding servant of middle age opened the door and stared at him sourly.

Jock began, "I am looking fer a physician tae tend a wounded boy, wha is in dire circumstances."

The servant said haughtily, "Doctor Anderson left instructions tae nae be disturbed." He began to shut the door.

Jock quickly inserted his booted foot, preventing the door from closing.

"I said," repeated the servant, coloring slightly and attempting to force the door shut, "that Doctor Anderson left instructions nae tae be disturbed."

Jock thrust his gloved left hand through the half-closed door and seized the servant by his cravat in an iron grip.

"And I said, my guid man, a boy's life is in dire circumstances. He may die wi'out yer master's help."

With his right hand, Jock reached down and drew his pistol. He raised the barrel and laid the muzzle against the man's cheek. Thumbing the hammer, he pulled it back slowly. The ratcheting sound of the pistol being cocked was loud in the doorway. The servant's eyes bulged, and he swallowed hard.

Jock ground the blued steel muzzle firmly into the man's cheek, shredding the soft inner flesh against his teeth. In an iron-hard voice, he grated, "As I said, dire circumstances. In addition tae the boy, there are several badly wounded men in a wagon coming south frae the battle. Now, I need yer employer and all o' his medical supplies immediately. Do ye ken my words, sir?"

The servant swallowed and nodded, a thin trickle of blood running out of the corner of his mouth.

"Aye," he croaked.

Jock released his grip on the man's throat but kept the pistol pressed hard against his cheek.

"Now, let us see what could possibly matter tae yer employer mair than the life o' the eldest son o' the Laird o' Abergeldie." With a hard lunge, he shoved the servant backward away from the door.

"Oh, sweet Jesus, prithee dinna hurt me, sire," the servant squeaked in a shrill voice as he stumbled backward from Jock's relentless pushing. He collided with the cherry cabinet on the opposite wall, knocking several pieces of crockery to the floor. The sound disturbed the dog, which resumed barking furiously. "Please put awa' yer pistol, guid master. I will do as ye say. The doctor was most insistent on nae being disturbed, sir, because he is…he is…abed."

"Weel then," Jock roared. "Let us find his chambers and awaken him!"

The servant bleated with fear. "The doctor is abed with the maid, sire, if ye mark my meaning."

"Weel," responded Jock, "when he hears why I am summoning him, he will nae longer be interested in continuing his midday dalliance. Now, bring him here in whate'er state o' undress ye find him!"

He pulled the pistol away from the man's face and aimed it between his eyes.

The whimpering servant whirled away and scuttled down a corridor leading from the entry toward the back rooms. Jock stood in the entry, listening to the sounds from the interior of the doctor's house in grim satisfaction, a woman's high-pitched but quickly muffled scream and then a male voice shouting, followed by silence. Even the dog had quieted.

In less than three minutes, a short, red-faced, fiftyish man in a half-buttoned waistcoat bustled through the door with a coat in one hand and bulging black valise in the other. Ignoring Jock for a moment, he retrieved hat, gloves, and heavy coat from a closet and then turned to face the old soldier, who stood glaring at him with his pistol still in his hand.

In several crisp sentences, Jock informed the physician of the seriousness of Peter's injuries and the nearness of a number of wounded soldiers. Minutes later, Jock trotted up the street with a one-horse carriage rolling along behind, driven by the tight-lipped Doctor Anderson.

They overtook the rear of Lord Ogilvy's Regimental column as they were passing Littlemill. The wagons conveying the wounded pulled to the edge of the road. Jock left the physician to swiftly examine the injured men. He trotted to the head of the column to find Captain Andrew Alford. After a short conversation, the captain agreed to leave Peter and the worst of the wounded to be cared for by Doctor Anderson at Abergeldie, with the risk that they might be captured by loyalist forces moving south. The captain waved the columns forward and then rode back to the wagons with Jock. By the time they arrived, Doctor Anderson had selected seven soldiers in addition to Peter to be loaded into wagons for emergency surgery as soon as they arrived at Abergeldie.

Jock turned to Captain Alford. "I will ride ahead tae Abergeldie to prepare them tae receive the wounded and the body o' General Drummond. I ken that ye need the wagons and drivers fer the rest o' yer journey, so I will hae men ready tae unload them. I canna speak the words tae properly convey my thanks. I wish ye weel on yer journey hame and that ye can avoid the clutches o' Cumberland."

Andrew Alford extended his hand and wrung Jock's. That done, the officer saluted smartly and wheeled his mount away to bawl commands to his troops. Jock retrieved his spare mount and, holding the reins in his right hand, spurred his horse to a fast trot down the road into the gathering gloom.

By the time he reached the turnoff and the bridge over the Dee, it was dark, with only a quarter moon rising through a gathering mist. However, the horses were sure-footed and knew the road. Jock paused momentarily on the short bridge to listen to the water chuckling and rushing beneath him and then kicked his horse into a gallop for the last quarter mile to the castle. Gravel sprayed from under the horse's hooves as he skidded to a halt.

Jock dismounted and tossed the reins to a groom, who had emerged from the dark pathway to the stables. He bounded up the stairs to the top landing at the castle doors and pounded on the ornate brass knocker. A butler pulled the door open, and Jock strode in, calling loudly for Charles Gordon and Euphemia Drummond to attend him. Both appeared almost immediately and saw the look of urgency on his face.

"My lord and lady, a troop is coming down the road but will bypass the castle, except that they are carrying twa stark burthens. The battle that we expected on Drummossie Moor hae happened, and it was a disaster fer the cause."

Servants and the older children huddled by the doors. A look of fear shot across Euphemia's face. Charles's face went rigid. Only their eyes betrayed their tumultuous emotions. In the shadows, Jamie gripped Will's hand tightly. Alison came into the entry and knelt, hugging the boys.

Jock continued rapidly. "Peter is found, but he is badly hurt. He took three balls, and I think that the physician hae some hard work ahead tae cleanse the wounds. He was not fechting but serving as courier for Viscount Strathallan, wha was killed at the height o' the battle."

Euphemia gasped, horror-stricken, and reached for a chair. She sat down and stared at her shaking hands before clasping them together tightly. "What about James and John?" she asked dully.

"Captain Alford of Ogilvy's regiment, wha brought Peter and the Viscount's body, kent nothing sairtan, but the belief is that they took their troops westward tae regroup." Jock repeated the story of the General's fall, Peter's attempt to save him, and how the MacDonalds and Ogilvies pulled him from the battlefield. Jock looked hard at Charles Gordon. "My lord, we hae little time afore the wounded arrive. They were only twa or three miles behind me on the road and anxious tae discharge their commitment before traveling on tae Braemar this nicht. I dragooned a physician, Doctor Anderson, frae Crathie. I expect that he will shoot me on sight fer putting a pistol in the face o' his servant and rousting him oot o' a comfortable bed, but we need him tae perform surgery tae save Peter and seven other badly wounded men. They are also bringin' the bier o' the Viscount."

Charles reacted immediately. "Aye, weel. The Viscount is already gone, so we will attend tae him later. We hae mair pressing business wi' the living. Alison, Euphemia, Jean, the physician will need ye all as nurses, as weel as any maids o' an age tae handle the blood and anguish o' the soldiers." He turned to his major domo and said crisply, "Mister Ruthven, hae servants clear the dining room and cover the table wi' linen. Place as many lamps tae provide light as possible. Hae them bring as many towels and spare linen as they can find tae tear into bandages. Hae servants fashion litters. Doctor Anderson will need their help tae transport the wounded inside. Find Mister Lindsay and instruct him tae bring grooms tae convey the bier of Viscount Strathallan tae the barn. Hae the carpenter construct a coffin oot o' spare lumber, and assign stablehands to dig a grave in the far corner o' the cemetery. It might be very late before we can hae a funeral service for Lord Drummond and inter his body in a temporary grave, but we will do so wi' all the honor we can give."

Just as Charles finished these instructions, there was a hail from a groom, who came trotting from the gloom at the end of the road.

"Wagons coming!" he shouted.

More grooms came forward with torches and lanterns. The group in the entryway streamed outside to await their arrival. Jamie, Will, and the other Gordon children watched from inside the doors. Wagons carrying the wounded, accompanied by that carrying the body of Viscount Strathallan, pulled up at the front of the castle.

As the grooms readied litters for the wounded, Doctor Anderson climbed down from his carriage to remark, "Laird Abergeldie? Terribly sorry fer the delay, but the journey up frae the main road, across the bridge, and tae the castle was unco rough. We were forced tae travel slowly fer the wounded, who groaned pitiably with every lurch and drop into a pothole. I was tempted tae stop tae administer laudanum, but I need them awake during examination for surgery. The young lad is awake once mair and in great pain."

Charles explained, "We hae set up our dining room sae that ye may use it as a surgery. My grooms and servants will get the wounded inside sae that ye may begin treatment as soon as possible. Please accompany Mister Ruthven. We will place the wounded in the hall close by. My wife, sister, and sister-in-law will assist in any way they can."

The doctor nodded assent. He returned to the carriage for his bag and then followed the major domo up the steps. In a few minutes, the wounded had been carried inside and the body of Viscount William Drummond tenderly placed on a litter and carried to the barn. Cooks brought steaming mugs of soup, bread, and beer for the drivers, who ate and drank quickly before clambering back onto the seats of their wagons. Replenished with as much as Abergeldie could offer, they urged their teams back to the main road so they could catch up with the regiment fleeing south.

With their mothers consumed in tending the wounded, Jamie and Will went up the hall to find Peter. They walked carefully past the litters lining the corridor. He was lying on the sixth litter on the floor of the hall. The dining room door was shut, although there were loud voices and groans emanating from inside. Alison and Charles were kneeling on the floor, holding Peter's hands tightly as he writhed in pain.

Because the entry points of his wounds were in his shoulder and hip, Peter lay on his stomach. His hair was damp and lank, his face sweat-streaked and haggard, while his body trembled in the throes of pain. Peter jerked his head to the side and saw Jamie and Will. Weakly, he called to them, and they stepped closer.

"Will, I'm sorry I lied when I sneaked awa'. It was a cruel thing tae do tae a brother."

Will's face revealed his shock at seeing his brother in such pain. He could not speak but nodded and reached out a hand to pat Peter's cheek. Peter continued talking, stopping every few words to grunt with pain through clenched teeth.

"Jamie, ye were right and I was wrong. I was a little impulsive and a lot foolish. I dinna ken how terrible a battle could be… watching many men die sae quickly. I am sorry that I could nae save yer grandfather. He died bravely, and I could do naething but get myself shot in the arse."

Peter tried to laugh, but it came out as a hoarse bark.

"Papa, can Jamie and Will come in with ye tae hold my hands when the doctor performs surgery?"

Charles shook his head grimly. "I think nae, Peter."

"Please, Papa. I need them. I need their strength."

He looked pleadingly at his mother. She looked at her husband's eyes and nodded slightly.

Charles took in a breath, held it, and then expelled it gustily. "Sae be it. But only sae long as they can bear it."

Peter looked at each of the boys in turn. Both nodded their assent but with uncertainty written in their faces. Peter stiffened and closed his eyes. He uttered a deep groan and then clenched his teeth to stifle another. Alison wiped her son's forehead with a wet cloth and bent to kiss his cheek. When she arose to return to her nursing duties, her face was streaked with tears.

It seemed to Jamie that a long time passed before the door of the dining room opened and his mother appeared to beckon servants to enter with an empty litter. They hurried forward and gently lifted an unconscious soldier from the table to the litter. They conveyed the soldier into an adjacent corridor.

Doctor Anderson busied himself rearranging tools and bandages while servants removed the blood-soaked coverings from the table and replaced them with a clean blanket and sheet. With that accomplished, Euphemia stepped into the hallway and spoke in a low tone to Charles, who had risen and now stood white-faced at the end of Peter's litter. Euphemia called for servants to bring him in. When that was done, she motioned to Jamie and Will to take chairs on either side of the table where Peter lay.

"Peter wishes ye here to help him, and ye must do what the doctor tells ye instantly. If either o' ye takes fright and decides that he canna bear the sights or sounds, he must leave. Do ye understand?"

Jamie and Will nodded agreement. Jamie felt his stomach churn. Fear constricted his throat so tightly that he had difficulty swallowing.

The doctor told a servant assigned to the surgery to remove Peter's boots and stockings and then cut off his trews as gently as possible. Peter was no longer groaning, but his breathing came in shallow gasps. His pasty face glistened in the yellow light. The doctor moved the lamps to get a better view of the wounds. He used a water-soaked cloth to gently remove the dried and encrusted blood.

Jamie looked up as Jock McRae entered the room with two bottles in his hands. He passed them to the attending servant and, looking around, found a seat in the corner and sat down.

"Hmm," was the doctor's comment as he looked at the angry redness and swelling of the rounded blackness of the entry wounds.

"Let's use the strap and let the lad squeeze the boy's hands."

He handed a leather strap to Charles, who held it up so Peter could see it. Peter nodded and opened his mouth to grip it between his teeth. He reached out his hands so Will and Jamie could clasp them. The doctor lifted one of the bottles on the side table, jerked out the cork, and splashed a stream of liquid over the wounds. Peter's body jerked. He shrieked piercingly as the alcohol in the brandy reached the open wounds. Jamie and Will jerked as well as Peter gripped their hands more tightly.

The doctor reached for a long metal probe and held it over the larger of the bloody holes. He said gently, "Now, Peter, I am going tae probe fer the ball, which might have shattered the bone when ye were hit."

He worked quickly, moving the probe inside the opening while blood and fluid trickled down Peter's writhing torso to soak the sheet.

"Ah. There it is." The sweating doctor grunted. "Mister McRae, if ye will assist me."

The doctor removed the probe and reached for a pair of tongs. Jock moved alongside the doctor and placed his large hands on Peter's uninjured shoulder and left thigh. The doctor inserted the tip of the tongs into the wound. As Peter's body bucked upward,

Jock's grip tightened to hold him steady. Peter howled with pain. His head lashed from side to side while he chewed on the leather strap.

"I hae it!" panted the doctor, pulling out the tongs. He deposited the ball in a bowl, where the metal clinked against the china. He set down the tongs, picked up the bowl, and moved it into the light to peer at the impact-distorted metal.

"It is somewhat flattened, but the ball is in a single piece, praise God!" He leaned over to speak directly to Peter. "That means that no fragments broke off, my brave lad. Now, I must probe once again to ensure that there are nae bone fragments-in this wound. If I find none, then we are assured that it will heal completely." He picked up a fresh probe and, inserting it, felt around for nearly a full minute. Peter gripped the strap in his teeth and made sounds that Jamie had once heard from a badly injured dog. Finally, the doctor withdrew the probe and uttered a sigh of satisfaction.

"Nurse, please swab with mair brandy. I dinna think that we need to suture this wound. It will heal and fill in new flesh on its own."

The doctor raised his head to address Jock and the others.

"Now, we must deal with the other wound, which frightens me. The swelling, foul pus, and discolored flesh indicate infection. The wound is small, which means that the swelling hae closed it somewhat. I must open it again and cut awa' some damaged flesh. Mister McRae, ye will please hold the lad tightly." The doctor looked at Jamie and Will and smiled crookedly. "Ye are both brave boys to help Peter. Now, ye must hold tight until I say enough. Can ye do that?"

Jamie swallowed and only nodded, not trusting himself to speak.

Will nodded and whispered, "Aye, sir. I will, fer my brother's sake."

"Guid lads!" exclaimed the doctor. "Now this will be difficult fer him, I fear. Are ye ready? Grip hard now!"

The doctor worked quickly, with deft and sure movements. Using a scalpel, he shaved flesh off the ragged edge of the wound, which immediately began to bleed and ooze discolored liquid. Peter lurched, spasmed, and fainted in mid-cry.

Jock, sweating profusely, muttered, "The puir lad hae swooned, doctor."

"Excellent! Ease up a little, lads, and I will hurry. Wi' some luck, we will finish before he regains consciousness." After a few more cuts with the scalpel, he dropped it to stain the towel and picked up another instrument. "This tool holds the wound open so I can probe fer the ball." He inserted the tool and twisted it slightly. "Here, nurse. Hold the extractor in ain hand while I probe."

Jamie saw his mother's steady hand reach across to grip the tool. The doctor reached into the wound with one finger and then two. Peter stirred. Jamie hissed. "He's waking up, Doctor."

"Hold on tight! That's a guid lad!"

Peter groaned and began to writhe under their hands.

"Steady, everyone!" shouted the doctor.

Peter emitted a high-pitched shriek and then another and another.

"It's oot! Nae! Damn!" Doctor Anderson grunted. "I only hae half o' the ball and ain bone fragment. I can feel another. If I can just get a grip on it! The rest o' the ball is lodged against the hipbone. Hold tight! He's slipping."

Jamie, with sweat running into his eyes, saw his mother brace herself against Peter's side.

"Thank ye, Nurse!" muttered the doctor, his vision fixed on the wound. "I canna see weel. Someone hold the lamp o'er my head!" he called.

A servant's hand lifted another lamp and held it high. The doctor dropped the probe and picked up the tongs. Peter fainted again, and his body collapsed against the table.

The doctor hissed, "God in heaven, where is it? Ach…there it is!"

He straightened slowly and exultantly held up the tongs in one hand and two small white objects in the other. Jamie felt faint as he saw bone fragments gleaming against the light. Firmly in the grasp of the tongs was the missing fragment of the musket ball. On the doctor's open palm, dripping blood, lay the shattered fragments of bone. The doctor stood shakily for a long moment and then dropped the objects in the china bowl.

"We must work quickly now. I see the furrow where the third ball grazed the lad's shoulder. Nurse, swab it weel and bandage it. It may suppurate a wee bit, but it will heal nicely. The second wound needs irrigating with brandy, and then I will suture it securely."

He nimbly drew the needle and thread as he talked while Euphemia bound up the shoulder wound.

"When the bandages are secure, ye can move him tae a bed. He must be watched carefully because I fear that he will hae a stiff bout o' fever before he is oot of danger. He will also hae a lot o' bone pain, fer the ball hit his hipbone. That is the reason for the loose bone fragments."

Charles asked in a trembling voice, "Will my son walk again?"

The doctor took a deep breath, which he exhaled gustily. Then he smiled. "Aye, my lord. He will live, he will walk, and he will also ride again, but it might be some time. He might always limp a little tae favor that hip. For now, we must worry aboot the risk o' gangrenous fever, fer he is already shows signs o' blood poisoning, and his color is nae healthy. Prayers, rest, and nursing are the best medicines. Now, I am going tae administer a little laudanum when he awakens and leave some here wi' instructions. The medicine will assure that he sleeps while his body heals. Now, we must move on tae the other wounded." The doctor turned to Jamie and Will. He clapped them on their shoulders. "Lads, ye are indeed brave. Ye hae a muckle spirit aboot ye. Peter will thank ye forever fer yer support. A guid nicht to ye, lads. Ye may depart." He turned to Jock and said, "This is going tae be a very long nicht fer the rest o' us. Will ye stay and aid me for a wee spell?"

Jock nodded.

"And will ye nae remember the circumstances o' my afternoon dalliance? A lonely bachelor needs comfort frae time tae time."

Jock smiled hugely. "Aye, my guid physician. I believe that I hae forgotten already. I hope that yer servant can forget my uncouth Highland manners in rousting ye oot. I was unco rough wi' him. I think that he might hae difficulty chewing his food fer a few days. Ye are a marvelous physician, Doctor Anderson. Bein' close by in Crathie, ye will be essential tae the lad's recovery. I dinna doubt that the Laird o' Abergeldie will reward ye handsomely."

The doctor put his arm around Jock's shoulder and said, "I believe that my flagging strength will improve, Mister McRae, wi' a tot o' yer marvelous French brandy."

Jamie and Will dozed off curled in a large sofa while the adults worked busily to aid the doctor in treating the remaining wounded. Sadly, there was nothing that the doctor could do for two of the soldiers, who expired shortly after their arrival at Abergeldie. The servants buried them next to the grave they had already dug for William Drummond. By eleven o'clock, the last patient had been treated, his broken leg splinted, and shell fragments removed from his back and side.

Servants placed the five surviving soldiers in makeshift beds in spare rooms and took turns watching them as they slept. The doctor exhausted his meager supply of laudanum on the wounded. He promised to return the next day to check on the soldiers and bring more medications. Charles expected that they would house the soldiers only a few days before either loyalist troops would come by to capture them or Lord Ogilvy or their families would send wagons for them.

The cooks prepared a late supper for the family, servants, and Doctor Anderson. After the children had been awakened and the family assembled in the freshly cleaned dining room, Charles Gordon stood to address them. Everyone quieted instantly.

"At twelve, we will assemble tae pay our respects tae William Drummond, Viscount Strathallan, wha died at Drummossie Muir the day before yesterday. We canna perform the proper services fer the dead, but we will pay our simple respects as family and friends. He will lie in our family cemetery here at Abergeldie until Strathallan is once again free o' the military units bivouacked there and the property restored tae the Drummond family.

"Once the service is over, we can all take tae our beds fer a weel-deserved rest. Thanks tae all o' ye, our dear Peter is hame again and will recover frae his terrible injuries. Also thanks tae ye, five soldiers will live and recover, although twa did nae survive. These puir lads will also lie in our family cemetery until we can notify their families. Let us gie thanks to God Almighty fer his great providence and blessings."

Every head bowed as Charles offered a heart-felt prayer.

As they entered the barn, Euphemia held Jamie's hand as they walked slowly toward the raised casket through a double row of torches to the muffled beat of a single drum. Charles, Alison, and the Gordon children followed and joined them in the front rank. Servants, grooms, gardeners, and nearby neighbors who had heard of the viscount's funeral gathered around three sides of the bier. A piper stood in the shadows and played a dirge-like piobroch.

Charles had not had time to search out a minister, so he gave the funeral oration himself. A tearful Euphemia followed him, citing remembrances of the many good deeds of her elderly father-in-law, his love of wife and children, generosity to servants and neighbors, and final act of devotion in serving as a general in battle at the age of sixty-eight, long past the time when old warriors retired to their comfortable firesides. She broke down and wept for several minutes. Everyone waited in silence.

Jamie listened to the sizzle and occasional pop of the pine-knot torches. Finally, it was time for him to pay his respects. Holding a single white lily tightly in his fist, he climbed a wooden step to gaze down on the body of his grandfather. William Drummond lay in his general's uniform, with a Drummond tartan draped over his shoulder and mostly covering the large bloodstain on his left breast. His sword, dirk, and blue bonnet lay by his side. Draped over his waist and extending to his feet lay the blue flag of Scotland with the white cross of St. Andrew. In keeping with ancient Scottish tradition, in the center of his chest lay a porcelain dish containing earth and a quantity of salt.

Jamie gazed dry-eyed at his grandfather's calm face and white hair. His mind went back to the time when he had sat at the old man's knee, listening earnestly to his impassioned words about honor, dignity, and duty. Jamie was struck by the inescapable fact that with his father and uncles elsewhere, although he was only eight years of age, he was the only Drummond male in attendance at the service. His eyes brimmed with tears, but he realized that he had to remain calm and do his duty to his family.

Jamie laid the white lily gently by his grandfather's side. He extended a shaking hand and willed himself to place it for a moment on his cold cheek. His resolve broke. He bowed his head and sobbed. His mother's arm came around him, and he felt himself lifted off the step. She supported him back to his place in the front rank, and knelt to enfold him in her long, dark cloak until the service was over.

As they left the barn, Jamie felt a big rough hand slip over his. Looking up, he saw Jock McRae towering above him. Suddenly, the old veteran reached down to sweep him up in his strong arms.

Late the next morning, after breakfast, Euphemia and Jamie walked to the Gordon family cemetery on a low rise two hundred yards from the castle. They gazed at the three fresh mounds of turned-over earth where the Jacobite soldiers lay, two privates and a lieutenant general. The servants had erected wooden crosses inscribed with their names and dates of death burned into the wood. All three graves were strewn with lilies and whatever other spring flowers the Gordon family members could find. They stood without speaking and then walked slowly back to the castle.

When they returned, there was news, for Peter had awakened to sip some water after a restless night. Within minutes, he lapsed once again into unconsciousness. His fever rose alarmingly, and those assigned to watch him bathed his body with cool cloths while he raved and tossed. The wounds in his hip were inflamed and leaking, requiring frequent changes of dressings and sheets. On the fourth day, the fever slowly subsided and Peter experienced a brief period of coherent wakefulness. He was wasted and weak but smiled broadly as Will and Jamie sat at his bedside. Alison hovered and did not permit Peter to talk more than briefly before shooing the boys away.

"Peter will recover, and then ye can hear the tale o' his adventures, but later," she warned.

By the fifth day, three of the soldiers were well enough to rise from bed and totter around their rooms. No messenger had come from Lord Ogilvy's regiment. Word came from Braemar that the regiment had disbanded and the soldiers had dispersed. Charles arranged for a servant to write letters for the men, to be posted to their families, informing them of their circumstances and location. Charles gave the letters to a groom to carry south to their homes, as well as notices for the families of soldiers who had died. Over the next week, families with wagons arrived to take home the wounded soldiers.

On the tenth day, a loyalist officer led a squad of mounted soldiers up the road to the castle. He asked to speak to the Laird of Abergeldie. With David Lindsay and Jock McRae attending, Charles received the officer in the entry. His assembled family,

Euphemia, and Jamie sat in an adjoining room, where they could hear every detail.

The officer began, "My lord, I have an order from General Cumberland for the apprehension of all persons who had taken up arms against the crown. If there are any on the grounds or hereabouts, you must inform me so that they may be taken into custody. If they give up their arms willingly and swear the required oath, they will be treated leniently." The officer paused.

No one said anything.

The officer continued. "I have word from reliable sources that you have been harboring rebels. Would you care to explain yourself?"

Charles nodded and spoke in measured tones. "Sir, the house of Abergeldie did not take up arms against the crown. A few days ago, a troop o' Lord Ogilvy's regiment came south frae Drummossie Muir conveying many wounded. They also delivered the body of Lord William Drummond, Viscount Strathallan, since his family is scattered, but his daughter-in-law is here. She is my sister, and when the Drummond family estates were seized by the crown, the family fled where they could find shelter. She came here wi' her son. We buried Lord Drummond in our family cemetery until he can someday be peacefully interred on his own estates, God willing." Charles paused and looked steadily at the loyalist officer. "We took in seven of the most badly wounded soldiers since we hae a local physician in Crathie who treated them. Twa died, and the other five recovered sufficiently fer their families tae retrieve them."

The officer interrupted brusquely. "I will need their names and the addresses of their families. You have them, I presume?"

Charles smiled indulgently. "I had them, but I did not make copies of the letters that my servant addressed and delivered. Ye may interrogate him, but I doubt that he will recollect such details, for he is scarcely literate. But they were all frae hamlets close around Braemar. None of the surviving five soldiers will be fit tae fecht fer many months, if ever, sir."

The officer waved his hand dismissively. "May I see the graves of the others?"

Charles nodded. "Certainly, sir. I will hae Mister Lindsay escort ye tae the cemetery. Do ye intend to desecrate the graves by disinterring the bodies?"

The officer shook his head. "There is no need for such measures, my lord. However, I insist on searching the castle and outbuildings, if you do not object."

Charles smiled blandly. "No objection at all. Mister McRae, will ye provide an escort to the stables, barn, byres, and storage sheds?"

They left to conduct the search. Alison and Euphemia released their tight grips on their son's arms and audibly exhaled.

"Gae upstairs and stay wi' Peter until the soldiers are gone," commanded Alison.

The sixth of May brought rain and wind from a storm that traversed the Highlands from west to east. The setting sun shone through breaks in the cloud cover, turning the sky a rosy color. Jamie sat before an east-facing window, staring at the pink-tinged clouds as twilight came on. He saw movement under the tall pines swaying in the wind. He stared at the spot and then glimpsed the silhouette of a lone rider on a black horse approaching from the wooded hills behind the castle. He leaped to his feet and raced off to find his Uncle Charles.

Charles sat in conversation in the solar with David Lindsay. Both men turned to stare at Jamie as he called, "Uncle Charles, beggin' yer pardon fer the interruption, but there is a man on horseback approaching the castle frae the east."

Charles leaped to his feet. "Frae the east, ye say, lad, and nae frae the main road?"

Jamie nodded his head firmly. "Frae the east he comes, and alone."

Charles brushed past Jamie toward a rear entrance, closely followed by David Lindsay, who lifted a musket down from its mountings. Jamie trotted after them but stayed inside the open door to watch the rider approach the castle.

The rider responded to David Lindsay's hail. "My name is Patrick Cameron, commissioned by my clan chief, Donald Cameron, tae bring letters. I come frae Loch nan Uamh in Lochaber and hae been three days on the road, dodging loyalist patrols."

Charles extended his hand to clasp that of the rider. "Three days? Ye must be done in. Please come inside while my grooms tend tae yer mount and feed him. Ye must be famished and thirsty after sae lang on the road."

Patrick Cameron staggered slightly as he dismounted. "Ach! I am near the end o' my strength. I need food and drink, but only a few hours o' sleep before slipping awa'. I hae mair letters tae deliver tae Tullibardine before returning tae Lochaber."

David Lindsay took the reins and walked off toward the stables while calling for grooms. Jamie slid into a doorway as Charles and Patrick Cameron came up the steps to the castle. The men walked down the corridor before entering Charles Gordon's study. Charles sent a servant to find Jock McRae. When the veteran arrived, they shut the door. Jamie, always curious for news, was stymied until his mother summoned him an hour later.

When he knocked at her door, she pulled him inside. Her eyes were shining.

"Jamie, I hae news frae yer papa! He is sailing tae France until it is safe tae return hame. It may be a very lang time, but he is safe! Now, sit while I read a portion o' his letter."

Jamie sat on the edge of the chair she pulled close to the sofa. She held up a sheaf of pages and adjusted a lamp.

"'My dearest wife, Euphemia,'" she began, and her voice caught. She paused for a moment to compose herself. "'It is now the first day of May, and John and I are on board the French frigate

Bellona. We sail with the morning tide, accompanied by a second French frigate, the *Mars*. They entered the loch yesterday, and we are deathly afraid that the Royal Navy might hae spotted them sailing in the Irish Sea to this rendezvous. If they attack us before we clear the loch, it will take all the sailing and gunnery skills o' the crews tae escape. We are assured by our French compatriots that they were nae detected. The crews are busily loading as much o' our arms and supplies that we brought with us tae this place as they can before we sail. It is doubtful that we will get all aboard by morning.'"

Euphemia stopped to squeeze Jamie's hand.

"'I am sure that ye hae heard from various sources o' the terrible outcome at Culloden. Cumberland's army was hot on the heels o' our withdrawing forces and eager to invest and capture the town o' Inverness. I marched my units westward tae the barracks at Ruthven, along with George Murray's forces and others with every intention tae regroup and make a stand tae the west. When we arrived at Ruthven, we numbered o'er fifteen hundred men wi' mair coming in every hour. Many dispersed, and others went north toward Fort Augustus. We hae every hope o' welding them with us, but the Prince intervened with contrary orders. Words tae express my disappointment with the son o' King James canna pass my lips, fer the imprecations that I would shout would be vile tae speak in the hearing o' patriots. He refused tae come tae Ruthven wi' us. He escaped tae the hills north o' Inverness. Lord Elcho was sae disgusted that he exclaimed when the Prince took his leave, "There goes a damnable Italian coward!" I hae seen the Prince's personal bravery many times in the past year, but I fear that he hae run through his stock and is now quite wanting in that commodity. The Prince sent word tae the leaders at Ruthven tae disperse and shift fer themselves. Fitzhugh's Horse and the Royal Eccossois marched back tae Inverness in a body tae gie themselves up. There are sae many rumors o' Cumberland's enforcement o' nae quarter that I fear fer their safety. Lochiel was sore wounded in the battle but recovering. He is defiant and hae taken the Camerons, MacKenzies, and other western clans into the hills, vowing tae fecht on. He told me he received an overture frae Cumberland to gie himself up, but he will nae hear o' surrender. His hope is that in time, French reinforcements will come and nae leave the clans in the lurch.'"

Euphemia turned the page and adjusted the light.

"'I am sorry tae say that John suffered grievous wounds, taking four balls and some quantity o' shell fragments frae the deadly accurate loyalist artillery. A surgeon removed the metal, as much as he could extract, and stitched up the wounds. However, John contracted a vicious fever and hae tae be carried in a litter aboard the ship. The surgeon provided him laudanum to cope wi' the pain, but John is suffering frae infections that hae brought on a high fever. He passes in and oot o' delirium. I understand that the *Bellona*'s surgeon is very competent and will do his best by John. He is young and strong, and I am hopeful fer his eventual recovery tae guid health.'"

Euphemia glanced at Jamie and smiled.

"'I am concerned for Jamie in my enforced absence, but I hae every confidence, my dear wife, that with the help o' yer brother Charles and Jock McRae, ye will do everything possible tae see the lad protected and educated as befits a young gentleman. I will miss ye both terribly, my dearest wife and son.'"

Euphemia paused and struggled to speak. She wiped away the tears that kept blurring the writing. In a high-pitched voice punctuated by occasional sobs, she continued.

"'And pray every day fer our eventual reunion on our native estates. Nae one kens the mood o' Parliament and crown in this matter. The precedents o' previous risings are all we hae to gae on. In those sad and unfortunate events, reasonable men saw the need o' moderation and reconciliation fer the guid o' the nation and the peace o' the Highlands. We can only hope that when tempers cool and reason prevails, some form o' amnesty will be offered, although there might be severe financial penalties fer a season. We must wait and see how events work themselves oot. I fear that many of those taken prisoner will be dealt with harshly, though I canna believe that execution awaits them fer following their consciences. I can certainly see large numbers banished tae the American colonies. This is a favorite practice o' the Hanoverians tae put those wha threaten them oot o' the way. Since the war with France continues, I can foresee that those wi' significant military experience will be recruited to replenish the government's forces fechting the French.'"

Euphemia turned to the last page.

"'They are calling fer us tae complete our letters. A lookout saw three sails near the entrance tae the loch. The captain fears that they are a Royal Navy patrol. I must finish quickly and put this in the hands o' the Cameron men wha accompanied us aboard tae take our letters. We must leave the remainder o' our stores on the shore and flee.'"

Euphemia looked at Jamie with a stricken face. "That is all. He signs the letter but leaves us in suspense aboot the outcome."

Her face crumpled, and she began to cry, flinging the letter on the low table and covering her face. Some of the sheets of the letter floated to the floor. Jamie bent to pick them up and arrange them. He put them carefully on the table. Sitting down on the sofa next to his mother, he wrapped his arms tightly around her.

They heard a tentative knock on the door. Jamie slipped off the sofa and reached for the knob. Euphemia raised her tear-streaked face.

"Should I open it, Mama?"

After the third knock, she nodded. Jamie twisted the knob and pulled on the door. Charles inserted a hand into the gap and peered at his sister.

"I am sorry tae disturb ye while ye are in such a state, Euphemia, but I hae been interviewing Patrick Cameron, wha brought the letter. He must depart soon, but wishes tae gie ye a message o' hope. Will ye come tae my study tae speak wi' him?"

Euphemia straightened at his use of the word *hope*.

"Aye. Weel. Gie me a moment tae restore my face."

When she was ready, she turned to Jamie. "Stay here. I will come back wi' whate'er news he gi'es tae me." She followed Charles downstairs.

After his mother left him, Jamie watched the large clock in the corner and occupied himself with counting the swings of the pendulum. Sometime after five hundred, he must have dozed, for he was startled into wakefulness when his mother threw open the door.

"Guid news, Jamie, my lad!" In her excitement, she extended her hands to grab his. She pulled him off the sofa and swung him around in a crazy jig. "Yer papa got awa' frae the English! Patrick Cameron was watching frae the shore. There were three Royal Navy ships attacking the twa French frigates. The ships sailed back and forth in the narrow loch, firing broadsides at each other fer six hours. The English ships withdrew tae make repairs, and the French sailed awa'. Unless mair English ships intercept them, they are safe! Patrick Cameron also said that the rebels left six casks o' gold coin on the shore. Much o' that is making its way tae Lochiel tae continue the fechting and feed the men, though gold tends tae slip through fingers and fall into thieving men's pockets."

☙

After the fever and pain of his injuries subsided, Peter mended rapidly. Within two weeks, he was able to sit up. The carpenter improvised a wheeled chair so Peter could leave his bed. The servants carried his chair downstairs, and Will and Jamie took turns wheeling Peter around the garden to enjoy the spring sunshine.

On a warm day in late May, Jamie and Will lounged on the lawn on either side of Peter's chair. Alison accompanied a servant, who brought a lunch hamper and large jug of cold cider to the boys. Excusing the servant, she spread a colored cloth on a small table and laid out plates of cold fowl, pots of farmer's cheese, bread, some of the last apples from the barrels in the basement, and large wedges of cake.

Jamie pulled Peter's chair close to the table. Alison took a seat next to her son and helped him load his plate. For a while, they ate in greedy silence. Finally, the last of the cake disappeared. On a signal from Peter, all three boys belched in unison.

Alison waved her hands and giggled. "If ye insist on bein' boys and makin' sech rude sounds, then I will return tae the castle. I hae many things tae do."

Will and Jamie helped her fill the hamper with the plates and remains of the lunch. They offered to carry the hamper back, but she insisted that they stay with Peter. When his mother disappeared, Peter began to talk.

"Will, before Mama came wi' lunch, ye were asking aboot my recollections o' the battle. Papa is still upset because I ran awa' and will nae ask me any questions. He is sae disappointed in me. I canna talk wi' him aboot it. Perhaps sometime soon I can, but nae now." He sighed and looked at the snow-capped mountains looming over Abergeldie. "It seemed sae simple and glorious tae fecht fer the cause. I learned that I was lucky to get tae Nairn and find the army without running into ain o' the numerous loyalist patrols ranging south frae Cumberland's army. I rode to tae the camp where Lord Murray's army was bivouacked. The sentinels intercepted me and led me tae his headquarters. I asked how tae find General Drummond. Lord Murray directed a junior officer to escort me. At first, he wanted tae send me hame, but seeing as I was firm in wanting tae serve, he assigned me courier duties, but would nae arm me. He said that it was fer my protection, in case I was captured. If I was unarmed, the loyalists would not treat me as a combatant. I rode wi' yer grandfather and his staff officers, Jamie, except when I carried messages. I found it odd that the

Prince was seldom involved in councils o' war. Those councils were unco heated affairs, wi' officers shouting and threatening each other. The evening before the battle at Drummossie Muir, the council decided tae hae the army make a nicht march tae surprise Cumberland's army at Nairn. The troops were already dead tired. The officers couldna make up their minds which way tae gae or wha would gae which way. Finally, at a late hour, they called off the attack, believing that the loyalists were expecting them. So they ordered the troops back tae Drummossie Muir after marching all nicht, where they almost fell down they were sae exhausted. The army formed up in the morning. We were on the left wi' the MacDonalds. We waited a long time in the drizzling rain 'til everyone was soaked. It was cold and windy. When the loyalists formed up across the muir, the ground was sae muddy that it was hard for the Highlanders tae charge in their customary way, but they tried again and again and paid a heavy price. The enemy guns and artillery cut them doon before they could even reach their lines." He stopped and swiped at the tears streaking his cheeks.

Jamie said softly, "Peter, dinna tell the story if it is sae hard fer ye."

"I must tell the tale, lads. I will remember those puir soldiers all the days o' my life. They knew they were losing and that they were going tae die, but they fought on as long as they were able. I saw sech bravery and sacrifice, foolish sacrifice fer honor's sake. I saw yer grandfather raise the banner o' the MacDonalds and urge them onward. They charged, were pushed back, and regrouped. Shouting, 'Claymore! Claymore!', they raised their broadswords and charged again. I was crouched doon with a small group o' officers when I saw General Drummond get shot in the chest. He fell backward and spun around, taking another ball. He was on his knees, trying tae get up, when twa mair balls hit him and he fell over onto his back. I leaped up and ran toward him but stumbled and fell down. It was safer tae crawl, and I did until I reached him. I tried tae cover his body wi' mine. Then something hit me like I was stabbed. It felt like fire burning in my hip. I dinna feel the ball crease my shoulder. Twa o' the MacDonalds crawled tae me and pulled me off the General's body. He was gasping and bleeding. I saw Colonel Sullivan squatting down next tae him. Then I lost consciousness. I woke up frae time tae time, but my memory is blurry after that. I remember waking while being carried in a wagon, lying in deep hay. I saw Jock McRae's face, and then I was lying on the dining room table."

Peter stretched out his hands and gripped Will's and Jamie's fiercely. With his voice breaking, he told them, "Ye are the best friends in the world. I know I'll recover and walk again wi' yer help."

Will cut in softly, "And ride afore summer is o'er."

Jamie looked at Peter and grinned. "We weel do mair than that, Peter. We are goin' up tae Lachin-y-Gair together, all three o' us, before winter."

Peter laughed until tears ran. Will and Jamie joined in, wringing Peter's hands tightly.

Peter's voice cracked as he told them, "I know we will. Naething can stop the three o' us."

Chapter Eight

By early July, when Lord Ogilvy disbanded his regiment, districts around Abergeldie returned to the peace they had enjoyed before the rising. The Duke of Cumberland's administration that was so punitive in Lochaber, northern Argyll, and the Great Glen was much more lenient in Badenoch, Mar, Perth, and Aberdeen. Yet it still raised resentment at how unjustly it was conducted. Charles Gordon rode weekly to the village of Crathie to collect news of events roiling the Highlands. He returned from one such trip and, at supper, expressed his opinion of events in vehement terms.

"The Duke o' Cumberland is being replaced soon by Lord Albemarle. Cumberland is returning tae the continent to fecht the French. Many regulars are taking ship tae replenish British forces in Flanders. Others are being withdrawn tae restore garrisons at Forts William, Augustus, and George along the Great Glen. Cumberland hae empowered the Highland Independent Companies tae pacify the countryside by whatever means they choose. Those men are mostly scum, violent townsmen, and riff-raff wi' little leadership, but they hae guns and the crown's authority. There are reports of punitive raids mostly in the west and north, evicting and imprisoning tenants suspected of hiding arms, torching their hames, confiscating cattle, and shooting or hanging anyone caught under arms. There is an ugly rumor that the soldiers split the proceeds frae the sale o' twenty thousand head o' such confiscated cattle while the rightfu' owners hae been left impoverished. No one expects the change in military command tae alter the ferocity o' the measures that Cumberland hae put in place to pacify the Highlands. Cumberland is punishing the entire population fer the acts o' the rebels. I fear the worst is nae yet o'er and mair punitive measures are tae come."

Alison Gordon raised her head and stared at her husband. "Please try tae calm yerself, Charles, and eat before the food gets cold."

Charles ignored her. "There is news frae Lochaber o' Donald Cameron dispersing the last rebel army wi'out offering resistance. However, his defiance o' overtures o' the Duke o' Cumberland tae come tae the king's peace means that Albemarle plans vengeance on all the western clans. Lochiel and his lieutenants hae fled tae France. The violence o' the Highland Independent Companies will fall on the heads o' innocent clansmen and their families." He stopped, fork in hand, and stared at his plate.

After a long moment of silence, he set down the fork and pushed the plate away. Jamie looked at Will and then at Peter, who slowly shook his head, his eyes on his father's face.

Charles sighed and said, "'Tis hard tae be eating meat when sae many are starving and without hames."

Alison said softly, "And what can we do, Charles?"

He chewed his lip before answering. "I fear, my dear, that there is little we can do without bringing down the wrath o' the government on our heads. But if these confiscations and reprisals dinna stop, there will be starvation or perhaps worse in the western Highlands by winter. Some of us who did not take up arms, with the help o' the clergy, could perhaps persuade Lord Albemarle to allow shipments o' meal and meat tae the affected areas. I will talk tae some of the lairds, but I fear that the government is intractable."

One morning, a servant reported that a small oaken cask had been found close to the entry of the castle, with "Lady Euphemia Drummond" inscribed on a fragment of parchment nailed to the lid. The servants left the cask untouched and notified Charles Gordon. Within minutes, David Lindsay, Jock McRae, and Euphemia had joined him in a circle around the cask. The children, burning with curiosity, huddled at the top of the stairs to watch.

"What do ye make o' it, gentlemen?" Charles inquired.

Jock knelt and picked up the cask. "'Tis heavy, which means that it is full o' something." He shook it gently.

Everyone heard a distinct gurgle.

Jock mused, "Indeed, a mystery. The markings on the cask signify that it contains French cognac, an excellent gift frae an admirer, Lady Drummond. Perhaps it fell off a ship and rolled its way here tae Abergeldie."

Euphemia giggled. "A feeble jest, Mister McRae. Someone who did nae wish tae be seen or answer questions brought it here last nicht. The watch should hae seen him but was clearly inattentive. But why cognac and why addressed tae me?"

Jock looked at Charles speculatively. "This mystery is reminiscent o' the technique used by followers o' Mary, Queen o' Scots, tae smuggle letters when she was imprisoned by Queen Elizabeth. I suggest, my lord, that we investigate the contents. Hae a servant tap the cask and decant the contents into glass bottles until the cask is empty and then take it apart carefully. I believe that we might discover another container. That container, I expect, we will find tae be sealed wi' a letter inside."

Charles scowled darkly and turned to Euphemia. "Sister, did ye hae any foreknowledge o' this?"

She turned red and retorted, "Fie, Charles! How could I?"

Charles scowled again. "I am familiar wi' circumstances o' yer husband's departure and probable whereabouts, dear sister, but I do nae like this skullduggery. If discovered by an agent o' this government, it could put our whole family in grave danger. What would we do if a Highland Independent Company comes here some day, dispossesses us, confiscates our stock, and burns down our hame? We must find a way tae discourage the sender."

He turned to Jock. "Get the cask open and confirm whether it contains a letter. Then bring it tae me."

Euphemia swung to face him. "The cask is addressed tae me, brother. I will read the letter, sir, not ye!"

She and Charles angrily faced each other.

Charles said softly, "Do not gainsay me in a matter that brings danger tae my family as weel as yers. I will agree tae desist, sister, if ye read the letter in my presence and out loud except fer personal and private matters."

Euphemia stared impassively into her brother's rigid face. At last, she nodded. Charles continued, but his voice took on a pleading tone.

"Sister, we canna hae mair o' these secret deliveries. If the letter is frae James, ye must find a way tae send him a message tae ne'er send another."

"I agree," she responded. "Let us discover whether there is a letter, and then we can consider what must be done."

Within a few minutes, Jock brought back a basket holding six bottles of an excellent quality of cognac and a flat metal disk the size of an oat cake and about as thick. He laid the disk on the desk in Charles's study. Charles hefted it and turned it over in his hands, peering at the edges. He passed it back to Jock, who attacked it with his dirk. By prying up the lid all around, he broke a wax seal. Peeling it back revealed a packet of thin parchment inside. Jock handed the parchment to Euphemia, who slowly unfolded it while looking intently at her brother. Jock made to leave, but Charles and Euphemia told him in unison to stay.

"Unless, Mister McRae, ye dinna wish to be a partner in this conspiracy…"

"I will stay, Lady Drummond," he rumbled. "I already hae done enough tae inflame the loyalists against me, except bear arms."

Euphemia smiled and spread out the letter, which proved to be four pages of script written in a precise hand.

"At least it is not encoded," said Charles with a sigh. "If it were and we were caught wi' it in our possession, that itself could condemn us, nae matter the contents."

After a few moments to quickly preview the letter, Euphemia began to read it aloud.

"It is frae James, as we suspected."

The bulk of the letter was about the battle in the loch, the French ship's narrow escape, and their voyage to Brest on the French coast. They had spent much time evading Royal Navy patrols in the Irish Sea and the Atlantic. James reported that his brother John had died of his wounds in mid voyage, after much suffering.

Euphemia looked up with tears brimming in her eyes. In a cracking voice, she sobbed, "He was not yet twenty-one years o' age."

Charles crossed himself but said nothing.

His sister continued reading. "The crew preserved his remains in a large cask until the end of the trip. I had him buried in the town cemetery in Brest."

James went on to name the other rebels who had taken ship with him. One man, John Daniels by name, had been killed by cannon fire during the fight inside the loch. He was buried alongside John Drummond. No one seemed to know the whereabouts of Bonnie Prince Charlie, who hae gone to ground somewhere in the Highland hills or the Hebrides. The letter ended with James's concern for his family and speculation on how long it might be before he dared return to Scotland. He said that on another piece of parchment was written the names and addresses of two reliable Jacobite agents who would see to it that return letters would reach him in France. Euphemia set down the letter. Charles held up his hand.

"Please stop. I dinna wish tae hear the names o' the gentlemen or their locations. I insist, dear sister, that ye send James a letter immediately to ne'er send another giftie o' cognac, brandy, Bordeaux, or anything else tae Abergeldie, nor a letter, coded or otherwise. If ye wish tae correspond wi' him, and I daresay that ye do, then arrange messages through those agents on yer own. They are ne'er tae come here. If ye travel tae ain o' the agents, ye must take care that ye are nae followed there or back."

Euphemia set down the letter and took her brother's hands. "Charles, look at me please. I will do naething tae endanger ye or yer sweet family. I could nae bear it. Perhaps it would be better fer me tae gae awa' and take Jamie somewhere else."

He said softly, "Ye are family and hae a place here. But we must think ahead. I wish ye tae investigate possibilities. Ye should look at Aberdeen or Perth or even, God forbid, Inverness, a sorry uncivilized place. But ye shouldna do anything precipitous. That alone might draw unwelcome attention."

She drew her dark brows together for a long moment and then nodded.

Jock spoke up. "I hae twa suggestions, Lady Drummond. Ye should memorize the agent names and locations and then burn this letter. Another suggestion is that we toast the health and guid taste o' my Lord Strathallan in this fine Hennessey cognac."

※

The fifth of August was hot and humid in Abergeldie. In midafternoon, thunderheads formed over the Cairngorms and threatened rain. Jamie read aloud from his birthday gift, William Hamilton's *The Life and Heroick Actions of the Renoun'd Sir William Wallace, General and Governour of Scotland*, while Will and Peter sat with him in the shade of the garden.

A visibly angry Euphemia Drummond stalked after her brother Charles along one of the garden paths, brushing past the boys. Jamie stopped reading and stared after his mother. She stopped suddenly and spun to face her brother. "Tell me mair about this Act of Proscription," she shouted, "forced upon us by that damnable Parliament in London!"

Charles stopped. "Euphemia, if ye please," he said placatingly. "I was merely reporting the news, not creating it. Please calm yerself and I will continue."

Euphemia crossed her arms and stood rigidly facing him. "Then proceed, sir, and I will do everything in my power tae remain calm." She said the last word with considerable emphasis. Charles leaned back against the smooth bark of a tree.

"It is primarily a restatement of the Disarming Act, which penalizes the bearing and possession o' arms with fines, jail, and ultimately transportation tae the colonies. However, there are new provisions that are troubling, fer they appear aimed only at destroying the Celtic culture o' the Highlands and nae tae preserving the peace."

He glanced down at the paper in his hand. He read slowly while the paper fluttered in the light breeze. "'No man or boy within that part of Britain called Scotland, other than such as shall be employed as officers and soldiers in His Majesty's forces, shall, on any pretext whatever, wear or put on the clothes commonly called Highland clothes—that is to say, the plaid, philabeg, or little kilt, trowse, shoulder-belts, or any part whatever o' what peculiarly belongs tae the Highland garb; and that nae tartan or parti-coloured plaid o' stuff shall be used for great coats or upper coats, and if any such person shall presume after the said first day of August tae wear or put on the aforesaid garment or any part of them…'"

"Exactly so," fumed Euphemia, her voice rising with every word. "Imprisonment without bail for six months and liable tae be transported on conviction for a second offence for wearing traditional Highland garb? Why nae lesser penalties allowed? Why should such acts be accounted criminal at all?"

Charles continued to stare at the paper. "It is not stated specifically in the act," he continued in even tones, "but those with whom I spoke in Crathie believe that it also prohibits the playing o' bagpipes, unauthorized gatherings, and teaching o' the Gaelic language."

"How so?" questioned Euphemia sarcastically. "Pray tell what logic dictates that such things ought tae be banned? Why is this group of legislative fools nae the laughing stock o' all Europe?"

"Because, dear sister, the act states 'any part whatsoever o' what peculiarly belongs to the Highland garb.' *Whatsoever* covers anything they wish."

"And our children must pray fer them?" she responded with derision. "Those who now enslave us?"

"Aye," said Charles in bitter tones. "The act requires measures tae prevent children frae being 'educated in disaffected or rebellious principles,' including prescribing daily school prayers for the king and royal family."

"They believe that such measures will stamp oot the spirit o' disaffection and rebellion that still smoulders in these Highlands? Why, they will fan it into a flame that will eventually devour them. Oh, Charles! What can we do? Must we flee our own country?"

Charles stood very still and finally said in a low voice, "We must outwardly comply tae protect ourselves and our children but cherish our hopes and beliefs secretly fer as long as necessary. God help us, but they are making hypocrites o' us all."

Euphemia glanced at the three boys seated on the shaded bench under the willows. "Aye," she said in a resigned tone. "Sae be it. We will be as the children o' Israel, bending but ne'er breaking, though they multiply our afflictions seven times seventy. Our children will see this monstrous tyranny fall, and great shall be fall thereof." In a choked voice, she sobbed, "I pray that our children see such a day, fer we surely shall ne'er see it." She turned on her heel to return indoors.

Charles stood uncertainly for a moment and then followed her.

Peter looked up at the tree overhead and asked a question that neither of his companions chose to answer. "Children of Israel?

Where will we find a Joshua tae lead us tae march seven times around London sae that God can make the walls fall doon, and London Bridge, fer that matter?"

︎⁂︎

It was a long time after the event when the news finally reached Abergeldie that Bonnie Prince Charlie had escaped the net that Lord Cumberland had drawn tightly around the Highlands of Scotland. Although the government had posted a massive bounty, no one would turn in the royal Prince.

Charles had brought the news that morning of how intrepid Flora, a MacDonald lass on the Isle of Skye, was lodged in the Tower of London for disguising the Prince as her serving girl and guiding him to where a French ship had taken him to safety.

Not so happy was the news of the Act of Attainder, which dispossessed named rebels of their titles, lands, and revenues. The Drummonds had been impoverished by royal decree except for what valuables they had in their possession. Euphemia put her arm protectively around Jamie and thought of the meager stack of gold coins that she had brought on her flight from Strathallan. She wondered if it would be enough to enable them to live in reasonable comfort and security, provide for Jamie's education, and enable her to send small amounts to James in France.

︎⁂︎

The grassy sward stretching down from the castle to the river sparkled with dew. The canopies of trees had already turned from green to russet, although leaves had not yet begun to fall.

Jamie expertly turned his mount onto a side trail where a weathered signpost pointed to Littlemill. Peter and Will rode on either side. Euphemia and Emilia led at a slow trot. Bringing up the rear were Jock McRae and David Lindsay, both of whom had decided that they would enjoy the climb, although their reason for coming was to provide security, along with grooms who would set up camp and tend the horses while the party climbed the remainder of the trail.

Jamie was confident that Peter was ready for the long-promised outing. He had trained nearly all summer with stern resolve, conditioning his body and restoring his abilities to ride and hike, following the serious gunshot wounds and infection that had almost claimed his life in April. Peter walked with only a slight trace of a limp when tired. He could mount and dismount a horse without aid, although he still felt some pain where the ball had torn away several chips of the hipbone. The ride and hike to Lachin-y-Gair would be proof to himself and others that he was fully recovered.

Jamie watched his mother riding ahead of him, wearing a garish red jacket, tan trews, and riding boots. In spite of protests that she was too old to ride as she had done as a girl, she had prepared herself by taking numerous short rides with Emilia, who had come to Abergeldie for the summer. Euphemia now rode with effortless smoothness, her slim body rising and falling to match her horse's gait.

Jamie jumped slightly as he felt rather than saw Jock McRae pull up abruptly on his left. His mount reacted by veering slightly toward the center of the road to make room for Jock's overtaking horse. As he came abreast, Jock looked at Peter questioningly. Peter grinned, and Jock nodded in approval.

"Ye look verra fine, lad. Do ye like yer mount? Is she a smooth ride?"

Peter transferred his reins to one hand and raised the other in a fist, which he pumped in the air.

"I take that gesture as an 'aye'," Jock said gruffly. Flicking his reins and digging in a spur, he galloped forward until he came abreast of the women and then matched their pace.

Will and Jamie moved closer to listen to Peter describe what they could expect on their ride and trek up to Lachin-y-Gair.

They came out of the woods in Glenmuik and turned onto the twisting trail up the Muick. They stopped briefly at Birkhaugh to water the horses and adjust girths and harnesses. The air grew warmer as the sun climbed the cloudless sky and dried the morning dew. Jamie walked to the edge of the clearing to stare at the tumbled ruin of an old castle. His mother followed and stood by him.

"Jamie, this valley o' the Dee and Muick hae an auld and turbulent history. The great king Malcolm Canmore camped near here before going on tae defeat the usurper Macbeth." She pointed up the rock-strewn hillside.

"Those are the ruins o' Knock Castle. My family, the Abergeldie Gordons, built it aboot a hundred and fifty years ago. It had a fine view o' the surrounding mountains and glens, but it was abandoned tae the elements because o' a tragic and violent event. There came a day on which the seven sons of Alexander Gordon were working here, supervising men casting peats, when they were set upon and slain by a raiding party o' Forbeses. When Alexander heard the news about his dead sons, he collapsed and fell down the stairs of the castle. He died, and the leader of the Forbes was beheaded, but nae before the Gordons sought and found vengeance and were despoiled themselves, their byres and hames burned doon around their heads. Many died on both sides before the feud burned itself oot. Our relations with the Forbes family hae always been uneasy."

"But, Mama, the Gordon family tutor is Oliver Forbes. He dinna seem bloodthirsty."

"He and my brother are both peaceable men wha dinna hold with auld grudges. Perhaps someday Charles will rebuild Knock castle."

They returned to the group and remounted. That late in the season, they encountered no other riders and only a few farmers hauling hay down from the upper meadows. The riders climbed steadily, their pace slowed to a steady plod to avoid tiring the horses. The Muick, which had been a slow-moving stream at Birkhall, from which they had watered their horses, was rushing noisily over the rocky bed in tumbled rapids. As the sun reached the zenith, they arrived at the Spittal of Glenmuick and led the horses into a grassy glen where David Lindsay, who had ridden ahead, greeted them at the campsite he had selected.

The group dismounted, staked their horses to graze, unsaddled them, and hung nosebags of oats about their necks. The horses whuffled softly and began eating. The grooms took leather buckets down to the stream and struggled back with them full and slopping. Jamie and Will helped by sharing out water to the horses. Euphemia and Emilia spread a large cloth and set out cold meat, cheese, bread, and other elements of their lunch along with jugs of cider and beer.

As they ate, David Lindsay said around a huge sandwich, "It is about a two-hour brisk walk tae Lachin-y-Gair and a mite less back. It is all downhill coming back, ye ken. If we leave soon, we should hae plenty o' time at the loch and still be back here before the sun sets. The grooms will hae the tents set up and supper bubbling in the pot. All we need carry up wi' us is water. Tomorrow, we will leave the camp at dawn and be back in Abergeldie in time fer lunch tomorrow."

Euphemia gazed at Peter with a questioning look. He responded, "I took a quick walk aboot, and my rump feels wonderful, Aunt Euphemia. Let's hurry and start."

Everyone laughed as Jamie and Will pelted Peter with morsels of bread.

Jamie was grateful for his sturdy walking stick as they progressed through the upper reaches of the forest. The mingled smells of balsam, pine, and cedar were redolent. They emerged from the trees and paused to look to where the rock-studded trail snaked up the steep slope in a series of daunting switchbacks. Taking a deep breath, Jamie challenged Will to be first to the top. The boys scrambled upward and were soon out of sight of the others.

Jamie's first view of the dark loch nestled in the hollow between soaring crags was from a doubled-over position, gasping to get his breath after racing Will up the harrowing switchbacks. When he could get enough air into his lungs, he straightened to gaze to where Will was pointing. A small herd of dun-colored white-tailed deer stood halfway to the loch, ears extended, tails switching, and looking directly at them. The boys stood as still as possible, but the others coming up the trail, unaware of the presence of the deer, were making a lot of noise. Spooked, the deer bounded away downhill in long, graceful leaps.

The mid-afternoon sun was well past halfway to the horizon, and shadows were lengthening in the volcanic bowl girdling the loch, which reflected the craggy summits and brooding cliffs in its glittering dark blue waters.

Peter was next to gain the summit, with Emilia on his arm. He whooped with delight and started down immediately. Peter was grimacing and limping noticeably. The group reached the pines and flopped down to rest. Euphemia remained standing to point out landmarks.

"See there." She pointed. "That mountain takes its name frae Lachin-y-Gair, 'the little loch o' the noisy sound.' Frae Crathie, the mountain is often in shadow and takes on a brooding appearance while here we are in brilliant sunshine." She took in a deep breath and let it out gustily. "I could easily see poets contending to provide the most appropriate description o' this lovely place."

Jamie, Will, and Peter applauded. Euphemia turned pink. Emilia took her hand, and they raced down to the loch's edge to dip their feet in the cold water. Jamie and Will urged Peter to follow, but he shook his head.

"Lads, it was all I could do tae get here, and I still hae tae walk back."

Will and Jamie sat down by his side. "Then we'll stay wi' ye, Peter."

Peter hugged them close and said in a low voice, "Thank ye both. It was our plan tae come here together, and we'll make it back together, assuming the pain dinna kill me."

Jamie suggested, "Mister Lindsay and Jock could carry ye back."

Peter grimaced. "I'd rather suffer any amount o' pain and make it on my own than be carried. But I would'na mind leaning on yer arm once in a while."

※

Winter came early to the glens of the Cairngorms, with late October gales and drifting snow choking the roads. Communication with the outside world became sporadic. One morning, Jamie was delighted with a story that his Uncle Charles read from his week-old newspaper at the breakfast table.

"'Two men report frae aboot Strathfillan, that they apprehended twa Highlanders in kilts and were bringing them to Loch Rannoch, but in passing near the village of Clifton, the inhabitants, mostly women, got hold o' ain o' the soldiers, and the prisoner made his escape. The other soldier wi' the man he had taken got some miles farther on his way, when the inhabitants o' another village, assisted by twa disbanded Highlanders, armed with cudgels, rescued the other. The disbanded Highland soldiers were extremely abusive and insolent and threatened the soldier verra much, wha hae only his side arms if ever he molested their neighbors again.'"

"That was frae July," remarked Euphemia, putting down her cup and reading over his shoulder. "I wonder how many other incidents hae taken place. I would think that no government troops will be comfortable traveling anywhere in the Highlands except in groups of ten or mair fer self-protection until this accursed act is revoked." She took up her cup with trembling fingers.

Peter looked up and broke the silence.

> Mourn, hapless Caledonia, mourn.
> Thy banish'd peace, thy laurels torn!
> Thy sons, fer valour long renown'd,
> Lie slaughter'd on their native ground;
> Thy hospitable roofs nae mair
> Invite the stranger tae the door;
> In smoky ruins sunk they lie,
> The monuments o' cruelty.

Charles looked up and folded his newspaper. "Where did ye learn that verse?"

"It is frae a poem published this year by Tobias Smollett, entitled 'The Tears o' Scotland.' I bought it off a student visiting Crathie frae Aberdeen."

Euphemia's grey eyes looked at Peter over her cup. She said softly, "And so the resistance tae this tyranny spreads. Ye must take care, Peter, lest a soldier find ye with such seditious literature. I dinna wish to rescue ye with a cudgel in my hands, but I would."

Exasperated, Charles rapped the newspaper on the table. "My son, I wish ye tae bring nae mair such writings here." He put his hands to his temples and rubbed them. "We canna hae soldiers searching our hame."

Peter grinned at his father, who scowled darkly. "The pamphlet is weel-secreted and not in the castle, so ye can rest mair easily, Father."

∾

Hogmanay was a family affair, with the turning of the New Year, 1747. In late February, a letter came to Euphemia from Lady Margaret Drummond. The government authorities had discharged her from what she described wryly as her "comfortable captivity" in the brooding gray castle high on the rocky craig above Edinburgh. Dispossessed and reduced to financial gifts from family members, she had elected to take a small suite of rooms in nearby Dunfermline in Fife. The letter was dripping with cynicism, but Lady Margaret was determined to survive as she could until she could repossess her home. Clementine had already joined her mother and brought what clothing and other personal possessions of her mother's she had managed to take from Strathallan. Lady Margaret desired Euphemia to visit and bring Emilia.

Jamie begged to accompany Emilia and his mother to Edinburgh. She finally consented and arranged for his absence with Oliver Forbes. The tutor loaded down the lad with books and assignments. Jamie also brought his precious copy of Blind Harry's Wallace, although he was now engaged in his second reading of the book, having completed a vocal reading with Peter and Will before Christmas. The book had a strange power over his mind to transport him in time and space to that age of noble deeds.

The weather did not cooperate until early March, and the journey still required three days of bouncing, jolting, and sliding on the rutted and miry roads and two nights in cramped and dirty accommodations with badly cooked meals in post houses along the route.

The reunion with his grandmother was joyous. Her health had recovered somewhat after her confinement, and she hugged Jamie tightly, leaking tears onto his cheek. They settled down before a crackling fire in a room that smelled of French lavender. After embracing Emilia and Euphemia, Lady Margaret settled herself in a large chair.

In a high and querulous voice, she said, "Hae ye heard how Cumberland's evil men abused my property?" She crossed her thin arms and shook her head sadly. In a choked voice, she said, "They stabled their horses in my beautiful courtyard and gardens. Horse dung in my roses! It will take years of cleansing tae remove the Hanoverian stink! They neglected the greenhouse, and all my lovely tropical garden is dead!" She wept quietly for a while and then sniffed loudly as she slowly recovered her composure. "If I must live until I am a hundred years auld, I will restore my home and outlive that fat little Duke and the repulsive German lairdie wha calls himself a king."

Euphemia confided that James had sent a letter in a cask of cognac and that she had the names of two Jacobite agents who would convey letters for her. Lady Margaret reached for a Bible and extracted a lengthy letter, begging Euphemia to send it to James.

Euphemia leaned forward. "Mother, I am going to confide in ye. There are spies and informants all o'er the Highlands. Patrols accost families in the middle of the night to search their hames for Jacobites and arms. I want so much tae communicate wi' James, but I canna endanger my brother, Charles, and sister-in-law, Alison. If James makes a clandestine visit tae Scotland, he canna come tae Abergeldie. I must leave soon and find another place for myself and Jamie."

Lady Margaret waved her hand. "Neither must ye gae anywhere near other Drummonds. Ye must gae tae some town or city where people come and gae frequently. Why not close tae where ain o' the Jacobite agents lives but not too close?"

Euphemia chewed her lower lip for a moment before answering. "That limits the choices tae Dumfries in the southwest or Inverness."

"Inverness? That muddy, disreputable cattle town by Loch Ness? It is right under the noses of the garrison at Fort George!"

Euphemia smiled conspiratorially. "Aye, Mother, right under their noses. I would much prefer lovely places such as St. Andrew's, Aberdeen, or Perth. But Inverness seems tae be my safest alternative. In the spring, I will undertake a search fer suitable lodging and schooling fer Jamie."

"No need tae make the search alain. Ye hae a Drummond of close relation living in Inverness wha can help ye. William's brother's son lives there, a barrister by the name o' Hugh, now well established in the town. Let us compose a letter tae enlist his aid. It will save ye a world o' traipsing around in the mud. As yer agent, he can find prospective accommodations and arrange all details o' a lease. With a house in Inverness, ye can still visit yer brother in Abergeldie at any time ye wish, wi'out the risk o' compromising his family's safety."

Euphemia smiled and hugged her mother-in-law tightly.

In late April, Charles brought news that the government's persecution of captured rebel officers had reached a peak. Simon Fraser, Lord Lovat, although already above the age of eighty years and sick with arthritis and gout, had been forced to mount the scaffold in London to be beheaded. His tarred head rested on a spike over London Bridge.

Eighty-three rebel leaders had been executed and over a thousand transported to the Indies to slave on the sugar plantations, where brutal conditions and disease made their demise only somewhat lengthier than the trip to the scaffold. A like number was transported to the Carolinas, where disease was not as prevalent.

Charles expressed hope that the worst of the persecution was over. Euphemia bit her lip, for she could not agree.

※

Jamie sat with Jock McRae on a stone bench in the wan spring sunlight in the center of the garden.

Jamie was disconsolate. His mother had brought the news that negotiations were complete. Cousin Hugh Drummond had signed a lease for a house in Nairn, near Inverness, and they would be moving in early June.

"I will miss this garden; my best friends, Will and Peter; and riding in the mountain glens. I will miss ye the most, Jock McRae." The boy's face was taut as he struggled not to weep.

"Ach, laddie. Change is part of life and growing. Ye should be welcoming it with nae regrets. Ye will hae new experiences, and sae will they. Ye are still cousins and share the same blood. Ye will see each other again many times. Arter all, Peter will be leaving for university in the fall."

"And what will ye do, Master McRae? Strathallan is still in government hands. Abergeldie hae nae need fer a master of arms. Will ye return tae the foreign wars?"

Jock sat whittling a small piece of wood. He stared at it as he carved off small chunks. Finally, he put the knife back in his boot, tossed away the stick, and slapped his rough hands on his knees.

"When I was young, I treasured my freedom, lad. I dinna want a lass encumbering me. Now that my hair is nae longer dark but grey and the cold creeps into my bones on winter nichts, I think that perhaps I dinna make the right choices when I was younger. I hae nae hame tae return tae. Perhaps my only choice is tae find a position as a forester on some laird's estate. I hae never minded the loneliness o' that life, but now…I canna think it pleasurable."

Jamie touched the old veteran's gnarled hand. "Why not find Maggie McLeod and tell her what ye really feel fer her?"

Jock slowly turned to look at Jamie in astonishment. "What did ye say, lad?"

"I said why not find Maggie McLeod and tell her ye love her? I could see last spring that ye still do."

Jock waved his left hand dismissively. "Ach. 'Tis far too late fer that, laddie. Love is fer the young."

"'Tis ne'er too late. Ye told me that yerself, that I could only fail when I gave up trying. Besides, my grandpa loved my grandma, and he was much aulder than ye. My grandma says that true love lasts forever."

Jock looked down at Jamie with a soft light in his eyes. "Yer grandma is a very wise woman, Jamie Drummond. Fer nine years auld, yer words hae muckle power tae penetrate a lonely man's heart. Ye are wise beyond yer years, laddie. But I fear that time hae taken a sad toll on both Maggie and me."

"Why not seek her oot and ask her? Perhaps she dinna think it too late," Jamie said softly. He put his hand over Jock's and squeezed tightly.

They sat silently for a long time. Suddenly, Jock sniffed loudly. Taking out a large kerchief, he blew his nose. Jamie noticed that he also used the kerchief to dab at the corners of his eyes.

Jock looked into the bare branches of the tree over their heads. "Where would I find her? She travels frae fair tae fair all o'er the western and central Highlands."

"She will be certain tae be at Crieff or nearby in late July or early August, but I think ye will find her earlier and farther west."

"What makes ye say that, lad?"

Jamie smiled faintly. "Perhaps it is a trace o' the sight. Perhaps she gave it tae me with my birthday present sae I can gie ye a gift."

Jock heaved himself off the bench. "Weel now. I canna pack all by mesclf. Ye must come and help, lad. Then I must talk tae the Laird o' Abergeldie and Lady Euphemia. I think I hae a long road tae travel."

Chapter Nine

A chill wind blew off the Moray Firth and churned up waves that broke in foam on the smooth, sandy beach. Jamie Drummond hid his face in his horse's streaming mane as he raced Andy Hay and Robbie Dunbar along the strand. He felt the blood surge in his temples and smelled the salt spray off the water. Jamie held the breakneck pace until he could clearly see two lengths back to the nose of Andy's gelding before easing up. He raised his right fist in exultation, pumped it twice, and pulled back on the reins. Spurts of sand shot from the hooves of all three horses as their riders slowed them to a trot. Jamie stood in his stirrups and turned halfway around to grin at his companions.

"Let's rest the horses a bit," suggested Robbie Dunbar. "Fort George is up there," he said, pointing ahead to where an earthen rampart stretched across the sandy point of Ardersier that projected into the Moray Firth.

They pulled their mounts to a stop well short of the broad ditch, beyond which stood the rampart of the fort, atop which they could see wheeled gun carriages in earthen revetments.

As they stood gazing at the wide wall of dark earth, one of the soldiers standing atop the rampart shouted, "Move on, lads, lest the patrol take ye fer Jacobite spies. Get along now."

They wheeled their mounts expertly and trotted away from the ditch. The redcoated soldiers stood watching them, then turned back to their slow progress along the rampart. The boys reined to a halt and turned around to stare back at the earthworks. Andy broke the silence.

"Fort George hae been here since shortly after the battle o' Culloden three years ago this month, though fortifications hae been here fer half a century. The army hae been hard at work tae finish the ramparts and counterscarp, and emplace the guns tae make it a real fort. My father says that they can put three thousand men into the new brick barracks. The grounds now cover fifteen acres."

"Aye, and stables fer hundreds o' horses fer patrols throughout the eastern Highlands, and byres, smithies, storehouses, and everything tae make a fortified place," added Robbie Dunbar.

They watched as a troop of blue-coated horsemen rode out of the gate a quarter mile to their left.

"We'd better leave," Andy said nervously as the troop moved toward them at a quick trot.

"Nae," responded Jamie. "They will think we are spying if we turn and run. Stand still."

The troop halted about twenty paces from them and wheeled to form a line. An officer rode forward. He stopped and faced them, staring impassively, his reins held loosely in his gloved hands. Several troopers wheeled around behind the boys, blocking their pathway down the strand toward Nairn.

The officer spoke in icy tones. "I am Lieutenant Ian Hamilton of the Twentieth Regiment. Wha is the ringleader here?"

The boys goggled at each other. Finally, Jamie urged his horse forward a few paces.

"We are nae a ring, sir, and we hae nae leader. We are lads frae the town o' Nairn. We were only riding along the strand tae exercise our horses, and the ramparts made us curious."

Lieutenant Hamilton's expression and icy tone of voice did not change.

"I would not find it unusual fer Jacobites to send lads tae do men's work tae spy oot the military capabilities o' this fort.

Perhaps ye would like tae visit our prison, to see the damp stone cells and chains and eat the meager fare o' prisoners."

The boys darted glances at each other. Jamie found his voice and spoke with downcast look.

"Nae, sir. We dinna wish that. Please let us depart, sir. We promise tae ne'er come back."

Lieutenant Hamilton shifted his reins to his left hand and, reaching down, gripped the hilt of his cavalry saber and drew it half out of the scabbard. He held the pose for long seconds. Jamie felt fear crawling up his spine and clutching at his vitals, but he forced himself to meet the officer's stare. Abruptly, Lieutenant Hamilton rammed his sword back into the scabbard with a rasping sound of metal sliding on metal.

"Very weel. I will allow ye tae leave without confinement or interrogation. See that ye stay weel awa' frae Fort George. I will nae tolerate idle curiosity frae the filthy spawn o' Jacobites. Otherwise, my soldiers may choose to use ye fer a little target practice. I saw how quickly ye came. I expect ye to depart even mair quickly. Now gae!"

All three boys wheeled their mounts, kicked their horses in the ribs, and threaded their way between the troopers. They raced down the strand toward the distant steeples and roof gables of Nairn. When they were well away, they heard the noon gun's muffled boom at the fort. All three looked back to see smoke drifting to momentarily obscure the union jack snapping on its pole and the troop of cavalry riding westward parallel to the ramparts. The boys slowed their tired mounts to a trot. Jamie glanced at his companions and shouted over the brisk wind.

"He's a new un, that Lieutenant Hamilton. Did ye get a guid look at his eyes?"

Andy shouted back, "Aye. The man is dangerous and hates all Highlanders as Jacobites. He came oot o' his way tae threaten us. We'd best stay far frae the fort."

Robbie Dunbar nodded agreement, and the boys rode directly for Nairn.

The three boys had been constant companions since Jamie and his mother had arrived in the town three years before. Robbie's father, Patrick Dunbar, was tutor to all three, as well as other children in the town. He had been a classmate of Oliver Forbes's, the tutor of Abergeldie, when they were students at the University of Aberdeen. Andrew's father had served in James Drummond's command in the rising. He had surrendered after Culloden and was pardoned after a short imprisonment. He operated a mercantile establishment in Nairn and was a frequent guest at the Drummond home in the prestigious western end of town.

Euphemia had retained Hugh Drummond, her husband's cousin, to find lodgings in Inverness, but he could find nothing suitable in that town, renowned in the north for its tawdriness. However, Nairn on the Moray Firth sixteen miles from Inverness was ideal. The weather was the finest in the northeast, and the town boasted a lovely kirk, stores, and a society that welcomed Euphemia Drummond and treated her as somewhat of a Jacobite heroine.

They lived in a large, three-storey house that Andy and Robbie called a mansion. It was a far comedown from the castles of Strathallan and Abergeldie, but comfortable and spacious. Euphemia retained only three servants: a housekeeper, a groom, and a gardener. Behind the house stood stables, a modest barn, a small but well-tended garden, and a tiny greenhouse. Jamie loved the well-stocked library, where he spent evenings reading while his mother wrote letters and worked on intricate stitchery of medieval scenes that she framed to adorn the house's walls.

Euphemia and Jamie moved out of the castle in the mountains at Abergeldie in June of 1747 but made frequent trips back, especially for holidays and summertime. Jamie and his cousins, Will and David Gordon, remained close friends, but Peter had matured quickly after he departed for university studies.

Only a few Drummond family members visited Nairn, chiefly Emilia and Clementine. Andrew, Henry, and William corresponded but did not visit. Euphemia missed them but understood their reluctance to be seen with the family of attainted Jacobites and the potential threat to their careers. Also, with their army and university studies, the long trip to the far north was difficult. Jamie and his mother visited Lady Margaret, who moved from Dunfermline to Perth, at least twice a year. She was the same fiercely unrepentant Jacobite and a fountainhead of stories of government abuses and Jacobite passive resistance to repressive government edicts. Jamie's favorite was the tale of the daring raid by Edward Halls, a Jacobite patriot who stole the heads of executed Jacobites from spikes on the gates of the English city of Manchester and brought them back to Scotland for secret burial.

Euphemia sought out Arthur Grant, who ran a small bookshop and coffee house in Inverness and served as courier between banished Jacobites and their families in the north. She hated making trips to that town, renowned for filth and squalor, but through Grant, successfully established an infrequent but vital contact with her husband on the continent. James lived in Paris for a time and then moved to Antwerp in the Low Countries, where he found employment in the import/export trade. Euphemia was convinced that her husband was involved in smuggling, but the government authorities either did not know or chose to tolerate it.

His letters were initially cheerful and full of hope, but gradually, a note of gloom crept into his correspondence. He reported that the French king had decided in June of 1748 to recognize the Hanoverian succession to the British throne. That event, for a time at least, dashed the hope that French troops and arms would support another rising. Later that year, the French had even taken the step of jailing and then releasing Bonnie Prince Charlie, who had gone to Rome after his eviction from France.

James Drummond's spirits sank very low when he reported that Donald Cameron, the Gentle Lochiel, had passed away in October of that year. The great clan chief never recovered from the wounds he suffered at Culloden. Jamie was overcome with grief when he heard of Lochiel's death. He thought of the big man's jolly spirit and could not imagine that he was no more.

"When will Papa come hame? It hae been such a long time."

His mother sat staring into space and shaking her head slowly.

"It is sae dangerous, Jamie. Yer papa is weel known by many men in Scotland. Because o' Fort George close by and sae many soldiers patrolling, he certainly canna come here or tae Strathallan or Abergeldie. Perhaps we could find a place fer a rendezvous somewhere south along the eastern coast, where foreign vessels dock. Ye hae given me an excellent idea, Jamie lad. Another assignment for Arthur Grant, my friend the bookseller, tae find us a safe house. We could visit on the way tae Perth. And yer papa would hae to visit in disguise."

Jamie watched his mother fold and put down the letter. She rose and came to sit next to him. "Jamie, I hae guid news for ye. Do ye recall the wonderful announcement that we received twa summers ago, about Jock McRae?"

"Aye, Mama. He looked all winter and spring for Maggie McLeod that year over the Highlands. He almost gave up tae return tae Abergeldie. Then he decided tae visit Eilean Donan castle tae see some o' his McRae kin. They told him that she was staying in Portree on the Isle o' Skye, so he crossed over and found her."

Euphemia clapped her hands. "He must hae been powerfully insistent, for she agreed to hae him, and they were married soon after. They both gave up their gypsy ways and settled down tae buy a tavern near the harborside. I miss the auld soldier and his gruff ways, but I am sae glad fer him and that he found love after all these years." She leaned back and closed her eyes. "Aye, true love finally won oot. It is a fairy tale."

Jamie nudged her. "And what is yer guid news, Mama?"

Euphemia opened her eyes, and Jamie could see little lines of amusement at their corners.

"There is a spring fair, a large gathering at Kilravock Castle in April, sponsored by the Rose family." She seized his arm in a tight grip. "Jock and Maggie are coming tae visit us. They will stay wi' us here, and then we will gae tae the fair wi' them!"

They jumped up, embraced, and danced around the room, to the consternation of the housekeeper, who had just entered the room to announce supper.

Jamie struggled to contain his rising excitement as March passed and April came. The long grip of winter loosened in the north, and finally, spring flowers pushed through the patches of snow and budded. Jamie worked hard to complete the seemingly endless stream of assignments imposed by his tutor, Patrick Dunbar.

In addition to lessons in mathematics, logic, French, Latin, Greek, and natural philosophy, Mister Dunbar had recently inflicted Gaelic. The tutor explained his reasoning one day to his struggling students.

"Nairn sits at the confluence o' cultures and languages, gentlemen. I can walk the High Street from ain end o' this town tae the other and hear English predominant at one end and Gaelic at the other. Ye canna live here without having respect fer the people and cultures that use each language. I care nae a groat fer the edicts o' a government that is trying tae strangle the whole o' the Celtic culture oot o' Scotland. They dinna live here, but ye do."

Jamie had acquired only a smattering of Gaelic from the children in the streets of Nairn. His friends were mostly from the west end, where English was predominant. While he excelled in other languages, he found Gaelic confusing in structure and pronunciation.

Patrick Dunbar looked directly at Jamie and asked, "*Am bheil thu ga mo thuigsinn?*" ("Do ye understand what I am saying?")

Jamie sat frozen in embarrassment, a slow flush mounting to his cheeks.

Patrick Dunbar asked again, softly, "*A bheil fhios agad?*" ("Do ye know?")

With a flash of inspiration, Jamie responded, "*Tha.*" ("Yes.")

The other students giggled.

Mister Dunbar looked at Jamie severely. "I think that yer answer should be, '*Chan eil mi a' tuigsinn,*' ("I dinna understand") and ye are only guessing. Practice will improve yer understanding, Master Drummond." He handed Jamie a sheaf of papers. "Here is a Gaelic phrase book. Ye will memorize it all by next Monday."

He turned his attention to the next student, who was only slightly better prepared and drew the same difficult assignment.

Jamie was engrossed in memorization late on Friday afternoon when the housekeeper announced that Jock and Maggie McRae had arrived. Jamie dropped the phrase book and bolted for the entrance, followed closely by his mother.

Maggie had not changed, but Jock seemed somewhat grayer to Jamie. Both greeted him with tight embraces. Jock teased Jamie about his gangling height. They lingered long over tea. The conversation drifted to activities of the government to suppress the Jacobites and effects on the local people. Jock shook his head sadly.

"It seems that Aberdeenshire and Mar hae been less affected than the west, although the proscriptions ye describe are onerous. Conditions are still severe in Lochaber and northern Argyll because o' resistance o' the Camerons in taking sae long tae surrender. Cumberland, his successors, and especially the Campbells hae perpetrated such excesses that people harbor murderous feelings toward the government. They are making it difficult for men tae make a living, so many o' the young bucks are bein' recruited into the regiments and bein' sent o'er the water tae fecht in the British army. Patrols seem tae be everywhere. If they find concealed weapons, they either pull down the house or burn it tae the ground."

At this point, Jamie related what had happened recently in their encounter at the fort. Euphemia's face betrayed her concern.

"Ye must stay far frae the fort, Jamie. I hae heard ugly stories about Lieutenant Hamilton. He hae taken tae making unannounced visits tae homes and shops and allowing his soldiers tae ransack them. He is seldom in Nairn, but folk in Inverness are nervous. There are bad feelings among the people and merchants o' the town toward the soldiers. They travel aboot only in large groups. I fear that someday soon, we might hear o' a riot and people beaten or killed."

Maggie changed the subject to Jamie's studies. She smiled with pleasure when Jamie told her how he treasured the history of Sir William Wallace that he knew came as a gift from her and had read it through twice.

"William Hamilton, wha compiled and translated the book, is now quite auld and lives in St. Andrews. I hae spoken wi' him many times o'er the years. Would ye like tae meet him?"

Jamie glanced at his mother questioningly. She said slowly, "Tis a long way, but I suppose we might arrange something."

Two days later, they rose and breakfasted early, in order to attend the country fair at Kilravock castle. The sky was cloudy with occasional drizzle, but they were familiar with the weather of northeast Scotland and not deterred. The carriage ride to Kilravock took a little over an hour, but they detoured so that Jock and Maggie could view the battlefield at Drummossie Muir.

They sat in the carriage, looking in silence at the nearly flat and barren heath. There was only a single cottage that had served as a field hospital during the battle to interrupt the dreariness of the terrain. The dead and their accountrements had long since been removed from the lonely windswept field. Jock and Jamie dismounted and walked around the low walls that had been key points during the attack. They stood in silence before three small rocky cairns that someone had erected. In front of the cairns lay piles of spring blossoms.

They walked to the left of where Jock said that the rebel line extended. He stopped and pointed.

"Aboot there is where yer grandpa was killed."

Although the day was mostly cloudy, a few rays of sunlight emerged and shone down. Jamie saw something glinting in the tall heather. Bending down, he scratched at the earth with his fingernails and extracted a metal button. Digging further, he pulled out a uniform epaulette. He gently brushed away the soil and held the objects up for Jock to inspect. When they returned to the carriage, Jamie wordlessly handed the items to his mother. She held them in her palm and then pressed them to her cheek.

Maggie put her hand over Euphemia's and said, "I dinna hae the sight regarding the wearer o' these mementos, except that this unknown soldier died bravely. This place tortures my soul, but I am glad that I came."

Jock requested that they drive to Leanach Farm a short distance away. When they arrived, he got out and stood silently for a long time. When he got back into the carriage, he said, "This is the spot where Cumberland's troops surrounded thirty Jacobite rebels in the barn. After barricading them inside, they set fire tae the barn. Twas a terrible crime that will cry oot as long as mankind hae a conscience."

After the driver pulled back onto the road, Jock pointed to a small house set back from the road behind a manicured garden.

"This is where a local woman hae taken in twelve wounded rebels. The government troops promised them medical aid if they surrendered. When they were disarmed, Cumberland's soldiers shot them doon here in the front yard, ain at a time."

Jock sat, with his eyes shut and his fists clenched, until the driver put his head in at the window to request instructions. Jock responded roughly, "Aye, drive on tae Kilravock Castle, if ye please. We hae seen enough o' this charnel house that justifies the dead and condemns the living."

He took out a large handkerchief, covered his face, and blew noisily. As the carriage approached Kilravock castle, they passed many family groups trudging toward an expansive meadow. Crowds of people had gathered in knots around two enormous canvas pavilions.

The driver pulled into an area where horses, wagons, and carriages were parked. When they dismounted, the people set up a cheer and streamed forward to greet Maggie, whose skills as a harpist and singer were renowned throughout the Highlands.

Jamie left the adults to converse. He soon found his friends, Archie Gordon and Johnnie Sutherland, from Nairn wandering the merchant stalls. It did not take the young men long to find other friends who had come with their families. They wandered the grounds in a happy knot, sampling food for a penny or two; looking at winsome girls who mostly pretended not to notice them; and enjoying the sports, particularly those involving archery, wrestling, and tossing the caber, a peculiarly Highland sport.

Suddenly, they heard a shout of warning from near the entrance. A dozen blue-coated dragoons trotted toward the merchant stalls. At their head, Jamie instantly recognized Lieutenant Ian Hamilton. The officer rode with his saber out of the scabbard, with the blade resting across the pommel. The crowd quieted, and the music stopped. The dragoons formed a loose semi-circle enclosing many of the people. Lieutenant Hamilton reined in and sat silently facing the crowd.

"An informant loyal tae the crown hae provided information that there is contraband hidden here intended fer Jacobite traitors. What say any o' ye tae refute that accusation?"

His ice-blue eyes surveyed the crowd. Jamie could see his mother, Maggie, and Jock McRae just outside one of the entertainment pavilions. Maggie sat on a stool, holding her harp. Euphemia and Jock stood on either side. Two older men stepped forward to speak to the officer. Lieutenant Hamilton ostentatiously ignored them. Wheeling about, he shouted a command to his troops.

"I declare this an unlawful assembly! Pull down the pavilions! Search the stalls fer contraband!"

The dragoons drew their sabers and commenced slashing at the guy ropes holding up the tent poles. A horseman veered toward Maggie with his saber out and swung for a rope near her head. She fell to the ground, cradling her precious harp. Euphemia seized her arm and helped her scramble out of harm's way.

Jock reacted by grabbing the dragoon's extended arm. The cavalry horse reared, whinnying. Jock dug in his heels and yanked the rider out of the saddle. The soldier crashed to the ground directly in the path of another horse, which swerved to collide with the riderless horse. Both went down under the collapsing canvas, entangled in the ropes.

An infuriated Lieutenant Hamilton charged Jock with his saber raised. Jock ducked under his wild swing and seized the bridle of the officer's horse. In the few seconds that these actions took, Jamie had sprinted across the field until he was on the opposite side of Lieutenant Hamilton's horse and struggling to reach his mother and Maggie. Lieutenant Hamilton wheeled his horse to the right in an attempt to break Jock's iron grip.

Jamie fell under the hooves of the turning horse, which kicked him in the shoulder. The boy howled in anguish as his left arm and side spasmed in pain. He heard the crowd's roar of anger as he scrambled away with his arm hanging limply. Lieutenant Hamilton pitched out of the saddle and dropped his saber as Jock hung grimly to the bridle of his horse.

Lieutenant Hamilton landed on the turf with a "whoof!" of surprise. As the officer tried to rise, he looked up wide-eyed to see the sharp point of his own saber hovering over his breastbone. Hamilton lay back as the point prodded his jacket fabric. Jock's voice was conciliatory.

"Steady, sir. Ye hae taken a nasty fall which hae undoubtedly addled yer senses. I suggest, sir, ye order yer men tae pull back and sheathe their sabers. Do it now, if ye please."

Hamilton saw no fear or uncertainty in the veteran's eyes. He shouted hastily to his men over the crowd's noise. They withdrew their mounts a few paces.

Jock's voice was steely and insistent. "Tell them tae sheathe their weapons now!"

Lieutenant Hamilton gave the order, and the men complied, with obvious reluctance. Jock withdrew the saber point about a foot from the officer's face. Hamilton sat up.

"There are witnesses here that yer dragoons attacked my wife and this lad's mother wi'out provocation. Yer horse hae injured this defenseless lad. I suggest that ye carefully consider yer actions and words going forward. If ye persist in committing an outrage against this unarmed crowd o' civilians, neither ye nor yer troopers will make it back tae Fort George alive. Certainly, ye will suffer casualties that ye must explain to yer commanding officer, and the mood of the crowd is such that they might well tear ye limb from limb. Ye might search fer contraband but will find naething, for this is a gathering o' country folk here only for amusement and commerce at the invitation of the Rose family o' Kilravock. Handbills were posted weeks ago in all local towns and villages announcing this fair. There is nae secrecy here, nae pipes, nae weapons, nae contraband, and nae reason for attacking innocent people. Now, sir, I suggest that ye see tae the lad, wha might need medical attention because ye steered yer horse o'er him."

Jock stepped back, permitting Lieutenant Hamilton to rise. He reached out a hand for his saber.

Jock shook his head slowly. "Arter ye see tae the lad and are ready tae leave, sir. I also require yer word as a gentleman that ye will do nae further harm tae these people."

Lieutenant Hamilton huffed, his face contorted with anger. "Ye demand my word? Ye are a fool, sir! I will see ye in irons and probably hanged for assaulting a king's officer!"

"I think ye weel do nae such thing, Lieutenant. I am a retired Captain o' the Black Watch and am nae rebel. I didna bear arms fer the Bonnie Prince. Yer trooper assaulted my wife at yer order, and I hae the right tae demand satisfaction. Are ye prepared to gie it tae me? I might be much aulder than ye wi gray hair and a weathered face, but I hae a fine eye and a steady aim. I am a dead shot wi' the pistol and expert wi' the cavalry saber. Shall we call fer seconds?" He stared calmly at the young officer, who could not hold his gaze.

Lieutenant Hamilton dropped his eyes. At length, he growled, "Let us see tae the boy."

They walked to where Jamie lay groaning on a blanket, where two hefty men had laid him and were holding him down. A third man, balding and wearing a leather apron, was massaging Jamie's shoulder. Euphemia hovered over him, and Maggie gripped his hands. They looked up as Lieutenant Hamilton approached.

The balding man said, "The lad is lucky, indeed, sir. The right shoulder is numb frae where yer horse kicked him, but I think that there are nae broken bones. I expect the shoulder tae bruise massively, howe'er. The joint will be numb fer some days, but the lad should recover completely. I suggest bathing the limb in cold water and applying a poultice o' tobacco leaves bandaged tightly as long as the swelling persists."

"Are ye a physician, sir, tae speak sae authoritatively?" Lieutenant Hamilton inquired haughtily.

The man answered mildly. "Nae, sir. We hae nae physician hereaboots. I am a groom expert in veterinary medicine, wha hae been around horses fer o'er thirty years and seen many o' these injuries."

Another man interjected. "Yer pardon, sir. But this lad's father is a viscount, who is unfortunately abroad at this time. Would ye care tae speak tae Lady Drummond, his mother?"

Lieutenant Hamilton paled perceptibly and spoke tonelessly. "Nae, nae. I believe that I will withdraw my troop and resume our appointed patrol." He held out his hand.

Jock McRae extended the Lieutenant's saber, hilt first, and asked softly, "If I gie ye this weapon, sir, do I hae yer word tae leave this assembly in peace?"

The officer nodded, his lips a thin line and his eyes blazing.

Jock said in a low voice, "Then, sir, I withdraw my challenge."

Lieutenant Hamilton took his saber and thrust it savagely into the scabbard. He turned to face his troop, who sat in a row, blank-faced. Mounting, he turned his horse away from the tumbled pavilions. Behind him, a sergeant bellowed commands to the dragoons to move out. The crowd watched silently as the troop trotted away with a jingling of harness. When they were well out of sight, the people cheered madly and surged around Jock.

After the patrol rode away, those attending decided to hurriedly close down the fair and disperse to their homes for fear of Lieutenant Hamilton returning with more soldiers. Within an hour, the grounds were clear. Jock and Maggie helped Euphemia make Jamie comfortable in the carriage and climbed in to return to the house in Nairn.

They put Jamie to bed and made him as comfortable as possible. He complained of achiness of his entire body except for the numbness of his shoulder and arm. The tobacco poultice applied by the groom at the fair was still snug. The bruising that Euphemia could see around the bandage was extensive, but there was not as much swelling as she expected. She gave Jamie a small amount of laudanum to enable him to sleep.

An anxious Maggie persuaded Jock to start for Portree immediately and to take a circuituous route home to avoid passing through Inverness, for fear of arrest. Before departing, she invited

Euphemia and Jamie to come to Skye during the summer, since it was obvious that Jock must avoid coming to Nairn as long as Lieutenant Hamilton was stationed at Fort George.

After their departure, Euphemia stayed up late, expecting soldiers to batter on the door at any time.

At a late hour, there was a discreet knock. When the servant opened the door a crack, a disheveled Hugh Drummond stood at the entrance. Euphemia invited him to her parlor and instructed the housekeeper to bring refreshments. The lawyer sat for a while, examining his fingernails. Euphemia waited. Finally, Hugh cleared his throat and began.

"My dear Euphemia. I am very sorry about Jamie getting hurt at that…ugly incident…at Kilravock today. I heard about it frae a client in Inverness and intended tae come straightaway. Howe'er, I thought it prudent to make a few inquiries before arriving. I understand that Lieutenant Hamilton o' the Twentieth Regiment is considered a vicious martinet, even among his fellow officers, most o' whom hae little love fer the people o' the north. Fort George is considered a hateful assignment, and mair than a few hae taken liberties in making the lives o' the people hereabouts miserable. Nothing as bad as conditions around Fort William in the west, however. Hamilton has compiled a bad record in his short few months here of bullying people. I hae it on good report that the troopers hate him, except for his bully boys, and are overjoyed at how Jock McRae humbled him. This is the first time that anyone hae resisted his abuses, let alone struck back. There is fear among the people o' Inverness and Nairn that there will be some form o' reprisal, but in speaking with the officials o' both towns, it appears that young Hamilton hae nae stomach fer facing the auld veteran."

Euphemia giggled. "Discovering that he is, indeed, a retired Captain o' the Black Watch undoubtedly set the lieutenant back a pace or twa."

"Indeed. But I think that he will wait fer an opportunity to retaliate in some underhanded way, especially when he discovers that Jock McRae is nae a resident of this district and hae already flown."

Hugh took a sip of tea and reached for one of the pastries on a tray unobtrusively left by the maid. He chewed thoughtfully and then said, "I'm sure that he now kens wha ye are and that yer husband is an attainted Jacobite. In spite of the discrete life ye hae lived here in Nairn, he will be watching fer an opportunity to seek revenge. I am sure o' that. However, I wouldna expect anything like the dustup that took place at the fair." He stopped and laughed gleefully.

"I sincerely regret nae seeing it. It must hae been a precious sight to see the lieutenant in his glorious uniform sprawled on his inglorious arse!" He chuckled and had to stop eating while both of them laughed uproariously.

When Hugh could continue, he leveled his finger at Euphemia and said, "I almost can persuade myself tae advise ye tae move south tae escape him, but ye are something o' a heroine hereabouts. That means that making ye a target would be a most unwise course o' action fer the lieutenant. While harassing Jacobites is a favorite pastime o' the enlisted troopers, the officers avoid such behavior fer fear o' offending the commanding officer o' the Twentieth Regiment, wha is trying to maintain a reasonable peace hereabouts. I understand that a new commander will soon be appointed, a freshly promoted officer currently assigned tae Perth. He is a lieutenant colonel by the name o' James Wolfe, whose father is a general o' some renown. While he dislikes Jacobites and Scots in general, he willna tolerate unjustified abuse o' the local people. Wolfe hae a sterling reputation in the army, having fought at Culloden under General Hawley. There is a rumor that he stood up tae General Cumberland and refused tae shoot a captured officer. He told Butcher Cumberland that he would resign his post before sacrificing his honor. Now there is a man o' integrity." He stopped and looked narrowly at Euphemia. "Yer pardon, my dear, I am prattling again. It is a very bad habit o' mine and made worse by being a lawyer. Ye must think on this situation and weigh the risks tae yerself and Jamie. Speaking o' the lad, how is he?"

"Resting comfortably, but he will bear the marks o' massive bruising fer several weeks."

"Ach. It is truly a shame. I understand that he was rushing tae yer defense when he was hurt. The lad is fearless and possessed o' a brave heart, but he is only twelve years auld, bless him. Keep him hame fer some time and oot o' sight o' the mad lieutenant. If ye need a bodyguard or an additional manservant, I have funds placed at my disposal by yer inestimable brother fer that purpose."

Euphemia touched his hand and shook her head firmly. "I thank ye, Hugh, but nae. It would only draw mair attention. I will be very discreet and not gae oot mair than once a month and ne'er tae Inverness. If I visit, it will be tae Abergeldie. What letters I choose tae post, I will send tae Arthur Grant through Jamie's tutor Patrick Dunbar, wha is a fervent Jacobite. He is very discreet and circumspect. Mister Dunbar is weel-acquainted wi' the bookseller, being a scholar and frequenter o' his stalls. I shall be safe enough, unless Lieutenant Hamilton chooses tae invade this house. Here, he will find nae weapons, nae letters, naething tae implicate me. If he tears up the furniture or burns down the house, ye must remember that it is rented."

They both laughed heartily again and talked a while longer, until the pastries were gone and the tea drunk. Cousin Hugh, reasonably assured that he had fulfilled his duties, brushed crumbs from his vest, called for his driver, bowed to his hostess, and departed for Inverness.

From the parlor window, Euphemia watched Hugh step into his carriage and wave to the driver. As they left, she noted that her groom, Alan MacAlister, stood near his quarters in the carriage house, watching. She nodded with satisfaction when she saw in the wavering light of the post lamp that he had obeyed her instructions and was wearing a brace of pistols in his belt. She closed the curtains and sat thinking for a very long time before changing for bed and blowing out the lamp.

Jamie remembered little of the first week of his confinement. The numbness disappeared slowly, followed by a nearly intolerable tingling as the nerves healed from the shock. The bruises changed color from dark-purple and black to a sickly green, followed by pale, blotchy yellow before disappearing. The pain in his muscles and joints took longer.

After three weeks, Jamie managed to make his way downstairs and back up again. His friends visited frequently to keep up his spirits. Many had seen the incident involving Jock McRae and Lieutenant Hamilton. They were in awe of Jock's bravery, and Jamie came in for his share of adulation. Patrick Dunbar came daily to check on Jamie's progress and provide tutoring through the end of the school year.

Within a day after the accident, Euphemia had engaged a local physician, William MacIntosh, to examine Jamie. He was well liked and had also been instrumental in hiding and treating several Jacobite officers after the battle on Drummossie Muir, which enhanced his status. His white hair and gentle manner made him popular with matrons and mothers alike.

The physician approved of the emergency steps taken by the groom after the accident. Jamie hated the tobacco poultice, and the doctor removed it after a week.

Doctor MacIntosh was also expert at manipulating the muscles, joints, and connective tissue to promote healing. Jamie bit his lip and groaned but resisted crying aloud as the doctor bent and twisted his tortured shoulder in what he called "modern therapeutic exercises." The physician also advocated cold soaks and wraps for the injured area to reduce the swelling and speed recovery.

Jamie was overjoyed when the day came that the doctor prescribed a regimen of walking, followed by running and, finally, riding. What confused him was the doctor's admonition for Jamie to spend at least thirty minutes a day at exercises such as forking hay in the stable, tossing a ball in the air and catching it, and twirling a rope.

"Nae objections now. These exercises are needful tae rebuild strength and flexibility in that damaged joint, lad. Come. I will watch ye fer the first set o' exercises. Twice a day fer twa weeks should do ye weel. If ye do as I ask, I will see ye on a horse soon."

In early July, while his friends, Robbie and Andy, were visiting, Doctor MacIntosh completed his examination. Euphemia stood by the door with her hand anxiously gripping the frame. The doctor pronounced Jamie healed sufficiently to mount and ride for the first time since the accident. She rushed forward to hug her son, and his friends cheered loudly.

The doctor beamed and said, "I think my work here is done, Lady Drummond. If the lad suffers a setback, please send fer me. It hae been a pleasure working with such an obedient and determined lad. He is a treasure, and ye must be unco proud o' him. The whole town is aware o' how he was injured."

By his mother's firm command, Jamie and his friends rode only in Nairn or in the countryside south of town, well away from Fort George. At no time did they encounter an army patrol, and the summer days passed peacefully. On a warm, breezy day, Euphemia and Jamie took the coach to Abergeldie. Peter, Will, and David Gordon were there, and they rode up to Lachin-y-Gair. As they lay in the meadow above the loch, a wide-eyed Will told Jamie of his late-night encounter with the ghost of French Kate in the hallway outside the kitchen of the castle.

Jamie was skeptical. "I thought she only appeared in the cellars."

Peter smirked. "Perhaps she was jealous about the apple pie ye were stealing frae the kitchen, Will."

At that jibe, David and and Jamie laughed gleefully, and Will chased Peter down to the shore. Peter seized his struggling younger brother and tossed him headfirst into the cold water. Jamie and David pushed Peter, who stumbled in surprise and fell into the shallow water. The horseplay ended when Will and Peter chased Jamie across the field and carried him struggling to the water's edge and tossed him in.

In August, Euphemia and Jamie journeyed by coach to Kylieakin on the west coast and took a boat across the channel to the sleepy harbor town of Portree on the Isle of Skye. Across the town square, they saw a tidy whitewashed two-storey inn with a large wooden sign displaying a seated woman holding a golden harp.

They walked into the cool dim interior. The scent of flowers filled the air, from the plentiful pots and basins arranged around the spacious entry and dining room. Jock came from around the bar to sweep both of them into his burly arms. Minutes later, they were seated before a pleasantly crackling fire with tankards of cider and a heaping plate of cakes and fresh berries. They whiled away the afternoon exchanging experiences. Jock was puzzled by the lack of response from Lieutenant Hamilton after the incident at Kilravock Castle. He agreed with Hugh Drummond's assessment and warned Euphemia to be vigilant.

"I hae heard guid things frae friends in Perth about Wolfe, the new commander o' the Twentieth Regiment. I hae also heard that he is staying tae the south and not coming tae Inverness, fer at least the present. So ye must remain on yer guard."

They spent an idyllic week roaming the town and the nearby Cuillin hills. Maggie had quickly gained a reputation in the community as a healer, dispensing herbs and roots gathered from the meadows and glens of the island, in addition to her other skills. Jamie loved tramping the fields with Maggie, pulling, cutting, trimming, and packing the variously scented plants into baskets for her. They feasted on roast lamb and fresh fish from the harbor and stayed up late listening to Maggie singing and playing in a corner of the packed dining room to a large and appreciative crowd while Jock manned the bar and kept serving wenches busy carrying foaming tankards of ale to the crowded tables.

On the evening before they left to catch the boat back to the mainland, Maggie rose to face the crowd in the dining room. She clapped for silence and announced, "This nicht, we hae posted twa sentinels in the square and closed the curtains tae contain the sound, lest there be a roving soldier o' the Hanoverian government outside."

The crowd hissed and thumped on the tables.

Jock rose and lifted his tankard of ale. "My guid friends, many hae fought and many hae died for our Prince and King. Let us drink tae their memory."

Everyone raised their glasses and tankards and drank silently.

"Here's tae our families, wha hae lost loved ones, hames, cattle, and crofts."

Again, everyone drank.

"Here's tae our Prince and King, tae their health and long life."

The crowd erupted boisterously and drank.

Jock smiled approval as he saw that Euphemia and Jamie were also standing. "Here's tae Flora MacDonald, that winsome lass wha loved her country enough tae help our Bonnie Prince escape at risk o' rope and ax."

The crowd went wild, with many slamming their tankards on the tables and stamping their feet.

"And here are the emblems o' our Celtic heritage, banned by the government in London."

The crowd was hushed, waiting expectantly. Maggie opened the doors to an upper cupboard, moved some dishes, and pulled up a false bottom. She reached in and took out lengthy swatches of red-and-green tartan cloth, which she draped over the bar. The crowd craned their necks to look when there came a loud thumping at an inner door. Jock flung it wide to reveal a piper standing in presentation kilts and full regalia. He marched in to the skirling sound of his pipes and paced up and down the floor through the passionately cheering throng. Jock flung open another door, and a second piper walked in. In seconds, the pipers were mingling their melodies. Jamie strained to see on tiptoe and then climbed onto a table. His mother held him steady as he clapped and stamped along with the crowd.

Jamie looked at Maggie, who was singing in Gaelic, her strong soprano voice rising clear above the pipes. Caught up in the song, he gazed at the faces in the crowd—fishermen, shopkeepers, farmers, shepherds, and their wives—many spellbound, others grinning, and some weeping, stamping and clapping to the martial sound of the pipes. Suddenly, the music stopped and the crowd quieted. The pipers nodded to each other and began a slow melody.

Maggie motioned to a group of young men and women to join her. She spoke to the crowd. "*Riaghladh goirid air an or, ach Riaghladh fada air an oran.*" ("Shared gold goes not far, but a shared song lasts a long time.")

Maggie picked up her harp and plucked the first stirring notes. The group began singing softly, quickly joined by the entire crowd, the haunting strains that brought to Jamie visions of the misty hills and seas of the western Highlands.

They followed this lovely melody with a long medley of traditional tunes. Jock opened the doors, and the pipers marched out to a thunderous ovation. Maggie resumed her seat in the corner. She sang old songs of the islands, and the crowd sang with her, swaying and holding hands with eyes closed. At last, Maggie stopped, touching the strings to silence them. She gently placed the harp on the bar and walked through the crowd, stopping to embrace each person. Jock blew out the lamps, and the crowd, in utter silence, filed out into the cool summer night.

Chapter Ten

At the house in Nairn on a cold Saturday morning in late October, the maid answered the knock on the door and accepted a letter from a courier. Euphemia broke the red wax seal and read the short letter, gasping in surprise. She strode into the breakfast room and snatched the bowl of porridge from Jamie, who sat in astonishment with upraised spoon in hand. She spoke with ill-concealed excitement.

"Ye must pack immediately. We must set out fer Peterheid at once! Yer papa is waiting!" She pushed the letter in front of him.

Jamie set down his spoon, swallowed, and read the short note in his father's ornate, flowing script.

Jamie was puzzled. "A shipment frae Antwerp? Mister Williamson waiting yer visit at Mintlaw, near Peterheid at yer soonest convenience, but not later than the first day of November, which is his sailing date. Wha is Mister Williamson, Mama?"

Euphemia giggled. "It is a code name tae protect us. Yer papa is James, and he is the son of William. Hence, James Williamson. Mintlaw is a shooting lodge owned by James Ferguson, a man wi' decided Jacobite sympathies. It is on Pitfour Loch in Buchan near Peterheid, where we will hae our rendezvous with Papa. The ship frae Antwerp arrived early. We hae only five or six days before his ship sails back to the continent. We must hurry."

Jamie gulped down the remains of breakfast and took the stairs two at a time. Euphemia called for Mister MacAlister, the groom, who would accompany them to Pitfour. She also penned a short note to Patrick Dunbar to excuse Jamie from class for a week.

The coach rumbled up the road through the red-and-gold beech trees to the Ferguson mansion house at Pitfour just as the sun was setting in the west. Mister MacAlister slowed the coach as it rounded a bend and pointed his whip at a herd of red deer browsing in a meadow.

Jamie's eyes shone. "Papa must hae selected this place because the hunting is guid."

His mother squeezed his hand. "The truth is that he selected Pitfour because it is secluded and one wouldna think tae look in such an oot of the way place fer him."

Mister MacAlister brought the coach to the mansion's entrance, where young footmen unloaded their luggage. The interior demonstrated its origin as an old shooting lodge with displays of ancient weapons—crossbows, wheel locks, and longbows—as well as an assortment of stag heads and antlers mounted on the carved dark oaken walls. Servants whisked away their bags and seated them in a secluded alcove in the dining room. Within minutes, a tall, bearded man dressed in baggy trousers and shooting jacket approached the table and slid into a chair next to Euphemia.

She looked puzzled for an instant and then quietly embraced her husband, leaking tears onto the lapels of his coat. It was several minutes before she disengaged. She held his face in her hands, tenderly stroking his beard and mustache in wonderment. Jamie instantly recognized his father behind the disguise, but it was a more somber and careworn face than he remembered from nearly five years before. James's hair and face were thinner and his eyes deep set. He stood to embrace his son, who, at twelve years of age, was only inches shorter than his father.

"Ach. Jamie, lad. Ye've grown sae tall. I can scarcely believe it. We canna talk much here in public, but after supper, ye hae much tae tell me and I tae tell ye." He sat and turned to Euphemia, who grasped his arm and laid her head on his shoulder. He reached for a printed menu. "This reunion calls for a feast. The kitchen hae wonderful venison and partridge, and the cellar hae fine wine. I hae missed guid Scottish game fer such a lang time."

Jamie enjoyed days shooting at clay targets with his father. When his father saw that he was ready, they went on an early morning walk with a pair of hunting dogs in the extensive meadows surrounding the lodge. They waded through waist-tall, dew-drenched grass with the dogs ranging ahead. After an hour of strenuous walking, they saw the dogs start a covey of partridge from cover that took flight, whirring up from the grass. James shot two, and Jamie one.

James reached for the bird and examined it carefully. "Excellent shot, son! See here." He pointed to where the shot had penetrated the feathers. "Verra little damage." He hefted the bird. "This will be excellent eating, indeed." He nudged Jamie's shoulder. "But three are nae enough tae feed a hungry crew like us. We need tae bring doon three mair." They reloaded their fowling pieces. James strung the birds and tossed them over his shoulder. They continued on their original course across the meadow toward a small pond.

After supper, Jamie curl up in front of the fire in their quarters, while James recounted his adventures since he had left Strathallan in the time before and after the final battle on Drummossie Muir in April of 1746. That story told, James began to tell of the fate of the refugees from the rising. He was present at the death of the Gentle Lochiel Donald Cameron and told the mournful tale of the loss of that good friend. Most of the rebels had found employment in French and other military services on the continent. Many returned home on surreptitious visits, as he had, only to eventually return to their refuges on the Continent.

Consumed in the gloomy aspects of the conversation, James finally said, "This summer, our Bonnie Prince went tae London in disguise tae visit wi' some members o' Parliament wha are hostile tae the Hanoverians in order tae make a startling proposal. He offered tae convert frae the Roman church tae the Anglican faith. They assured him if he hae made such a bold proposal before he landed at Eriskay in forty-five, he might hae succeeded in causing a great defection in King George's party and won much support." James sat back with a deep sigh. "They told him that it was far too late, but he did plant a seed o' disaffection tae grow and fester. It was a very dangerous act, tae gae tae London that way, but bold, and they must respect him fer that act o' courage."

Euphemia sat up and put her hand gently on his knee. "Dearest husband. Ye know that we will keep faith wi' ye as ye keep faith wi' the cause. But it hae been nearly five years now. Surely, if Parliament and the crown were going tae grant pardons and restitution, they would hae made an overture by now. Perhaps it is time fer ye tae petition them and seek an accord that will bring ye hame. We are losing the best years o' our lives in a cause that appears tae me tae be irretreviably lost."

James' gaunt face grew stern. He shook his head doggedly.

"Nae. Honor forbids. As long as there is even a slender chance tae succeed, I will nae submit and I will keep faith. Nairn appears tae be a safe refuge for ye and Jamie."

Euphemia's face fell. She crossed her arms tightly and struggled to maintain her composure. Finally, she nodded but would not speak again.

James turned to his son. "Jamie, lad. We hae only a few days here. I must be awa' soon back tae Peterheid and ye back tae Nairn. The captain hae notified me that the cargo packing is on schedule and the winds remain favorable. Yer mama hae suggested that we ride tae Latrick tomorrow tae visit auld William Hamilton, the man wha published that marvelous book that Maggie McLeod gave ye, *Blind Harry's Life of Sir William Wallace*. He is getting along in years and might nae be around much longer. It will be the privilege o' a lifetime tae meet the man." James reached over to tousle his son's hair. "I also want ye tae ken that as

James Williamson, the successful Antwerp-based importer and exporter, I may be able tae come tae Pitfour several times a year on business. Let us enjoy these respites as we can."

On the return ride from the vicinity of Glasgow to Pitfour, Jamie reflected on their visit. They had been graciously received by tall, white-haired, and bent William Hamilton, who claimed that he was suffering the cumulative effects of his eighty-five years. He confided that he was somewhat abashed by the popularity of his editorial efforts on *Blind Harry's History of Sir William Wallace*. He wryly observed that critics had severely treated the book.

"Aye, they describe it as bloody on every page, violently and unfairly anti-English, grossly embellished, vulgar and disgusting, clumsy and stilted, in short, a literary failure in every sense." He sat back in his rocking chair and smiled. "Yet, nearly thirty years later, here we are. That book, whose original author is nearly nameless tae us, is next tae the Holy Bible, the second most popular book in Scotland. I was merely the translator and editor of the writer's large and unwieldy mass o' material. The genius was Blind Harry's or John Blair's before him, nae mine. I would ask ye, but ye hae already solved the enigma, especially this young laddie. I leave it tae others tae wonder, but the secret is this." He paused and leaned toward Jamie with intensity in his blue eyes under their white shaggy brows. "It speaks tae the love that burns in every true Scottish breast, the love o' freedom that is achieved only when we hae patriot heroes wha sacrifice fer the guid o' all."

A thrill shot through Jamie. He waited until William Hamilton stopped speaking and then said with intensity, "William Wallace was such a man. He continues tae inspire patriots. Because o' him, sir, Scotland's identity as a nation will ne'er die. In spite o' what the critics say, sir, that is why the book is an epic."

Euphemia's eyes widened and her mouth formed a silent oval of surprise. James smiled broadly, and William Hamilton slowly clapped his gnarled hands.

"Our young scholar sees what the foolish critics ignore. He and others like him gie me assurance that Scottish love o' freedom will live on." He pointed to the book that Jamie held in his hands.

"If ye will pass that volume here, Jamie Drummond, I will gladly sign it fer ye. God bless ye, lad."

When they returned to Pitfour, they had two quiet days together, and then James was gone, back to Peterhead to board the merchant ship to Antwerp. He had announced before departure that it was unlikely that he would be able to make another crossing before winter settled into the north but that he would be back in the spring for another rendezvous.

However, there was no trip to Pitfour that spring. In January, James wrote that the Royal Navy, desirous of stamping out smuggling of arms and other contraband, had stepped up patrols and searches of merchant vessels on the oceans surrounding Great Britain. James decided that the risk was too great to attempt a visit. Euphemia was forced to agree, especially since she discovered that after nearly thirteen years, she was pregnant and due at the end of July. Jamie was terribly disappointed, but his mother had agreed that they would spend a month in Abergeldie after the baby was born.

At the end of May, Euphemia's pregnancy was well advanced, and her younger sister Jean came up from Abergeldie to run the household. Patrick Dunbar brought news that William Hamilton had died on the twenty-fourth of May. While the critics did not mourn, Jamie was greatly affected, since he had grown to appreciate the old man's book and love of country.

On a warm afternoon at the end of July, Jamie felt the utter uselessness of a young man with the coming of his mother's labor. The household erupted in female activity, in none of which he was involved or understood, except that his mother was in great distress. He could not leave since the burden of being uncaring was too great, so he stayed below and tried to read and write to stay busy while feet tramped up and down the staircase with hot water, hot towels, cold towels, midwife, midwife's assistant, and finally, around midnight, a plaintive little cry followed by female shrieks of, "It's a girl!"

A half hour later, as he fought off sleep, he was finally invited upstairs to see his red-faced baby sister, held out to him by his exhausted but ecstatic mother. He took the infant in his arms and looked down at the puckered little face.

Euphemia said, "Gently now. Her name is Margaret. Ye canna understand my great happiness, my son, to hae this infant in my arms after sae many years since ye were a wee bairn. Her father canna be here fer her, so ye must bear the weight o' being a father fer a while, in addition tae being a brother. Now, gie her back tae me and get ye tae bed before ye fall doon."

By the end of September, baby Margaret was sleeping through the night, and Euphemia's spirits and level of energy rose, though she had little time for Jamie. He immersed himself in what little time his tutor permitted in sports and riding with friends. Patrick Dunbar was fond of telling them, "The De'il leads idle minds astray."

Snow came early to the Moray coast that autumn, with a storm that coated the streets and gardens of Nairn and the surrounding fields on the last day of September. On October third, Lieutenant Colonel James Wolfe, the new commander of the Twentieth Regiment, rode through Nairn with his escort, which had accompanied him from Perth to his new headquarters at Fort George.

Patrick Dunbar recessed his students so they could watch the entourage passing through town. Jamie stood on the top step of Master Dunbar's dwelling with his friends, watching a tall, rather ungainly officer riding past. James Wolfe wore a heavy cloak wrapped tightly around his slender frame, and his nose and cheeks were reddened from the cold wind. Jamie stepped back into the recessed doorway and turned away to avoid being recognized, for he saw Lieutenant Ian Hamilton riding on the left of his new commander.

Within days, it became clear to those living in Inverness and the surrounding towns and villages that Lieutenant Colonel Wolfe did not much like his assignment in the north of Scotland or its inhabitants. He issued orders to be read at the Mercat Cross of each town and posted wherever people gathered, renewing the requirements for army-issued passes for people entering or leaving the area, restricting gatherings, and imposing a curfew of eight o'clock at night on all residents without the required passes. These restrictions had been previously imposed but only loosely enforced. With the new commander's coming, the orders stated that harsh penalties could be exacted on the sullen populace. However, stricter enforcement proved difficult to achieve, since the winter weather kept most people indoors, except for essential tasks.

Patrick Dunbar had gone to Fort George to obtain a pass enabling him to visit Arthur Grant's shop in Inverness to obtain books and periodicals for his school. He returned to Nairn with gossip that Lieutenant Colonel Wolfe, already in poor health, was bundled up in his quarters before a roaring fire with ague, headaches, racking cough, and a nose that ran like a faucet. Without his direct supervision, there were few patrols on the roads and in the towns, except for those led by the indefagible Lieutenant Hamilton.

Unfortunately, Patrick Dunbar himself came down with the ague and missed his rendezvous with the bookseller. Euphemia grew impatient since Arthur Grant had sent a message that he had in his hands a packet of letters from James Williamson of Antwerp. After waiting two days for the tutor to recover, she impulsively decided to borrow his pass and make the sixteen-mile trip to Inverness herself.

While the streets of Nairn were still covered with snow and thin streaks of ice, travelers coming east from Inverness reported that the roads were easily passable. Euphemia ordered Mister MacAlister to hitch up the carriage. She handed baby Margaret to the nurse she had hired to help her care for the baby. She took down a pile of blankets and coverlets to keep herself warm in the carriage and left the house shortly after breakfast.

Jamie, the nurse, and housekeeper grew anxious when late afternoon came and the carriage did not return. Jamie bundled up and walked the short distance to the house of his friend Andy Hay and asked for his father. Archibald Hay had served in James Drummond's regiment in the '45. When Jamie explained what his mother had done, Archie Hay's face grew grave. He ordered Jamie to go home to wait while he sought information from the town magistrate.

The eight o'clock curfew passed with no word. Jamie fell asleep in his mother's sitting room. He awoke briefly in the dark to find that someone had thrown a blanket over him. Distantly, he heard baby Margaret crying and footsteps pacing in the hall. He woke in the cold dawn when he heard loud knocking. The housekeeper responded to the knock, and Archie Hay strode in, tracking snow across the carpet.

"Ye must get up, Jamie. Yer mama is in terrible trouble. An army patrol stopped her carriage on the outskirts o' Inverness yesterday and took her and her groom tae Lieutenant Hamilton at Fort George. He saw immediately that her pass was issued tae Patrick Dunbar. He declared it invalid. He confiscated the carriage and horse and imprisoned the both o' them." He sat down heavily while Jamie searched for his boots. Archie pulled off his bonnet and combed back his wet hair distractedly.

"Ach, what a disaster! It took me all nicht tae discover their whereabouts. Lieutenant Hamilton is holding a drumhead court this morning and will surely find them guilty o' traveling wi'out a proper pass."

"What will they do tae my mama?" shouted Jamie, his voice rising.

Archie hung his head dejectedly. "The order calls fer up tae a hundred lashes at the Mercat Cross." He rose and put on his bonnet with shaking fingers. "Come, lad. We must gae tae Fort George tae request a meeting wi' Lieutenant Colonel Wolfe. It might be their only hope, tae plead mercy fer a mother wi' a new bairn."

Chapter Eleven

Archie Hay and Jamie rode to the guard kiosk before the gate of Fort George and requested permission to speak to the commander. The soldiers manning the post searched them for weapons and then took them to the captain of the guard. They waited in the cold for long minutes until Captain Holmes returned from his tour of the guard posts. The officer, bundled in his great cloak from the bitter cold, looked at the man and boy with ill-concealed contempt.

"Colonel Wolfe left the fort on a midday ride and is not expected back until this afternoon," he said brusquely.

Archie Hay asked, "Is Lieutenant Hamilton at the post?"

The captain shook his head. "He left over an hour ago with an escort of horse to take prisoners to Inverness to inflict punishment on them at noon. I do not expect him back until some time after that."

His final words were said to their backs as Archie and Jamie rushed for their horses. They had forgotten that they needed travel passes and were at risk of punishment themselves if stopped by a patrol. They pushed their horses hard on the frozen road to Inverness twelve miles distant but did not catch up with Hamilton's troop. As they neared the Mercat Cross in the center of town, they saw mounted soldiers, a horse-drawn cart, and townspeople gathering, their breaths smoking in the frigid air.

Jamie, filled with dread of what was about to happen, dismounted near the crowd and tied his horse to a post. Archie slid off his horse and dropped the reins, knowing his horse well enough to know that she would not stray. He walked with stiff strides until he could pluck at Jamie's sleeve.

"Stay, lad. It is too late. Ye can only do yerself harm in tryin' tae interfere wi' this proceeding."

Jamie pulled away. "But I must save my mama!" He sobbed.

"Ye canna do anything, lad. The soldiers will put yer back tae the lash as weel as hers or, worse yet, just shoot ye if ye get violent." He seized Jamie in a tight grip and held him close.

Jamie struggled but finally subsided, breathing hard.

"They canna do this!" came out in a hoarse whisper.

"Aye, they can, and they will," Archie growled.

Lieutenant Hamilton stood facing the sullen crowd. He raised a sheet of paper and loudly announced the infraction and the prescribed penalty, one hundred lashes. Soldiers pulled Alan MacAlister and Euphemia Drummond from the open cart and pushed them, stumbling, toward tall posts before the Mercat Cross. Both prisoners stood bareheaded in the wind that whipped at their clothing and stung their faces. In moments, they were untied and shackled to the posts with their hands pulled above their heads. A soldier unsheathed a knife and cut away the groom's coat and shirt. The wind picked up the ripped pieces of clothing and blew them away across the square. The cold air immediately reddened the white skin of the groom's back. Euphemia stood quietly and glared at the soldier.

A burly corporal reached into a bag and extracted a knotted rope. He swung it whistling around his head and advanced to take a stance behind Alan MacAlister. The groom stood stolidly, with his forehead against the post. The corporal braced his feet on the icy pavement and lashed the rope against his victim's back with a loud snap. Jamie winced and pulled back as he heard the smack and saw the scarlet welt left by the knot on the groom's broad back. A gasp escaped Alan's lips on the fifth stroke, and he cried out on the ninth. On the fifteenth stroke, the groom's taut skin broke and flecks of blood flew from the rope to spatter on the snow.

After the twenty-first stroke, a voice called out in stentorian tones. "By order of the regimental commander! Stop this proceeding immediately!"

All heads turned, and the corporal froze, arm raised. Alan MacAlister hung limply by his outstretched hands, moaning softly. Two officers sat their mounts in the street, enveloped in steam rising from their horses' nostrils. Jamie recognized the sharp features and tall form of Lieutenant Colonel Wolfe, in spite of his being heavily bundled in a great cloak. The other officer dismounted and strode to confront Lieutenant Hamilton, who saluted smartly.

"Captain Easton, sir. These prisoners were caught yesterday with a travel pass issued in the name of another person. They were found guilty and punishment assigned this morning, a hundred lashes each."

"One hundred lashes…and who imposed the sentence?"

"I did, sir."

"I see…and who conducted the judicial review of the sentence?"

Hamilton swallowed nervously, his Adam's apple bobbing. "None, sir. There was nae need."

"No need? Are these recalcitrant or defiant persons with previous violations?"

"Nae, sir."

Wolfe dismounted slowly and handed his reins to a nearby soldier. He walked toward the prisoners and stood looking at Euphemia, who stared back at him with calm dignity, in spite of her cold, reddened features and wind-tangled hair. Wolfe turned toward Lieutenant Hamilton, who paled visibly under his new commander's scrutiny.

"Lieutenant, it seems that these prisoners would deserve the maximum punishment for repeated offenses but hardly for a first offense, which would do little more than antagonize a town where we are commanded to maintain order. I do not see incorrigible rebellion in the faces of these prisoners. I insist on conducting a judicial review myself before approving this punishment. Return them to confinement in the fort. Since one of the prisoners is now without a coat or shirt in this inclement weather, you will see that he is reasonably clothed. After we return to Fort George, report to me in my quarters immediately to present the evidence of their violations and perfidy. Now, disperse this crowd of onlookers."

He spun on his heel and, returning to his horse, mounted and rode slowly away, followed by Captain Easton. Lieutenant Hamilton flushed furiously and stiffly saluted the departing officers. Turning about, he repeated Wolfe's orders to his soldiers and then stalked away to his horse. The soldiers unshackled Euphemia and Alan MacAlister and nudged them toward the cart. A coat appeared, and Alan shrugged into it. The mounted soldiers surrounded the cart, and the entourage began the return journey to the fort. When they were out of sight, Archie Hay relaxed his grip on an exultant Jamie.

"Mister Hay, did ye see what I saw? Lieutenant Colonel Wolfe will dismiss the charges. I ken."

"Perhaps, lad, but perhaps he will do nae such thing. He is a stern one, I hae heard, wi' little liking fer the people o' the Highlands. But I hae heard o' his sense o' justice, and we might hae seen it at work here. We must get back tae Nairn, afore we are caught by a patrol and find ourselves shackled tae those posts."

They plodded the last miles to Nairn through freezing rain and sleet. Archie Hay took Jamie to his house and ordered him inside while he put away the horses. Plump and motherly Cecilia Hay bundled Jamie into a warm blanket. She handed him some of Andy's clothes and towels.

"Get ye up tae Andy's room and change oot of those wet things. Hot soup, fresh bread, and tea are waiting for ye in the kitchen, ye puir thing."

Archie sent a message to the Drummond's housekeeper and nurse to relieve their concern over their mistress's and Jamie's whereabouts. With a full stomach, Jamie fell asleep before the fireplace and awoke only when Andy Hay shook him roughly. Disoriented, Jamie looked around blearily. Alan MacAlister stood in the doorway.

"Lad, yer mother is at hame, safe and sound, although monstrously indignant at her ill treatment and imprisonment. By order o' Lieutenant Colonel Wolfe, we were released this afternoon and our carriage and horse restored. He reviewed the evidence presented by Lieutenant Hamilton and dismissed the charge. Jamie's face clouded with concern.

"Are ye all right, Mister MacAlister? We were there on the edge o' the crowd and saw ye beaten and bloody in the freezing cold."

"Aye. I am a Highlander, Master Drummond, and used tae cold and privation. The lashes are another matter. They will heal slowly and always remind me o' why I hate this government fer its treatment o' our people. The ride in the cart was nae what I would call comfortable, but I hae experienced much worse. I was mair concerned fer yer puir mother, except that she was sae angry and indignant that I think she scarce noticed the weather."

Archie Hay came into the room with the bundle of Jamie's wet clothing and a coat.

"Ye'd best be getting along, Jamie. Ye can come back another time tae tell us all about yer mother's stay in the fortress and the King's meager hospitality."

Jamie found his mother in her sitting room, nursing the baby. She was red-eyed but calm. She handed the baby to the nurse and embraced Jamie, shivering a little from the snow clinging to his coat. She said nothing for a long time, only held him close. Then she pulled away and brushed at the tears on her cheeks.

"I am sae sorry tae hae brought such a cruel punishment on puir Mister MacAlister. It was my own foolishness that led tae this."

"Nae, Mama! It was that vicious Lieutenant Hamilton. He is the officer wha chased us awa' frae the fort that summer. It took Jock McRae tae stop him frae hurtin' people at the fair. He twisted the new commander's orders tae arrest ye and try tae whip ye and Mister MacAlister, as he hae been doing tae others since we hae been here. Everyone in Inverness and Nairn knows that he encourages the soldiers tae persecute the people."

In a quavering voice, she said, "I will ne'er gae tae Inverness again. I will not permit ye tae gae there either. We must move awa' as soon as we can find a new place tae live. Perhaps we should gae back tae Abergeldie. I will write my brother this nicht. Oh, I miss yer papa sae much!"

Her voice grew thick with emotion. She sat down on the sofa and put her shaking hands together tightly. She fought for control but lost, weeping in great, wracking sobs. A miserable Jamie hugged her shoulders for a long time until she quieted.

The next day was Saturday, so there were no classes. Jamie devoted his time after breakfast to study. Euphemia sat with him, working on embroidery. The housekeeper answered a knock on the door and then brought a note to her mistress.

"Yer pardon, mum, but the servant wha brought this note is waiting fer yer reply."

Euphemia opened the note and exclaimed, "It is frae Lieutenant Colonel Wolfe, requesting the privilege o' calling on me today at twa in the afternoon." She looked at the ceiling and asked, "Why would Lieutenant Colonel Wolfe wish tae make a social call?"

Without waiting for Jamie to reply, she rose, seated herself at her writing desk, and penned a reply. She handed the note to the housekeeper to pass to the waiting servant.

Jamie set down his copy of Virgil's *Aeniad* and looked at his mother. "He is coming here, Mama? I dinna understand."

"Neither do I, lad. But I think it wise tae listen tae him, considering the power he holds o'er us. Given the trouble we hae been through, if he is coming tae present an apology, I will think mair kindly on him and his fort full o' lobsters."

"Since he is coming, perhaps I shouldna be here. I can gae tae Andy's house."

His mother shook her head. "I want ye here, Jamie. Ye hae knowledge o' Lieutenant Hamilton's harassment, and I need ye tae support me."

At two o'clock, Euphemia and Jamie sat, waiting. Both had taken pains to dress well since it was a formal visit by the officer. The housekeeper answered the knock and swung the door wide to welcome Wolfe's arrival. She escorted him to the parlor. Euphemia rose demurely.

"Lady Drummond, how kind of you to accept my request." Wolfe swept off his ornate officer's hat and bowed over her hand, brushing it with his lips.

Jamie rose and stood facing him, stiff and expressionless.

Wolfe nodded and murmured, "Master Drummond. My pleasure, sir."

Euphemia motioned to an upholstered settee and turned to sit on an end of the matching sofa. Wolfe sat and laid down his hat. Jamie sat in a chair next to his mother.

"It is a cold and raw day, sir. May I interest ye in a warm punch or glass o' port?"

Wolfe smiled. "Ordinarily, I do not partake of spirits while on duty. However, this is principally a social call, so I will accept the offer of port. Here in this frigid place, it might make my stomach think that it is in Portugal."

Euphemia smiled and told the housekeeper to bring a carafe and glasses. When they arrived, Euphemia unstoppered the carafe and poured two full glasses and a third with a finger's depth of liquid. She passed a full glass to Wolfe and the partial to Jamie.

Wolfe sipped appreciatively and set the glass down on the low table. He leaned forward, rubbed the side of his nose, and cleared his throat. Euphemia waited, her face impassive.

"I felt, Lady Drummond, that our meetings yesterday were awkward for you, indeed, given the circumstances into which ye were thrown. I requested this meeting to clear the air and to persuade you, if possible, to accept my apology for your apprehension and detainment by one of my officers, as well as your suffering in the open in such beastly weather."

He looked at Euphemia expectantly. She gave him a slight smile but sat very still.

He reached for the glass; took another sip; and, still holding the glass between thumb and fingers, continued his explanation.

"That officer is part of my command, and I am responsible for his conduct and judgment. My command is the Twentieth Regiment, and I have orders to maintain the peace throughout the Highlands, to include all towns, villages, and countryside. To ensure that objective, I must maintain order and suppress any residual activities of the erstwhile rebels. One of my orders is to restrict the free and easy movement of people who might either be rebels or in collusion with rebels."

Euphemia held up her hand. "Colonel, may I call ye by that rank? Lieutenant Colonel is such a difficult title."

Wolfe nodded, and she continued.

"I am completely responsible for violating that order, sir. Ordinarily, I ask Mister Patrick Dunbar, who is my son's tutor, to pick up letters when he travels tae Inverness. Mister Dunbar came down very ill and, although possessed of a pass, was too sick tae travel. As ye may know, sir, my husband is in France, and I was most anxious to receive a letter that he hae sent me."

She looked down and said in a low voice, "I was impulsive and took Mister Dunbar's pass, resolved nae tae wait fer him tae recover or tae seek a pass of my ain."

Wolfe shifted in his seat. "I know those particulars, my lady, but such a whimsical act is not sufficient reason for an officer to violate established protocols governing judicial proceedings and exacting of penalties. That is why I conducted a thorough investigation not only of this act but others over the many months that Lieutenant Hamilton has been at Fort George. I was very disturbed by what I found, a consistent pattern of prejudicial behavior and—"

Jamie piped up. "Injustice, sir."

Wolfe's eyebrows shot up. He looked squarely at Jamie. "Exactly, Master Drummond. How old are you?"

"I was thirteen years auld last April, sir. I am the only son of James Drummond, Viscount Strathallan. I am James William Drummond, but everyone calls me Jamie."

Wolfe put down his glass of port and sat back. "I know who you are, Master Drummond, as well as the identity of your father. I know that he was a viscount briefly after the death of his father at Culloden. He was attainted and is no longer deserving of that title. But you are not responsible for the acts of your father, nor the prohibitions that surround his relationship to the rebels. I also know that you are uncommonly brave, witnessed by your attempt to protect your mother and others during an incident at a country fair last year at Kilravock. I have spent more time than I can spare questioning my officers and men about disagreeable incidents taking place since April of seventeen forty-six. Many of the punishments meted out following these incidents were deserved by those involved, but not all. I agree with you, Master Drummond, that the stink of injustice is present in some of the incidents. I am resolved as the officer responsible for maintaining peace to do so with justice and equity. I cannot undo the punishments carried out unjustly, but can expunge records of convictions and instruct members of this regiment to treat civilians with respect unless they forfeit it by their own actions." He stopped and looked intently at Euphemia. "I have heard no accusations that you or anyone in this house has harbored rebels or provided arms or other material support to them. Is that correct?"

Euphemia looked at him steadily. "That is true, Colonel, but my heart is tied to the traditions of my Highland hame, and it endorses the rightness of the Jacobite cause. I still love my banished husband, the father of my children. While my heart supports the cause, I live in relative seclusion here in Nairn and dinna entertain rebels or pass military information to their agents. I am bereft o' income frae the family estates and must live on the money frae my dowry and my brother's charity."

Wolfe smiled. "I am not in the business of controlling hearts and minds, my lady, only actions. It is by actions that I must judge in this land, for which I confess little liking. However, I have hospitable friends who are Scottish. My intercourse with them is enjoyable and conducted in an atmosphere of trust. I cannot expect everyone in this land to love my King, but I can expect them to obey his laws or deal with the consequences of rebellion and defiance. Do we understand each other, madam?"

Euphemia said nothing but nodded, her eyes locked on Wolfe's.

He sat thoughtfully for a time and took another sip. "This is truly an excellent port, madam. May I beg you for another glass?"

Euphemia smiled winsomely and reached for the carafe. "I sense, sir, that ye are leading up tae some momentous pronouncement."

He shook his head. "Not momentous, Lady Drummond, but I do have a proposal to make. But first, let me inform you of what is happening with the irascible Lieutenant Hamilton. He has been transferred to Fort William to remove him from contact with a populace which might well murder him if presented with an opportunity. That event, while welcome to his detractors, who are many and include even some officers and men of this command, would cause reprisals that would be most unfortunate to this populace. Before his departure, he was forced to endure the most severe tongue-lashing that I have ever administered and notice made in his official records of the reprimand and reasons for it." Wolfe chuckled. "The lieutenant knows my reputation for brutal frankness and its withering effect on those receiving it. I doubt very much if he will stray far from a strict code of conduct in his dealings with the people of Lochaber. I do wonder, however, if he will have a second encounter with that acerbic old Black Watch officer who withstood him so severely when he attempted to break up the country fair last year. I understand that the old veteran is now living in Portree on the Isle of Skye. I pity Lieutenant Hamilton if he does or if he ever chances to meet Flora MacDonald. She is an uncommonly brave lass, although an incorrigible Jacobite and quite spirited in her beliefs. The King was most charmed by her."

Euphemia looked at him archly. She was well aware of the nearly legendary girl who had smuggled Bonnie Prince Charlie out of Scotland from under the noses of Cumberland's forces. Wolfe stretched his long legs and leaned back. Euphemia and Jamie remained silent, waiting for his proposal.

"Lady Drummond, you are to be commended for your staunchness and bravery. You are raising a young gentleman without benefit of his father or even of an uncle or guardian. That is a difficult task and an unfortunate liability for your son. He has uncommon qualities that need training and manly influences to make him a gentleman and a blessing to his family and nation. When I was scarcely a year older than he is, my father obtained for me a commission in the Royal Marines. I had the benefit of his guidance and training to prepare me for that role. I would like to see your son benefit in such a manner. Assigned here without wife or children and not of a frivolous nature to waste time on cards, quadrilles, or similar activities, I have a proposal for you to consider. I desire a young companion who will ride and shoot with me, although I do not see very promising grounds for hunting hereabouts. I would also undertake to teach him as much of the art and science of swordplay as I have mastered. I understand that your son is also adept in algebra and geometry, which I have undertaken as an area of study, under the tutelage of a Mister Barbour of Inverness. Perhaps I could benefit from your son's knowledge as he benefits from mine."

Euphemia looked at Jamie and back at Wolfe, but her expression was inscrutable.

The officer raised his hand somewhat defensively. "Let me assure you, madam, that I am a man of integrity regarding children. I realize that mothers are justifiably wary of the intentions of bachelors with respect to their young sons, but I have perfectly normal feelings for the tender sex and few opportunities for pursuing matrimony have come my way in my postings. I abhor those who take advantage of close relationships with children to do ought other than cherish and protect them in their innocence."

Euphemia responded quickly. "Nae, nae, Colonel. I was thinking nae such thing, and I respect ye for putting a mother's mind at ease. I was thinking about how such a relationship would be viewed by those of yer ain command, as weel as the townspeople."

Wolfe frowned, and then his expression cleared. "I think that there might be some suspicions about my intentions among your neighbors, but I can periodically invite other young men from Nairn, Inverness, and other towns to participate, as well as some of my own officers. It might gae a long way toward reducing the tensions and suspicions between the soldiers and the townspeople. Let us label it an experiment."

Euphemia turned to Jamie expectantly.

"I think that it a guid idea, Mama, but we should be engaged in activities in full view o' the people in the countryside round aboot and not only in the fort."

Wolfe smiled when Euphemia nodded agreement.

"An excellent suggestion, Master Drummond. That will help establish confidence in all concerned. Give me a week or two to talk to others, and I will extend an invitation." He frowned. "Of course, we are victims of the most beastly weather with which I have had to contend in Scotland. The first few encounters might be trials in perseverance. My health at times is not the best, but I can rely on some of my officers to assist. Major Robert Dalrymple and Captain Benjamin Easton are fine officers and excellent horsemen. I also rely on a fencing master who lives in Inverness. He is a French Protestant who is a wizard with the blade and the best instructor I have ever met. Everard Gascoyne is a tyrant but an unparalleled teacher. You will love him and hate him, Jamie. But he will make you a master with the blade." He set down his empty glass and stood.

"It is getting late, and I am expected back at Fort George shortly."

Euphemia rose and extended her hand. Wolfe bowed over it and then straightened his thin frame and smiled warmly. Jamie came to his mother's side.

Wolfe disengaged his hand and gripped Jamie's. "Thank you for accepting my proposal, Lady Drummond. I believe that it will be of mutual benefit and will also greatly advance your sense of security, madam, which you richly deserve after such trials as you have had. I have great expectations for your son, and I look forward to many happy hours afield. You can expect to receive word of our first engagement by the end of next week. Good day."

The next day, a courier dropped a post from James Williamson of Antwerp, notifying Euphemia that after a year in which patrols of the Royal Navy had made it excessively risky to enter Scotland, he had arrived and desired to see his family. Within a day, she made the necessary arrangements and they departed for a week in the lodge at Pitfour. They had missed the best hunting season, since it was already mid-November, but they enjoyed the warm fire in the cozy lodge which they shared with only a few other visitors. James took great delight in his three-month-old daughter, Margaret, whom he affectionately named "my little Meg." She had just learned to smile and delighted Jamie and his father, who doted on her. The week disappeared too soon. James expressed confidence that the relaxation in the government's vigilance toward the banished Jacobites would continue. They parted in high spirits with the promise of a reunion when the lodge reopened in late March.

Good to his word, shortly after their return, James Wolfe sent a message arranging a rendezvous for a ride with Jamie in the countryside south of Nairn on a day that turned out cloudy but unexpectedly mild. Captain Benjamin Easton accompanied Wolfe. He turned out to be a pleasant and affable Lancashire man in his mid-twenties. Wolfe chose to talk about his mathematics lessons with Mister Barbour in Inverness. He shook his head woefully.

"I pride myself on my ability to solve most problems through application and sheer tenacity. However, the logical exercises imposed by Mister Barbour baffle me. I have read the texts 'til I am grown perfectly stupid and have worked away the little portion of understanding that is allowed to me." He laughed goodnaturedly. "They have not left me even the qualities of a coxcomb, for I can neither elocute, nor sing, nor talk an hour upon nothing. The latter of these is a sensible loss, my lad, for it excludes a gentleman from all good company and makes him entirely unfit for the conversation of the polite world."

Jamie's spirits soared, for he was enjoying the ride and appreciating having a prominent adult treat him as a companion. When Wolfe fell silent and Captain Easton had nothing to say, he offered a comment.

"Well, sir, ye can make a neighborlike appearance hereabouts with only a moderate competency o' knowledge, for people hereabouts know naething aboot mathematics, except for a few engineers, and they are quite scarce in yer social circles. If ye speak with the gravity appropriate tae yer station, it will supply the deficiency."

Both officers reined up and stared at Jamie in astonishment.

Easton slapped his knee and exclaimed, "Sir, the lad has the wisdom of Solomon, for his advice is perfectly sensible. You can also invest a bit of time with those whom society esteems to be learned and wise, such as clerics, and your stock will rise quite high. You will most assuredly and deservedly obtain a reputation for great wisdom and discretion."

Wolfe looked at both of his riding companions with his brows knit, and then a slow smile broke over his sharp features. "As you undoubtedly know, Captain Easton, I correspond with my parents nearly weekly and have been struggling to express my feelings on this topic, but this conversation is worthy of the old gentleman's attention. I don't always understand myself and can't, therefore, wonder that I am sometimes unintelligible to others. However, you gentlemen have put my thoughts into a framework that is dazzlingly clear." He took off his hat and bowed to them both.

They resumed their ride.

Wolfe turned to Captain Easton. "My good Benjamin, my astonishment at your wisdom is moderate since you are paid to advise me." He gestured toward Jamie. "However, this worthy lad is a jewel since, without recompense, he has given me much food for thought." He turned in the saddle to regard Jamie. "What else can you tell me about mathematics?"

Jamie turned to look at Wolfe. "Only this, sir. Every problem in algebra and geometry yields an answer if ye apply the proper axioms and postulates to its solution. The principles apply the same way every time. They canna be true ain day and false the next."

The normally reserved Wolfe whooped in delight. "He is more than a jewel, Benjamin. When we return from our ride, my lad, I will buy ye dinner if ye will look over the exercises I owe to Mister Barbour tomorrow." In high spirits, he picked up the pace, singing a marching song as they trotted down the road.

As winter settled down on the northern Highlands, there were fewer opportunities for Jamie to ride with Lieutenant Colonel Wolfe, his officers, and other boys, but he continued to assist the commander with his mathematical studies. There were several cancellations since Wolfe's fragile health took occasional downturns. However, he was good to his word about arranging fencing lessons with the Huguenot master Everard Gascoyne since he was unable to devote time himself.

Gascoyne had rented a large house close to the town center with living quarters above and the bottom comprising an office and a large room that resembled nothing so much as a warehouse. Mister MacAlister accompanied Jamie on the long ride from Nairn and was mystified by the piles of equipment in the large room, where Gascoyne was engaged in fencing with a tall young man of about seventeen. Gascoyne was a slender, swarthy man in his late thirties with a hawklike visage, sharp features, and dark eyes. The young man was fencing with great vigor, but Gascoyne moved effortlessly, parrying the other's vicious slashes. Finally, he noticed that he had visitors and ended the bout quickly, disarming his opponent with a swiveling blade, followed by a spin and riposte, the tip of his blade hovering over the young man's breastbone. Wide-eyed, the youth dropped his rapier and raised his hands. Gascoyne stepped back and lowered his blade. The young man bent to retrieve his weapon.

"You have made much progress, Mister MacIntosh. We will work on converting your enthusiasm into killing strokes in next week's lesson. Now, I must attend to my visitors."

He shifted the blade to his left hand and extended his right to grip Alan MacAlister's. Gascoyne escorted them to his office, poured tea, and offered a plate stacked with small cakes. The Frenchman took the letter of introduction from James Wolfe and read it slowly.

"You must excuse me, monsieurs. I read English somewhat slowly. Ah! It is from *mon ami*, the excellent Lieutenant Colonel Wolfe."

Jamie sat in silence, sipping tea and looking around while Everard Gascoyne read. On a wall hung rapiers, fencing foils, dirks, and cavalry sabers. Surmounting the display of light weapons was a lengthy two-handed Scottish claymore. A heavy desk piled with papers, a bookcase holding a dozen books, five chairs, and two tables completed the austere furnishings.

When he finished the letter, Gascoyne dropped it on the desk and, rising, lifted down two rapiers from the wall. He motioned his visitors to follow him into the vacant, large room. He handed both blades to Alan MacAlister. Turning to a pile of clothing in a corner, he rummaged until he extracted a small leather jerkin, which he slipped over Jamie's head and cinched up several straps. Then he took a mask with a wire-mesh facing from a wall hook and fitted it over Jamie's head. Gripping one of the rapiers, he stepped away until he was two paces from Jamie.

"I must find out what, if anything, you know about swordplay, *jeune ami*. Raise your blade and take a fencing stance."

Jamie had seen mock sword fights several times at Strathallan and Abergeldie. He took what he felt was the correct stance, turned sideways with his blade up and his other arm raised and foot extended. Gascoyne faced him and raised his blade. Mister MacAlister reclined his tall form against the wall to watch.

"Come now, young sir. Attack me." The master advanced a step and extended his sword arm until the blades touched.

Jamie stared at the fencing master's face. Gascoyne was utterly expressionless. Jamie rolled his wrist and flicked the tip of the blade toward Gascoyne's shoulder. The Frenchman's parry was effortless, almost lazy, yet Jamie could feel the force up his wrist and forearm. Jamie swung the blade down and then up toward Gascoyne's middle. Gascoyne leaned away, and Jamie's blade swung up harmlessly. Suddenly, the tip of the master's blade snaked out and rapped hard against Jamie's. The shock of the impact flew up his arm, and he almost lost his grip.

"Again. On the attack."

Jamie took a step forward and lunged suddenly. Gascoyne flipped Jamie's blade away as one would swat a fly and then executed a swift spiral with his blade so that the tip caught in Jamie's guard. The rapier went flying across the room to clatter against the wall. Jamie stared down at the tip of the master's blade pressed against the leather of the jerkin over his sternum. Mister MacAlister snickered and then stifled it with a discreet cough.

"Touché!" Gascoyne lowered his blade and stepped back. He looked sympathetically at Jamie. "*Moi jeune ami*, my young friend, you are not yet ready for lessons with the blade, but you showed me courage by trying. You need exercises to increase your agility, for you waddle like a hog in a pen. You must learn to float and dance like an acrobat. Your wrist is weak, and your arm is soft, like butter. It must be like oak and your wrist like a steel spring, strong yet resilient. I did not test your wind, but I suspect that you would not last long in a bout with a blade of any size."

He walked over to retrieve the fallen rapier and then returned to gently pull the mask from Jamie's face. Jamie was downcast at Gascoyne's criticism, for such he felt it to be.

"Master Gascoyne, are ye saying that I canna learn tae fence? Ye will nae teach me?"

The Frenchman's dark visage softened, and his face split in a wide grin that showed large, even teeth. "*Mais oui*, I can teach, and you will learn, *mon ami*, although your body might wish sometimes to be dead. My good friend Wolfe desires it, and he is as good a friend in this godforsaken land as I have. He brought me here from Fife, where he was stationed and I was teaching young aristocrats. He extracted me from a discovered dalliance with an earl's wife, so I cannot go back there, so here I must stay and make what living I can, until I can find more pleasant and safer surroundings. I cannot go back to France, for I am Protestant and not Catholic. I have no taste for the wild American frontier that has drawn so many of my countrymen. If you have the courage to do what I will compel you to do, you will become supple, agile, and strong. I will teach you the principles and techniques of the Italian master Ridolfo Capoferro. They will give you great pleasure and perhaps save your life one day.

Oui, if you can endure my lessons and your mother will pay me a reasonable stipend, I will teach you."

"Oh, my mama will agree tae pay ye. We discussed it last nicht, Master Gascoyne. Send her a letter with the particulars, and she will invite ye tae visit to agree on the details."

The fencing master glanced at Alan MacAlister, who nodded. "Excellent! We should not waste our time this afternoon. We will begin by demonstrating exercises that ye must perform every day at home, although we will meet only once each week."

"Performing these exercises diligently will improve your wind and agility as well as strengthen your wrist, arms, legs, and torso. If you are diligent, young master, you will be prepared within a month to begin learning the use of the blade, tempos, and footwork essential to the discipline. It is not enough merely to understand the art of fencing. Once you have mastery of the basic techniques, I will match you with other students. Only through repetition will you become adept and grow in skill. However, if you slacken the exercises, I will know it and require additional exercises. This is a contract between me as your master and you as the pupil. Are we agreed?"

Jamie nodded vigorously. A half hour later, however, he began to wonder whether he would survive the exercises demanded by the fencing master. First, Gascoyne required him to practice a series of dance steps while the master hummed and kept the beat on a small snare drum. Jamie felt foolish, but the only spectators were the master and Alan MacAlister, neither of whom snickered or laughed at his clumsy footwork. The next exercise was to pick up a heavy weight in one hand and run up and down a staircase many times until he was quite winded. Gascoyne tossed him an India rubber ball and insisted that he squeeze it hard a hundred times in his fist, resting briefly after every ten squeezes.

When he was finished, Gascoyne tossed Jamie a large ball and ordered him to grasp it between his hands and squeeze them together, again a hundred repetitions. Before he was finished,

Jamie's hands and wrists were aching. The last exercise was enjoyable since it involved balance. Gascoyne handed him a long stick. Then he swung a three-inch metal ring suspended from a hook mounted in the ceiling like the pendulum of a clock. The objective was to spear the ring with the stick while keeping at least one foot in place. Gascoyne kept changing the trajectory and speed of the ring's motion, but Jamie was very accurate in spearing it. Just as Jamie was developing confidence, Gascoyne changed the exercise. He placed a board with a spring-mounted axle on the floor, similar to a child's teeter-totter, and invited Jamie to climb aboard and balance himself. Jamie felt unsteady but managed to achieve balance after a few trials. Gascoyne handed him the stick and then set the ceiling-mounted ring swinging an arm's length away. Jamie gauged the speed and trajectory of the ring, lunged to spear it, and promptly fell off the balance board. He sprawled on the dusty floor, muttered a curse under his breath, and then climbed back on. It took Jamie several trials before he was successful in spearing the ring. However, his aching knees and elbows bore witness that it would be some time before he mastered that exercise.

After he finally speared the ring, Gascoyne exclaimed, "Bravo! Well done! This is a good beginning. As you can see, Master Drummond, these are exercises to improve your wind, agility, and strength. I will give you equipment that you can take home so that you can repeat them every day, except for the Sabbath. We will meet again a week from today at the same time, if Mister MacAlister can arrange it. I have additional students arriving soon, so I must bid adieu."

Alan MacAlister helped Jamie set up the equipment in the stable and Jamie was faithful to his commitment to exercise daily after classes.

Monsieur Gascoyne's exercises increased in weight, repetitions, tempo, and variety. Jamie grew to despise the ferocious pace and intensity of the drills, but his internal criticism ceased on the day in March that Gascoyne pronounced him ready to begin fencing drills with a wooden sword.

Gascoyne faced Jamie and extended his rapier to touch Jamie's wooden weapon. "The first principle from Capoferro consists in understanding tempo. Tempo comes to signify three different things. Chiefly, it signifies a length of movement or stillness that I need in order to reach a definite end for some plan, without considering the length or shortness of that tempo, only that I finally arrive at that end. Now, there are four tempos: primo, dui tempi, mezzo, and contra tempo. Primo tempo is when I can strike my adversary with one movement of my sword. Striking dui tempi requires at least two movements. Mezzo tempo is when I strike my adversary in his advanced and uncovered arm with a thrust or cut or when I strike my adversary as he moves to strike or perform some other action. Redoubling of blows is usually done in mezzo tempo. Contra tempo is when at the same time that the adversary wants to strike me, I encounter him in shorter tempo. One needs to know that all movements and responses of the adversary are tempos. Now, let us practice."

Later, after a brief rest, Gascoyne taught Jamie another principle. They faced each other en garde. The fencing master stamped his leading foot. Jamie's eyes flicked to the movement, and Gascoyne rapped him on the shoulder with his blade.

"If you find yourself with an adversary, always have your eye on the other's sword hand, not the eyes, for they mirror only intent or hope but not action; nor the feet, for the feet are often used to mislead; and not the head, elbow, or unarmed hand. Paying attention to the armed hand, you will see the stillness and all movements that it makes, and from what that hand does, you can judge what you must do. Only actions of the armed hand can cause you harm." On another occasion, the fencing master admonished him. "Practice as often as opportunity affords and always with those who know more than you, for by learning their techniques, you will become a more perfect fencer."

Every session consisted of such comments, lectures, and exhausting application of techniques, both defensive and offensive. Gascoyne, as a teacher of Capoferro, emphasized the defensive aspects of the art over the offensive. He also insisted on repeating lessons until he was satisfied that the learned technique was deeply ingrained. A favorite technique was to make Jamie fence on a floor littered with obstacles, advancing and retreating around or vaulting over them.

"In a real fight, the space will almost never be clean. You might battle on a street where there are fences, walls, steps, trees, stumps, animals, dead bodies, or piles of *merde*. Indoors, there will be furniture, stairwells, lamps, chairs, even women, all obstacles that threaten your ability to move freely. If you can conquer such obstacles and your opponent cannot, you will have so much the advantage. If you or your opponent cannot, one of you will make a fatal mistake and end up an easy victim of the other's blade."

After two months of weekly private lessons, Gascoyne deemed Jamie ready to practice with other students. On the first such occasion, Jamie was surprised to find at least a dozen young men donning jerkins, gloves, and masks. Most of the students were older, ranging in age from fifteen to twenty, and most were taller and of longer reach. Two were Jamie's age and size, and only one was smaller.

Gascoyne paired the students by size and age. Jamie found himself facing fourteen-year-old Michael Fraser, a short, dark-haired lad whose family lived on the outskirts of Inverness. After all students had been paired, the fencing master paced up and down the double line of partners while, in a loud voice punctuated by occasional profanity always uttered in French, he led them through the various guard positions, feints, parries, and attacks. He occasionally stopped to point to feet, arms, heads, body posture, and weapons with the tip of his rapier. The drills increased in tempo as he led them through the movements. After an hour, he granted a brief rest and allowed the sweating students to refresh themselves from jugs of water.

The master called on two older students for a demonstration of a fencing bout. When they were finished, he called the two youngest students to step forward. The bout ended with a clumsy fall by one unfortunate student, roundly cursed by Gascoyne. After three tries, he cut off the bout and the crestfallen students retreated. Then he called Jamie and Michael Fraser. They advanced, went through the preliminaries, and engaged. Fraser went on the attack almost immediately. Jamie parried and circled cautiously. Gascoyne waved his arm and shouted for him to attack. He parried again and went on the attack at a faster tempo, beating Michael backward. They locked weapons, breathing hard. In the back of Jamie's mind, he realized that although younger, he was much stronger than his opponent.

After the second disengagement, Jamie attacked, driving Michael backward until he stumbled. One lunge and the bout ended, with Jamie's point pressed down over the fallen boy's chest. The other students applauded.

Gascoyne shouted, "Touche! Step back and let him rise! An excellent match!" Gascoyne critiqued them and called for the next pair.

Jamie stepped away, flushed with pleasure, and lightly tapped Michael on the arm with his fist. The losing boy flashed a grin, which signaled the start of a warm friendship.

In late March, Lieutenant Colonel Wolfe recovered enough from his chronic illnesses to recommence twice-weekly rides that usually involved several other boys from Inverness and Nairn and two or three other officers from the garrison at Fort George. At least half the boys were students of Everard Gascoyne as well. On one ride, Wolfe suggested that the fencing students demonstrate their skills at a fair that he would sponsor, and invite the townspeople. Other events would include horse racing, exhibitions of riding skills, shooting at targets, rope tugs, and the traditional Scottish athletic contests.

"We will hold the event in late April, about a month from now. The snow should be gone and the weather sufficiently warm so that people can enjoy such outdoor activities. It will be my last opportunity to express my thanks to the garrison and the townspeople before I depart."

Jamie and several other boys reined up to stare at the tall officer. "Depart? When? Why?"

Questions poured out. Wolfe smiled and waited until they ran down. He sighed and began his explanation to those who sat their mounts in a circle around him.

"I am not a good officer for a garrison in a time of peace, spending time in reviewing, administering, and driving a quill filled with ink across paper. I was always an officer of action and happiest when I am presented with opportunities to be active. My time in Inverness is drawing to an end. I must repair to Fort Augustus next month to observe construction at that place, and then I will be taking a long-hoped-for leave of absence by traveling, probably to Ireland. While I have not enjoyed the Highland winter and freezing weather, which settles into my bones and aggravates my distempers, I have made some fast friends in this land."

At that point, he turned in the saddle to gaze on his fellow officers and the boys in the group.

"While I cannot stay to further tutor or engage in friendly pastimes with you, let me assure you that I am leaving you with adequate tutors. I shall miss our association, for there is nothing more satisfying to the heart than friendship with those whom one can trust." He glanced down, rubbed his horse's neck, and then looked around at everyone in the circle. "One never knows the future, and it might be that the paths of some of us may cross again. I sincerely hope that they might, for you are all good companions. My advice to you all is to do everything in your power to be men of action and not drawn off into indolent practices. I pray that our paths cross in a more hospitable clime."

A chuckle ran around the group.

Captain Easton pointed forward and called, "Then let us enjoy the time we have left together with our good commander. We will ride every day on which we have the opportunity and agreeable weather."

There were shouts of "Aye! Every day!" as the group moved off.

Before the ride was over, Wolfe took Jamie to the side to tell him that he had assurances from Everard Gascoyne that he was planning on remaining in Inverness for at least the next several years. The fencing master had confided to his old friend that he had formed a romantic liaison with a well-situated and youthful widow of strong Protestant persuasion in the town. Gascoyne had promised Wolfe that he would continue to tutor Jamie until he moved away to attend university three years hence.

The fair was a resounding success since the townspeople had come to value and appreciate Wolfe's administration for justice and equity, albeit sometimes harsh to recalcitrant malefactors. Jamie amazed himself and others with three excellent fencing matches and a group demonstration of skills. He won all three matches and a small prize for target shooting. He happily engaged in a rope tug over a mud pit, from which he emerged splattered and grimy from being dragged through the mire on the losing side. Euphema made a point of approaching Wolfe during the fair to express her thanks for his intervention with Lieutenant Hamilton, befriending Jamie, and for arranging lessons with the fencing master.

"He is growing sae fast, Colonel, and now needs strong men tae guide him in ways that I canna. I will ne'er forget what ye hae done fer him."

Wolfe bowed and bent over her hand. "I will not forget him, either, my lady, or you. You have exactly the qualities that I search for in the young ladies I encounter. I pray that someday I may find someone with the same qualities of honesty, loyalty, intelligence, and love of family."

Euphemia curtseyed. "I am sure that ye will, Colonel, for ye have the same qualities that women admire in a man."

Wolfe's popularity with the townspeople grew greatly from an incident in early April during a visit to Inverness by Lord Bury. The provost and councillors requested his presence at a celebration of the Duke of Cumberland's birthday. Bury observed that he was delighted to find the inhabitants of Inverness so loyal. But he believed that there was another occasion at hand whose celebration would give his Royal Highness even greater pleasure, the sixth anniversary of the Battle of Culloden. Consternation appeared on the faces of the deputation from Inverness. They retired, saying that they would consult their colleagues. Another deputation waited upon Lord Bury and stated that they declined to celebrate the fall of their sons, brothers, and kinsmen. They stated that no one with a particle of manhood could agree to such a suggestion. Bury threatened the townspeople with a military outbreak because of the disappointment his soldiers would feel. This frightened the poor provost and deputation into compliance, but Wolfe refused to take part. That act, more than anything else that he had done in his tenure at Fort George, won him the admiration of the townspeople, for he demonstrated that he respected their values and beliefs. By early May, Lieutenant Colonel Wolfe had left for Fort Augustus, but Jamie was quickly distracted by news that James Williamson had arranged to visit Pitfour in mid June.

With Wolfe's departure, Captain Easton took the lead in the weekly rides. With the advent of good weather, the fencing master created new exercises for his students. Chief among these were leading students in running lengthy courses along the shores of the Moray Firth and Loch Ness. Jamie was mystified one day when Monsieur Gascoyne canceled his weekly lesson in favor of a boating trip on Loch Ness. They rode to the loch in Gascoyne's carriage. The master shouldered a bag and led the way down to a dock, where three weathered rowboats with cracked and peeling paint lay moored, bobbing gently on the dark blue water. He untied the painter of one rowboat and invited Jamie to step in.

"Rowing is an excellent exercise to improve the wind and grow muscles of the shoulders and arms. Have you ever rowed a boat?"

Jamie shook his head. "Only a little, Master Gascoyne, but I hae been swimming in lochs and streams most o' my life."

"I will demonstrate for you. You sit on the thwart, like so. Then you put the oars in the locks and dip them in the water perpendicular to the surface. To row straight, all I must do is to pull the oars toward myself, raise them out of the water, push the oars away, then repeat the action. To steer in a particular direction, I put more force into one oar than the other and the prow of the boat moves in the opposite direction, like so."

Gascoyne rowed for a few minutes until they were well away from the dock. Then he insisted on shifting places so Jamie could row. Within a few minutes, Jamie demonstrated sufficient skill that Gascoyne could lean back to enjoy the ride and call a tempo of increasing rapidity while Jamie rowed the rest of the way across the loch. When they reached the other side, they tied up at a dock and Gascoyne insisted that a gasping Jamie rest for a few minutes while he prepared for the next exercise. Jamie flexed his shoulders, which had tightened with the unfamiliar exertion.

The fencing master opened the bag that he had brought from the carriage to extract a small wicker hamper, from which he lifted a bottle of cider, another of Madiera, and two glasses. He held up a large wedge of cheese, sniffed it appreciatively, and put it back in the hamper. He passed the bottle of cold cider and a glass to Jamie and invited him to drink. While Jamie sipped, Gascoyne pulled a leather harness from the bag and began attaching a length of rope to it.

"Now for the best exercise of all. Master Drummond, you will take off your clothing, except for your small clothes, and put on this harness. I will explain this exercise, which marvelously develops the wind and shoulder muscles of the fencer. I fasten the buckles so the harness is snug across your shoulders and the rope trails from this swivel at your back. I will hook the other end of the rope to the front of the rowboat. I know that you are familiar with swimming, but undoubtedly somewhat out of practice after a long winter. The distance is not long for a first pull, only back to the dock on the north shore. You will enter the water and take strong strokes, like so, and the boat will move through the water behind you. When we reach the other side, I will unfasten the harness and we are finished. You must stroke smoothly so that the boat does not upset, eh? If you need to rest, you may float alongside the boat. As you gain wind and strength, you will be able to pull the boat across the loch several times. When you fence, you will be amazed at your ability to engage in long contests and strike again and again without weariness. Let us begin."

The water was chilly but not as cold as Jamie expected. He lay just below the surface, cupping his hands to improve the power of his strokes and using a flutter kick to keep his body level. After a few strokes, the boat began to move. Gascoyne lay back and called the tempo. Jamie managed to keep up for a while, but gradually felt his strokes getting weaker, and his breath coming in ragged gasps. His strokes became uneven, and he veered to the right. He stopped to rest, hanging on the gunwale of the boat until his breathing returned to normal. Looking up, he could see that the north shore was noticeably closer. He felt the cold deaden his feet and legs and began to doubt his ability to pull the boat the rest of the way.

"Master Gascoyne. I am nae sairtan that I can gae the rest o' the way."

Gascoyne reached over to feel Jamie's arms and face. "Nonsense, *mon ami*. You are my star student, and I know your heart. You have great courage and determination. They will carry you when your muscles do not think that they can do any more work. You must force them and be their master. If your body cannot perform, I will know it and pull you into the boat. You must face your fear of failure and seize control. Your mind is the master of your body. Control your breathing and keep your strokes even, long, and strong. Now, swim and do not upset the boat. If you do, there will be no Madeira and cheese for Monsieur Gascoyne, which he will share with you when the boat reaches the dock. Now, stroke one, stroke two, stroke three…"

Jamie resumed swimming and drifted into a state in which he was conscious only of cramps growing in his tired arms, aching shoulders, and fluttering feet. It seemed that time ceased to move. He swam with his eyes squinting against the glare of sunlight on the water. He was so tired that his chin barely cleared the surface. He choked when a ripple submerged his face and flailed to keep from sinking.

At last, Gascoyne stopped counting and shouted to him to stop swimming. Jamie was stunned to look up and see the dock over his head. He had literally swum under the dock and the boat was bumping against it. Jamie drew ragged breaths into his tortured lungs and rolled over onto his back. He could not feel his legs. Gascoyne pulled in the rope and grasped Jamie, shaking from the cold and exhaustion, under his arms. He pulled him into the boat and wrapped a thick towel around him. When Jamie had warmed up, Gascoyne spread a cloth on the grass nearby and laid out cheese, bread, and pieces of cold chicken.

Jamie swore to himself that he would never again tow Master Gascoyne's rowboat on Loch Ness. However, four days after the ordeal, with his muscles and stamina recovered, he changed his mind. The following Saturday, he repeated the performance for the benefit of three awestruck younger students, in far less time than required for his first crossing. Two weeks later, he skipped the rowing and towed the boat across the loch in both directions.

Jamie progressed so rapidly in his fencing skills that Master Gascoyne pronounced him ready to battle his older students. He quickly bested all except eighteen-year-old John Barclay, the mayor's eldest son. Barclay sat silently watching Jamie defeat the other students with his aggressive style. When he and Jamie faced each other, although Barclay was taller and with a longer reach, he responded to Jamie's attacks defensively, with parry after parry. A puzzled Jamie shifted between high and low-line attacks, but Barclay's response was always defensive. Finally, the younger Jamie began to tire. Barclay moved quickly to the offense, with a withering series of thrusts and cuts that Jamie struggled to parry. Barclay's relentless attack beat down Jamie's guard. Jamie circled desperately and gave ground until his back was against the wall. He dropped his point in submission as the watching students cheered John Barclay's victory.

Later, Master Gascoyne led Jamie aside to critique his performance. Embarrassed and disappointed, he could not meet the master's eyes.

"Listen to me, Master Drummond, and learn. Fencers in actual battle who are defeated have no chance to correct their errors. It is difficult for a fencer in a mock battle to learn from a victory, but it is very important that he learn from defeat, *mon ami*. You have not lost enough times to discover your weaknesses. You were far too aggressive in attacking, so Master Barclay took advantage by using simple parries. He allowed you to tire yourself. He looked for your arm to weaken enough for your parry of a high-line attack to be too slow."

Jamie looked up. "But the defense canna win. Only the offense affords that opportunity. Is that not so, Master Gascoyne?"

"*Oui*, provided that you and your opponent exchange enough offensive and defensive blows for you to learn his strengths and weaknesses. I saw that Mister Barclay took advantage of every opportunity to watch how you fenced with others. However, you did not watch him. That inattention caused you to lose. You rained blow after blow on your opponent, not knowing if any had a chance to be effective. They did not. Do you now begin to understand the lessons he allowed you to painfully inflict on yourself?"

Jamie hesitated, but finally nodded slowly. "Aye. I understand that he did not defeat me. I defeated myself. Johnnie Barclay only took advantage of my own weaknesses. I ken the lesson, and someday soon, I will do the same thing tae him."

Master Gascoyne's dark eyes twinkled. He clapped Jamie on the back and smiled. "Come. There is another lesson. Master Barclay and I will demonstrate new techniques in fighting with rapier and dagger together."

Chapter Twelve

On a warm afternoon in the late summer of 1754, on a dusty trampled field alongside the inn in Portree, Jock McRae and Jamie Drummond maneuvered their sweating horses, exchanging cuts and parries as they circled. Jock McRae dismounted and stood leaning on his cavalry saber, breathing heavily. Jamie grinned widely and sheathed his rapier. He smoothed back his damp hair.

"Are ye pleased wi' my skills, Master McRae? I am thinking that I set ye back a pace or twa."

"Aye, ye are quick and hae excellent skills in the fine points o' fencing, laddie. Ye demonstrated them afoot and just now on horseback. Master Gascoyne, although he be a French froggie, hae taught ye weel. Your skills will win ye points in a bout between gentlemen. But the fine points will nae save yer life in a dirty fight wi' an unprincipled opponent determined tae kill ye, wha accepts nae rules."

Jock motioned for Jamie to dismount and face him. He gestured with his blade at Jamie's rapier. "Lad, this is nae a weapon. It is a gentleman's mark o' distinction and will serve weel only in a fair fight wi' another gentleman." He held up his own saber. "Now, this is a soldier's weapon, as is the basket-hilted broadsword. They hae heavy blades that shear through the thinner metal o' a rapier or shatter it in a single blow. Ye must train yer wrist and arm to wield such a blade. Ye are stronger than most lads o' sixteen, but ye are still slender and not yet braw." Again, he gestured at Jamie, the point of his sword hovering over his mid-section.

"Lad, ye must change yer thinking. Ye are the weapon, yer hands, elbows, feet, knees, and body. A blade is only an extension o' ye, designed tae increase the reach o' yer arm and lend sharpness and power tae yer blows. What makes a man dangerous tae his opponent is more than body and blade. His mind is the most dangerous part o' a man, which gies him purpose and determination tae attack or defend. And ne'er turn yer back on a wounded or disarmed enemy. Ne'er assume that a man, even when wounded and-down, is defenseless. Nearly every soldier carries mair than a single weapon. Even wi'out a blade, a man is dangerous. A swift kick or a gouge in the eye can disable an enemy as weel as a sharp point." He rammed his saber into the earth, knelt, and scooped up a handful. "Distractions can kill. A handful o' dirt or sand flung in the eyes o' an opponent is enough tae blind a man and enable ye tae rearm and strike him. Something thrown will distract, the stamp o' a foot, or a surprised look might make him look behind and leave himself open tae attack." He let the dirt pour out between his fingers and gripped his saber.

"See the hilt, lad? It is as much a weapon as the other end. A knock on the head or a blow in the face wi' the hilt will stun yer opponent. Ye can use a pistol butt the same way." He chuckled. "And ye dinna hae tae stop tae reload!" His face grew grim. "A man fighting by himself fears two kinds o' attack." He pointed the tip of his saber to Jamie's face. "The first is tae his head, his face, and eyes especially. The second..." Jock turned the point toward Jamie's crotch. "The second is right there, my lad. A man whose crotch is threatened might uncover his torso and face tae protect it. That provides ye an opening. Another principle is tae use only what is necessary tae win. If ye hae a sword with a blade thirty inches long or a twelve-inch dirk, ye dinna need all o' that steel tae kill a man. Quickly in with only as much as ye need, a guid twist, and then quickly oot."

Jock slid his saber into the scabbard. "None o' these tactics are part of a gentleman's code, but in war, if ye follow that code strictly and yer enemy cheats, ye will die. The principles o' war reward decisiveness, surprise, speed, and shocking force. Soldiers seldom fight alone. They fight as teams. Drill as a team is what makes soldiers effective and enables them tae stand their ground under a strong leader. Soldiers must learn tae trust their mates. Ye might fight a man tae yer left because yer mate is guarding yer right, just as ye are guarding another man's."

Jock extended his gloved right hand to grasp Jamie's. He smiled affectionately at the sixteen-year-old, grown almost to his own height. "Aye, ye are fast becoming a man, Jamie lad. I canna remember ye growing sae quickly. Ye are slender wi' supple muscles, but yer shoulders are already broad, wi' promise o' great strength. Ye will be a strapping and formidable warrior someday, lad, if ye are called upon tae fight. Another thing I wish ye tae think aboot. Nae mair talk about how much ye dislike yer tutor. He is a hard man only because ye are somewhat rebellious and disliking o' his assignments. I understand yer reluctance tae sit in a musty room studying when the outdoors calls ye. Most lads yer age yearn for the saddle and wind blowing through their hair mair than reading or driving a quill o'er paper." He put a rough hand on Jamie's shoulder. "Master Dunbar strives tae make ye what ye yerself desire, tae be a man o' distinction, a gentleman prepared to take his place in the world and lead others."

Jamie shook his head. "But my father canna gie me titles or lands. What is tae become o' me, Master McRae?"

Jock stopped short to gaze at Jamie's face for a long moment.

"All the mair reason for ye tae study and improve yer mind. A birkie wi' social advantages can muddle through life wi'out thinking much. Yer future is nae clear, but for a bright, intelligent lad wi' learning, there will be unco possibilities. The best way ye can prepare for the future and honor yer parents is tae excel, lad, excel. So, work tae please Master Dunbar's expectations. Ye willna hae him lang. I understand frae yer mama that ye will be going tae university next year." Jock slapped Jamie's back affectionately. "Come. Let us find my darlin' Maggie and fill ye up wi' fine victuals. Ye need plenty o' food just tae keep yer fires stoked with all this exercise. Maggie and I hae enjoyed your visit here in Portree these ten days. 'Tis a pity ye canna stay longer, but we understand yer mama wanting ye back wi' Master Dunbar tae start the new school year. Ye must promise tae return soon."

They unsaddled their horses and finished feeding them just as Maggie appeared at the stable door to announce that dinner was ready.

Jamie returned to Nairn, resigned to a final difficult year of study and avoiding clashes with Master Dunbar. He settled into a routine that permitted few distractions. He enjoyed weekly rides with his friends and occasionally with Major Easton and other officers of the Twentieth Regiment, but winter came quickly, and the end of good riding weather. Weekly fencing lessons, drills, and competition arranged by Everard Gascoyne were the only other pleasures he allowed himself.

On a Saturday in early November, at the conclusion of a lesson, Master Gascoyne called for quiet as the students were casing their weapons. He called for them to seat themselves on the floor in a circle around him. Without a word, he savagely impaled the rapier in a sack of oats on the floor. The grain spilled through the rent in the burlap and cascaded to the dusty floor as the shocked students sat silently regarding him.

Gascoyne reached up with his gloved hand to grasp a ceiling joist. He grimaced and shook his head. Tears stood in his dark eyes.

"And so, it ends. This fencing school is closed. I will leave Inverness within the week."

There were shouts of dismay from many students, including Jamie, who leaped to his feet.

Gascoyne released his grip on the beam and waved his hands. "Sit, sit. I owe you an explanation. I do not leave because I wish to do so. I leave because I must. My arrangement with a certain citizen of this town has come to an end, and it is better that I quickly find other accommodations well away from Inverness. My good friend Lieutenant Colonel James Wolfe has a friend in England who has engaged my services at a military academy near London. I am very sorry to leave so many excellent students, but I have sent letters of recommendation for all of you to other fencing instructors in the town. You are all my good friends, and I bid you adieu, hoping that we will meet again." He turned away as a hubbub of comments and questions erupted from the circle of students. Suddenly, he turned back to point at Jamie and John Barclay. "I wish to speak privately with both of you. Please wait until the other students depart."

Minutes later, both young men were sitting in Gascoyne's business office. The fencing master reached up to take down a rapier with a jeweled hilt. He extended it to John Barclay, who reached for it uncertainly and then withdrew his hand.

"I…I canna accept this, Master," he stammered.

Gascoyne's dark eyes glittered. The fencing master persisted until Barclay took the weapon. He reached for another rapier, only slightly less ornate than the first, and extended the hilt toward Jamie.

"These are gifts of remembrance, *mon frères*. They are by Andrea Ferrara, of Italian craftsmanship, the finest in the world." He bent to point to the blade of one. "There you can see the crown, the mark of a genuine Andrea Ferrara. You are the best students I have ever taught, and I would have you remember me and the long hours we have spent together as you wear them. I am ready to weep for your loss, for I cannot recommend you to any of the fencing teachers of this place. They are not experienced enough to help you, and I am indeed sorry to leave you like this. I exhort you to drill together and seek others of similar skill, if you can find any hereabouts." He sat down and leaned toward them, tears glistening on his cheeks. "The bald truth, gentlemen, is that

I am leaving Inverness because I am a deeply flawed man. I have lived with a woman whom I love deeply and who embarrassed herself by offering me her hand in marriage. She was stung by my refusal, and I cut her heart deeply by engaging in a dalliance with a serving wench. One of her relatives informed her. It was only an encounter of two or three times, I forget how many, but she refuses to forgive me. She wishes me out of her sight, and I am certain that some of her powerful relatives will take steps to ensure that I am gone quickly, either to heaven or hell with a knife in my back or they will challenge me to a duel that will kill either me or one of them. I am not afraid to die, but I heartily do not wish to kill any man because of a woman's jealous rage. I have already done so once. And so, I must leave. If you ever travel to London, look for me at the Royal Military Academy in Woolwich." Gascoyne gave them both letters affirming his gifts. Deeply affected, he embraced and kissed them on both cheeks before escorting them to the door. Within days, he was gone, and the fencing school was vacant.

Shortly before Christmas, Euphemia received a letter from Archibald Thomson, who had ended his long sojourn in Geneva and accepted a faculty position to teach natural science at Kings College in Aberdeen. Although nine years had elapsed since the summer of the '45, he remembered Jamie fondly. He encouraged a visit to the college, expressing a strong desire to recruit Jamie for matriculation. Euphemia urged her son to respond to Doctor Thomson's letter, and he did so, promising a visit to Aberdeen in early spring.

On a blustery night in mid November, Jamie sat studying Latin grammar by the fireplace. His mother sat by the fire, crooning to little Margaret. A maid entered and bent over Euphemia to whisper a message.

"My lady, there is a Captain Queernabs outside the back door tae the stable, the shabbiest wastrel I hae e'er seen. He is a tall, bearded man by the name of James Williamson."

Euphemia's eyes widened in surprise, and she sat up abruptly, waking her daughter, who began to cry. "Hush, child!" she scolded, and passed the girl to the maid. She strode swiftly to the back entrance to the house, where a heavily bundled man stood leaking puddles of rain onto the bricks. Euphemia stood facing him, arms akimbo.

"Ye are indeed a pitiful sight, James Drummond!"

At that remark, Jamie dropped his book and bolted for the door. "Papa!" he shouted and rushed into the man's embrace.

After a long moment, James Drummond, for it was he who had mysteriously appeared, using the alias James Williamson, merchant of Antwerp, at the house in Nairn.

"Ye are taking such a terrible chance, my dear James!" Euphemia scolded. "What if ye were discovered? Ye would be in chains on yer way tae the Tower by morning."

James replied affably. "If I were tae come in a fancy carriage, wi' driver and footmen, loudly acclaiming my name and titles, I would be seized. But no one pays the slightest attention tae a tatterdemalion skulking at the back entrance, begging a crust o' bread. I am safe as long as none in this household talks and I dinna gae oot or meet anyone here. I will stay at most three days and be off again. There is nae danger, especially in such wild weather."

Euphemia pulled herself away. "Ye must be wet through and starving fer hot food and drink. Come upstairs this instant to doff those wet things. I will hae food prepared and brought in. Jamie, continue yer studies until yer papa hae changed into dry clothing. We will be doon again shortly."

While he ate, James talked desultorily of affairs on the Continent and the state of his prospering import/export business. He stopped to wipe the crumbs from his beard, now showing a few traces of gray. "Business is excellent, but I must consider adopting a new strategy because war hae become inevitable."

Euphemia's breath caught, and Jamie put down his Latin grammar.

"Aye, war between Great Britain and France is now certain. While relations are cordial here in Europe, there is already conflict in North America. The signing o' the Treaty of Aix-la-Chapelle six years ago ended conflict between Britain and France and the prospects that King James hae harbored o' French support fer a rising in Scotland. However, affairs in North America were nae settled, although a peace commission tried tae seek a resolution. In addition tae disputes o'er territory in the interior, there was disagreement over the Atlantic fishing grounds. Every summer, there are outbreaks o' violence between ship crews." James stopped to drink deeply from his tankard of ale. He wiped his mouth and continued.

"In the spring o' last year, the French sent a twa thousand man force and Indians tae the Ohio country. Their orders were tae protect French trading interests in the Ohio Valley frae the British. However, the French commander did something that previous expeditions hae never done. He constructed and garrisoned forts. The first was Fort Presque Isle on Lake Erie's southern shore. He drove off or captured British traders, alarming the local Indians, the powerful Iroquois. The Iroquois chiefs sent messengers tae the governor in New York. They insisted that the British abide by their obligations and block French expansion. When Governor Clinton dinna provide a response that satisfied the tribes, their chiefs proclaimed the Covenant Chain between the Iroquois Confederacy and the British broken. Governor Dinwiddie of Virginia found himself in a predicament. He was ain o' the investors in the Ohio Company, which stood to lose if the French held their claim. Tae counter French military presence in Ohio, in October o' last year, Dinwiddie ordered a young colonial major by the name o' George Washington to warn the French tae leave. When Washington's expedition reached the first French fort, Jacques Legardeur de Saint-Pierre invited Washington tae dine with him. He presented the commander a letter frae Dinwiddie that demanded an immediate French withdrawal. Saint-Pierre said, 'As tae the Summons ye bring me tae retire, I dinna think myself obliged tae obey it.' He told Washington that France's claim tae the region was superior tae that o' the British, since La Salle hae explored the Ohio country nearly a hundred years ago."

At that point, James looked directly at Jamie, who was following his words with intensity. "Even before Washington returned, Governor Dinwiddie sent men tae construct a small stockaded fort. Governor Duquesne sent additional French forces last spring tae force oot the British. After Washington returned tae Virginia, Governor Dinwiddie ordered him tae lead a larger force back tae protect men building another British fort. He surprised the French and opened fire, killing and wounding many. Following the battle, Washington pulled back and built Fort Necessity, which the French attacked in July. French regulars and Canadians easily overpowered Washington's colonials. News o' the battles reached London in August. The Duke o' Newcastle's government dithered all autumn but hae now resolved to send an army next spring to dislodge the French. The French intelligence service intercepted those plans and is sending regiments tae New France." James stretched his long legs. Taking up the tankard, he gestured with it to emphasize his points.

"Within a year, this colonial territory dispute will become open warfare. The conflict will pour back o'er the Atlantic. There will be naval patrols a' o'er the Atlantic and North Sea. French ports will be blockaded, and possibly those o' the Dutch, wha will be forced tae declare themselves. Military forces will be drawn down across England, Scotland, and Ireland as the British army sends troops tae America and possibly the Continent. By this time next year, conditions might permit resumption o' the Jacobite rising."

"Stop! Stop! In God's name, James!" Euphemia jumped to her feet, eyes blazing, and fists clenched. "Nae! The time fer armed rebellion in the name of King James is o'er! The clans and families o' Scotland hae bled enough. What guid can possibly come frae such thoughts? Ye would bring doom on yer ain son and those o' the loyal clans? O'er half o' them are already in British regiments. Our lands are forfeit, and many families are destitute. Oh, James!"

He reached out his arms for her, but she backed away and burst into tears.

Between sobs, she shouted at him, "Dinna touch me! I must tell ye what is in my heart! Ye hae been gone nearly ten years, James. We hae lived a life o' grief and loneliness and miss ye terribly. My children need a father, nae a vagabond wha comes and flits awa' in the middle o' the night. Please gie up this rebellion and make an accommodation with the Hanoverians. In such a time o' crisis, with war looming, they will be forced tae be reasonable. Ye can come hame, James, tae yer family, and rebuild our lives." She looked around wildly. "It willna fadge, James. I hate it here by the cold sea, sae far frae family and frae Strathallan and Abergeldie and my beloved mountains. Do nae leave me again, James!"

She rushed to him and curled up on the floor, hugging his knees and crying unconsolably. He bent over to hold her close. Jamie struggled to his feet and rushed from the room. Outside, he stood looking at the leaden sky while the cold rain poured over his upturned face to wash away the hot tears that kept coming.

Jamie sat morosely in the wan morning light, stirring his cooling porridge and watching the rain sluice down outside while the wind buffeted the house. The tension between his parents was thick, with few words exchanged in front of the children and servants. On the previous night, a sleepless Jamie noted that the light shone from under their bedroom door long after the servants had doused the lamps in the rest of the house.

After breakfast, James ushered his son into the sitting room for a private discussion. It went badly. James refused to answer his angry son's heated challenge to explain his allegiance to what his mother had labeled a lost cause. Their meeting ended suddenly. Both leaped to their feet.

"Papa! Ye canna love the cause mair than us!" Jamie took a stumbling step backward. His face contorted and he whispered, "Ye dinna love us, and I canna understand, Papa!" He balled his right fist and raised it threateningly.

James held up a hand defensively. Jamie whirled and fled from the room. He seized his heavy coat and hat from a hook.

James followed him to the door. "Jamie! Come back, son!" he called hoarsely.

Jamie ignored him, stepping into the rain. Hands shaking in rage, he walked quickly to the stables and saddled his horse.

Mounting, Jamie savagely spurred the mare up the muddy street, dodging potholes. His emotions boiled, ranging from profound sadness to rage. He felt powerless to stop his father's foolish and dangerous behavior and secret visits. He wished that his father would simply stay away rather than raise his family's hopes and fears during his visits. It was Jamie, not his father, who had to deal with his mother's fall from wild elation to profound depression after each appearance.

With his father's stubborn allegiance to the Jacobite cause, Jamie saw no solution. James was implacable and would soon be gone again, leaving Jamie to deal with a mother who had lost her youthful exuberance as she bore the grief of near-widowhood and obligations of raising children without husband or family. Jamie knew that soon, he would be leaving for university, forcing his mother to cope with only his four-year-old sister and the servants for company.

Jamie trotted down to the strand and reined up to watch the wild water crash noisily on the black shingle and listen to the wind whispering in the tall sea grass. In the distance, he watched a fishing boat beating a slow path back to port. He envied the crew their simple lives struggling with the wind and weather to bring home their catch. Suddenly, he realized that he was soaked through and the afternoon light was fading. The mare whinnied and shifted restlessly. With foreboding, he realized that he had to return to face his father and apologize for running off. Reluctantly, he turned the horse, pulled his hat down over his eyes, and rode slowly into the buffeting wind.

All the way back, he fought rising dread that the impending war was closing in on him and that he must soon choose, caught between his father's unswerving devotion to the Jacobite cause and his mother's revulsion to it. As he splashed his way back to the stable, he saw Alan MacAlister slide the door open. Jamie rode the horse inside and dismounted. Alan reached for the reins, but Jamie shook his head. "Nae, Master MacAlister. I took her oot in the rain and rode her hard because I was angry. It is my responsibility tae care fer her."

The groom stood regarding Jamie speculatively. "'Tis a servant's chore, sir. But I see that ye need some time before ye are ready tae speak wi' the master. Let us work together and prolong the time until ye are ready tae gae back inside."

Jamie nodded, filled with appreciation for the older man's consideration.

As they worked silently, patting and brushing, Jamie warmed up. He doffed the heavy coat and slipped on a dry woolen jacket that Alan handed him. Finally, the groom spoke.

"Master Drummond seems tae be a man beset by many troubles. He handles them in a manner befitting a great lord, fer such I consider him tae be, regardless o' the Bill o' Attainder." He looked intently at Jamie as he continued grooming the horse. "Pardon my presumption, Master Jamie, but I must say that ye are worried overmuch about yer father's reaction tae yer outburst."

Jamie winced and looked down. "Aye, my outburst, as ye put it, is the first in my life. I love my father, Mister MacAlister. But I hae strong feelings about the danger in which it puts my mama and how she is sae lonely and…" His voice trailed off, and he resumed brushing.

"Aye, lad. I understand. There comes a time in the life o' every father and son when the son pushes back against the father's authority, questioning, challenging, and expressing his independence. Every father and son gets angry at that clash, which takes place aplenty in most families. Ye, on the other hand, hae grown up wi'out that opportunity. One clash is naething. Most fathers and sons hae many clashes o' will, sometimes even coming tae blows. Yer mama will want peace between ye, sae it is best that ye both say ye are sorry, although ye are nae truly sorry. Ah. Here is yer opportunity. Yer father is approaching."

While they were talking, James appeared at the stable door. He stood watching Jamie and the groom work for a while before clearing his throat. Alan MacAlister glanced around as if noticing James Drummond for the first time, tugged his forelock, and bent to gather up the brushes.

"Guid evening, my lord."

James nodded wordlessly in acknowledgement. The groom turned to Jamie.

"I will clean the bridle and saddle, Master Drummond, and feed the mare."

Jamie turned away to clasp Alan's rough hand and give him a slight wink. He faced his father and waited. James inclined his head toward the light streaming from the rear entrance of the house. Jamie accompanied him across the yard. The rain had stopped and the dim light glinted off the puddles. As they neared the doorway, James stopped and faced Jamie.

"Ye were gone a long time, son."

"I was angry, Papa, and needed time tae think."

"Aye, weel, I hae been thinking too." With sudden emotion, he laid a hand on Jamie's shoulder. "Ye might nae think that I am much o' a father to ye, lad, and ye would be right. I ken ye and yer mama hae both sacrificed much. I hae suffered every day since I took an oath tae support the rightful king. It cost me my father, brother, title and lands, my family, and everyone and everything I hold dear except my immortal honor." He bowed his head in the shadows, and his shoulders slumped. At last, he straightened.

"God help me, I canna sacrifice that, even at the cost o' all else, nae while there is a chance tae fulfill my oath. That time is here. Perhaps it is the last time. One year, twa, nae mair. If the war with France dinna produce a rising within twa years, I will return and accept the terms meted oot by auld King George. I promise."

Jamie swallowed, his throat taut with emotion. He nodded and embraced his father hard. They stumbled slightly with the force of it, slapping each other on the back inarticulately. Suddenly, Jamie felt his mother's arms around them both.

His father left as surreptitiously as he had come, slipping away behind the stable in the wan light of dawn. The family farewells were courteous and controlled, neither joyous nor sorrowful. It was as if everyone had a tight rein on their emotions, except for little Margaret, who wept copiously when her father departed.

Everyone agreed that Jamie should attend Kings College in Aberdeen. Patrick Dunbar, Archibald Thomson, and Oliver Forbes sent letters to recommend him for matriculation. On a bright spring day, Jamie and his longtime friend Andy Hay tossed up their luggage and boarded a coach in Nairn for the journey to the historic coastal city of Aberdeen.

The rutted road loosened the binding on the axle, and the coach lurched as the wheel went spinning away. As young gentlemen travelers, they were not expected to labor to reattach the wheel and repaired to a nearby post house for a leisurely lunch of bread, meat, cheese, and a pot of ale while a simpering serving wench hovered over them with a flirtatious twinkle in her eye. Both of her youthful patrons were tall, well dressed, handsome, and willing to stare boldly in return. Before matters could move beyond flirting, the red-faced driver appeared and loudly announced that the Aberdeen coach was repaired and ready to depart. Andy and Jamie paid and hastily retreated to the waiting coach, leaving the crestfallen serving wench to stare after them.

The next morning, after a sumptuous breakfast at the modest inn, they toured the town before their midday appointment with Doctor Thomson, who had promised to escort them about the campus of Kings College and the adjoining Marischal College.

They decided to walk from the inn into Old Aberdeen, crossing the bridge over the Don. The ivy-bedecked buildings of the colleges dominated the cloud-covered skyline. At first, they walked the High Street from one end to the other, admiring the architecture of the fifteenth-century town. The street was filled with busy tradesmen and shoppers. Many pedestrians were students wearing their distinctive academic robes and caps entering or leaving bookshops and stalls and making their way in and out of inns. A few were already in a state of obvious intoxication. Clearly, alcoholism among students was far from a rarity in Aberdeen.

They stopped before the Crown Tower to admire the college's coat of arms. Jamie recited the motto emblazoned below the shield.

"*Initium sapientiae timor domini.*"

Andy Hay looked puzzled. "My Latin is nae sae guid, Jamie. What does it mean?"

"Mine is nae sae guid either, but this I ken. It says, 'The fear of the Lord is the beginning o' wisdom.' It dates back tae when the university was training divines, nae lawyers and other scholars."

They entered the Quadrangle and gazed at the venerable buildings. A bell tolled twelve times in the Crown Tower, marking noon. Two students were strolling past and stopped to listen. As the bell ceased ringing, one of the students, thin to the point of emaciation, addressed them.

"I see that ye are strangers tae Kings College." He gestured to the tower. "This is Kings Chapel, the oldest building on the campus, founded in the fifteenth century. The Collegium Regium Abredonense is the third oldest in Scotland and fifth oldest in all

Britain. In fourteen ninety-five, William Elphinstone, Bishop o' Aberdeen, petitioned Pope Alexander the Sixth to create it tae cure the ignorance he had witnessed in Aberdeen and the north generally. Of course, our English and Lowland cousins still view the north as massively ignorant. Why should we gainsay them? The best course tae follow is tae study a little, sleep a little, eat a little, and drink a lot."

He and his companion guffawed with mirth.

Jamie smiled thinly. "Aye. We saw some students engaged in that activity in the High Street just now. I thought that gentlemen were mair circumspect and restricted their imbibing tae later hours."

The students shook their heads.

"Nae. They are anxious tae place themselves in the proper frame o' mind. It is far easier tae study when the mind is loose and the imagination expansive."

Jamie shook his head in wonder at such an obvious contradiction in logic. "Indeed, they can imagine themselves wise, I suppose, and see the world mair favorably frae the bottom o' a bottle. But the headaches the next morning and the curses o' the professors! I think it would bring on a bout o' suffering nae worth the pleasure o' the nicht before."

"A pox on such opinions, sir. Ye are strangers and not true scholars, who hae infinite capacity for great ideas and gluttony all in the same day."

All four young men laughed uproariously. Their hilarity came to an abrupt halt at the approach of a tall ungainly figure in black academic robes, whom Jamie recognized instantly as Doctor Archibald Thomson.

The students quickly excused themselves and hurried away.

Doctor Thomson extended a slender hand and shook Jamie's warmly. "Master James William Drummond! It has been a very long time, and you have grown considerably. You must be seventeen now, stand at least six feet tall, and weigh nearly thirteen stone."

Jamie grinned. "Ye are most precise, Doctor Thomson, on all accounts. Allow me to introduce my good friend Andrew Hay, frae Nairn. He also is planning tae matriculate at Kings College, tae study law."

Andy inclined his head, and Doctor Thomson offered his hand.

"Excellent! Excellent! And yourself, Master Drummond? What piques your interest? Could it be natural science? I remember your avid interest and ability in that subject when I was your tutor in Strathallan."

Jamie answered uncertainly. "I am interested in science, Doctor Thomson, but am somewhat uncertain how tae divide my time in expanding my education across the arts and pursuing the goal of an employable profession. Ye see, my father was attainted, and the Drummond lands and titles taken frae the family. I hae nae legacy, sir, and must make my ain way in the world."

Archibald Thomson's features softened as he regarded Jamie. He cleared his throat to break the awkward silence. "A difficult and sad situation, indeed, with no resolution in sight, though there is always hope where there is life. I strongly urge you to pursue both eventually, but preparation for every worthy profession rests solidly on the foundation of a broad education in the classics, including philosophy and natural sciences. Connections and relationships are also critical in life. Those that you make here at the college among faculty and students will be vital to a successful future." He extended his long arm in a sweep around the Quadrangle. "Come. I promised you a tour, and a tour you shall have. Let us start with Kings Chapel, and then proceed to the Cromwell observatory of the sixteen fifties."

They spent the afternoon touring the buildings, grounds, and living accommodations. Doctor Thomson lectured extensively on the history and facilities of the college, its library, its rivalry with the newer Marischal College, and occasional feuds and fights between the students of the colleges that disrupted the town. They finished back at the Quadrangle but extended their discussion over roast beef and a fine Bordeaux in an upscale inn near the campus.

Archibald Thomson checked his watch and leaped to his feet. "I must depart. I have a meeting with the Chancellor. Let us meet tomorrow morning at ten. I would like you to meet some of my colleagues before you depart for Nairn."

Andy and Jamie spent the early evening looking over the library and talking to students about the housing arrangements. While students at Marischal College lived in town, those enrolled at Kings College were required to live in run-down dormitories. The students complained of the cold, cramped quarters and poor fare but were free to supplement their meals with provisions from town to the extent that their personal purses permitted.

At the end of their visit, both young men were enthusiastic about student life at Kings College, the venerable facilities, quality of the professors, and proximity of the town of Aberdeen. Doctor Thomson warned them of the dangers and pitfalls of the town, its taverns, women, tradesmen, and workers, many hostile to students. Their great disappointment was that they would have to wait until September to experience them.

*

Jamie finished classes with Patrick Dunbar in June. Euphemia was well along in her pregnancy, travel for her was out of the question. She was due to give birth shortly before Jamie left for Aberdeen in late August. The MacRaes invited Jamie to spend a month in Portree and agreed readily to his suggestion to bring along Andy Hay. Jock had known Andy's father, Archie, since he had served as an officer in James Drummond's regiment during the '45 rising. Before they departed, Jamie's mother confided that his father was coming to Nairn in his usual disguise as James Williamson to be with her while Jamie was away. Jamie would see his father for only a few days, but it would be an excellent time for little Meg to be with her father.

The month in Portree passed too quickly. Although Jock and Margaret had outwardly aged, both retained an almost youthful energy and zest for life that was infectious. Their circle of friends in the small harbor town of Portree was large. The whole community took in the young visitors as if they were family. The local lads and lasses were friendly, and the lads from Nairn spent many days riding in the Cuillin hills and sailing on the bay. Evenings they spent dancing and wandering under the stars with a shifting set of girls. Several times, Maggie appeared at an awkward moment to crook a finger and remind Jamie or Andy sweetly that it was past time to walk the girls home. Once Andy came to blows with a local lad, but an adroit lass smoothed it over and remained friendly with both. Jamie's height and physique were enough to keep him out of clashes with local lads, who were well aware of his prowess with the sword.

Shortly before their departure, Maggie McRae approached Jamie to suggest an evening walk along the harbor. When they reached the end of the breakwater where small boats lay moored, she sat down and invited Jamie to join her. They sat for a while, enjoying the glint of sunset on the still water of the bay. Jamie marveled at how youthful Maggie's features appeared, although her hair was now completely white. Her clear blue eyes were kindly and her voice soft and melodious.

"Jamie Drummond, I owe ye sae much. Because of yer advice, my dear Jock came tae find me and bless my declining years with a love I can scarce understand. Ye were only a wee lad tae be sae wise. Ye were seven, I believe, when I met ye at the cattle fair in Crieff. Ye were such a bonnie lad."

"Aye, it was a marvelous event. I remember being entranced by yer music and voice. I can ne'er forget how ye prophesied that day."

"It was impulsive o' me tae say those things, but I felt the sight come o'er me stronger than ever before. I dinna ken why, except I knew that it was important that I tell ye what I felt in my heart. Ye are destined tae perform great deeds." She reached up to touch his cheek tenderly.

"Ye said that I would face great adventures and travel far. Later, ye wrote that the adventure hae already begun."

"Aye, lad. But dinna think that the adventure and travel will all be pleasurable. It pains my heart tae say it, but I saw sorrow and difficulty fer ye as weel. All the talk here in Portree is o' the coming o' war with the French. I fear fer ye, Jamie. Ye are an unco intelligent and brave lad. The only advice I can gie ye is tae be wary and keep yer wits aboot ye."

Jamie chuckled. "Aye. 'Tis the motto o' the Drummond clan, 'Gang warily.' I will follow yer advice with exactness. I am going tae Kings College in Aberdeen next month. I intend tae stay weel clear o' recruiting sergeants."

Maggie gripped his arm with an intensity that surprised him. "These are dangerous times, lad. Stay awa' frae yer father as much as possible. He is up tae nae guid. I hae heard rumors that he is still trying tae provoke a rising in the Highlands. That is dangerous behavior. There are mair military patrols operating out o' Fort William and Fort Augustus than in many years."

Jamie looked at her incredulously. "I know that Papa is still loyal tae the Jacobite cause, but he is mostly in Antwerp, except when he visits us. He runs an import-export business there."

Maggie shook her head slowly. "He tells ye that, lad, and it is partially true. But in the past year, men hae seen him in Lochaber, Wester Ross, and Sutherland. He travels in disguise and under assumed names." Maggie stood up suddenly. "Gae tae Aberdeen and immerse yer nose in books and lectures. See yer father as rarely as ye can wi'out offense. Pay nae attention tae the troubles o' the outside world as long as ye can, lad. But I fear that we will nae see ye in Portree for a guid lang while." She took his arm and turned toward the inn. "What will come will come. Let us enjoy the guid life while we can. This nicht, we eat, sing, and rejoice."

Although Euphemia was due to deliver in mid August, the baby did not come. Neither did James. The weather was hot and humid, with little wind from the sea to dissipate the heat. Jamie watched his mother struggle with her ungainly burden. She whiled away the time with stitchery but frequently stared at the swinging pendulum of the large clock and nodded as if to urge a faster passage of time.

A courier brought a letter from Mister Grant, the Inverness bookseller. Eagerly, Euphemia ripped open the wax seal and read, only to toss the letter on the floor with a little cry of despair. Jamie reached down to retrieve it. The letter was curt, stating that James Williamson had missed the sailing from Antwerp and would attempt to reach Nairn by another route. With a stab of apprehension, Jamie remembered Maggie McRae's warning about his father's clandestine activities in the Highlands.

The maid tapped on the door to Jamie's room shortly before midnight six days before he was scheduled to depart for Aberdeen. He heard the soft rap and sprang to his feet, dropping the slim volume of poetry he had been attempting to read.

"It's time, sir. Yer mama hae started contractions. Please gae upstairs tae sit wi' her. Mister MacAlister is readying a carriage tae bring the midwife. I will prepare everything needful and bring them upstairs."

Jamie felt a sudden fright. "But I hae nae idea o' how tae help her. What if the baby comes while ye are awa'?"

The maid smiled and shook her head. "Ach, sir. Babies dinna come that quickly. It will be hours yet. She needs someone tae hold her hand and comfort her during her pains."

His mouth went dry, so he merely nodded. The maid scurried off, and Jamie bounded up the stairs to his mother's suite. The next few hours were a blur. His mother squeezed his hand every few minutes but was not feeling any discomfort. The portly midwife arrived with her daughter to assist her. They joked about Jamie's discomfiture and gently shooed him away. He hovered outside the suite for a while but heard nothing but murmurs and occasional giggles through the panels of the closed door. He pulled up a chair to the lamp and tried to read but kept nodding off.

He jolted awake and shot to his feet just before dawn when a series of loud screams erupted on the other side of the panel. He could distinguish his mother's high cries from the shouted instructions of the midwife. Torn between a sense of duty and fear, he pounded down the steps to stand uncertainly at the bottom. Another loud shriek brought him up the steps two at a time to the closed door behind which his mother was crying in distress. He repeated this maneuver twice more before Alan MacAlister plodded slowly up the steps to place his arm around Jamie's shoulders.

"Come, lad. Downstairs, we will find a hot pot o' tea. It will do ye guid. Standing here, ye can do naething. Come. This is women's work, and they do it unco weel."

"But my mama is in pain. Surely I can do something tae help her."

The groom reassured him in soothing tones. "She is fine, lad. This is entirely normal, and the child will be born soon. Then she will rest. Come."

Jamie allowed himself to be led downstairs to the kitchen.

About an hour later, the maid, flushed and breathless, appeared in the kitchen doorway. "Another girl, Master Jamie. Yer mama is fine. She is a strong woman wha handled the whole affair beautifully. The baby is perfect and crying lustily."

Jamie shifted in his seat and shook his head. "But I heard my mama cry in such pain. It tore my heart tae hear her."

The maid waved her hand in a dismissive gesture. "Ach. It sounds alarming tae ye, being inexperienced in such things, but the shouting, crying, and swearing helps the mother tae relax. Believe me, sir, she is weel and will see ye soon."

Euphemia fell asleep, and the midwife refused to wake her. She brought a wet nurse to tend the child. Four-year-old Margaret danced around the house excitedly. An exhausted Jamie fell asleep on the sofa. Around ten in the morning, the maid answered the rear door, where a haggard James Drummond stood with Alan MacAlister. James walked in to wake Jamie, who bolted upright as soon as he opened his eyes.

James pushed himself back from his son's embrace. "I hae been three days on the road frae Newcastle. I missed the ship in Antwerp and had tae travel by coach all the way tae Hamburg tae find a ship coming this way."

"Jamie looked at his father narrowly, but detected no guile in his expression.

"Yer mama and I decided last year that if she had a girl, we would name the bairn Elizabeth Marie. She and little Meg will be wonderful company fer each other."

In the ensuing days, the little Drummond family settled in to enjoy the new baby. Jamie listened carefully to his father's news from the continent. James avoided speculating on prospects for a rising to avoid provoking his wife, who had passionately made her feelings clear the previous winter.

One evening, they sat comfortably while James talked of information he had received from French contacts about affairs in the New World.

"After the skirmishes wi' the French in the Ohio country, the British formed an aggressive plan o' operations fer this year. General Braddock led an expedition tae the headwaters o' the Ohio River, tae Fort Duquesne, while the governor o' Massachusetts fortified Fort Oswego and attacked Fort Niagara on the northern lakes. Johnson attempted tae capture Fort St. Frédéric in New York, and Lieutenant Colonel Monckton attacked Fort Beauséjour on the frontier between Nova Scotia and Acadia. Braddock led an army of twa thousand regulars and provincial militia in June tae take Fort Duquesne. The expedition was a disaster. At a battle on the Monongahela River, Braddock was mortally wounded. That colonial colonel frae Virginia, George Washington, once again saved the British army by leading an orderly retreat. He undoubtedly saved hundreds frae death or capture. One consequence o' the British debacle was that the French acquired a copy o' the British war plans." His relish in telling the tale of British bungling and defeat was obvious. "Word hae come tae France by fast courier ship shortly before I left Antwerp, reporting the British defeat. It puts the whole o' the British colonies in America in jeopardy. It is now the end o' August, and there is nae word o' what transpired since then. The British did capture Fort Beauséjour in Canada in June, cutting off the great French fortress at Louisburg frae land-based reinforcements. Losing a copy of their war plans tae the French puts the British at a great disadvantage. They canna defend their colonies or attack Louisburg without a massive shipment o' regular army units and a significant portion o' their fleet tae the New World. This Colonel Washington is a lion in battle, although scarcely into his twenties. If the British were tae promote him, he would be a highly effective general. But I canna see that the British army, wha loathes and mistrusts colonials, will e'er give him command."

Euphemia shook her head. "And what will ye do, James?"

He looked at her face searchingly, but her expression did not change. James pushed out his lower lip and chewed on it before answering.

"War will come tae Europe. It is too late fer the British or French crowns tae back doon. The French will be desirous o' providing arms and money tae support a rising, but the British navy is powerful and able tae blockade any attempt. The Highland clans can scarcely rise wi'oot help, but if military forces in the north are drawn down significantly, it might be easy tae overwhelm them with only modest support frae the French. Conquering the

Lowlands and England would be oot of the question without a French invasion."

Margaret began squirming, and James put her down to play.

"The keystone tae French support is the extent tae which the French monarchy believes that King James and the Bonnie Prince are capable allies. King James is now sixty-seven, and his mind is auld beyond his years. Our prince is bonnie nae longer. I canna believe how he hae declined toward dissipation. Five years ago, he laid the groundwork fer a rising in England by visiting London where he conferred with Jacobite leaders as well as converting tae Anglicanism in a failed attempt tae sway some in Parliament. The English Jacobites were clear that they would move only wi' French assistance. Andrew Murray o' Elibank was principal liaison between Prince Charles and the clans. He came tae believe that was nae hope o' French help and ended the conspiracy, but by then, Prince Charles had sent two exiled Highlanders tae prepare the clans. They were betrayed by Alistair Ruadh MacDonell o' Glengarry. Ain was arrested and now languishes in the Tower. I barely escaped. Charles responded by denouncing the effort and continuing wi' his drunken debauchery and abuse o' his mistress. His behavior continues tae be erratic, ranging frae brilliant clarity and leadership at ain moment tae drunken stupor and petty meanness the next. If French support is nae forthcoming soon, there will be nae Stewart worthy o' the throne and nae loyal men inclined tae put him there."

Jamie watched his mother's face, but she was tightly in control and betrayed nothing of her feelings.

Three days later, on a bright, warm day, Jamie prepared for his trip to Aberdeen. He paged through the book on William Wallace, his treasured gift from Maggie McRae, and placed it in a bundle of books accumulated through the years. He packed his fencing equipment and held up the well-worn rapier with which he had drilled with Everard Gascoyne. He drew the blade from the scabbard, and held it up to the light, revealing a multitude of scratches and nicks. He exulted inwardly, remembering how those marks had been made. He knew that there were fencing clubs at Kings College and wondered if he would find opponents there the equal of his friend John Barclay. That young gentleman had gone south to Edinburgh six months before to accept a clerking position for Barclays bank. Jamie packed the rapier and saber but left behind the treasured Andrea Ferrara given him by Everard Gascoyne. Jamie feared theft in the insecure lodgings at Kings College and could not bear the thought of losing such a fine gift. Tossing the weapons case over his shoulder, he buckled the last strap on his trunk. He dragged it and his bundle of books down the stairs to the entry.

The farewells were tearful, especially with little Margaret, who clung to Jamie tightly until her father gently disengaged her arms. Patrick Dunbar gripped Jamie's shoulder and pumped his hand vigorously. Alan MacAlister stood to the side, as befitted a servant, but Jamie approached and pulled him into a strong embrace.

"I'll miss ye, Master MacAlister. Take care o' my mama," he whispered.

"Aye, that I will right weel. And I will miss ye, Master Jamie. I will ne'er forget how ye came when yer mama and I were chained up and I was whipped in Inverness, nor when ye stood up tae the dragoons at Kilravock and got knocked arse o'er. Ye are a brave and true young gentleman, and I wish ye weel." He wiped his eyes and stepped back.

The post coach made the turn from the High Street and rumbled to a stop. Family and servants crowded around for final hugs and words of advice. Jamie handed up his trunk and bag of books to be stowed in the boot but extended the long case containing his weapons up to Andy Hay, who reached out from the passenger compartment to receive it. Jamie pulled open the door and climbed up to his seat. Laughing, he leaned out the window for a final embrace from his mother and a kiss on the cheek from little Margaret, held up by her father. The burly driver took his seat, adjusted his hat, and reached down to release the brake.

"Ready tae depart, my lady."

Euphemia stepped back reluctantly. James took her arm. Both waved cheerily.

The driver tipped his hat. "All clear! Next stop, Elgin!" He cracked his whip over the heads of the lead horses, and the coach moved off.

End Notes

In writing this novel, I was committed to remaining faithful to the history of Highland Scotland during the last Jacobite rising and its bitter aftermath. Creating this novel required a meticulous timeline of historical events. I spent many hours poring over old maps and charts to ensure that details of people, events, and geography were consistent. The number of details that had to be researched and checked was nearly endless. Clothing and fashion, climate, road conditions, rates of travel, castle layout, music, weapons, traditions, slang, and foods are only a few examples. Getting the details right became an endlessly enjoyable pastime. A passion for historical and geographical accuracy is essential to successfully drawing the reader into mid-eighteenth century Scotland.

Strathallan and Abergeldie are filled with reminders of their early history, with standing stones thousands of years old, carvings left by the Southern Picts, crumbling ruins, and castles. The members of the Strathallan Drummond family and the Gordon family of Abergeldie, with the exception of Jamie Drummond, were also real and endured many of the events depicted in this novel. Anecdotes of events that took place during the '45 rising and persecution of Highland families by the victorious forces of the Duke of Cumberland are extracted from journals of the period.

Viscount William Drummond died at Culloden in the manner described, John Drummond perished on the way to France, and

James Drummond fled to France and then the Low Countries, with only occasional visits to his long-suffering wife, Euphemia. The Drummonds of Strathallan were attainted and dispossessed of titles and properties for over forty years for their participation in the rebellion.

Lieutenant Colonel James Wolfe (later Major General Wolfe – the great hero of the Battle of Quebec) served in Scotland early in his military career, including a tour in Inverness, and left an extensive collection of letters recounting his experiences. A portion of his conversations in this story come from those letters. Jock McRae, Maggie McLeod, Archibald Thomson, Lieutenant Ian Hamilton, Oliver Forbes, Patrick Dunbar, and Everard Gascoyne are all fictional but exemplify characters living during this period.

Traditions of Highland life during the eighteenth century, such as Hogmanay, 'first foot', and saining are ages old and practiced in many Highland households to this day. Old beliefs do not really die. French Kate still haunts Abergeldie castle, according to witnesses who have stayed overnight, and Highland families still talk reluctantly about the sight and places where they claim mysterious appearances take place. Bards and musicians are still highly esteemed, for they preserve the poetry and song that are an essential part of Highland culture.

In closing, I felt that a brief explanation is proper for introducing a simplified form of the Doric or Broad Scots dialect spoken by mid-northern Scots into the story. Simply writing the dialogue in modern English would have failed to convey the sense of "Scottishness" that I felt was essential to the novel.

Book Two

Trial of Honor continues the adventures of Jamie Drummond, as the young student of Kings College, Aberdeen and son of the attainted Viscount Strathallan is unknowingly drawn into his father's Jacobite intrigue. His mind is challenged by professors influential in the Great Scottish Enlightenment, that great intellectual outpouring that fueled not only the American Revolution, but modern political thought in Great Britain.

By reluctantly agreeing to courier letters for his father, Jamie endures betrayal, pursuit, capture, and confinement in Newgate, England's most notorious gaol. Faced with a lengthy prison sentence or worse on the eve of the Seven Years War, he reluctantly accepts impressment into military service in Britain's Royal Marines. He scarcely completes training before the outbreak of the Seven Years War. Only honor, courage, and unwavering faith in an old prophecy about his destiny sustain him through harrowing battles with the French and Barbary pirates, storms, and shipwreck.